June,

Unlike Before

J.B. VAMPLE

Thank You

Happy Reading

ISBN: 978-1-7374279-7-1 (Hardcover)
ISBN: 978-1-7374279-6-4 (Paperback)
ISBN: 978-1-7374279-5-7 (eBook)
Library of Congress Control Number: 2024902243

Author name: J.B. Vample, 1981
Title: Unlike Before
First edition

Published by: Jessyca B. Vample
Imprint: Jessyca Vample Publishing
Address: PO BOX 21313, Philadelphia PA, 19141
Email: info@jbvample.com
Website: jbvample.com

For those who refuse to give up on their dreams, and for myself.

Author's Note

Unlike Before is a story about falling in love and finding happiness. It is also about healing from past trauma.

With that said, this story contains heavy topics, including domestic abuse and PTSD.

Please read with care

Also by J.B. Vample

Chapter One

HEAD RESTING AGAINST A CUSHIONED spa pillow, Patience Harvey exhaled deeply as the light scent of lavender filled her bathroom. Submerged in the heated, bubble-capped water in her bathtub, soft music played through her small speaker, and candlelight flickered from the scented candle on the sink. Closing her eyes, she allowed her mind to clear, taking in the solace of her perfectly planned moment of calm.

The peace lasted only for the length of a single song, as the sound of her cell phone cut her mental decompression short.

Patience sat up, glaring at the open bathroom door as the ringtone blared from her bedroom. "God, *why* does it take so damn long for the thing to go to voicemail?"

After the long, trying week she'd endured, the last thing Patience wanted to do on her Friday evening was talk on the phone. *Especially* if it was one of her clients, who had no respect for her after work hours.

"Finally," she muttered when the ringing stopped. Leaning back, she closed her eyes once again.

When the phone rang again, Patience let out a sigh of frustration. Then her eyes snapped open as the realization hit her. "Shit," she hissed, quickly getting out of the tub. Grabbing her plush towel from a rack, she wrapped it around her body and bolted to her bedroom.

She snatched the phone from her bed, eyeing the name as she answered the video call. "What's wrong? What happened?"

A woman's glowing, deep brown face stared back, a boisterous laugh erupting from her. "Why does it look like your eyes are about to pop out of your head?" Toni Harvey-Blake asked. Seeing the annoyed stare coming from Patience, the amusement cleared from her face.

Patience rolled her eyes. "Because you called back-to-back instead of just leaving a damn voice message." She rubbed her face. "Anyway—what's up Toni?"

"What are you doing right now?"

Patience adjusted the large butterfly clip holding her curly hair in place. "Relaxing...*trying* to anyway."

"Stop lying, you don't know what the word relax even means." Toni let out a chuckle. "I'm teasing," she added when Patience made a face. "Listen, I know you planned on staying in tonight. But this man of mine is irritating me, kid is on my nerves, and I don't feel like cooking so... Let's go out to dinner."

Arching an eyebrow, Patience placed a hand to her hip. "*Both* kids are on your nerves?"

"Oh no, not my angel..." Toni shook her head. "The *other* one."

Patience smirked. "The *other* one is *yours*."

Toni flicked her hand in the camera. "Girl hush, I don't need the reminder."

"Stop it," Patience chortled. "Why is my brother-in-law on your nerves?"

Stalling, Toni's eyes lifted as if she were looking to the ceiling for an answer. "I *want* to say it's because he left his dirty socks on the bed, but I feel like the *real* reason is because I'm PMS'ing."

Pinching the bridge of her nose, Patience shook her head. "Not surprised."

"Hell, neither is *he*." Toni shrugged. "Anyway, come hang out and eat some good food with your favorite sister."

Patience let out a heavy sigh. "Sis…this week kicked my ass. I just want to try to unwind."

"And you will…*tomorrow*," Toni pressed. "*You* could use the night out too, just admit it. I promise I won't keep you out too long."

Patience hesitated. Her sister was right; she *could* use the night out. Even if it was just for a meal that she didn't have to cook.

Sensing her pause as hesitation, Toni put a hand up. "My treat."

"Oh, you thought it *wouldn't* be?"

Toni let out a laugh. "Fair enough… I'll meet you at your house in an hour— Wait, do you plan on drinking?"

"No."

"Good, because *I do*. I'll cab it to your house." Toni smiled sweetly, a hopeful look on her face. "Would you mind driving?"

"Do I *ever*?" Patience sucked her teeth when Toni did a happy dance. "Girl—I'll see you in an hour." Patience ended the call before Toni had a chance to say anything else. Tossing the phone on the bed, she stretched her neck from side to side. "This damn food better be worth it."

Touching up her lips with a sheer chocolate-tinted gloss, Patience gave her beautiful golden-brown reflection a look in her bedroom mirror. She removed the clip from her hair, letting her long, brown, naturally curly hair tumble past her chest. Tossing the clip on the dresser, she ran a hand through her locks, fluffing it out before glancing at the silver watch on her wrist.

It was a half hour past the time Toni was supposed to arrive. "She better come the hell on before I go to sleep."

As if on cue, her doorbell rang. Grabbing her purse from an accent chair, Patience headed downstairs. Looking out of the peephole, she shook her head at the huge grin on Toni's face. Pulling open the door, Patience met Toni's gorgeous face with an unenthused stare. "You're late."

Toni moved in for an embrace. "I apologize. The girls couldn't find that damn movie they love to watch and almost had a meltdown." Parting from the brief hug, she stepped inside. "Turns out it was still where I hid it."

Closing the door, Patience squinted in confusion. "Why would you *hide* it?"

"Because I got tired of hearing that shit play over and over—" Toni held her hand on the door, preventing it from shutting. "Wait a sec."

Patience's brow furrowed in concern. "What's wrong?"

"I umm…" Toni ran her hand along her jet-black, shoulder length bob. "Angela is on her way in."

Eyes darting outside to the curb, Patience saw a woman stepping out of a car. She shot a stern glance Toni's way. "Seriously?"

"Look, she called me after you and I got off the phone, and I happened to let it slip that I was going out with you," Toni whispered. "I felt bad, so I invited her to come with us."

"Perfect," Patience grumbled, watching her eldest sister walk up the pathway.

Tapping her arm, Toni shot her a warning look. "Be nice, Pace."

Patience's eyebrows shot up. "Aren't I *always*?"

Walking up the front step, Angela Bishop flashed a dazzling smile. "Hey Patience," she greeted with an air kiss.

Patience offered an indifferent half-smile. "Hi Angie." Sighing, she grabbed the door handle, gesturing Toni outside. "Let's go before I change my mind."

Patience sat at the seafood restaurant table, quietly sipping her seltzer with lemon as her sisters chatted. They'd been at the restaurant for nearly an hour, and she was practically fighting to keep her eyes open.

Removing the blackberry garnish from her berry martini, Angela pointed to Patience's glass. "Patience, why didn't you order a cocktail?"

Patience set her glass back down. "I drove."

"It's *one* drink," Angela pressed, setting the berries on a napkin.

"It's one too *many*," Patience countered, a twinge of annoyance in her tone. "I don't chance stuff like that."

Angela scoffed. "And everybody thinks *I'm* the uptight one, huh?"

Patience narrowed her eyes, but didn't bother giving a reply.

Toni pointed her fork in Angela's direction. "Oh, make no mistake you *are*." She grinned at the taut look on Angela's striking brown face, before turning her attention to Patience. "Pace, Angie *did* offer to drive us here in *her* car."

Raising her glass, Angela tilted it in Patience's direction. "*Exactly.*"

Shooting a blank look Angela's way, Patience once again chose not to offer a response.

Angela rolled her eyes as she returned her drink to the table. "God, Patience, are you *still* in your feelings?"

Patience cocked her head to the side. "Yep."

"That's fine, punish me because I set you up on a date," Angela mocked,

"Oh, you mean the blind date you *tricked* me into?" Patience threw back. "I thought you invited me over so you and I could have dinner one-on-one—You know, spend some *actual* time together?"

Angela crossed her arms in a huff.

"Imagine my surprise when I walked into a damn double date with you, your husband and—*that.*" Patience shook her head at her sister. "I should've known something was up. I can't remember the last time you invited me over, or even hung out with me."

Tossing a hand up, Angela puffed out a loud breath. "Patience, as always, you're being dramatic."

"No, Angie, that *was* foul," Toni jumped in before Patience could fire back.

"What? I was just trying to *help*." Angela fixed her wide eyes on Toni. "And as *usual*, our baby sister decided to be rude."

"No, that *bastard* was rude, arrogant, insulting and did I mention *rude?*" Patience fussed. "*And* had the nerve to be unattractive as *fuck*."

Toni snickered, quickly covering her mouth with her hand.

Angela's mouth fell open. "Was the language necessary?"

"*Yes*," Patience hissed.

"Look, he's *successful*, and successful men are a bit crass sometimes. It comes with the territory. You could've at *least* given him a chance." Angela eyed the two-karat diamond wedding band on her own ring finger. "God *knows* you could use the help in the romance department."

Patience inhaled deeply to keep her temper in check. "*Help* I don't need Angela. However, *you* staying out of my personal business, I could use a *lot* of."

Angela threw her hands up. "Fine, sue me for trying to introduce you to a fitting suitor." She tapped her own hand. "*Bad* Angela."

"Yeah, 'cause the *last* one you introduced me to worked out *so* well," Patience sneered, tone heavy with sarcasm.

Making a face, Angela stared her down. "Girl, whatever. Fine, do you." Her shoulders rose with a blasé shrug. "*Obviously*, you're satisfied with riding your little *situation* out."

Folding her arms, Patience shot her a challenging look. "*Which* situation exactly, Angela?"

Angela smirked, but didn't reply. She just picked up her glass, taking a sip before eyeing her wedding band once more.

"Okay now," Toni put her hands up. "Angela, trying to

insinuate that there is something wrong with Patience's life as *is*, is bullshit," she chastised. "She's doing *damn* well for herself."

"Being a thirty-five-year-old divorced—"

"You might want to stop," Patience warned.

Brow creasing in agitation, Angela leaned forward in her seat. "Look, as the eldest sister, and frankly a mother figure since Mom died—"

"Now *that's* a goddamn stretch," Toni cut in, perplexity heavy on her face. "You stay taking that three-year age difference between you and I and running with it. Mom passed away ten years ago, and your *mothering* tendencies towards us haven't changed." She was unfazed by the daggers that Angela was shooting with her eyes. "I love you, but stop telling people that. Just say you're the oldest and sip your drink."

Angela curled her lip up at Toni, but refused to respond. She instead turned her attention back to Patience. "Anyway, I just want what's best for you, and—" She put a hand up. "This is going to ruffle your feathers I'm sure, because apparently everything I say *does*—"

Patience's searing stare had not waned as she prepared herself for whatever nonsense Angela was about to spew.

"But what was *best* for *you* Patience, was staying in your marriage."

Toni's head jerked back, astonishment on her face. "Angie are you kidding—after *all* the shit that man put her through?" she argued. "Patience was *right* to leave Greg's controlling, narcissistic, *deadbeat* ass. *I* would've done the same thing."

"I'm sitting right *here*," Patience stepped in, tone even. The last thing she wanted was for her divorce to be the topic of conversation.

Once again, Angela raised a hand. "Fine... I apologize for bringing that up," she directed to Patience. "I guess I didn't know *exactly* how unhappy you were in your marriage to Greg."

Patience rolled her eyes. "Um hmm."

Angela casually fluffed the natural coils of her short, auburn-tinted hair. "Anyway—" Her phone rang, and she immediately grabbed it from her designer purse, answering. "Yes Trevor... I'm out with my sisters, are you home? ...I'm coming back ...No, it's fine, I'm on my way."

Patience shot Toni a side-glance.

Toni just put a hand up to silence any remark that Patience was about to make.

Angela tossed the phone back into her purse. "Ladies, I hate to cut this gathering short but—"

"Your husband finally made it home, and you're running to make sure he doesn't go anywhere else, we know. Go," Patience finished.

Toni pursed her lips. "Hmm, told not *one* lie."

Angela stood from her seat, slinging her purse over her shoulder. "Don't sound so bitter Patience. At least I still *have* a husband."

"Yeah, that's not really the flex you thought it was," Patience calmly shot back.

Squinting her eyes at the snide remark, Angela was about to fire back, but Toni's cackling threw her off. She shot a side-glance Toni's way. "Antoinette—"

Toni looked up at her, amusement still on her face.

"Don't mock me." Angela pointed at her. "You know if *your* husband worked as much as *mine* does, you'd spend as much time with him as possible when he's home."

"*Mine* actually works when he *says* he is and comes home when he's *supposed* to, but go off big sis," Toni dismissed.

"I don't know what the hell you're insinuating, but I'm over the both of you." Angela yanked a few twenty-dollar bills from her purse, tossing them on the table. "Enjoy the rest of your evening... Don't bother paying me back for this extra money."

Sucking her teeth, Toni snatched one of the twenty-dollar bills from the table next to Angela's unfinished plate of shrimp and scallop pasta. "Girl, take this lonely ass extra twenty and run along," she said, pushing it into Angela's hand, who in turn put it back into her purse.

Snapping her purse closed, Angela waved a dismissive hand at them before trotting off.

"*That's* why I drove my own car," Patience commented to Toni, who dug her fork into her remaining salmon steak. "She'd leave us stranded in a minute."

"That girl knows exactly what I was *insinuating*," Toni griped. "Trevor's ass is hardly ever home." She shook her head. "And she thinks because he makes good money that that shit is acceptable."

Over the entire conversation, Patience just offered a nonchalant shrug.

Toni went back to enjoying her meal, until she looked up at Patience, who was picking at the roll on her plate. "Aside from that raggedy ass dinner date Monday, how *was* your week sis?"

Patience let out a long sigh. "It was…nothing I'm not used to." She rubbed the back of her neck. "I took on a few more properties to sell."

Toni's eyes lit up. "Yeah?" Patience nodded. "Good for you. Those commissions are nice, aren't they?"

Patience laughed. "They *do* pay my many bills… Including the abundance of new art supplies that I have to keep buying."

"Again?" Toni chortled. "How much drawing are you *doing*?"

"It's not just *me* doing it."

"Yeah, that apple surely didn't fall far." Toni took a sip of her pinot noir. "Did she wind up joining that art club?"

"Yeah."

"Good for her," Toni beamed. "I'm trying to get Jordan to join dance club."

Patience stretched her neck from side to side. "I take it she's not trying to hear it?"

Toni rolled her eyes. "Of *course* not," she grumbled. "Talking

about she doesn't like the idea of being told when and how to dance."
Patience laughed, causing Toni to squint her eyes. "It's not funny,
your niece is a mess. It's amazing how a nine-year old—who pays
not *one* bill—can be such a damn diva."

Patience laughed again. "And you're *shocked* by that?" she
teased. "You *do* know you're her mother, right? You remember how
headstrong and opinionated *you* were at her age…hell, at *every* age."

Toni pointed a finger at her. "Hey now." Her face displayed a
hint of amusement. "You aren't some quiet, sweet wallflower your-
damn-self."

Hand over her eyes, Patience shook her head. "This, I know."
She folded her arms. "Mom would always say that I had the worst
attitude out of the three of us."

"Nah, that was a whole lie. Everyone knew it was Angela."

Patience laughed quietly. "Agreed."

"Anyway, off the topic of mean ass big sisters and crazy kids,
I'm taking on a new client." Grabbing her fork, Toni once again
speared her food. "Meeting with him next week."

A warm smile appeared on Patience's face. "Nice,
congratulations T… Your firm is still trusting you with people's
money huh?"

Toni playfully flipped her the finger, earning a giggle from
Patience. "Thank you, and yes, they *are* because I'm a damn good
accountant." She placed the fork full of food in her mouth, chewing.
"I hope he's not an asshole… It'll be even better if he's attractive."

"Something is wrong with you." Patience's voice was laced
with humor.

"No, for real you have *no* idea what it's like sitting across from
someone who's not only irritable because someone tore his taxes up
the year before, but then has the nerve to look like a damn foot."
Toni set her fork back down. "Like the *last* client I had, before he
decided to cut ties with the firm because he was pissed that he owed
back taxes. Like it was *our* fault he hadn't filed correctly in four years."

"He might've been the same guy your sister tried to hook me up with," Patience brought up. "He was...*both*."

"I wouldn't be surprised." Toni raised her glass to her lips. "You know her taste in men has always been questionable."

Nodding in agreement, Patience dug her fork into the partially eaten crab and spinach stuffed shells on her plate. Turning her lip up in disgust, she tossed the fork back down without eating it. "You know, I was trying to be polite, but the food here is trash."

Toni nearly spat out her wine with laughter. "Yeah, I didn't want to admit it. My face was screwed up eating this shit." Setting her glass down, she grabbed her purse. "I still owe you something to eat and this won't count." She pulled out her wallet. "You want to head to the sports bar next door? I'm sure their hot wings taste better than this." When Patience shook her head no, Toni grimaced. "I have half a cheesecake at home, you want some of *that*?"

Patience chuckled at the guilty look on her sister's face. "Sure, why not?"

Relieved that her offer was accepted, Toni grinned. "Okay, cool."

As she went to signal for the waiter, someone approached their table. Both women eyed the patron with curiosity.

The man's bulging pectoral and bicep muscles were clearly noticeable under his two-sizes two small, long-sleeved T-shirt. Judging by the form fitting jeans hugging his skinny legs, he clearly hadn't focused nearly as much time on building *those* muscles. "Excuse me ladies, I couldn't help but notice you two sitting over here alone."

Patience and Toni shot each other confused glances. Patience then looked back at him. "I'm confused as to why you said that we're alone when it's clearly two of us sitting here."

Closing her eyes, Toni lowered her head, shaking it. *Jesus.*

The man smoothed his hand down his shirt. "There's no *man* sitting here with you."

"Oh, my mistake," Patience bristled. Rolling her eyes, she turned away from him, earning a snicker from Toni.

"So, can I buy you ladies a drink?" he pressed.

"No, we're fine, thank you," Toni politely shot down.

He leered at Patience, who was blatantly ignoring him. "You sure?"

Patience frowned at him. "My sister just told you no." Her tone failed to hide her disdain. "Is there a reason why you didn't just take that and go?"

"I peeped her wedding ring. It makes sense that *she* turned it down." He pointed to Patience's left hand. "I don't see one on *your* finger though."

Patience fixed him with a blank stare. *Note to self, get a fake wedding band.*

"So… What do you say? Can I buy you a drink?" His lips twisted into a smug smirk. "It might loosen that attitude up a bit."

Hand smacking the table, Toni scowled at him. "Now hold the fuck up—"

Patience quickly put a hand up to stop her sister's rampage. "It's fine T." She returned her attention to their unwanted company. "You really want to buy me a drink?"

He nodded, eager. "I sure would."

"You probably want to fuck me too, don't you?"

Toni shot her a stunned look. "Pace, what the hell?"

Pulling an empty chair out, he plopped down. "I mean I wasn't going to *ask*, but hell *yeah*." He grinned. "You down for that?"

"Well… It might help with my attitude, so I guess." Patience leaned forward. "But only if you promise to take me home to my five children when we're finished."

His eyes went wide. "Wait you— You have *kids*?"

"I just said that I have five," Patience quickly reminded. When his mouth fell open, she tilted her head, her unblinking deep brown eyes staring into his soul. "Does that bother you? The fact that I have five children?"

He looked like the words had gotten stuck in his throat. "Uhh— Umm."

"Oh, I'm divorced too, and quite possibly emotionally damaged, so there's that."

Toni turned away to not laugh in the man's face.

"And you should know that I don't do one-night stands, so if you fuck me, I'll expect you to stick around," Patience goaded. "You down for that? Picking up the pieces of my shattered heart? Being a stepdaddy to my five children?"

The man scooted his seat back so hard, he practically fell out of it. "Umm, you ladies have a good evening."

"Is that a *no*?" Patience called after him as he scrambled away.

Unable to hold it in any longer, Toni erupted with laughter. "You damn near gave that fool a heart attack."

"His swole ass should've taken the initial no and rolled." Patience grabbed her purse, slinging the strap over her shoulder. "Let's get the hell out of here."

Toni shook her head, amusement still written on her face. "Yeah let's, before you hurt anyone else's feelings." She signaled for the waiter.

Chapter Two

EXCEPT FOR THE R&B MUSIC coming through the car speaker, the thirty-five-minute drive from downtown Maple Glenn to the Virginia suburbs was quiet. Pulling in front of Toni's two-story single home, Patience put her late model silver sedan in park.

Toni peered over at Patience, who was rubbing her eyes with her fingertips, and gave her arm a light nudge. "You still want the cheesecake, or do you want to head home to sleep?"

Patience shot her a weary look. "Stop trying to get out of giving up the damn cheesecake."

Giggling, Toni grabbed her purse. "Whatever." She opened the door. "You want to come in for a moment while I pack it up?"

Shaking her head, Patience leaned back against the seat. "I'm fine waiting out here."

"Okay. Hang tight."

"Sure." Patience watched Toni trot inside, before lowering the volume on her car radio. Eyeing the dash numbers illuminating eleven-thirty p.m., she let out a deep breath. "My bed is definitely calling my name right now."

After a few moments, her phone rang. She grabbed it from her purse, placing it to her ear. "Are you *remaking* the damn cheesecake, Toni?"

"Listen, I was packing it up for you, but Noelle walked in and

14

was being nosy, so I told her what I was doing and who it was for, and now she wants to see you," Toni quickly fired off.

Patience removed her seat belt. "Not surprising." She opened the car door. "Tell her 'here I come'."

Patience walked up the lit path and opened the door, stepping foot inside of the house. Crossing through the living room, she entered the kitchen to be greeted by a child darting straight for her.

"Mommy!" the girl squealed, practically tackling her.

Amused, Patience wrapped her arms around eight-year-old Noelle Harvey. The adorable little girl was a spitting younger image of Patience, down to her brown complexion. "Hi baby."

Humored by the scene, Toni shook her head. "Little girl, if you don't stop acting like you didn't just see your mother earlier today."

Patience shot a narrowed-eyed glance Toni's way. "You leave my child alone." What Patience had told the man at the restaurant wasn't an entire lie. She did have a child—*one*, not five.

Toni flagged her sister with her hand.

Pulling back from the embrace, Noelle—standing at the middle of her mother's waist—stared up at her. "Did you have fun with Aunt Toni?"

Patience winced. "Sure," she slowly drew out.

Toni ran a hand over her hair. "Aunt Angie ruined it before it even started."

Patience waved a hand at her. "It was fine."

"Cool. Did you come to take me home?" Noelle asked, playing with the silver butterfly pendant hanging around her mother's neck.

Patience opened her mouth, but was drowned out by Toni. "Nope, you're staying here until Sunday," she said. "Your mama deserves a break."

Patience flashed Toni a stern look. "Toni."

"*What?*" Toni threw back, eyes wide. "These kids know they're a handful and a hot, energy filled *mess*."

Noelle giggled. "You're silly Aunt Toni."

"Yeah, she's *something* all right," Patience muttered. She looked at Noelle. "Do you *want* to come home?"

"What did I just say?" Toni jumped in.

"Toni, shut up." Patience's command earned a snicker from her sister.

Noelle shrugged. "No, it's okay. I'm having fun with Jordan."

Patience smiled. "Good."

Toni folded her arms. "All right little girl, you've seen your mom, go back up to bed."

"Aww, can I stay up a little longer?" Noelle's brown eyes pleaded.

Patience patted the top of Noelle's unruly, curly ponytail, a contrast to the neat style that Patience had dropped her off with. It was clear that Noelle had been rolling around with her cousin all evening. "No baby, go get some rest." She leaned down, giving Noelle a kiss on her cheek. "I'll call you tomorrow."

"Okay. Good night Mommy," Noelle relented, before leaving the kitchen.

"Good night Bunny." Patience followed her progress until she heard footsteps go up the stairs. "She's such a night owl."

"It isn't just *her*, that niece of yours is too," Toni said. "But Rob promised to take them to the indoor bounce park tomorrow, so Jordan figured that her going to sleep on time for once would make the day get here faster."

Patience laughed a bit.

"The girls always have fun when they're together," Toni added. "You need to let us give you a break more often." Only a year apart, Jordan and Noelle, like their mothers, were close.

"I hear you, but—"

"Aht, no 'buts'. I mean it." Toni pointed to a seat at the kitchen table. "You might as well sit for a minute."

Conceding, Patience set her purse on the chair next to her, before taking a seat.

Toni placed a hefty slice of cherry cheesecake on a plate, then sat it in front of Patience.

"Thank you," Patience replied.

"Of course." Toni grabbed her own slice and sat down across from her sister. They ate in companiable silence, before Toni finally spoke. "So... Tonight was interesting, huh?"

Patience swallowed her bite before speaking. "You mean the moron, or that dumb guy?"

Toni nearly choked on her food, trying not to laugh. "You know Angie would slide down a wall if you called her a moron to her face."

"I'll be sure to put that on my to-do list," Patience jeered, lightly jabbing the fork into the remaining cake. "You know I haven't been able to tolerate her for years now. She's just so..."

"Uppity? Inauthentic? Judgmental?"

"It's like..." Patience sighed. "Whenever I'm in a good place in my life, she finds a way to irritate me," she explained. "She never even *asked* me if I was ready to date yet, she just ambushed me with the most irritable person she could find."

Toni let out a weary sigh. Though she was used to being in the middle of her sisters' lifelong feud, she still hated it. "Maybe if you two talked more—"

"I've tried in the past, doesn't work, so no."

Toni put her hands up in surrender. "Okay, let's drop Angela from the topic of discussion." Patience nodded in agreement. "But since you mentioned dating—*some*what," Toni amended, noticing the perplexity on Patience's face. "*Are* you ready to date?"

Patience grimaced. "Do I *have* to?"

Stifling a giggle, Toni shook her head. "No, you don't *have* to date, but it *has* been a while sis," she reminded. "You've been divorced for nine years, and I know you took the first few years after it was finalized to heal from that entire ordeal and get used to being a new mom— understandably." She scooped some more cheesecake onto her fork. "But the last time you even *mentioned* a date was what, four years ago?"

"*Five*. If you could *call* that a date. I couldn't even tolerate the man through dinner. And before *that* it was just a few conversations here and there." Patience set her fork down, folding her hands on the tabletop. "Toni... I know you're married, so you don't get this. But the dating pool has piss in it—"

Swallowing her bite, Toni choked out a laugh. "Oh, *come* on Pace."

"And frankly, some shit too," Patience finished. "I don't want to go through another talking phase that will go absolutely nowhere." She leaned back in her seat. "And I *refuse* to bring any raggedy prospects around my daughter."

The hilarity left Toni's face. "I can understand that; you not wanting to introduce Noelle to anyone you're not serious about."

"Exactly." Patience offered a shrug. "I'm at a point in my life where I'm *fine* with being by myself. I'm content with it; I'm *used* to it." She stared down at the napkin on the table, toying with it. "Besides, what free time do I really *have* to entertain dating with a child?"

"You can have *lots* if you give yourself a break," Toni mentioned. "I told you, Rob and I will get Noelle anytime you need us to."

Patience just shook her head.

Toni sighed once again. "Well... If you don't want a stepdad for Noelle, how about at *least* someone who can crack your back for a while?"

A bemused smirk crossed Patience's face. "You said that shit with a straight face too."

"Look, I know you. You're not out here having one-night stands, so I *know* you're aching for some right now." Toni pointed her fork in her sister's direction. "And before you say anything about a vibrator, it's not the same."

"Shit it's *better* in some cases."

"Well... I can't argue there," Toni agreed, laughter in her voice. "You remember some of the guys I dealt with before Rob." Dropping her fork to the plate, Toni clasped her hands. "Okay, but in all seriousness. If a nice, handsome, established man who loves children, has no baggage—"

"Wouldn't it be a bit hypocritical for me to expect no baggage from a man, when I, myself have my own set of bags in the garage?" Patience questioned.

"Nah, *you* threw *your* trash—*Greg*—away a long time ago, and I'd never consider my beautiful niece, baggage, so you are in your right to want that."

Patience waved a dismissive hand her sister's way. While she knew Toni had a point, she was over the topic altogether.

Toni waved one right back. "Okay fine let's say someone who has *little* to no baggage, and loves a challenge, i.e. dealing with *your* smart-ass mouth, comes along—would you be open to date him?"

Patience stared for a moment. Then her brow gathered. "Toni, don't you *dare* pull that shit."

Eyes bulging, Toni brought a hand to her chest. "*What?*" When Patience shot her a knowing look, Toni sucked her teeth. "It's not like I *know* anybody—"

"So, you're saying that if you *did*, you'd try it?"

Glaring, Toni sucked her teeth. "Don't do that Pace, I wouldn't set you up like *Angie* did."

Patience pointed, her eyes flashing. "You *would*."

"Okay, I *would*. But unlike Angela, *I know* your type."

Shaking her head, Patience pushed her half-eaten plate back. "Good night, Antoinette."

"So, is that a *yes?*" Toni harped as Patience grabbed her purse. "'Cause if it *is*, I'll certainly be on the lookout."

"That's a 'if you try to hook me up with anyone, I'm going to choke you'."

Toni snickered at Patience's departing back. "Fine… Call me when you get home, baby sis."

"I will."

Chapter Three

MICHAEL CARTER SURVEYED THE FLOOR plans laid across the table. Picking up a pencil, he made a few notes near some of the photos.

"What do you think?" Dante Carter asked, folding his arms.

Michael made another correction. "This is a simple structure. Three bedrooms, two and a half baths, kitchen, living room and den—we can get this built in about nine months, maybe shorter."

Dante nodded.

"The second home on that twin project out in Clearview is on schedule to be completed in a few weeks..." Michael put a cap on his marker, setting it on the table. "So we can put this on the books to start soon after."

"The second home already has offers in and it's not even *finished* yet," Dante mused.

Rolling the table-length blueprints, Michael put them in the cylinder case. "I'm not surprised. The first one sold before completion too."

"Yeah, you're a beast with the floor plans."

Michael offered the man a smile. "Thanks." The owner of his own construction company for nearly fifteen years, Michael had a proven reputation and talent for both designing homes and building them. He wasn't just the face of his company; he was also hands on.

"At this rate, we might as well go ahead and sign a few more contracts." Dante tapped his chin with his finger. "There's a wait list, you know."

"Appreciate the enthusiasm, but don't get ahead of yourself," Michael replied. "We have plenty of work that'll hold us over for a while."

Dante quickly mulled over his hectic schedule. "Yeah, I guess you have a point." Younger than his older brother by six years, Dante had worked within Michael's company as a contractor for the past seven. As such, he knew well enough that his brother was not about to bite off more than he could chew. Besides, Michael was right; they had more than enough work, and the company made plenty of money. "*Speaking* of houses...how's everything going with your realtor?"

Michael looked up at him, a stoney expression on his handsome dark brown face. "I'll let you know when she actually shows me a *house*."

Wincing at Michael's sharp tone, Dante ran a hand along the back of his neck. "Umm... She's new to this bro—"

"I *know* that, and I'm being patient—as patient as I *can* be," Michael cut in. "But I've been doing most of the work *for* her." He lightly tapped his fist on the table. "Look, I know she's your lady Dante, but I don't have many more missed properties in me—"

Dante's hand shot up, halting his brother's words. "I get it, and if it means *anything*, I appreciate you giving her a chance to do this for you," he said. "Please don't cut her loose just yet. I'm sure she'll find you something great."

Michael raised an eyebrow. The last thing he wanted to discuss was the struggles with his realtor...also known as his brother's girlfriend. As soon as Michael had announced that he was in the process of purchasing a home, tired of the luxury high rise condo he'd been renting, his brother hadn't hesitated to press him to take on his girlfriend as his realtor. Something that Michael had since regretted. But because she was family, he hadn't done what he'd *wanted* to do after she dropped the first ball three months ago—fire her.

"She has *one* more chance," Michael warned as the conference line rang.

"You're the best." A grateful smile flashed across Dante's brown face. "She says you're the *nice* in-law… Unlike the *other* one."

"Nice to know," Michael muttered, peering at the caller ID. Seeing that it was his receptionist, he answered the phone. "Yes Cassie? …Okay. Yes, please send her in… Thank you—and take your lunch."

Dante eyed Michael as he hung the phone up. "A new client?"

Michael sat down at his desk. "Nah, Kenya is here."

"The *other* one," Dante grunted, gathering up the cylinders. "And that's my cue to get the hell out of here."

Michael shook his head as Dante grabbed his baseball cap, placing it on his head. "You two still at odds, huh?"

"Well, Lori is still upset, so I guess *so*."

Michael ran a hand along the top of his short, tapered coal black hair. "Damn."

"Right—"The door opened, interrupting Dante's rant.

"Hey guys." Kenya Carter's tone was cheerful.

Michael offered a wave. "What's up sis?"

Kenya smiled at him. But as she spotted Dante trying to get past her towards the door, she grabbed his arm. "Seriously? I just got back from vacation yesterday, and you're not going to speak to me?" she charged. "I can't get a hug? Acknowledgment about my flawless tan? *Nothing?*"

Michael snickered a bit at his sister's pressing questions. Though her light-brown skin was clearly favored by the Bahamian sun over the past week.

"Nope," Dante scoffed.

Narrowing her eyes at her baby brother, Kenya folded her arms. "This wouldn't happen to be because of your little girlfriend, would it?" she assumed. "Don't tell me she's *still* upset that I gave my opinion about her cooking?"

Dante tossed an arm up in agitation. "She spent all *day* on that roast, just for you to tell her that it was the worst thing that you'd ever tasted."

Letting out a sigh, Michael rubbed his temples with his fingertips. *Dear God.* He'd had a long night and a hectic morning. He was in no mood to endure a feud between his brother and older sister.

Kenya stared at Dante, unfazed. "It *was*, and it was *three weeks* ago. I think she should be over it by now."

Dante loudly huffed, "Bye, yo." He punctuated his words by storming out of the room, shutting the door behind him.

Kenya shook her head. "Michael, our little brother is *still* so dramatic."

Michael fixed Kenya with a stern gaze. "May*be* Kenya, but you can't keep talking shit about and *to* the man's girlfriend, and think he's not supposed to *say* anything about it," he chided. "He's right to defend her against you."

Kenya rolled her eyes. "Oh please, I haven't said *half* the shit I've wanted to say to that dippy girl." A scoff sounded from her throat. "Hell Dante knows she's flaky too, he just doesn't want to admit it."

"Kenya, enough." Michael's tone was flat. "They've been together five years now."

"Five years and he has *yet* to propose to her. That should tell you something."

Michael pinched the bridge of his nose. "How they choose to navigate the progression of their relationship is *their* business."

Waving a dismissive hand, Kenya approached the table. "Okay fine, I didn't come here to argue with you," she said, smoothing down her red pencil skirt. "I have an hour, so I came to see if you wanted to go to lunch… Well, I wanted to go with *both* of you, but…"

"I appreciate the offer, but sorry, I can't," Michael shot down. "I ran over on a few meetings earlier, so I'm just eating a quick lunch here in the office while I finish up what I need to, before I clock out for the day."

Kenya placed a hand to her hip. "You own the company, you can leave whenever you want."

"Yes, and I *want* to leave *after* I get done what I need to get done." He ran his hand down his royal blue button-down shirt. "I refuse to leave these records that I still have to pull, for tomorrow."

Shrugging, Kenya leaned against the table. "I understand. As a fellow business owner, I know how much work and time it takes to keep things running." The owner of a lucrative wedding planning company, Kenya did indeed know. "But I *also* know when to set business aside and have some fun...unlike *you*."

The not-so-subtle dig drew an eyeroll from Michael; he could see where this was going. "I *do* have fun, know-it-all. *Building houses* is fun for me."

Kenya pursed her full lips. "Just what I thought a grumpy, old, millionaire bachelor would say."

Squinting his eyes at his sister, Michael leaned back in his seat. "I am *not* one of those characters in those romance movies you watch—" He chuckled when Kenya dissolved into laughter. "I'm *far* from grumpy, and I'm three years younger than you. So if *I'm* old, so are *you*. Millionaire is a *stretch*—"

"Oh please, not hardly." Kenya's voice was laced with humor.

"I'm financially *comfortable*, I'll leave it at that," he countered. "And yes, I'm a bachelor. But that is by choice."

Kenya gathered some of her waist-length braided hair, moving it to one side. "Um hmm."

"And you and I are *both* single, if you recall."

"I'm single and *dating*," Kenya corrected.

Confusion masked Michael's face. "What does that even *mean?*"

"That I'm single until I'm *not*," she shrugged. "Until then, I'm having fun. Like *you* need to." Her head leaned to the side. "Nobody is telling you to get *married* Mike, but hell, at least *date*."

"I *have* dated," he reminded her. "But it was hard trying to maintain a relationship while I was building my business—"

"No, you just *chose* wrong. A *real* woman wouldn't have left you when you weren't available to her twenty-four seven." Kenya folded her arms. "Like you said, you were building your business."

Michael's brows shot up. "Umm…yeah, I know you're a bit biased because I'm your brother and all, but women *deserve* quality time and attention. So, they weren't *wrong* for stepping off because I couldn't give it to them."

Though Michael was no stranger to dating, he had a point. Between grad school, and building his business, he hadn't been the most attentive partner in the past. Which led to the dissolution of those relationships. Three years ago, he'd sworn off dating entirely.

"Okay fine, but you have the time *now*, and you won't find the right woman with your lackluster everyday routine," Kenya harped.

Folding his arms, Michael stared at Kenya with an emotionless face as she ranted on about *his* love life—or lack thereof.

"What are the odds that you're going to meet your future wife at a construction site, this office building, or that old ass coffee shop you go to every morning?" Kenya put a finger up. "I'm taking you to a lounge this weekend."

"Neither *one* of our old asses need to be looking for love in a damn *lounge*," Michael sneered, earning another laugh from his sister. He pointed to the door. "I love you and appreciate your concern, but I'm just fine being by myself. Now I have work to do, so with all due respect… See yourself out."

Kenya lightly flung her wrist in his direction. "Okay fine."

"And apologize to Lori please," he ordered. "The last thing our parents need is tension between their children."

Letting out a loud breath, Kenya adjusted the purse on her shoulder. "*Fine.*" She threw a wave his way. "See you. Stop over my place for dinner later if you can."

"See you. I will," he said at her departing back.

Once the room was empty, Michael grabbed his laptop. As the system booted, his mind wandered. He hadn't exactly told his sister the truth. While Michael was glad that he'd taken his dating hiatus, he was now at a point in his life where he yearned for companionship again. But he often wondered if by waiting until his late thirties to want to settle down, he'd missed his opportunity to find the woman who would be his forever.

Hearing the email notification from his laptop snapped him out of his wandering thoughts. Adjusting his tie, he sat up in his seat, eyeing the message. "Nothing like a last-minute meeting request to take my mind off of my loveless life," he joked.

Pulling open the freezer, Patience retrieved a box of frozen waffles. Removing four, she placed them in the double toaster, then grabbed two plates from the overhead cabinet.

While waiting on the waffles, she rinsed off a handful of strawberries in the sink. Patting them dry with a paper towel, she placed a few on one plate and the rest on another. Glancing at her watch, she headed for the kitchen entrance.

"Noelle," she called. "Come eat breakfast."

"Okay, here I come."

Once the waffles popped up, Patience moved swiftly to butter each one before dividing them between the two plates, alongside the strawberries. After cutting the waffles on one plate into smaller pieces, she retrieved both from the counter and transported them to the kitchen table. Placing a bottle of syrup down, she peered at her watch again, sucking her teeth. "This little girl," she huffed, spinning around. "Noelle—girl!" Startled, Patience clutched her chest as Noelle stared at her with wide eyes. "Why is it that you're only quiet when you're sneaking up on me?"

Noelle giggled. "You should've seen your face."

"Oh, that's funny, huh?" Patience questioned, slightly tickled.

Removing the satin scarf from Noelle's braided hair, she guided the little girl to the table and prepared herself some coffee.

Noelle squirted a generous amount of syrup on her waffles. "Ooh, can I have whipped cream on my waffles?"

"Sorry Bunny, we're out."

Placing a fork full of waffles into her mouth, Noelle just shrugged.

Her favorite hand-painted lavender mug in hand, Patience sat down at the table. Then began to eat her own breakfast, in between a few quick sips of her coffee. "Are you ready for your test today?"

"Yes," Noelle answered. "Are you showing a new house today?"

Patience set her coffee mug down. "No, I'll be confined to the office."

"The next time you show a house, can *I* go?" Noelle's eyes were bright with hope.

"No ma'am," Patience shot down. "I don't think clients want to see an eight-year-old running around, while trying to decide whether to buy a house or not."

Noelle licked the syrup from her fork. "Well… Maybe if *they* have children, and they bring them, I can play with them and that would make the children happy," she pondered. "And if the children are happy, then the *parents* will be happy, and it'll make them want to buy the house even more, because I'm awesome."

Patience shot a humored look her daughter's way. "Yes, you *are* awesome. You're also, beautiful, intelligent, and the best daughter in the world, but you're still not going."

Noelle smiled despite having her request denied. Her mother praising her wasn't new, but it always made Noelle beam every time she heard it. "Okay." She grabbed a strawberry and bit into it. "But if you change your mind, I'm here."

"I'll be sure to keep that in mind." Patience eyed Noelle as the girl ate. Though she'd gone through a lot during her failed marriage to Noelle's father, the one thing Patience never regretted was having *her.* And though things were tough at times as a single mother, the sweet, smart, charismatic little girl was Patience's pride and joy.

Noelle set her fork down. "Finished."

Patience took her last sip of coffee. "Good job. Now go grab your bookbag and jacket so we can get going."

Pushing her seat back, Noelle stood up. "Can I take my stuffed bunny to school for show and tell?"

"Which one?" Patience muttered to herself, rising from her seat. Her daughter had a ton of stuffed toy rabbits. "Wait, they still have show and tell in the fourth grade?"

"Yes," Noelle threw out, scurrying out of the kitchen.

"Interesting," Patience mumbled, loading the dishes into the dishwasher. "But no. God forbid you lose one of those things. Take one of your drawings or something."

"Can I take one of *yours?*"

"Sure." Patience wiped the counter down with a dishrag.

"I have the picture. I'm putting my shoes on now," Noelle announced from the living room after a few moments. "Are you almost done in there?"

"Yes." Patience shook her head. "Now, *she's* the one rushing *me.*" When her cell phone rang, she swiftly grabbed it from the table, giving the screen a quick eye. "Yeah sis?" she answered. Pausing short of walking out of the kitchen, Patience's eyes became slits as Toni spoke. "What—girl, I won't have time to stop for no goddamn—"

"Mommy, I'm ready!"

"I'm *coming* Bunny." Patience held the phone to her ear as she hurried out of the kitchen.

Chapter Four

MICHAEL MOSEYED DOWN THE TREE-LINED street of downtown Maple Glenn, en route to his favorite coffee shop. Each morning, he'd drop his briefcase off at the office, before taking the short stroll to get the exact same order. This Monday was no different.

The early crisp mid-March breeze cooled him down as Michael stopped short in front of the coffee shop. But instead of being greeted by the vibrant "open" sign, he was met with a paper notice stuck to the glass door.

Fredrick's coffeehouse is closed for renovations. We apologize for the inconvenience.

Letting out a sigh, Michael ran a hand over the back of his head. "Great," he grumbled. He peered at the platinum watch on his wrist. "I guess I'll be drinking that cinnamon hazelnut mess that Cassie keeps buying for the office."

"Excuse me, son."

Curious as to who had interrupted his solo complaint session, Michael spun around. He laid eyes on a brown-skinned man, who clearly surpassed him in age by at least thirty years. "Yes sir?" Michael answered, politely.

The gentleman gestured towards the shop. "I saw you reading the sign here."

Michael nodded. "I was. It's my usual spot. Not exactly pleased that it's closed."

"Well, if you're looking for another coffee spot while they're being renovated, you should check out Jessy's Bakery and Café."

Michael's brow raised. "Oh yeah?"

Nodding, the man displayed the large coffee cup in his hand. "They've been open for a few weeks now. Just a few blocks up, and they make a mean crumb cake."

Michael offered a warm smile. "I appreciate the info." He pointed up the street. "A few blocks this way?"

Nodding once more, the man gestured. "Four to be exact and get one of those crumb cakes while you're there." He grinned. "Tell them Earl sent you."

Michael chuckled as the man moseyed away. "Will do."

The extra four block walk up the street took Michael less than ten minutes. He scanned the block looking for a sign, then glancing across the street, he saw it—Jessy's Gourmet Bakery and Café, nestled between a florist and an antique shop.

The moment he stepped inside, Michael was hit with the sweet scent of pastries and the rich aroma of brewing coffee. Approaching the counter, he eyed the generous assortment of baked goods enclosed in glass. Their selection was much more abundant than his old coffeehouse. He saw the crumb cake the man had mentioned, but being more of a brownie man, his eyes drew to the fudge square on the shelf above it.

Too early for something that rich, but I'll definitely be back for this later, he thought, still eyeing the selection.

"May I help you?"

The barista's pleasant tone snapped Michael out of his trance. He peered up at her. "Yes. I apologize for spacing out."

The woman stared with her mouth open for a second, then gave him a toothy smile. "No apologies necessary. I wasn't rushing you."

Michael smiled back; the way she was ogling wasn't lost on him. Michael was a tall, handsome, well-built man; looks of admiration, he was used to. "Okay then." He stepped forward. "This might be a silly question, but do you have breakfast sandwiches?"

"Yes, of course."

"Perfect, I'd like a large coffee—black, and a beef bacon, egg, and cheese sandwich on a plain bagel." He waited for the woman to enter that order as he scanned the menu on the wall behind her. *Might as well get something for the office.* "Before you ring that up, can you add two dozen donuts? —You can mix those any way you recommend. Also, six blueberry muffins, six coffee crumble muffins, six banana nut muffins, and—do you do coffee by the box?"

The woman eagerly rang up the haul. "We sure do."

"In that case, please add two boxes of coffee—one medium roast and one dark roast—to the order." He pulled his wallet from his trouser pocket. "Thank you."

"You're welcome." After ringing up everything, she read Michael his total to which he promptly paid with his debit card. "We'll get started on your sandwich right away, and I'll get your coffee now." She handed him back his card with receipt. "It'll be a bit of a wait for the bulk order. Would you like to come back for that, or do you mind waiting?"

"I can wait." Michael took a ten-dollar bill from his wallet and placed it into the tip jar, to which the barista thanked him profusely.

Stepping back from the counter, Michael returned his wallet to his pocket. He'd have to thank Earl should he ever see him again; somehow the miracle of his usual order had still come through.

Glancing at the receipt, he chuckled to himself. "As expensive as these specialty donuts and muffins are, they better eat every last one," he mused in a low voice, pocketing the receipt. He was so preoccupied with his thoughts that he didn't hear the shop door open and close.

"I can't understand why you couldn't just stop by here on your lunch break," Patience huffed into her phone. "I told you *earlier* that I didn't feel like this." She examined her sculpted, painted nails as the person on the other end of the line rambled. "Okay fine, I'm here now so what do you want me to pick up for you?" She stood behind the gentleman in front of her. "Toni—I'm not carrying all of that through these crowded ass streets. *Please* just pick one or two things." She rolled her eyes at her sister's reply. Noticing that the man had yet to move up, Patience pulled the phone from her ear. "Excuse me sir, are you in line?"

Michael turned around preparing to respond, but the words had gotten caught in his throat. Going completely still, his eyes broadened. *Whoa!* The breathtaking woman before him had certainly stunned him into silence.

Patience's brow knitted when he didn't provide an answer. *Are you going to stare, or answer?* She held her stern gaze on his face. "Did you hear me?" she asked, finally.

Realizing that he was getting lost in her alluring eyes and the delicate features of her face, Michael snapped out of it and quickly moved aside. "No— Uh, I mean, *yes,* I heard you." He could've kicked himself for his blunder. He gestured with his hand for her to go ahead. "I've ordered already. Please go ahead."

Offering a half smile, Patience approached the counter, putting the phone back to her ear.

Standing in the small space, Michael surveyed the artwork on the walls as Patience placed her order. Yet the pieces—as interesting as they *were*—failed to hold his attention. His eyes kept being drawn back to *her.*

He focused on the softness of her voice as she spoke to the barista, the subtle way she moved her head, sending her long, curly hair away from her face. His eyes slowly scanned her figure, noticing how the black, high waist flared skirt failed to hide the soft curves of her hips and behind. Or how the lavender long-sleeved blouse accentuated her ample chest and slender waistline, the color complementing the golden flecks of her skin. His eyes moved back up to her face, lingering on her profile. *She is absolutely beautiful—*

perfection... And you're staring at her like a damn creep. Blinking quickly, he turned away, hoping that she hadn't noticed.

"It'll be a few moments," the barista told Patience as she handed her the receipt.

Patience put her wallet back into her handbag. "Thank you." She backed away from the counter as a few more patrons walked in. "I got your raggedy pastries," she sneered into the phone. "I guess I can be nice and drop them off to you on my lunch break—" She scowled, "*No*, I can't come now—don't you have a client to see this morning?" Sighing at Toni's rants, Patience rubbed her forehead. "How is it that *you're* the annoying one? *I'm* the youngest sister, that's supposed to be *my* job."

Michael snickered at the comment.

Patience shot him a quizzical glance. "I'm sorry, was I speaking too loudly?" she asked him.

Meeting her stare, Michael's eyes widened, this time in panic. *Shit!* "No, no, you weren't," he sputtered. "I just have impeccable hearing."

Skeptical, Patience raised her eyebrow. "Uh huh," she slowly drew out.

When Patience turned away from him to continue her conversation, Michael had to stop himself from smacking his palm against his face. *Great. First you gawk at her, now she thinks you were eavesdropping on her conversation.*

"I'll call you later," Patience said, before hanging up. She'd had enough of her sister's nonsense for the morning.

As Patience placed her phone into her handbag, Michael felt the need to speak. "Excuse me," he said.

Patience shot a curious look his way. "Are you talking to me?"

Michael nodded, amazed at the contrast of her kind tone of voice to her stern face. "I just want to apologize if you felt that I was being a bit inappropriate earlier."

A bewildered frown scrunched her face. "Other than

potentially eavesdropping, he hadn't done anything wrong. "*What* was inappropriate exactly?"

"Staring at you when I first turned around."

Folding her arms, she took note of the smoothness of his baritone voice. Quickly scanning his rich dark-skinned frame from head to toe, she *also* took *note* of his thick, solid stature—and the perfect way the tailored gray suit hung on it. He was at least eight inches taller than her own five-foot-seven frame. His chiseled features were only enhanced by his tamed facial hair. Though he was clearly clean-cut, he could be rugged too if need be.

Quit eyeballing the man! she chided herself. Pushing her attraction to this man out of her mind, Patience raised her brows. "Do *you* think that was inappropriate?"

"I don't, nor was that my intention," Michael answered, honest. "However, it *could've* been if it made you uncomfortable."

She moved some of her hair over her shoulder. "I'm used to being stared at. In a *few* cases it has creeped me out, but in yours, it didn't, so… Don't worry about it."

Michael smiled, breathing a sigh of relief. "I'm glad."

Patience gave a nod. *He has such a beautiful smile… Look away.* Turning around, she faced the counter once again.

Michael stood back, trying to focus on the artwork for a second time. He'd completely forgotten about his sandwich and coffee, which seemed to be taking quite a long time. In this case, he was grateful for the delay; it allowed him to remain in the presence of this woman who had damn near taken his breath away.

"So…" he began after moments of silence. "Do you come here often?"

Patience turned towards him. A quiet laugh escaped her. "Sir… Is that a *pickup* line?"

Michael let out a laugh. "No, it was a genuine question," he assured. "A question with the intention of striking up a conversation."

She tilted her head. "Is there a difference?"

Michael shrugged. "*I'd* like to think so." Amusement was clear on his face. "Because for the record, my *actual* pickup lines are ten times better than *that* one."

"Are they really?"

"No," he immediately answered with a quick shake of his head.

This time, Patience let *out* a melodic laugh. "Well, at least you're honest about it."

"Yeah, lying was never something I was good at."

"It takes practice," Patience joked in return, earning a chuckle from him. "But to answer your question, I wouldn't say that I come in here often. Maybe a few times since they've opened," she said. "But my *sister* does, and she talked me into picking something up for her this morning."

Michael nodded, secretly thanking her sister, his normal coffee shop for being closed, *and* the elderly man who told him about this place. "This is my first time here," he revealed. "I was referred by Earl."

Stalled for a moment, Patience squinted. "I—I don't know who that is."

"Neither do I," Michael quipped, drawing a giggle from Patience. "No, he was just a random guy who saw me looking salty outside of my regular coffee spot, which was closed... He suggested this place."

"Well, here's hoping that it doesn't disappoint."

Michael's glossy eyes fixed on her. "No, it surely did *not*," he replied, tone dropping an octave. When her brows furrowed then released, he cleared his throat. *Dial it back, Mike.* "So umm, since you've been here more times than I have, do you recommend anything?"

Patience smirked; *a chatty one he is.* Normally she wasn't one for casual conversation with strange men. But it was something about this man—Patience didn't know what it was, but she found herself less...on guard in his presence. Maybe his kind eyes and easy smile were the culprit.

Glancing back at the pastries, Patience pondered the question.

"Frankly, it's a bit difficult to suggest something when one has no idea what the person is fond of."

"I'm not hard to please," he crooned.

Patience shot him a side-glance, but didn't say anything. Though for a moment, she felt a warmth go through her. *What the hell is wrong with you? He didn't say anything seductive... Stop acting juvenile.*

Michael took a step forward. "What do *you* like?" When her eyes met his, he amended his question. "What I mean is—what's your go-to treat?"

"Right." Patience adjusted the purse strap on her shoulder. "Anything lemon." She folded her arms once again. "Lemon strudel, lemon Danish, lemon pound cake—*anything* with lemon flavored icing—that's my go-to."

Nodding, Michael's eyes moved towards the display. "Fancy."

"Far from it. But it's what I like."

Michael eyed her intently. "A woman who knows what she likes is definitely a good thing."

Her full glossed lips curled into another smirk. "Right," she repeated. "And *your* go-to treat is?"

"Brownies—well, anything chocolate really." He let out a light chuckle. "Basic, I know."

Giggling, Patience threw her hands up. "I didn't say anything."

"You didn't have to, I *know* it is," he joked. "But I'll certainly give *your* suggestion a try." When Patience simply smiled at him, Michael felt his heart flutter. He opened his mouth to say something else, but Patience had turned her attention back to the barista, who was *finally* bagging up orders.

He'd had a casual conversation about pastries with this woman and he couldn't help but want to talk more. To get to *know* her more. But before he could muster up the courage to ask for her number, he needed to know her *name*. Adjusting his tie, he inched towards her. "Excuse me—"

"Sir, your order is ready."

Michael silently cursed that voice. Closing his eyes, he exhaled deeply—he'd lost his nerve. "Thank you," he said, approaching the counter.

"So sorry about the wait. We had a problem with the warmer, but it's all fixed now."

"No problem." Michael retrieved his coffee, along with the two paper bags which held the rest of his massive order.

"Do you need help with that?" the barista asked.

"No, I got it, thank you." Michael headed for the exit but stopped, gazing back at Patience, as she retrieved her box. "Have a nice rest of your day," he said to her. "It was nice talking to you."

Peering back at him, Patience's eyes crinkled in the corners. "You as well... Likewise."

Feeling his face flush, Michael willed himself to reply. "Thank you." When she turned away once again, Michael walked out of the shop. He looked back through the glass doors, catching one last glimpse of Patience. "Damn..." he whispered to himself. "It's just as well, I'm sure she's spoken for anyway." Resolved, he walked down the street.

Chapter Five

SOMEHOW BETWEEN CARRYING THE BAGS and his coffee, Michael had managed to scarf down his breakfast sandwich by the time he'd made the journey back to his office building. During the walk back, he couldn't stop thinking about that woman. *Damn, I should've asked her name before I started talking about pastries and shit. I'm thirty-seven, I should be better at this.*

His solo berating session would have to be put on hold; his receptionist was waiting for him.

"Michael, your nine o'clock is here," Cassie informed him, typing on her laptop. "She's in the conference room. Oh, and your meeting with the property owner over on Charleston has been pushed back to one."

"Thank you, Cassie," Michael replied in passing.

Cassie peered at the bags in his hands. "Umm, do you want me to take those bags?"

Michael paused. "My mind must be scattered today because I almost forgot I had these," he joked. "It's okay, I'll put them in the kitchen. But if you could take everything out of them, I'd appreciate it. It's coffee, donuts and muffins for the office."

"Still not a fan of the cinnamon hazelnut coffee, huh?" Cassie chortled, rising from her seat.

Michael laughed a bit. "No, but *you* like it, so I don't complain."

"Appreciate you, boss." Cassie zoned in on the name on the bags with glee. "Ooh, Jessy's. I *love* that place."

"Help yourself to whatever you want." After placing the items in the kitchen, Michael made a beeline for his office. Setting the coffee on his desk, he grabbed his laptop and headed for the conference room.

Giving the cracked door a quick knock, Michael entered. "Mrs. Harvey-Blake?"

Looking up from the folder in front of her, Toni flashed a smile. "Yes, but please call me Toni." She stood from her seat as Michael approached, hand outstretched. She shook it. "I'm pretty informal, Mr. Carter."

Michael smiled back. "Same. Michael is just fine." He gestured to her seat with his hand. "Please."

Toni gave a slight nod as she sat back down. As Michael took a seat across from her, Toni quickly sized him up. *Hmm, attractive man...very attractive.* Though she was happily married, she wasn't blind. "So, your last accountant retired?" she jumped right in.

"I guess you could say that," he answered with a nod. "He decided to switch careers. I'm happy for him of course, but he was great at what he did and while I'm skilled at doing my personal taxes, *business* taxes are a different story and I choose not to tackle that."

"I don't blame you, trust me. Business owners have *enough* on their plate." Toni folded her hands on the table. "Well, lucky for you, *I'm* also great at what I do."

"I don't doubt that." Michael adjusted his tie. "*He's* the one who recommended your firm."

"Perfect," Toni beamed. She opened her folder and clicked her pen.

Toni took an abundant number of notes over the next hour as they discussed Michael's company, finances, processes, procedures, and expectations. "Okay, so I'd like to have a meeting with your bookkeeper to go over your finance records in depth."

Michael raised his hand slightly. "That would be…me."

Toni's head leaned to the side. "Oh okay." She set her pen down. "That's a huge undertaking with everything else you're doing. Are you thinking of delegating that task in the future?"

"Not as of right now. I like the idea of knowing everything that's going in and out of here," Michael answered. "I have a system, and software that keeps me organized."

Toni gave an approving nod. "Makes sense." She glanced at her watch. "Since we're running short on time, we'll set up another meeting to go over your record keeping process."

"Sounds good."

"As part of my job, I like to meet with clients quarterly to go over finances, projection— things of that nature,"Toni continued. "I also keep records of my own, and as a courtesy I go back and check the tax preparations from the past few years." She studied Michael's face for any sign of protest. "Would you be okay with that?"

"Oh of *course*," Michael replied, pleased. "Whatever you feel is best. I'll be sure to provide you with everything you need."

A grin crossed Toni's face. "Despite the novel of notes I just wrote, I can tell you're going to make my job very easy."

Michael chuckled as he pulled his laptop closer to him. "That's a *good* thing, I assume."

"Absolutely." Toni caught a glimpse of his left hand as he opened the device. *No wedding band that I can see.* She tapped her pen to her notepad. *He seems polite, respectful, owns his own business— He'd look good on my sister's arm.* She quickly shook the thought from her head. *Patience would kill me if I tried it.*

"I'm checking my calendar now," Michael announced, completely unaware of whatever plan Toni had brewing. "I have some availability between projects next week."

"Okay great. When I get back to the office, I'll check my calendar as well, then give you a call so we can set a time to meet," Toni said. "I believe I have a few mornings open."

"Sounds like a plan." Michael closed his laptop. "I'll come to *your* office this time around. It's over on Marley Street, right?"

"Yep, just five blocks from here." She closed her folder. "Got to love working in Center City. Every major company is within blocks of one another, *and* they have some of *the* best food places down here."

Michael smiled, then it quickly faded as he thought of the café he'd just been to…and the intriguing woman he'd probably never see again. "I agree." He rose from his seat as Toni rose from hers. "It was great meeting you Toni. I look forward to working with your firm."

"Likewise, Michael."

Gathering his laptop, Michael headed for the door, opening it for Toni to pass through. "Have a good day."

"You as well," Toni returned, heading down the hall.

Michael retreated for his office in the other direction. Entering, he sat at his desk and set his laptop down. Eyeing the cold coffee, he was once again reminded of everything he should have said. He sighed. *Why can't I shake her face from my head?* Shaking *his* head, he opened his laptop once again.

Patience opened the oven, peering inside at the bubbling cheese in the large glass dish. *It could use a few more minutes.* "How are you doing with that garlic bread over there, Bunny?" she asked, closing the oven door.

"Good." Noelle sat at the kitchen table, plastic butter knife in hand, smearing a generous amount of butter on to a slice of Italian bread. "I'm covering the entire piece of bread this time."

"Good jo—" Spinning around, Patience stalled when she laid eyes on the massive pile of butter. "J—job." She ran a hand over the back of her neck. "Umm, baby… Are you *sure* you meant to put that much butter on there?"

Noelle lifted the piece of bread, examining it. "Is it too much?"

Patience opened her mouth to confirm, but hesitated. Noelle often helped with small tasks while dinner was being prepared, and

Patience didn't want to be discouraging, but she didn't want to lie either. She grabbed a butter knife from a drawer and went to the table. "Uh—it's a *tad* bit excessive, but it can be fixed," she softly said.

Patience proceeded to take some of the butter from the slice of bread, smearing it onto another one. "See?" Noelle leaned forward, studying what her mother was doing. "Only a light layer is needed."

"Oooh." Noelle stuck her plastic knife in the container of butter, then gave her mother a thumbs up. "Got it."

Patience winked at her, before moving for the counter, where her chopped salad veggies were waiting.

"Mommy, how come *I* can't use the metal knife?" Noelle asked, working on another piece of bread. "I already use the *fork* and *spoon*."

"Because knives can be dangerous, even *butter* knives," Patience explained, rinsing out a large glass bowl. "I just feel that you're still too young to use one now." Hearing a distinct smacking noise, Patience spun around. Eyebrows lifting, she fixed Noelle with a challenging look. "Did you just suck your teeth at me little girl?"

Noelle's eyes expanded; she didn't think her mother had heard it. She vigorously shook her head. "No—" she lied. When Patience's eyes narrowed, Noelle scratched her head. "I'm sorry Mommy, I won't do it again."

"Um hmm." Since it was Noelle's first offense, Patience elected not to harp on it. She instead returned to her salad making. "Saturday I'm taking you to the arts and crafts store, so we can get you some new art supplies for your club," she brought up after a few moments of silence.

Sighing heavily, Noelle finished buttering the last slice of bread. "Okay."

Picking up on the sullen tone of Noelle's voice, Patience turned around yet again. "Is something the matter?"

Noelle just shrugged.

"Noelle, you *do* know," Patience replied, tone soothing. "Come on, tell me."

Setting the knife back in the tub, Noelle folded her arms on the table. "I guess… I guess I'm a little mad because my teacher said that before we start drawing, we have to learn about art history and stuff."

Patience fought the urge to smile at her voice. Though clearly irritated, it was still adorable. "While I understand why you might feel a bit annoyed by that, you *should* learn the history of art." She rested her back against the counter. "It might not be an extensive history, but you should learn *something* about it."

Noelle plopped her elbow on the table, then leaned her head in her hand. "It just sounds boring," she pouted. "I just want to draw and paint and stuff."

"I hear you Noelle, but it's necessary," Patience maintained. "And I want you to go into it with an open mind and enthusiasm, okay?"

Noelle nodded.

"You promise?"

Noelle nodded again. "Yes."

"Good." Patience returned to her vegetables, tossing them in a bowl and mixing them before covering the finished salad with saran wrap. "I'll finish up here, go start your homework," she ordered, facing Noelle. "I'll call you when dinner is ready."

Leaving the table, Noelle scampered out of the kitchen. A moment later, the doorbell rang. Pausing in the middle of the staircase, Noelle peered back at her mother, en route to the door. "Ooh, can I see who it is?" she asked, eyes full of enthusiasm.

Patience pointed up the stairs. "No child. Homework. Go."

"Okay." Flinging her braids over her shoulder, Noelle ascended the steps, sulking in the process.

Peeking through the peephole, Patience unlocked the door and pulled it open. She greeted the visitor with narrowed eyes. "I ate your damn pastries."

Toni let out a laugh. "You know damn well that's a lie. You don't even *like* coconut."

Moving aside to let her sister in, a bright smile crossed

Patience's face when her niece walked in. "Hey baby." She extended her arms for a hug, to which the girl jumped into.

"Hi Auntie Pace," Jordan Blake eagerly greeted.

Patience glanced towards the staircase. "Noelle, come see whose here!"

It only took mere seconds for the sounds of running to sound through the house. And a moment after for Noelle to appear down the steps. She gasped, joy on her face. "Jordan!"

Toni and Patience watched the two girls run for each other, hugging.

"Like looking in a damn mirror, isn't it?" Toni quipped in an aside to Patience.

Patience nodded in agreement. "Um hmm." Just like Noelle favored Patience, Jordan favored *her* mother, including the dark brown skin tone.

Shaking her head at the girls' giddiness, Toni folded her arms. "They just talked on the phone earlier," she mumbled, earning a nudge from Patience. "Yeah, y'all are cute and all...*sickening*, but cute."

"Leave them alone." Patience pointed to the steps. "You two go upstairs."

"Can Jordan help me with my homework?" Noelle asked.

Patience tilted her head. "Do you want *me* to help you?"

Noelle shook her head. "No, that's okay," she politely shot down. "You don't know how to do the new math."

Toni busted out laughing at the astonished look on her sister's face.

"*I* do," Jordan boasted, raising her hand. She took hold of her cousin's as she put it down. "Come on. When we finish, we can color."

Toni waited until they'd disappeared up the steps, before turning to Patience. "That's okay, *I* don't know how to do that shit *either*," she said. "And I have an accounting degree."

"Why the fuck do they need *blocks* to solve simple math

problems?" Patience grunted, moving through the living room with an amused Toni following.

The aroma of food wafted up Toni's nose as soon as she stepped into the kitchen. "Smells good in here."

"Thanks. It's lasagna." Patience checked the dish in the oven. "And it's almost finished. You and Jordan are welcome to stay and eat with us if you want."

"Oh, girl don't waste your food on us. We met up with Rob after he got off work and went out to eat." Toni sat down at the table. "I didn't feel like cooking."

At the table, Patience placed the buttered bread on a baking sheet. "I don't blame you."

Toni watched her sister work, a gleam in her eye. "You know, I commend you for always taking the time out to cook every day."

"Oh trust me, it's not every day," Patience said. "But thanks. Noelle likes to help a lot and I consider it a bonding moment, you know? One of many."

"She *is* a helpful child," Toni praised. "Reminds me of you with Nana as a kid… You were the only one who wanted to be in that kitchen with her. *Especially* when she baked." Her eyes lowered to the table; she gave it a light tap. "God, I miss that lady."

Patience sighed as she put the bread in the oven. "I remember, and me too." Gathering the unused cooking items, she placed them back in the refrigerator. She then grabbed a white box from a shelf, before closing the door with her hip. She handed it to Toni. "Here."

Toni clapped her hands in delight. "Thanks sis, my mouth has been watering for these all day." Setting the box on the table, she flipped the top open. "Ooh, you got the French toast cookie."

Patience sat down at the table beside Toni. "Yeah, yeah," she dismissed. "I ended up getting myself one of those too. Had it with lunch, it's pretty good."

"Coming from the lemon queen, if you say it's good, it must be amazing."

Patience chuckled. "Cute, real cute."

Toni broke a piece and took a bite. Closing her eyes, she savored the decadent flavor. "Oh my God," she breathed between eager chews.

Patience stared at Toni, fighting the urge to laugh at the look of ecstasy on her face. She shook her head instead. "You're so dramatic," she jeered, earning a full-mouthed laugh from her sister.

Playfully tapping Patience's arm, Toni swallowed her food. "Anyway." She broke off another piece of the treat. "Sorry I couldn't meet you for lunch today. I had back-to-back clients, then like two meetings that could've been emails."

"Ah, it's fine," Patience replied with a wave of her hand. "I got caught up with a few meetings myself."

Toni took another bite. "Ooh girl, *speaking* of clients," she began after swallowing. "Remember I told you that I had a new client?" Patience nodded. "Well, I met with him this morning and let me tell you that man was fine—*fine* I said."

Patience laughed at the hungry look on her face. "Should you even be *looking*?"

"I am married, not *blind*." Toni adjusted her position in her seat, facing Patience. "Anyway, he owns his own construction company—a *successful* one at that."

"Hmm, if he's successful, that would mean he's an *asshole* according to your sister," Patience said.

Toni sucked her teeth. "Girl, you already know not to listen to her ass."

"Yeah, I do."

"But no, he didn't have that cocky shit going for him," Toni filled in. "At least from what *I* could tell, and I'd like to think that I'm a good judge of character." She glanced up at the ceiling as she thought. "*Most* times anyway." She shook her head, bringing the focus back. "But yeah, in that hour of meeting with him, I've already paired him with you in my head."

Patience frowned at her. "Toni—"

"Don't worry, I wouldn't set you up in real life." *Though I've thought about it on more than one occasion.* "But it was nice to imagine for you."

"Umm hmm." Patience stood from her seat, then grabbed her oven mitts from the counter next to the stove. "There must've been something in the air today because I ran into a fine one my*self* this morning."

Toni leaned forward, intrigue all over her face as Patience took the lasagna out. "Do tell."

"There's nothing to tell," Patience shrugged. "I saw him in line at that bakery, and we exchanged a few words while I waited for my order." She placed the piping hot pan on the stove. "No wait, *your* order."

Toni moved her hand in a rapid motion, gesturing for her to keep going. "And?"

Patience eyed her, bewildered. "And *what?*"

"And did you get the number?" Toni pressed.

"No."

Tossing her hands in the air, Toni threw her head back. "God, have I taught you *nothing?*"

Patience flung the mitts on the counter. "Besides how to cry my way out of a speeding ticket? No."

Toni successfully concealed a laugh. "I saved you an ass whoopin' from Mom for that, smart ass," she reminded, pointing. "Let you have come home with a ticket on her car, when she didn't even know you had driven it in the first place."

Patience rolled her eyes, waving a flippant hand in the process.

"Anyway, *here's* the lesson…" Toni counted on her fingers. "After a pleasant exchange, check the ring finger—if bare, get the number."

"That's stupid," Patience bristled. "A bare ring finger doesn't mean that someone isn't involved. Girlfriends and boyfriends don't walk around with *rings* on."

"You ever heard of a promise ring?"

"*Grown.* We're talking about *grown* people here, Toni," Patience stressed.

Toni put a finger up, halting her would-be comeback briefly. "Good point." She folded her arms. "But for real, I just want you to get *somebody's* damn number."

Patience rolled her eyes yet again, sucking her teeth. "God girl, *drop* it already."

"No, I *won't* drop it." Toni stated, unfazed. "You deserve a good, healthy relationship and some premium dick."

Patience's mouth dropped open at the crass comment. "Toni!"

"Mom. What's premium—"

"Shit!" Toni shrilled as both she and Patience snapped to the kitchen entrance. "*Shoot*, I meant shoot," she quickly amended as they found both Jordan and Noelle standing there.

Patience shot Toni a rigid look, before turning back to the girls. "Whatever you two heard, forget it and don't repeat it," she firmly said. "Got it?"

"Yes," the girls spoke in unison.

Hearing noise from Toni, Patience turned to see her sister's hand over her face. By the way Toni's shoulders shook, and the shrieking coming from her, Patience knew her sister was in tears laughing. "You are a horrid, crass individual, *middle* child."

Toni's laugh grew louder. "Oh my God, I *am*."

Shaking her head, Patience signaled to Noelle. "Dinner is ready."

Chapter Six

"MOM, YOU ALL RIGHT OVER there?" Michael asked as he pushed the lawnmower.

Jill Carter, seated in a cushy chair on her patio, lifted her glass of lemonade. "Yes son, I'm perfectly fine."

Nodding, Michael went back to his task. Finding himself with some free time that Saturday afternoon, he'd decided to pay his parents a visit. When he'd noticed that their lawn needed tending to, he'd gotten right to work. He'd trimmed hedges, touched up the mulch around the landscaping, and now was mowing the grass.

Finishing up, Michael wiped the sweat from his brow with his t-shirt, then proceeded to empty the lawn clippings into a garden bag.

Jill sipped more of her lemonade, watching him work. "Michael honey, you know your father will have a conniption when he finds out you're doing this," she called out to him.

"He'll be fine. I'm almost finished anyway." Grabbing the filled bags, Michael placed them along the fence, intending on putting them out in front for trash pickup before he left. After returning the mower to the garage, he headed for the patio.

Jill's smile illuminated her pretty, dark brown face as her son stood before her. "Thank you for taking care of this for us."

Michael returned her smile with one of his own. "You're welcome Mom, anytime."

Setting her glass down, Jill shook her head. "Your father *insists* on still trying to tend to this big yard on his own."

"Pop has yet to learn to relax." He removed his gardening gloves. "I'll talk to him when he gets back."

"If he won't listen to *me*, you know he's not going to listen to *you*," Jill joked, earning a chuckle from her son.

Michael rubbed the back of his neck, stretching it from side to side. "Yeah, you're probably right," he agreed, humor still lacing his voice.

"I poured you a glass of lemonade." She gestured to the full, frosted glass on the patio table. "Sit with me."

Michael obliged, taking the seat right next to her. "Thank you." He took a long sip. The cool liquid, paired with the breeze, offered a much-needed reprieve.

Jill eyed Michael. "Are you hungry? I have some left-over pot roast and mashed potatoes from last night's dinner."

"No thanks. I actually have a pot roast slow cooking at home as we speak."

Patting his arm, she grinned. "Knowing how *you* cook, your roast will be ten times better than mine."

He shook his head vigorously. "Come on now, I could never outdo the one who taught me."

Jill waved a playful hand at her son. "Oh please, no need to lie. Just bring me a plate when you get a chance."

Michael laughed a bit. "Of course I will."

A few moments of relaxed silence passed as Jill finished the rest of her lemonade. Setting the empty glass down on the table, she leaned back in her seat. "So…how've you been?"

Staring out at the yard, Michael sighed a bit. "Busy," he answered. "But I'm not complaining. Business is good."

"I'm glad." She beamed, "I'm so proud of you."

Michael gave her hand a gentle pat. "Thanks Mom."

Folding her arms, she lightly rocked in her chair. "So…career is great. You have your health…" She paused momentarily. "Any update on the romantic front?"

Michael slowly turned, fixing her with an unblinking stare.

"Any future daughters-in-laws I should be meeting?"

Yeah, I knew that was coming. He wasn't new to the question. "No Mom, I'm not dating right now."

Jill tilted her head. "No?"

"No."

"Michael—how long has it been since you've been in a relationship? Since you've been on a *date?*"

"A few years." Michael shrugged. "And I'll tell you like I told your nosy *daughter—*"

"Oh stop it, I'm not that bad," Jill cut in, pointing a manicured finger at him.

"You *are*," he maintained. "But in all seriousness, after the dating history I've had, I think choosing to take a break for as long as I have has been good."

Brow creasing with sympathy, Jill let out a sigh. "I hear you sweetie," she said. "Trying to find a soulmate in a sea of mess I'm sure is difficult…*especially* nowadays."

"Yeah, you and Pop really lucked out in the soulmate department." Michael returned his attention to the swaying trees in front of him. He didn't talk about it much, but he hoped to have a marriage as loving as his parents. *Should* he ever decide to get married. In the meantime, he was desperate to change the subject. "Well, I might not have a girlfriend, but hopefully I'll have a *house* soon."

Excited, Jill gasped. "You found one?"

"Still looking," Michael clarified, relieved at the smoothness of the subject change. "I've been searching for homes in between meetings and projects." He took another sip of his beverage.

"Well, when you finally get one, I'm coming to hang curtains and I'll hear no protesting from you." She patted his shoulder. "You hear me?"

Michael flashed an amused grin. "Yes, Ma'am."

Giving a satisfied nod, Jill settled back. "First the house, then the relationship." She smirked, "Then *grandchildren*."

Good Lord. Michael rolled his eyes. "Mom—"

"I can hope, can't I?" She laughed. "To be honest, you're my only hope for a wedding, and a grandbaby."

Rubbing his face with his hand, Michael released a sigh as his mother prattled on.

"I mean Lori is nice enough… A bit all over the place, but a lovely girl nonetheless," she mused. "But frankly, I don't know how much longer she's going to stay with Dante's behind if he doesn't propose to her."

"Maybe he's waiting for *her* to be ready."

Jill shot him a knowing look. "Please," she scoffed. "That girl has dropped more hints than a little bit—*including* taking him to a jeweler to get her ring size."

Michael shook his head in amusement.

"Dante is dragging his damn feet."

Michael chose not to respond. Instead, he finished his drink. As far as he was concerned, the love life of his siblings wasn't any of his business.

"And Kenya seems to be enjoying *testing the waters*, so, I doubt *she'll* get married any time soon," Jill added. She moved some of her thick, coiled, salt and pepper hair back from her face. "As long as she's safe and enjoying herself, I can't and *won't* complain."

Michael shook his head yet again. "Any chance you're going to believe me when I say that *I'm* fine being single?"

"No, because *you're* lying," Jill refuted, earning a snicker from Michael. "And you were never *good* at it, so I don't know why you even try."

"Point taken and noted." He took a deep breath, the humor leaving him. "I hear you, and I guess you're right. I *have* reached a point where I could see myself being in a relationship but… I want what I want, and if I don't find it, then… I'll just have to be fine with being alone."

"You'll find someone." Jill placed a hand on her son's shoulder. "Who knows, maybe you already *have*, and you just don't know it yet."

Michael rolled his eyes to the patio umbrella above them. "Like I *also* told your daughter, my life is not one of those sappy movies you like watching."

Jill sucked her teeth. "Oh now you cut it out." She folded her arms to her chest as she crossed her legs. "And there's nothing wrong with a sappy movie. You could learn a thing or two from them."

Slightly humored, Michael leaned over, kissing her cheek. "Love you, Mom."

"Love you too, smart behind." Hearing a voice coming from inside the house, both Jill and Michael turned towards the glass door. "I'm outside Gary," she said.

Michael rose from his seat as the door slid open, smiling at the brown-skinned elderly man stepping through. "Hey Pop."

Gary Carter greeted his son with a grin and a hug. "It's good to see you, son."

"You too." Michael stepped aside, allowing his father access to the seat he just stood from. "Here, have a seat."

Gary flagged away the gesture. "Boy please, I don't need to sit—" He paused, surveying the manicured lawn.

Both Jill and Michael exchanged knowing glances.

"Michael, did you—"

"Yes, I did Pop, and I'll *continue* to do it until you let me hire a gardener for you," Michael affirmed, folding his arms. Gary shot him a wide-eyed look. "That's right, I said it, and I *mean* it."

Jill dissolved into a fit of laughter, earning a flabbergasted look from her husband. "You heard what the man said." She pointed to the empty chair. "Now sit your behind down."

"Pace, can you hand me that glass, over there?" Toni requested, hand outstretched. "On the coffee table."

Patience glanced over at Toni, seated next to her on the couch. She then eyed said glass on the table. "You mean this empty one?"

Toni looked up from her laptop screen. "Damn it, I forgot I drank it all." She craned her neck towards the kitchen. "Babe!"

"Yes?" Rob Blake returned.

"Can you please fix me another drink?" Toni took a quick glimpse at the other half-empty glass of lemonade. "And bring Patience some liquor to put in her lemonade, please?"

Patience cut her eye at Toni. "Patience doesn't *need* any Rob, thank you."

Toni's lip curled in judgment. "Prude," she mocked, earning a nudge from Patience.

That Saturday evening, after running errands and taking an excursion to the movies with Noelle, Patience had decided to make a pit stop at Toni's for a visit.

Within a few moments, Rob emerged from the kitchen, margarita on the rocks in hand. Noelle and Jordan were giggling and running behind him.

Toni smiled at her handsome, brown-skinned husband as he handed her the drink. "Thank you love." Eyeing the girls with their hands full of cookies running for the stairs, she turned towards them. "Aye, you two stop running before I trip you."

Concealing a laugh, Patience nudged Toni once again, who in turn snickered.

"No, but I'm serious, and Jordan don't get those cookie crumbs on your floor!" Toni harped.

"I won't," Jordan promised from upstairs.

Patience giggled. "She's lying."

Toni shook her head. "Chile'—that's okay, because her little butt will be vacuuming the entire upstairs."

Rob ran a hand over his low-cut hair, "Okay ladies, you enjoy yourselves. I'm headed out to watch the game." He leaned forward, kissing his wife's lips. "Love you."

"Love you too, be safe. And if you don't win the bet, just take the money off the table and run like I taught you," Toni said.

Rob busted out laughing. "Silly ass." He tapped Patience on her shoulder on his way. "Later sis."

Patience waved at him. "Later bro."

Toni watched as her husband walked out of the door, shutting it behind him. "He thinks I'm playing Pace, he better come home with that money."

"How much do they bet on those stupid basketball games?"

"Like twenty bucks. For a bunch of lawyers, they're all cheap." Toni shrugged. "But still."

Patience shook her head, taking a small sip of the remaining beverage in her glass. She then pointed to Toni's laptop. "You know your rude ass has been on that thing since I got here."

"I know, and I'm sorry." Toni sipped her own drink, then set it down. "I was organizing some files, then got caught up looking at this event."

"*What* event?"

Toni turned her laptop around, grin on her face. "*This* one."

Patience studied the elegant invitation on the screen. "Diamonds & Pearls Mixer," she read aloud. "Come down to the Lux ballroom, sparkled and dressed in your best all white attire. Mix, mingle and have dinner with the city's elite." She leaned back against the couch cushions. "And who the hell do they consider 'the elite'?"

Toni smirked. "Anybody who pays the hundred and fifty dollars for this ticket."

"Um hmm." Patience ran a hand through her hair. "Sounds cute though." She took another sip of her drink. "Why are you looking at it?"

"Because we're going to it."

"Who? You and Rob?" Patience asked.

Toni turned the laptop screen back towards herself. "Nope, *you* and *I*."

Patience's head snapped in her direction. "I'm not paying a hundred and fifty damn dollars to mingle with a bunch of fuckin' strangers."

"We get *dinner* too," Toni reminded, pointing to the screen. "And don't forget the 'mix' part." Seeing the annoyed look on her sister's face only made Toni laugh. "No for real, we're going. I think it'll be fun."

"You have a whole husband! Go with *him*."

Toni rolled her eyes. "I love my man with every ounce of my being, but he'd be dry," she said. "No, I want to go with *you*, and you need the fun."

Patience let out a whine as she set her glass back down. "Take Angela."

"We *both* know she won't come out," Toni scoffed. "And even if she *did*, she'd run home as soon as that bastard calls her." When Patience turned away mumbling under her breath, Toni gently nudged her. "Come on Pace, you're my partner in crime. So, let's dress up and go have some fun."

Straightening up in her seat, Patience faced Toni. She pinched her fingers together, sternness in her eyes. "Antoinette, I am not *paying* a hundred and fifty dollars for that."

Toni shrugged. "You don't have to." Confusion set in on Patience's face as Toni showed her the screen once again. "I bought your ticket."

Eyes lowered, Patience saw the confirmation message. One ticket in Toni's name, and the other in hers. When she looked back at her sister, she only found Toni's satisfied grin. "You raggedy bitch," Patience grunted.

"Ooh, you're such a disrespectful little heffa." Toni's voice was laced with laughter. "But that's fine, I'll be that." She closed her laptop. "And *you'll* be my date for this beautiful event in two weeks."

Patience gritted her teeth. "I don't own anything white."

"I just *said* it's in two weeks, you have time to get something." Toni moved her finger within inches of her *clearly* annoyed sister's cheek. "Your face is red. You're hot with me huh?" She gestured to Patience's glass. "Drink the rest of that, it'll cool you off."

Patience smacked her hand down, then bolted from the couch. Toni followed her progress as she moved towards the stairs.

"Noelle, come on, we're leaving," Patience called up the steps.

Toni's mouth fell open. "You're really going to be that petty? You haven't even been here that long."

Not saying a word, Patience flipped Toni the middle finger. Extending her hand closer to her, she didn't take her eyes off the steps.

Toni shook her head as Noelle came trotting down. "See you later Bunny," she said to her niece, who came over to give her a hug. "Love you."

"Love you too," Noelle returned, then headed for the door.

Toni looked over at Patience, waiting in the entryway. "Love *you too* Patience."

Patience simply cut her eye as she walked out of the house.

"Mommy, you're not going to say it back?" Noelle asked, following.

"Not right now," Patience muttered, closing the door.

Chapter Seven

"WHEN DOES THE LISTING AGENT plan on scheduling showings for those houses?" Michael asked into his cell phone as he maneuvered along the crowded sidewalk. Listening to the person talking, he scowled. "What do you *mean* you haven't followed up with them yet?" He pinched the bridge of his nose at the poor excuse of an explanation. "Lori—I hope you're aware of how unprofessional and *unacceptable* this is... I can't continue to overlook this because we're family..." He shook his head; he was over the conversation. "Look—I have to go. I'll call them myself, and *we'll* talk later... Right. Bye."

Ending the call, Michael slipped the phone into his trouser pocket. "What the hell was I thinking, agreeing to this?" he muttered to himself. He'd been trying to get in contact with his so-called realtor since yesterday morning, regarding the homes he'd sent her to verify. Only for him to finally get ahold of her fifteen minutes ago, to find out she'd dropped the ball once again.

Approaching the office building, he shook the frustration off. Entering a set of glass doors, he greeted the receptionist warmly, before being directed down the hall to the designated suite. Shifting the briefcase in his hand, he knocked on the door, then entered upon being given the okay. "Good morning," Michael said.

Toni returned a smile. "Good morning Michael, good to see you again."

"You as well." He took a seat in the chair that Toni gestured to.

Keeping with their promise to schedule a second in-person meeting to go over a few more items, Michael had journeyed to Toni's office that Tuesday morning.

"I've had a chance to start going over some of your previous records and returns." Toni clicked a few keys on her laptop, before shifting her attention back to him. "Was actually just double-checking one when you knocked…"

Michael shot her a curious look when she paused. "Did you find any discrepancies?" he asked. "Do I owe *more* money?"

Clasping her hands on the desk, Toni gave her head a light shake. "No."

"Oh thank God," Michael breathed out, earning a giggle from her.

"You were right, your last accountant was excellent," she praised. "I still have a few more returns that I want to go over, but I honestly don't see any issues arising."

Relief resonated on Michael's face. "You have no idea how happy I am to hear that. I needed some reassurance today." Opening his briefcase, he retrieved a few folders and handed them off to Toni. "Here are my receipts and expenses for this year so far."

Toni flipped through the pages. "Organized, I love it."

"Thank you. I have my parents to thank for that." Feeling his phone vibrate in his pocket, Michael retrieved it. Eyeing the email notification, his brow pleated. "Please excuse me, I have to check this message. It'll take less than a minute."

"Oh sure, go ahead. Take your time." Toni studied a page. Yet as she heard an exasperated huff come from Michael, curiosity piqued her interest enough to look up. "Is everything okay?"

Michael put the phone away. "Yes, sorry." He rubbed the back of his neck. "As experienced as I am when it comes to working on houses, I didn't think that trying to find one to *live* in would be so difficult."

Toni grimaced. "Ugh, sorry to hear that," she sympathized. "Bad housing market?"

"Bad *realtor*," he grumbled. Massaging his temples with his fingertips, he let out a sigh. "I apologize. My personal problem isn't a topic I should be discussing."

"Oh please, no need to apologize," Toni assured with a wave of her hand. "I told you, we're informal, so if you need to vent, go right ahead."

Michael released a quick, quiet laugh. "Thanks, I appreciate it."

"Of course." She folded her arms on her desk. "I remember *my* first realtor. After working with the guy for a week… Let's just say I had to take my business *elsewhere*."

Michael shook his head. "Yeah," he sighed again. "I know it's time that I seek out a new one… I have no *choice* at this point, I want to move as soon as possible." He put a hand up. "But enough about my housing crisis, let's get back to business."

Toni held her reply. The more Michael explained, the faster the wheels in her head were turning. A gradual grin crept across her face. *If this isn't divine intervention, I don't know what is.* Grabbing her purse from the windowsill behind her, she stuck her hand in. "Before we get back to work, may I offer a suggestion? Or should I say, a referral?"

Michael gestured for her to go ahead. "Please."

Toni pulled out a business card. "*This* realtor is who you need working for you." She handed it to Michael, who eagerly took it. "Trust me."

Michael eyed the name. "Patience Harvey; Clayborn Realty."

"She is *amazing*," Toni raved, eyes *and* smile gleaming. "She'll get you the exact house you're looking for—she sold me *my* home, so I should know."

Throwing a grateful smile Toni's way, Michael pocketed the card. "Great, thank you. I'll be sure to give her a call."

Toni gave a crisp nod. "You're very welcome." *I sure hope you do.* Satisfied with her efforts, she went back to reviewing receipts.

"Do you think they call this a starfruit because it looks like a star?"

Patience turned, looking at her coworker with deadpan eyes. Her eyes drew down to the slice of star-shaped fruit on his plate, then back up at him. "Do you... Do you really need me to answer that Jerry, or do you really not know?"

A booming laugh emitted from Jerry's lungs.

Patience, on the other hand, was far from amused. Turning away, she cursed under her breath. She never minded interacting with fellow coworkers, but Jerry, she avoided like the plague. He was obnoxious, corny, and often spit when he talked. The latter was *especially* irritating to Patience, because he always tried to converse with her during lunch.

"I love working for this company," Jerry continued before biting into the fruit slice. "The free lunch *alone* was a selling point."

"Yeah, I'm sure it was," Patience mumbled, moving away from him. She surveyed the trays of hot and cold food displayed in the kitchen. She rarely ate the provided lunch, opting to eat outside of the office. But her fatigue had made her not want to take any excursions this afternoon. Settling on a delicious looking chicken parmesan, Patience grabbed a plate.

"Ooh, they have the chicken parm from Judy's today!" Jerry barreled over. "The sauce is the *best*, you'll love it."

"I'm sure I will, Jerry."

Sidling up next to her, Jerry pointed to the pan. "And the *parmesan*—"

Patience's eyes shot down to the moister that had fallen upon her plate. Sickened, she glowered. *I swear to fuckin' God!* "Jerry—" pausing the rant she so desperately wanted to spew, Patience slammed her plate in the trash, blowing out a loud breath in the process. There was no way she was going to eat anything in that room with him in there. "Enjoy the food, Jerry." Heading for the exit, she passed another coworker.

"Ooh, they ordered Judy's—"

"Jerry just *spit* over it," Patience grunted in passing.

Stopping short, the woman's eyes widened. "Patience *please* tell me you're lying."

Keeping her stride, Patience glanced back at her. "I'm not."

The woman stomped into the kitchen, eyes blazing. "Damn it, Jerry! You don't get to eat until everybody has had their share," she hurled. "This is getting ridiculous."

Patience entered her office, grabbing her purse just as her cell phone began to vibrate. Giving the screen a quick look, she answered. "Hey sis."

Toni immediately picked up on the frustration in her sister's voice. "What's wrong with you?"

Patience slung the purse strap over her shoulder. "Because this buffoon ass coworker of mine who can't keep the saliva in his big ass mouth, *insists* on talking over the fuckin' food, I have to take my tired ass *out* for lunch today," she fumed, voice low. As Patience stormed out of her office, she was met with Toni's silence. "You're about to laugh, aren't you?"

Toni's high-pitched laughter erupted through the phone. "I'm sorry, I tried to hold it in, but—*what?*"

Exiting the glass doors, Patience shook her head. "Forget it."

It took a moment for Toni to compose herself. "Anyway, you said you're tired. Long night?"

"Yeah." Patience ran a hand over her ponytail, pushing the curls behind her shoulder. "Noelle had a science project she needed help with and because both she and I are *perfectionists*, we were up half the night working on it."

"She waited to the last minute, huh?" Toni assumed.

"No, its due next week." Patience rubbed her eyes with her fingertips. "Anyway, what's up?"

Toni stalled for a second. "Huh?"

"You called me," Patience reminded. "What's up? Did you want to meet up for lunch or something?"

"Oh girl no. *My* coworkers don't spit on food, so I ate what the office ordered for us."

Patience couldn't help but smirk. "Fuck you."

Toni chuckled. "No, but I was just calling to see how you were…and to see if you received any new clients today?"

Navigating the sidewalk, Patience adjusted her blazer. "No, I haven't. Why? Do you know something I don't?"

"Oh no, no, not at all," Toni sputtered. "Was just asking. Because you know *I* have a new client, so I was just…"

Puzzled by Toni's weird line of questioning, Patience frowned. "You sound crazy right now."

"Yes, I am aware," Toni replied. "What else is new?"

"Well—" Patience paused. Hearing ringing from her purse, she pulled out another cell phone. "Let me call you back. I'm getting a call on my work phone."

"Oh yeah sure, go ahead."

Patience ended the call with Toni and put the other phone to her ear. "Hello, this is Patience Harvey."

Michael, seated at his office desk, held the business card that Toni had given to him earlier that morning. "Yes. Good afternoon Ms. Harvey, my name is Michael Carter. I'm currently looking for a realtor, and I was referred to you."

Patience stopped walking, moving aside to let people pass. "Hi Mr. Carter. Well, I'm flattered for the referral." She didn't need to ask who'd referred her; she'd had many satisfied clients over the past five years. It could have been anyone. She backed against a building wall. "Are you looking for a residential property or commercial?"

Michael stalled for a moment, his brows gathering slightly. He couldn't put a finger on it, but the soft, dulcet voice sounded familiar. Shaking the thought from his head, he cleared his throat. "Residential," he answered. "A house, for myself."

"Okay." She adjusted the purse on her arm. "Are you close to the downtown Maple Glenn area? We can set up an appointment to meet at my office."

Michael smiled, eyeing the work address on the card. It wasn't far from him, just blocks away. "Yes, I am. That sounds like a plan," he replied. "I have my pre-approval letter and everything else you'll need."

"Well, you're already ahead," Patience mused. "When I get back to the office, I'll check my calendar and give you a call back to set up an appointment. Is this number you're calling me from the best one to reach you?"

"Yes, this is my cell phone." He tapped his hand on the desk. "I look forward to hearing from you Ms. Harvey."

Patience nodded, though he couldn't see her. "Talk back shortly."

"Okay. Goodbye." Hanging up the phone, Michael expelled a light breath. He was feeling good about this decision. He'd called his *former* realtor as soon as he'd left Toni's office a few hours ago, to let her know that they would no longer be working together. Michael didn't know if his brother would be upset about it, nor did he care. He was eager to get the process started, and could only hope that Patience was as good as Toni said.

Two days later, at three o'clock in the afternoon, Michael sat waiting in the reception area of Clayborn Realty.

"Patience will be with you in just a moment," the receptionist announced from his desk. "Would you like a complementary beverage and a snack?"

Michael peered up from the papers in his hand, offering a gracious smile. "No thank you." Shifting his focus out the window, he took in the specs of sunrays peeking between the tall buildings that lined the downtown area. His gaze was still fixed on the view as the sound of high heels clicking along the wood floor approached him.

"Mr. Carter?"

Michael rose from his seat, coming face to face with the voice.

Any answer to his name being called was immediately halted as he froze. His eyes nearly bulged out of his head, "Oh shit," he blurted out. He recognized her—the beauty from the bakery—*her*.

Patience's head flinched back at his reaction. "I'm sorry?"

Michael quickly shook his head. "I didn't mean to say that… out loud." He was surprised to say the least. He'd never imagined that he'd see her again, and in a little over a week's time. *What are the odds? This is crazy…in the best way possible.*

He recognized the same look on her face that she'd given to him when he'd been gawking at her *then*, and cut the barrage of inner thoughts short. He extended his hand, clearing his throat. "What I *meant* to say was yes, that's me—Michael, Ms.—Mrs. Harvey."

Returning a warm smile, Patience shook it. "*Ms*. And Patience is just fine."

Michael hoped that Patience didn't sense the absolute relief he felt at that moment. *She's not married. Thank God.* He released her hand.

Patience's brow gathered subtly, her eyes scanning him from head to toe. "Hmm," she muttered, in a voice so low she was certain only she could hear. She gestured towards her office. "This way."

Giving a nod, Michael followed her as she proceeded down the corridor to her office.

"I apologize for the brief wait," Patience said, closing the door behind him.

"Oh no need to apologize." He waited until she'd sat down before taking the empty seat in front of her desk. He glanced around the space…mostly in an effort to not stare at her. "Cozy office."

Patience hit a few keys on her laptop. "Thank you."

Michael's eyes lingered on the small art piece hanging behind her. "Nice art piece," he complimented, gesturing to it.

Patience looked behind her, briefly smiling at it—it was one of her daughter's first attempts at finger painting. She was amazed at how many people thought that the colorful splatters of a then five-year-old was an expensive painting. "Thank you. It's priceless."

"I'm sure," Michael mused. His attention left the picture and went to Patience, who was busy typing on the keyboard. He had recalled her face many times since their chance meeting, but seeing her again… She was even more beautiful than he remembered. When she looked up at him after moving her laptop aside, he wondered if she'd remembered *him*. Then he quickly dismissed the thought. *Yeah, I think this memory is one-sided Mike.*

"So." Patience clasped her hands on the desktop. "Fill me in on what you're looking for in a house."

Michael straightened up in his seat. "A two-story single home, with a generous front and backyard," he began. "Three to four bedrooms, two and a half bath, open concept floor plan, living room, dining, den, kitchen of course, finished basement, garage…"

Patience diligently jotted notes as he ran down the list of requirements. "One car or two?"

"One is good. Though I'd like to be on a block that has plenty of available parking—*without* a time limit."

"Ahh, you've been to some of these 'you have two hours to park in this spot, and if you try to move your car up a few spaces on the same side of the street, you'll get a fifty-dollar ticket' residential streets, huh?" Patience's question was tinted with amusement.

Michael let out a chuckle. "One too many," he confirmed. "Can't count how many times I've found a perfect spot on my brother's block and said to hell with it, because I refused to drive around to look for another one."

She jotted down something else. "Yeah, I don't blame you. Luckily, I don't have to deal with that where I live. The perks of living just outside of the city." She tapped her pen on the notepad. "So, a block with no businesses on it, or near any major transportation stops."

Michael nodded. "Someplace quiet. Outskirts of the city or suburbs preferably… I'm around noise all day at work, so quiet where I live would be welcomed."

Patience sat back in her seat, eyeing him. "That's right, you work in construction," she recalled from their brief chat when she'd returned his call to set up the appointment.

His eyes gleamed with pride. "That's right."

"So that being said, are you looking for a fixer upper? Or do you want something move-in ready?"

"Oh, move-in ready most definitely." He watched her write down a few more things.

"How much are you looking to spend? How much do you have to put down? Or if you don't *plan* on putting anything down, how much do you have at your disposal for closing costs, and other associated fees? Lastly, how soon are you looking to move?" she fired off.

Michael delayed his response for a moment, shooting an impressed look her way. *Yeah, she definitely knows what she's doing.* "I'm looking to spend no more than four hundred thousand, I have fifty thousand at my disposal, and honestly I'd like to move as soon as possible."

Patience nodded as she finished writing. "You said you have the pre-approval from your bank?"

Michael swiftly handed her the papers in his hand. "Yes." He gestured to them once she took them. "I believe everything is all there."

Patience quickly scanned through the pile. "Looks like it is." She rested the papers down in front of her. "Okay then Michael, I have quite a bit of information here, which means that I can start looking into some properties for you." She glanced over at her laptop. "I have a few in mind already."

Michael's smile was bright. "Perfect. Should I call you in a few days to see what you have?"

"You *can*, but trust me it won't take that long. I'll call you as soon as I pull a few and confirm showing times." She smirked. "You'll get tired of me blowing up your phone soon enough."

Trust me, you don't have to worry about that. He just grinned. "In that case, I look forward to working with you."

She gave a stiff nod. "Likewise."

Chapter Eight

UNFOLDING A PAIR OF WHITE trousers, Toni held them up at eye level. "How much do you want to bet that once I put these pants on my ass, they'll be see-through?"

Patience examined the fabric, before placing a hand inside one of the pant legs. "Don't need to bet, they *will*." She showed Toni the hint of her brown skin through it.

Sucking her teeth, Toni returned the pants to the shelf. "I *hate* white clothes," she fussed, much to Patience's amusement. With the Diamonds & Pearls mixer a week away, Patience and Toni had taken a trip to the mall that Saturday with their children in tow.

"This is nobody's fault but your own," Patience reminded, eyeing the elegant pieces on display.

"Yeah yeah." Pulling a dress from a rack, Toni mumbled a profane word under her breath. Her examination of the garment was interrupted by her daughter shaking her arm. "Yes, child?"

"Can I have this dress for my school dance?" Jordan asked.

Toni peered down at the glittery pink sleeveless dress in her daughter's hand. She tossed a hand up. "How is it that you were able to find a dress before *I* did?"

Jordan shrugged. "Maybe because you keep complaining about stuff to Aunt Pace, instead of looking around for more clothes."

Offended, Toni's eyes narrowed. Hearing a loud snicker come from Patience, she turned, glaring.

"Well…she has a point," Patience joked.

"Shut up." Directing her gaze back to Jordan, Toni pointed to a cushioned bench by the wall. "Go sit over there with your cousin and put that dress back."

Slinging the dress over her shoulder, Jordan trotted off.

"That dance isn't until the fall," Toni said in an aside to Patience. "It'll be just my luck that I get that dress now, and the girl shoots up a foot in height."

Patience shook her head, taking a pair of pants off a shelf. "What kind of dance is it?"

"A father-daughter dance," Toni answered. "Needless to say, she's excited about it… *Rob* is too. That's his little princess."

Patience smiled. "That's sweet. I know they'll have a good time, and I can't wait to see what the mini fashionista picks out." She picked up a top, tilting her head to examine it as the smile left her face.

Letting out a sigh, Toni gently tapped her sister's arm. "Hey."

"What's up?" Patience wondered, still eyeing the items in her hands.

"I'm sorry."

The unexpected answer drew a perplexed look from Patience. "For what?"

"For mentioning the dance," Toni clarified. "I know that that might be something Noelle will hear about and might want to be a part of—"

Patience's face relaxed as Toni explained.

"And I can only imagine how difficult of a conversation you'll have to have with her."

Patience slung the clothing over her arm as she gathered her thoughts. "Okay listen," she began. "Don't ever feel the need to apologize about the fact that Jordan has a father—a *wonderful* father at that. Or about the fact that you're *married* to her father."

Toni's eyes lowered to her shoes.

"You have every right to be happy, just like Jordan has every right to be excited about that dance," Patience added. "It wouldn't be the first time that I've had talks with Noelle when it came to the father topic, and it won't be the last... And I'm okay with that."

Toni shot a sympathetic look her way. "What do you tell her about Greg? I mean... Does she know anything about him?"

"She knows his name, and that I was married to him at one point before she was born." Patience shrugged. "And umm... I just tell her that the reason he's not around is because he lives out of the country."

Toni's head bobbed with a slow nod. "You're not going to tell her that he's *actually* a piece of shit, who refused to be part of her life because you left him?"

"She doesn't need to know that at this young age." Patience tucked some of her hair behind her ear. "I don't mind carrying that burden on my own."

Toni folded her arms. She was well aware of what her sister had gone through during her five-year marriage; as far as Toni was concerned, her ex-brother-in-law was still due some bodily harm. Nevertheless, she praised Patience for being able to bounce back from it. If it were *her*, Toni wasn't so sure if she could be that strong. "Well, if it means anything, you're amazing, and Noelle doesn't want or need for anything."

Patience returned a faint smile. "Thanks... Though I'm not naïve to believe that she'll *never* want a father figure in her life, especially as she gets older." Smile fading, she let out a heavy sigh. "That's something I can't fulfill for her..."

"Patience, I don't believe for a second that you'll be single the rest of your life," Toni placated. "I know you're not worrying about that *right now*, but I'm just saying," she quickly added when Patience opened her mouth to protest. "There's someone out there. Someone who'll be the man you deserve and the dad *she* deserves."

"If you say so," Patience dismissed.

"Oh, I *do*, and I believe it too." Eyes lowering to her wrist, Toni adjusted her charm bracelet. "*Speaking* of men, how's it going with that new client—Michael is his name, right?"

Patience raised an eyebrow. "I told you his name?"

Caught off guard, Toni's eyes shifted. *Shit! She didn't. Damn it, pull it together.* "Yes. You mentioned it when you called me back after you got off the phone that day," she lied. "Come on, I know you were tired and pissed about that man spitting on the chicken parm, but *surely* you can remember our conversation." She breathed a subtle sigh of relief when Patience just shrugged it off.

"Anyway, it's going well. I showed him a house yesterday and will be showing a few more this week."

Toni stood there, eagerly waiting for Patience to go into more detail. When she failed to do so, Toni tapped her arm. "So?"

"So, *what?*"

"Tell me about him… Is he cute?"

Patience glared at the clown-like grin on her sister's face. "I am trying to sell this man a *house* Toni, not size him up for my *bed*."

Toni shot a knowing look. "Soooo you *have* thought about it?"

"What? —*No*." Patience put a hand on her head, shaking it. "Girl—I will *not* have this conversation every time I interact with an attractive man—shut up." She hissed when Toni pointed at her, eyes wide with glee. "I found my outfit. Good luck finding yours."

Toni's mouth fell open as Patience retreated for the dressing room. "Are you going to help me find *mine?*"

"No. And your child was right, you talk too damn much," Patience hurled back.

"You know what—shut up Jordan," Toni directed to her child, who was busy laughing at her, along with her niece.

Moving his mouse, Michael studied photo after photo of the property on his laptop screen. "*Damn* this is nice," he said to himself.

He'd received another property option from Patience via email, with her sending a backup text confirming his receipt of them. Michael didn't hesitate to put a pause on his lunch making to check it out.

Picking up the phone, he sent a text back.

Michael: I'm liking this one already, Will they allow a showing this week?

The reply came almost immediately.

Patience: I'm glad you like it. Yes, they have an opening for a showing this coming Wednesday at five. Is that okay with you?

Michael: Absolutely.

Patience: Perfect. I'll lock it in. Let me know if you have any questions, or if you find any properties that you want to add to the list.

Michael: Sounds good and your picks have been on point. I have nothing to add.

Patience: Good to hear. Talk back later.

Michael: Talk later.

His eyes lingered on the text exchange. While he was excited that the house hunting process was running smoothly and quickly with Patience as his realtor, he wished that their conversations didn't have to always be business related. As much as he tried, he just couldn't shake his infatuation with her.

"Ooh, nice house," Dante spoke, startling Michael.

Putting the phone down, Michael snapped his head around; Dante was standing over his shoulder. "And what's the reason for being all up in my face, bro?"

Dante shrugged. "Just wanted to know what had you so focused." He gestured to the device. "I couldn't see what was on your phone, so I opted for the laptop instead... But yeah, nice house."

Michael shook his head. The brotherly banter and pestering

didn't seem to wane as Dante aged. "Thank you." He closed his laptop.

"Is that the one you plan on buying?" Dante plopped down at the kitchen table across from him.

"I *hope* to." Michael then fixed Dante with a glare. "Oh, and if it weren't for the fact that you're my brother and I love you, I would kill you."

Dante's eyes expanded with feigned horror. "For *what?*"

"For making me waste my time with Lori," Michael spat. "I've had this new realtor for mere *days* and already she's sent me several homes and *shown* me one… No more professional favors for family."

Putting a hand over his face, Dante sighed. "I know, and despite the fact that she was salty about being dropped by you—she *did* cry by the way—I understand why you dropped her."

"Well, I certainly didn't want her to *cry*, but…" Michael folded his arms. "At least you're both mature about it."

Tapping his fingers together, Dante grimaced. "I umm… To make her feel a bit better, I told her I was coming over here to kick your ass for firing her."

Michael stared at him, eyes burrowing through him like a laser. "You're going to kick my ass, huh?"

"Nope. Can't do it, won't even *try*." Dante dramatically flung his hands up in surrender. "I saw your ass wrestle them big dudes at your high school matches… I'm good." He threw a hopeful look Michael's way. "Can I at *least* tell her I cussed you out or something?"

Shaking his head, Michael rose from the table. "Grow up."

Rolling his eyes, Dante leaned back in his seat. "Yeah, she wouldn't believe that shit anyway."

Michael opened the refrigerator, pulling out a pack of pepper jack cheese, some lettuce, and a tomato. "Anyway, the realtor that I have now—Patience—" His lips curved into a smile. "She's perfect."

Dante stared at his brother with a squint.

Michael frowned back. "Why are you looking at me like that?"

Smirking, Dante placed his hands behind his head. "Yep, you like her."

Moving the pan of reheated breaded chicken breast from the stove range, Michael shot him a perplexed look as he set it on the counter. "Where did *that* come from?"

"The change in your voice and that far off, gleaming look in your eyes when you said her name," Dante teased. "Dead giveaway."

It was the truth, but Michael wasn't about to discuss that with his nosy little brother. "So listen, I'll need you to work at the Malvern site this week," he said, smoothly changing the subject as he prepared himself a sandwich. "The team over there could use the extra hands."

Dante gave a nod. "You got it."

"Cool." Michael finished preparing his sandwich and glanced over at Dante, who was staring at him. Or better yet staring at the *food*. "Would you like one?"

Jumping from his seat, Dante bolted over to the counter. "'Ihought you'd never ask." He pointed to the bread slices. "Is this your homemade ciabatta bread?"

Michael grabbed his plate of food, along with a glass of juice, and stepped away from the counter. "Yes, and please don't take half the loaf home like you did last time."

Dante busted out laughing. "I couldn't help it, it's the best bread I've ever tasted." Removing a butter knife from the drawer, he pointed it in his brother's direction. "You cook better than Mom, you know."

Michael shook his head. "She pretty much told me the same thing," he said. "You're *both* exaggerating."

A knock at the door interrupted their conversation and sent Michael straight for it. Pulling it open, he welcomed his guest in. "Hey Kenya."

"Hey bro." Leaning against the closed door, Kenya removed

the strapped stiletto heels from her feet. "Feels *so* good to get these off," she breathed, following an amused Michael into the kitchen.

Dante turned around, bite of bread practically hanging out of his mouth as his siblings entered. "Yo sis, you want a sandwich? Mike made the chicken and his own bread again."

Kenya waved a hand in his direction. "No thanks. Just left a lunch date."

Dante shrugged as he finished creating his masterpiece.

Michael looked back and forth between them. "I take it you two finally made up?"

"Yeah, she called Lori and apologized for the insult," Dante confirmed, tearing a piece of aluminum foil from the holder.

Heading for the table, Kenya nodded. "Yeah, considering how bad she must feel after Michael fired her for being incompetent, I figured it was the right time to do so."

Covering his face with his hand, Michael shook his head. "Lord," he muttered.

Spinning around, Dante pointed at Michael. "Mike, you *told* her about that?!"

Throwing a taunting grin Dante's way, Kenya twirled a braid around her finger. "No, *Mom* did."

Dante scowled at Michael. "You told *Mom?*"

Michael's broad shoulders lifted in a shrug. "What? She asked how things were going. You know I can't lie right."

Letting out a huff, Dante stalked for the door, taking his sandwich to go. "Damn it, now I gotta go convince her that this wasn't my damn fault." He grabbed the doorknob. "This family talks too much."

Hearing the front door close, Kenya turned to Michael. "It's nobody's fault that the girl is scatterbrained," she ground out.

"Kenya, come on now."

Waving a dismissive hand, Kenya sat down at the table, eyeing the computer. "Anyway, since your laptop is out, can I use it for a sec? I want to show you something."

Michael sat down at the table across from her, then pushed the device in her direction, taking a bite of his sandwich. "What is it that you want to show me?" he asked after swallowing.

Kenya typed away, then after a moment, turned the laptop around. "There's this event coming to the city next week that I heard about from one of my employees." She smiled. "I think we should go."

Michael leaned forward, eyeing the screen. "Diamonds & Pearls Mixer," he read. "That's a party or something?"

"Somewhat." Kenya spun the laptop back towards her. "Think of a grown and sexy get together with food, drinks, great music, and ambiance."

Michael gave a blank stare. "So…a *party*."

She giggled a bit. "Fine, yes a party." She hit another key, showing him the screen once again. "The tickets are only a hundred and fifty dollars."

"Thanks for the invite, but I'll have to decline."

Narrowing her eyes, Kenya folded her arms. "I know *damn well* you're not scoffing at the price, when you've spent more money than that on *cologne*."

Confusion masked Michael's face. "I never mentioned anything *about* the price," he argued. "I'm just not in the mood for socializing. I *told* you that when you suggested that lounge."

"First of all, whatever lounge I would've taken you to, wouldn't have been some janky dive," Kenya shot back. "You should know me and my taste better than that."

"Whatever."

Kenya made a face at him in retaliation. "I refuse to argue with you. I want to go to this, and you and I are going together, so hush up and buy your damn ticket."

Michael narrowed his eyes at her as she slid the laptop in his direction. He didn't want to attend. However, the energy he'd need to go back and forth with his pushy elder sister could be better used on something else. "Fine Kenya, I'll go. But if I have a lousy time, you'll owe *me* a hundred and fifty dollars."

She gasped. "You wouldn't really make me pay you, would you?" Seeing the serious look on her brother's face, Kenya sighed. "Fine, I'll take that wager. You'll have a good time."

"Um hmm," Michael grunted. "When is this thing anyway?"

"This coming Saturday."

"Perfect," he drawled sarcastic.

"Oh, and everyone has to wear white." Kenya busted out laughing when Michael let out a loud groan.

Chapter Nine

YOU HAVE ARRIVED AT YOUR *location*. Though Michael could already see the familiar property, the confirmation from his GPS was welcomed.

Turning his car off, Michael exited the vehicle and stepped up on the sidewalk. There he stood, eyeing the two-story single-family home in front of him. Scanning the gray and white structure from top to bottom, he took mental notes along the way.

Brick structure, bay windows, walkway with stairs leading to the front door—great start.

His eyes did a quick scan of the landscaping. *Spacious yard, healthy grass, good shade from tree.* Peering over at the attached one-car garage, he nodded in approval. Turning to the street, he scanned the tree-lined block as far as he could see, taking in the neighboring homes with their own manicured yards. "I'm already impressed," he mused aloud.

"I'm glad to hear that."

Michael spun around at the sound of Patience's voice. A lively smile appeared on his face. "Hi."

"Hi," she smiled back. "Did I startle you?"

"Not at all." He placed a hand in the pocket of his jeans. "I figured you were around here somewhere."

That late Wednesday afternoon, as previously confirmed, Patience had Michael meet her at the suburban property for a walk-through.

Michael had looked forward to the meeting. Not only because this house was high on his approval list, but because it was yet another opportunity to see Patience again.

"Yeah, I was checking something around back." Patience gestured to the door. "Shall we?"

"Yes." Michael kept in stride with her up the walkway.

She shot him a side-glance. "The drive wasn't too bad, was it?"

"It wasn't bad at *all*. I enjoyed the scenic route," he beamed. "A half hour from my parents, forty-five minutes from my office building—" He looked at her. "Based on that and the outside *alone*, this place is already showing promise."

"Good to hear."

Approaching the step, Michael stood by as Patience opened the door. "It reminds me of the house I grew up in," he mentioned.

Stepping through the entrance, Patience peered back at him. "Well, thank goodness your childhood home holds pleasant memories for you," she quipped. "Otherwise, this could've been a disaster."

Stepping in behind her, Michael chuckled a bit. "No, *nothing* you've shown me has been a disaster."

She flashed a smile. Compliments of her job performance were always welcomed, but for some reason they seemed to mean more coming from Michael. As Michael's eyes roamed the space, Patience found herself leering at him. Her eyes traveled lazily up his frame, lingering on the profile of his face. *This man is a freakin' work of art— Girl! Do your job!* Her inner voice snapped her back in focus.

Clearing her throat, Patience pushed her hair over her shoulder. "So, before we take the tour, I just want to let you know that there's still a bit more work to be done on the property." She glanced around. "So, you'll see some unpainted walls, and some rooms don't have flooring down—things of that sort."

Michael waved a stiff hand. "Trust me, I know how to tune that stuff out."

Patience nodded. "Good." She tapped the folder in her hand. "As previously discussed, this is a four bedroom, two and a half bath property."

Michael stood, listening intently as she spoke.

"Living room, den, open concept kitchen and dining area, laundry room on the second floor, finished basement, one-car garage, plenty of yard space—front and back." She handed him the folder. "Ready for the full tour?"

Michael took it, and tried not to think about what it would feel like to take her hand. "Absolutely."

Over the next hour, Patience showed Michael every nook and cranny of the property from the inside to the outside, to back inside. Now standing in the kitchen, Michael was examining the cabinets.

"The wood type and color they chose for these is excellent," he said.

"Yeah, I've always loved the richness of dark cherry wood." Patience ran her hand along the light gray marble countertop, as she watched Michael closely study an open area. "It looks like you'll be able to fit a double-doored refrigerator there."

"Oh most definitely," Michael agreed. "The location of the space is great too. Both doors would be able to be opened, without one of them smacking against a wall."

Folding her arms, Patience nodded in agreement. "I currently have that problem with *mine*," she said, a slight inflection of amusement in her voice. "It's hell trying to get the shelves out to clean."

Michael grimaced. "Yeah, I can imagine." He paused and turned to face her. "You know, if you ever need any spaces widened or say, your whole *kitchen* remodeled, I could do that for you."

Patience smiled warmly. "I appreciate it, but judging on how much you make, I don't think I'd be able to afford you."

Michael folded his arms. "I highly doubt that." He shrugged.

"But even if that *were* true, I'd gladly give you a discount." *Hell, I'd do it for free if you needed me to.*

Moving over to a window, Patience shrugged some hair behind her shoulder. "As much as I appreciate you being willing to take a hit to your fee for me, I'm fine with my kitchen as it is for now," she said. "Besides, I'm renting my house, and as much freedom as I have to do as I wish with the property, I don't want to invest that much in a house that I don't own."

"Yeah, that makes sense." He propped himself up against the counter. "Not interested in snagging one of these beautiful homes for your*self* huh?"

"*Eventually*," she answered. "When I was looking for a place years ago, owning wasn't a priority." She peered out of the window. "My priority was just to find a place nice enough for me and my child." As soon as the words slipped out of her mouth, Patience's eyes went wide. *Shiiiit!*

Michael stared at her, blinking several times. That was the first time he'd heard her mention this. "You have a child?"

Patience was so focused on the thoughts screaming in her head, it barely registered that Michael had asked her a question. *Did I just tell this man my personal business?* Patience never discussed Noelle with any of her clients. Not even those who had children of their *own*. She kept her personal life private, yet for some reason, she'd just let this information fly.

Her silence confused Michael; so did the fact that she hadn't looked at him. "Patience?" he softly called.

Patience finally met his eye. "Yes?"

"You said that you—"

"Yes, I have a child," she cut in. "A daughter... She's eight."

Michael stood still, eyes fixated on her. "I'm sure she's amazing."

"Thank you. She is." Patience allowed a smile to come through. "The best thing in my life."

"I'm sure she is," he replied, sincere. *Wow, she's a mother.* While

81

that was the last thing he expected to learn about Patience today, he couldn't help but be more intrigued. "I'm *also* sure you weren't expecting to share that with me—"

"No, I wasn't," Patience confirmed, tone even.

He nodded again, eyeing her intently. "Nevertheless, I'm honored that you *did*."

Patience glanced down at her black stiletto heels for a moment. "Well…" She returned her gaze to him. "I hope you feel special."

Though he sensed she'd meant that as a deflective joke, it still made him smile. "I do." It was the truth. "Now I guess it's only fair that *I* share something with *you*." He gestured towards her. "Feel free to ask me something."

Patience's eyebrow arched. "It wouldn't be professional of me to do so."

"I won't tell your boss, if *you* don't." His easy joke earned him a giggle from her. "But seriously, you can… I'm an open book."

Patience pondered the proposal for a moment. "Okay, if you insist." She shifted her weight from one foot to the other as a question came to mind. "Do *you* have children?"

Michael shook his head. "No," he answered. "Not that I don't want—"

Patience put a hand up, halting his words. "You don't need to explain."

"I know but I *want* to," he insisted. "Children…a *family*, is something that I see in my future." He paused momentarily. "I guess I should say I *hope* to see in my future."

"I'm sure it'll happen whenever the time is right, and with the right person."

"Perhaps." Michael wondered if he should ask his next question. "Was…" He stalled. "Was *yours* with the right person?"

Patience's brow furrowed. *Fuck! I knew I shouldn't have engaged in this.* Her ex was the last thing she wanted as a topic of discussion.

Her jaw tightened. "I was married to her father, and now I'm not," she bristled. "That should answer your question."

Michael's eyes went wide for only a second before he schooled himself. *Divorced...she's also divorced.* "Oh... I—" Not only had Michael never fathered children, he'd also never been married. He couldn't imagine what it would be like to share vows with someone, just to have it not work out in the end. "Patience... I'm so sorry—"

"Don't be, it was necessary. Do you want another walk-through of the house?"

Michael focused on her words. *It was necessary.* He was curious as to who this mystery man was, and what he had done to Patience. He wondered how he'd treated her, how he'd treated his child. Unfolding his arms, and with a look of concern on his face, he took a step forward. "Patience, what—"

"Go do your walk-through Michael." Though her tone was stern, her eyes pleaded with him not to probe any further.

Michael sighed. The last thing he wanted was to upset her, yet clearly, he'd done just that. "Okay."

"I'll be outside." Patience punctuated her curt reply by walking out of the kitchen, leaving him standing there in silence.

Taking the alone time, Michael did in fact do a final walk-through of the house. Using his contractor expertise, he closely examined everything. At least what he *could* examine without proper tools. Already mentally noting what he'd have added to the customizable finishes.

Standing in the den, taking in the space one more time, he expelled a deep sigh. He liked the house, yet he couldn't allow his mind to fill with excitement over the fact that his long home-search journey could finally be coming to a close. Patience hadn't yet returned inside the house, and he couldn't help but be a little nervous to face her after their tense exchange. *You shouldn't have asked her anything else. Now you've upset her.*

"Michael?"

Startled, Michael spun around to see Patience standing in the den entryway. He'd been so busy berating himself that he hadn't heard her footsteps. "Yes?"

She stepped in, fiddling nervously with her fingers. "I wanted to apologize for my attitude earlier."

Sincerity on his face, Michael put a hand up. "No, please, you don't have to apologize. I shouldn't have tried to push you to talk about something that wasn't any of my business."

"Well, be that as it may... It was unprofessional of me," Patience replied. "So, I'm sorry."

Michael placed a hand on his chest. "*I'm* sorry." He hesitated, studying her face. "Are we okay?"

She nodded. "We are."

A sigh of relief escaped him. "Good to hear."

Folding her arms, Patience took a deep breath. "So," she commenced. "What do you think of the house? Do you have any further questions? Do you want to see any other properties?"

Michael looked around. "I like this place. It's what I've been looking for... I could see myself settling in here."

It was Patience's turn to study *his* face. She couldn't help but feel there was something he was leaving out. "But?"

He looked at her, curiosity resonating. "What do you mean?"

"I have a feeling that you're hesitating for some reason."

Michael shook his head slightly. "It's not that..." He gazed at her. "Tell me...what do *you* think about this place?"

"*I'm* not the one buying it."

"But if you *were*." He took a step towards her. "If *you* were looking to settle down somewhere—looking to make a home somewhere...would this be it?"

Patience's eyes wandered around the space. "I'd have to say yes."

Michael let out a chuckle. "I'm not asking you to look with realtor eyes."

Patience met his eye with perplexity.

"With *your* eyes." The humor erased from his face. "When you look at this house...what do *you* see?"

Patience crossed her arms. "I see..." She stood before him in silence, clearing all the realtor training and tactics from her mind. Closing her eyes, she expelled a deep breath before reopening them. "I see a yard where I can watch my daughter play, while I tend to the flower garden that I've always wanted..." She paused. "I see my dream kitchen where I can bake all of the cakes and pies that my grandmother taught me. I see a dining room where I can put a table big enough to hold an *entire* Thanksgiving dinner..." She looked over at the bay window. "I see a spot right by this window where I'd put a cozy chaise lounge and a bookshelf. I'd sit there after a long day, light one of my lavender scented candles, and read some sappy romance novel while drinking tea." She gestured to the living room entrance. "I see a fire going in that fireplace when it's cold outside, I see where I'd put a Christmas tree. I see the perfect spot in the living room where my daughter and I would sit and watch our favorite movies while drinking hot chocolate. I see space to *grow*, I just..." Her eyes settled on Michael. "I see a home." She shrugged. "So... there you have it."

Michael hesitated to speak, though the heartfelt smile that appeared on his face spoke volumes. He'd hung on to her every word, imagining, wondering, and *hoping*. "Thank you for that Patience," he spoke finally. "I see a home too."

Her eyes brightened. "Really?"

"Really... This is it. I'm done searching." He took a deep breath. "I want this." *In more ways than one.*

Patience clasped her hands with delight. "I'm so happy to hear that." She then cleared her throat, wiping the giddiness from her voice, bringing the realtor back. "Okay so, since this area is in high-demand, I would suggest starting the offer at their asking price. I typically don't push my clients to *over* offer at first, but I always give the disclaimer that a counteroffer over asking price might be needed, depending on how big the competition for the property is," she said. "And just as a reminder with this property, you're able to customize all of your flooring, which will be installed before closing."

Michael grinned, giving her a nod of approval. "Sounds perfect... Let's do this."

Patience returned a smile. "Perfect. I'll get an offer in for you."

Chapter Ten

PATIENCE PLACED HER CRYSTAL CHANDELIER earrings in her lobes and fluffed her carefully styled curls. Stepping back, she examined the lace, sleeveless top in the bathroom mirror. Touching the fabric around her neck, she squinted. "Toni," she called.

Toni shuffled into the bathroom, securing a diamond tennis bracelet around her wrist. "Yeah?"

"Necklace or no necklace?" Patience asked.

Toni gave her sister's two-piece outfit of the sleeveless, white blouse with white wide-leg slacks, a once-over. She pointed to the shirt. "The fabric comes up to your neck, no necklace."

Patience nodded in agreement. "Okay."

"You look pretty," Toni complimented, gently prodding Patience aside to allow herself access to her mirror. She fingered the curls of her own hair. "Still wish you would've traded me outfits."

Patience quietly laughed. "Thank you, and no." She eyed Toni's white satin cocktail dress without envy. "You look perfect in what you have on. Besides, the way my hips are set up, I'd be pulling that dress down all damn night."

"Girl please. Your hips are no bigger than *mine* and we have the same sized ass. You would've been fine." Toni gave Patience a soft nudge with her elbow. "Thank you though."

"You're welcome... For the record, I still hate you for dragging me to this."

Saturday had arrived, which meant that the anticipated mixer event was upon them. While Toni was excited, Patience was not. She'd much rather be home, curled up on her couch with her favorite mug of lavender and honey tea, reading a book.

Toni waved a dismissive hand. "Get over it. We're going to have a good time tonight."

"Yeah well, I guess I have no choice," Patience muttered. "You paid for the tickets *and* got Angela to babysit the girls—I'm still shocked she did it."

"Angie might be an anal nut job, but she loves those girls." Toni carefully applied her mascara. "Besides, that husband of hers is on a 'business trip'—" She shot Patience a knowing look as she gave air quotes. "So, she was more than happy to watch them. Maybe they can loosen her ass up some… Teach her to dance—*something*."

Patience shook her head, but didn't reply. She didn't doubt that her sister loved her daughter. She just wondered if Angela would speak badly about her to Noelle, or worse, bring up business she had no business bringing up.

"But to confirm your words—no you don't have a choice." Toni grabbed a bottle of expensive perfume, giving herself several sprays. "Who knows, you might meet your next husband there."

Patience rolled her eyes, leaving the bathroom without a word.

Amused by her reaction, Toni trailed close behind. "I'm just saying, you never know."

"Get away from me Toni."

Dressed to impress in his white trousers and button-down shirt, Michael got into his car. Pushing the start button, the late model luxury vehicle purred to life as he dialed a number on his cell phone. "Hey Kenya, I'm on my way—" He frowned at his sister's reply. The expression grew deeper as she continued to talk. "So let me get this straight…" He rubbed the bridge of his nose with two fingers. "After you talked me into going to this event—an event I had *no* desire to attend—you're standing me up because you have a *date*?" He couldn't believe his ears. "So after that whole speech you gave about us hanging out together, you accepted this date for tonight, *knowing* you had plans with me? ...Uh huh." He gritted his teeth. "You know what—I'm hanging up."

Michael ended the call, tossing the phone on the passenger seat. He was seething. "I *knew* I shouldn't have let her ass talk me into going to this shit in the first place."

He turned the car off with every intention of going back inside. His leftover beef ribs with rice pilaf, a glass of scotch, and a good book were calling his name. However, as he grabbed hold of the car door handle, he remembered that he'd already paid for the ticket. After going through the trouble of getting ready, he shouldn't let the evening just go to waste. At least without Kenya there, he could leave anytime he wanted.

Running his free hand along the top of his freshly cut hair, he released the handle and pressed the start button. "Hopefully this shit is worth it," he grumbled, pulling onto the street.

Toni tucked her gold clutch under her arm. "I'm starving, I hope this food is good," she said as Patience placed the valet ticket into *her* clutch. "Shit, it *better* be."

Patience walked towards the Lux hotel, keeping in stride with Toni. "I'm sure it'll be fine." Her lackluster tone was far from convincing.

As the pair passed through the lobby, they noticed the sign directing them to the grand ballroom. Side by side, the women entered the luxurious space with several other guests around them.

"Well damn," Toni whispered, awestruck.

Different assortments of white flowers and crystals were the focus of the decorated hall. Countless round tables, which were adorned with crisp white linens, candles, and flowers filled the room. The white satin drapery, with the sparkle of the crystals paired with rhinestone accents, gave a dazzling "diamonds and pearls" effect.

White-gloved servers carried an assortment of hors d'oeuvres, while two bar stations kept the top-shelf drinks flowing. The DJ was playing the latest grown and sexy tracks that had many guests out on the illuminated dance floor. Soft lavender up-lighting and crystal chandeliers added to the ambiance. A sea of guests dressed in their best white outfits were already enjoying themselves.

Patience moved her hair over her shoulder. "It looks beautiful in here."

"I know right? The décor *alone* is well worth the money." Toni craned her neck, peering at the nearest bar. "I bet the *drinks* are too. Let's go get something pretty."

Patience grabbed Toni's arm, stopping her hasty approach. "Eat something first."

Toni sucked her teeth. "I am *not* in college girl; I can hold my liquor." Patience shot her a sharp look, to which Toni put a hand up. "I just had flashbacks of Rob's birthday party last year, you're right."

Patience chuckled as Toni waved down one of the servers.

"Swedish meatball?" the smiling man asked.

"Yes," Toni answered as she and Patience grabbed a serving. When the man walked off, Toni promptly scarfed it down. "Let's go find a table—no wait, let's go take a picture first."

"Okay." Patience followed Toni to the photo area. The 360-camera booth was decorated with flowers, a lit event sign, and hosted plenty of props. The sisters took several fun, gorgeous shots, before going off in search of a table.

"As soon as they post those pictures on their site, I'm stealing them," Toni vowed. "I know how to remove a watermark."

Patience laughed. "Print me some copies too."

"You know I will."

The two women moved through the crowd en route to the

seating area. Luckily for them, a few of the tables had yet to be claimed. Choosing one, Patience sat down, placing her iridescent crystal-covered clutch on the tabletop. She picked up a menu card. "They have some nice entrée selections." She held the card out for Toni to see. "Here look, your picky ass might *actually* be pleased."

"I'm not the picky eater, *you* are, and I'll look at that thing in a minute. I'm going to the bar first." Toni bobbed her head to the music. "Ooh, this is my jam." She looked back at Patience as the song blared. "What do you know about this song youngin'?"

Patience scrunched her face. "Toni, stop using our two-year difference as a flex," she sneered. Toni laughed. "And you only started *liking* this song because *I* kept it on repeat back in high school, so come on now."

Toni flagged her with her hand. "Yeah yeah. What do you want to drink?"

"Something with*out* alcohol." Knowing her sister all too well, Patience rolled her eyes. "Never mind, I'll come with you."

Toni placed a hand on Patience's shoulder. "No, I'll be fine, it's right over there." She gestured to the area. "Besides, you need to stay and watch this table. These people are circling for empty seats like vultures."

Patience chuckled as Toni headed off, making sure to keep a watchful eye on her while enjoying the music. After a moment, she found her eyes drawn from the bar to the crowd. Chatter, laughter, dancing, cameras flashing—everyone seemed to be having a good time. She found herself smiling at what she could only assume were the couples—both young and seasoned—as they danced together.

Her smile diminished as she held her focus on those beautiful couples; she let out a deep sigh. *Must be nice.* As much as Patience had tried pushing the desire for companionship to the back of her mind, seeing couples up close and personal, laughing and smiling together, made her long for it.

"Hey sexy, is this seat taken?"

Patience swiveled her head around at the voice that had drawn her out of her daze. "Excuse me?"

The older man ogled her. "Is this seat taken?"

Patience opened her mouth to say "yes" but decided against it. *Don't jump straight to rudeness Patience, he probably just needs the extra seat.* She and Toni were only occupying two of the four chairs. He looked to be in his mid-fifties; maybe he just needed a place to rest. "No, it isn't, you can have it." Patience planned on turning back to the crowd, but the man sat down in the empty seat, his eyes locked on her. She stared back at him. "Umm…you're not planning on sitting here the *entire* time, are you?" she asked him.

He adjusted the watch—the large, *gaudy* gold watch on his wrist, as he grinned at her. "Yes." His response, just like the look on his face, was crammed with confidence. "Figured a woman as fine as you shouldn't be sitting alone."

Patience fought the urge to visibly cringe at the oversized, unnaturally whitened veneers in his mouth. "I'm *not* alone actually," she corrected, both tone and eyes deadpan.

"Well…right *now* you are." He rubbed the stubbly unconnected beard on his jaw. "So…let's chat. You look like someone I'd like to get to know."

Patience's eyes tightened; her jaws clenched. "I assure you, you don't want that."

"Oh, I'm sure I *do*." He leaned forward, winking. "I love a challenge."

Closing her eyes, Patience silently cursed herself for not accompanying Toni to the bar like she *wanted* to.

Reopening them, she fixed the pushy man with a stern stare. "Sir—"

"Cristian," he cut in. He extended a hand, showing off his gold rings…one on each of his ashy fingers.

She glanced down at his hand, before returning her eyes to his face. "Germs," she shot down. The man promptly lowered his hand.

"*Cristian,* while I'm flattered by your attention, I'm not interested in conversing with you. I'm just here to enjoy the event with the person I came here with," she spelled out. "So, if you wish to take the chair with you to another table, please feel free to do so. If not, then leave it here and *leave.*"

Cristian glowered at her. "What's your damn deal?" His voice rose with frustration, "You're too good to *talk?* What, are you here with your *man* or something?"

An icy gaze formed in Patience's eyes. "I'm here with my *gun,* now get the fuck away from me."

Eyes bulging, Cristian rose from his seat. "You bitter, lonely bitches are all the same."

"Aww, male fragility, how shocking," Patience mocked, flipping him the finger. "Bye Cristian," she further taunted as he sulked away.

"Screw you wench," Cristian tossed over his shoulder.

Rolling her eyes, Patience shuddered to think what the next woman he'd encounter would have to deal with. "Fuckin' raggedy ass Y chromosomes."

Michael pocketed his valet ticket and straightened his shirt collar, before walking into the hotel. Taking a deep breath, he made his way down the marble hallway to the ballroom entrance. Browsing the space and hearing the music playing, he couldn't help but be impressed. "Well, I can see why it costs so much," he mused aloud. He vowed to at least *try* to enjoy himself.

As Michael tried to decide which bar to head to, he was approached by a server.

"Mini steak roll?"

Michael eyed the roll on the small plate, then grabbed it along with a napkin. "Sure, thank you." The server nodded then walked off as Michael stuffed the entire small bite into his mouth. *Not bad.*

Strolling up to the bar, he signaled for the bartender. "Scotch neat please." He removed his wallet, pulling a few bills from it.

"You know this is open bar, right?" a woman's voice said.

Michael looked over at the woman who'd appeared next to him. "I'm sorry?"

"It's open bar," she repeated, then sipped her martini.

"Yes, I'm aware," he replied, polite. The bartender sat the drink in front of Michael, who in turn handed the man a tip.

The woman's rose-tinted lips formed a haughty smile. "My mistake." She stood perusing Michael up and down. "So…here with friends tonight? A girlfriend? *Wife?*"

"None of the above. Just…enjoying a night out solo."

"Well, a man as attractive as *you* should *not* be out at these types of events alone," she purred. "The women are already swarming."

Michael chuckled a bit. "I appreciate the advice, but I think I'll be fine." He was cognizant of the stares of admiration, but meeting someone wasn't on his agenda that evening. Especially when there was only *one* woman consuming his thoughts.

She raised an eyebrow. "You know," she said as he went to turn away. "I'm here with my friends, but I'm sure they wouldn't mind if I brought *you* to the table."

Michael faced her. She was practically drooling over him. "Thank you, but I'll probably walk around for a bit before sitting down to eat, so—"

"Oh, I'm sure you're skilled at—*eating.*"

The brazen comment drew a smirk from him. "Uh huh." He tipped his glass at her. "You have a good evening." Walking away, he couldn't help but shake his head in amusement. "Wow," he said to himself, leaving the woman gawking at his departing figure.

Placing a lamb skewer into her mouth, Toni read the menu card. "The honey glazed salmon steak sounds good," she said upon swallowing her bite. She took a sip of the purple drink in her glass, then winced. "God*damn.*"

Patience looked at her. "You went overboard, didn't you?"

"Just a tad." Toni coughed as the burning in her chest intensified. "I read 'whisky and bitters' and *still* ordered it because the shit was purple." She patted her chest.

Patience shook her head, taking a sip of the virgin version of the purple drink—or what she *thought* was the virgin version. As the liquid spilled down her throat, she nearly gagged. Pushing her glass away, she backhanded her sister across the arm.

"Ouch!" Toni quickly rubbed the stinging area. "That was uncalled for."

"If *I* get drunk, who's going to drive us home?" Patience fumed.

"It was an *accident,*" Toni threw back. "Come on, I'd only sneak and get you drunk at *home.*"

Patience's eyes formed into slits. "Remind me not to go anywhere else with you."

"Hush," Toni dismissed. "I'll go get you and I *both* something else. Then we'll get some real food in you, because this finger food isn't enough to keep your ass from being evil."

"Let me go, *you* watch the table."

Toni pointed a finger as Patience went to stand. "Look here, this dress costs *way* more than I wanted to spend, so I'm going to make sure everybody gets a gander at my fine ass *wearing* it." She bolted from her seat. "So sit *your* ass down and watch the table, while I go to the damn bar."

Patience made a face as Toni sauntered away. "Vain ass," she mumbled to herself.

Michael had roamed the hall for a little over twenty minutes, sampling finger foods and enjoying the music. "I should probably find somewhere to sit." Craning his neck, he searched for the main dining area.

As soon as he found it, he did a quick scan with his eyes. Not one empty table in the house—not that he was shocked by that. The place was packed.

Damn, he thought. *I guess I'll go back to the main section and fill up on hors d'oeuvres.* Just as he turned to head out, resolved to spend the rest of the evening on his feet, someone caught his eye. *Hold up.* He began making his way to the table to be certain. Getting a closer look, his face lit up. Once at the table, he lightly tapped it. "Excuse me."

Patience, whose sight was fixated on the bar, let out a huff. *Not another one of these bastards.* "The seat is not taken, but the table *is*, so—" She turned, locking eyes. "Oh shit, *Michael?*"

Her response caught him off guard. "Yeah…" He gave a nervous chuckle. "Is it safe to ask to sit?"

Patience shielded her face with her hand. "Yes, I apologize." She gestured to him to sit. "I thought you were—"

"An asshole?" he finished, taking the empty chair.

"Precisely." She shifted towards him, "I had a brief run-in with one not too long ago, so I'm on high alert."

Setting his half-empty glass of scotch on the table, Michael's brow gathered. "Is he still here?" he charged. "Let me know who it is, and I'll make sure he doesn't—"

"No, no it's fine," Patience cut in, putting a hand out. "I'm sure my attitude scared him off."

"Are you sure?" Michael had no problem handling anyone who dared to cause Patience any sort of problem.

"Yes, I'm sure." Patience offered a grateful smile. "Thank you though."

The concerned frown dissipating from his face, he returned her smile with one of his own. "No thanks needed." Michael had last spoken to her the previous afternoon. She'd informed him that the offer he'd put in on the house was still being mulled over. He hadn't expected to see her again until either the offer was approved, or if he needed to see new properties due to the offer being rejected.

So, the fact that he'd ran into her here, spotting her in a crowd this big, could only mean that this run-in was meant to happen. "So." He folded his hands on the table. "How did you hear about this event?"

"My sister dragged me here." Patience revealed, amusement in her voice. "She's over at the bar now, probably telling the bartender to sneak some liquor into my drink."

Michael chuckled. "That's a sibling for you."

"You've got that right." Patience adjusted the silver bracelets on her wrist. "So, what about you? How did *you* hear about this?"

"Like you, *my* sister told me about it... Though yours is ten times better than mine, because *mine* stood me up for a date," Michael put his hand up when Patience shot him a sympathetic look. "Nah, it's fine. I might be here solo, but I'm glad I came." *Now, more than ever.*

"Yeah, it's a nice ambiance." Patience scanned the space with her eyes. "It's been a while since I've been out in a crowd like this. So, despite my initial reluctance, I'm glad I came too."

As she spoke, Michael found himself mesmerized. Like the other times when he'd became spellbound, he willed himself to speak. "So... Since we're out in this causal setting—"

"I wouldn't exactly call an event with ten ice sculptures *casual,*" she joked, facing him.

Michael expressed a quick laugh. "True. But that being said, I have a slightly intrusive question?"

"Just a slight one, huh?"

"Minuscule at best." He put his hand up. "Feel free not to answer."

After pondering for a moment, Patience gestured for him to proceed. "Go ahead." She'd already revealed the fact that she had a child, and that she was divorced. Any question he came up with couldn't get more intrusive than that.

"Has it been a while since you've been on a...date?" he asked.

"Again, you don't have to answer," he quickly put in when she hesitated.

Patience's head leaned slightly to the side. "*Why* are you asking?"

"Making conversation." He took a deep breath. *Be honest, Michael.* "And because I'm curious."

"Fair enough." Patience toyed with the napkin cuff on the table. "Honestly...it's been a while."

"Honestly...same for me."

Lips pursed, Patience rolled her eyes. "Liar."

Michael couldn't help but find her reaction a bit humorous. "I'm *not* lying."

She folded her arms at a leisurely pace. Patience knew why *she* had put dating on the backburner, but she highly doubted that this gorgeous man before her, who she was *sure* had women throwing themselves at him, hadn't been on a date in a minute. "Umm hmm."

"I'm serious," Michael insisted. "Come on, do you really think I'd lie to you, when you were just honest with *me*?"

Patience shot him a shrewd look. "Do you really need me to answer that?"

"No. But I *am* being honest with you."

She raised an eyebrow. "Okay. If you say so."

Michael shook his head, amused. She clearly didn't believe him, but that didn't worry him. The humor left his face as he contemplated his next question. He almost didn't want to ask it, but it was gnawing away at him. "I have one more question, if you don't mind."

Moving her hair over her shoulder, she braced herself. *You better not ask me the last time I had sex.* She didn't want this man *that* much in her business. "Sure," she granted, despite her concern.

"This is a long shot, but... Do you remember meeting me before I walked into your office?"

Patience hesitated briefly before squinting her eyes. "I'm sorry?"

Her confused reaction disappointed Michael, though he successfully hid it from his face. *Yeah, I had a feeling she didn't. I guess I didn't make much of an impact.* "Don't worry about it. Forget I even asked." He tittered a bit as he gestured to his glass. "Blame this scotch."

Patience's eyes lowered to the glass, then rose back to him. "You're tipsy?"

"No, I was trying to deflect from my stupid question," he admitted, subtle humor lacing his voice. He planned on changing the subject, but his attention was caught by something in his peripheral. Or rather, some*one*. Turning his head, Michael fixated on the man lumbering in their direction from across the ballroom. "Hmm," he muttered.

Noticing the seriousness on Michael's face, Patience grew concerned. "What's the matter?"

Michael's steely gaze was focused as he rotated in his seat. "Some guy is heading over here," he replied. "And he doesn't appear to be in a good mood."

Patience followed his line of sight. Then her eyes widened. "The fuck?"

"Do you know him?" Michael asked her, eyes not leaving the culprit.

Patience grabbed her clutch from the table, sticking her hand inside. "No. But that was the asshole I encountered earlier."

Michael's brow drew into a deep frown. "Say no more." Pushing his chair back, he stood. "I got you."

Cristian, half-empty glass of bourbon in hand, aggressively pointed in Patience's direction. "I got one more thing to say to you—"

"Nah, say that shit to *me* bruh." Michael stepped straight in the man's face, halting his approach. "What's up?"

Aghast, Cristian's head jolted back. He was so focused on

giving the woman who'd bruised his ego a piece of his mind, that he hadn't noticed the man sitting with her. The one who was now standing in front of him, looming over his head. And from the menacing look on his face, he could snap him in half at any moment. "Wait, who the hell are *you*?"

"I'm a problem I *promise* you don't want," Michael threatened, staring the man down. "What the fuck did you come over here for?"

Patience sat in stunned silence, watching the exchange with her hand in her purse, clutching the mace she carried. Watching this poor excuse of a man be put in his place by a *real* one. Though she was on guard, something told her that she wouldn't need to use her weapon. Her eyes quickly darted to the crowd. *Where the hell is Toni?*

Cristian put a hand up in submission. "Look man, I—I don't want no trouble. I just w-wanted to say—"

"Say *what*?" Michael barked, causing the man to flinch. He jerked a hand up, silencing Cristian's would-be reply. "And I'd advise you to think long and hard before opening your mouth."

Swallowing hard, Cristian backed up. "Nothing... I wasn't going to say anything," he lied. "My fault brother. I didn't know she was with you." He took another step back. "I'll just go on my way."

"Make sure it's out the fuckin' door." Michael clasped his hands in front of him. "Since it's clear you don't know how to conduct your sleezy ass in a respectful manner towards women, you don't need to be here." He shrugged. "So, either you leave *willingly*, or I'd be more than happy to assist you."

Taking Michael at his word, Cristian simply nodded. Being sent to the hospital was not on his to-do list that evening. "You're right I umm, should probably go sleep this liquor off." He scurried away, nearly colliding with another party goer on his way out the door.

Michael followed his progress until he disappeared out of sight, exhaling deeply to calm himself down. It angered him to think of what that idiot might have tried to do to Patience, had he not been there to intervene. Shaking it off, he turned to Patience with a gentle hand on her shoulder. "Are you okay?" he asked, making no attempt to hide his concern.

Leaving the mace in her purse, Patience nodded. "Yeah, I'm good..." She locked eyes with him. "Thank you."

"No thanks needed." Michael returned to his seat. "Somehow I don't think he'll be a problem anymore."

"Well yeah, I'd agree with you." Patience smoothed her hair away from her face. "He looked like he nearly shit his pants when you stepped to him."

Michael couldn't help but laugh a bit. "That tends to be the outcome when I confront assholes." He placed a hand on the table, the amusement leaving his face. "But are you sure you're good?"

She nodded. "I'm sure."

Michael opened his mouth to speak, when a woman appeared next to Patience at the table.

"Girl, I'm sorry I took so long—"

Patience's head snapped in her direction, her eyes blazing. "Where the hell were you?"

"I was at the bar," Toni explained, two drinks in hand. "This lady was talking about her business, and when I mentioned that I was an accountant, she went off on this tangent about how her friend almost landed her in jail for tax fraud." She set the drinks down. "*Then* she started telling me about her man and that she had to leave him home because his whites didn't match... Cussed his ass out because his shirt was cream."

"Toni?" Michael blurted out.

Patience looked at Michael the same time that Toni did. While Patience shot him a questioning look, Toni's eyes enlarged in shock.

"Michael! Oh, umm—hi," Toni stammered. *Ooooh shit!* She was so focused on her sister that she hadn't seen him.

Michael smiled, oblivious. "Hi, how are you?"

"You two know each other?" Patience jumped in, pointing between the two.

Michael gestured to the speechless Toni. "Well, I wouldn't say we know each other on a personal level, but I *do* know her. She's my accountant." He looked at Patience. "You two are—"

"She's my sister," Patience finished.

Taken aback, Michael's eyes widened. "Oh wow… Small world."

Toni let out a nervous laugh. "Yep small. Patience is my baby sister, and I am your accountant," she sputtered, fiddling with her bracelets. "Have I told you how great your record keeping is?"

Michael's brows creased in confusion by Toni's nervous behavior. "Uh, yes, you have."

Patience was quiet as she reflected, thinking back to the conversation with Toni about her new client weeks ago. She agreed with Michael, it *was* a small world. *What a coincidence*—she paused her thought as something else crossed her mind. "Michael," she called, eyes still fixed on Toni.

"Yes?" he answered.

"When you called me to set up an appointment the first time, you mentioned that someone referred you to me." Patience looked at him. "*Who* referred you?"

Michael opened his mouth to answer, but was drowned out by Toni.

"You know what, I think they put alcohol in your drink again Pace. I should go back and get you another one."

Patience reached up, gripping Toni's arm as the woman tried to make a hasty departure. "No, I think you need to sit your ass right *here*," she demanded, pulling Toni down in the seat next to her. She fixated on Michael as she kept her tight grip on her sister's arm. "Go ahead Michael."

"You're hurting me," Toni hissed, trying to pry Patience's hand off.

Patience remained unfazed. "You'll make it worse if you keep moving."

Michael was clearly bewildered by what was going on between the sisters. Nevertheless, he had no problem answering. "Toni did."

"*Did* she?" Patience asked through clenched teeth.

"He said he was looking for a new realtor and *you're* a realtor, so I referred him to you." Toni once again tried to move Patience's tightened fingers. "Is there a crime in that?"

Patience fixed Toni with a stern glare. She knew Toni well enough to know when she was playing stupid. The questions about her new client, the constant pushing about her giving dating a try again—Toni had pulled an Angela and set her up.

"Well, Patience she *was* right about you," Michael stepped in, hoping to diffuse any tension. "She said that you were excellent, which you *are*. She even said that you sold her *her* house."

Closing her eyes, Toni lowered her head as Patience returned her sight to Michael. "Damn it Michael," Toni mumbled.

"She told you that I sold her her house?" Patience repeated. Michael nodded. "Toni purchased her home years before I even *thought* about becoming a realtor."

"Oh shit," Michael chortled, putting a hand over his face.

Feeling nails dig into her skin, Toni let out a yelp. "Okay now *look*, if you make me bleed on this white dress, you're *paying* for it!"

Patience released her arm, then nudged her.

Rubbing her skin, Toni checked for scratch marks. "I will *not* apologize for my exaggeration. You got hired, *didn't* you? And he's on the verge of getting his dream home, which means commission for *you*, so…"

Patience rolled her eyes. "Girl, just stop it."

Toni faced Michael, who was clearly trying to hold in his building laugh. "I don't exaggerate at work, so please don't worry."

Michael put his hands up. "I'm not worried."

Toni tossed her arms in the air. "Well, I'm already in trouble, so since we're all here together, we might as well eat." She grabbed her menu. "Where's the waiter?"

Michael locked eyes with Patience. He snickered, while she just shook her head in annoyance.

The next hour and a half had gone by, and the three table mates had enjoyed their meal and conversation, though Toni's temper rose when she'd learned of the situation her sister had to endure over that—*fool*. However, after being reassured by Patience that she was okay, and how Michael had stepped up for her, Toni was able to breathe a sigh of relief.

She'd resorted to being a happy spectator during most of the conversation between Patience and Michael. As far as she could tell, her sister was enjoying his company. And the way Michael interacted, engaged with, and *looked at* her sister, Toni had no doubt that he was enjoying Patience's company as well. In her mind, this match—though sneaky—was a success.

"That food was amazing," Michael commented, setting his fork on his empty plate.

Patience reached for her glass of water. "It *was*." Feeling a vibration in her purse, she left the glass on the table to grab it.

Toni dabbed the corners of her mouth with her cloth napkin. "Now that we've eaten, why don't we—*you two* hit the dance floor?" She gestured back and forth between Patience and Michael. "Nothing works off a meal like slow dancing."

Michael shook his head, amused. "You're not subtle at all, you know that?"

"I am when I'm not tipsy," Toni countered, earning a snicker from Michael.

Patience put her hand on Toni's arm as she eyed her text messages. "We have to go," she said.

Disappointment hit Michael at her words. He was looking forward to a dance or two. However, he remained silent.

Toni looked at her. "Why? The event isn't over yet."

"I know, but Noelle just texted me and said that the power went out on Angela's block for some reason. It won't be back on until the morning, and Jordan doesn't want to sleep there with no lights, because she's scared of those antique dolls," Patience explained.

Toni rolled her eyes. "God, I *told* Angie to put those goddamn ugly things in the *basement*," she huffed. "*Mom* didn't even like them, what would possess *her* to keep them?"

"Who knows, but Noelle said that *she* was fine with still sleeping there without lights, until Jordan started saying that she saw the dolls' eyes following her. Now *my* baby is scared."

Toni stomped her foot on the floor like a child. "*Why* does it always have to be *my* child with the dramatics?" she whined.

Patience put the phone back into her purse. "Yeah, not going to even respond to that." She pushed her chair back as she locked eyes with Michael. "It was good seeing you again, Michael."

Michael stood as she did. "Likewise."

Sighing, Toni stood up, smoothing her dress down in the process. "Well, it was fun while it lasted." She gave a nod to Michael. "Have a good night."

"You too." Michael turned, watching as Patience moved around the table following Toni.

Patience paused her departure, turning to face him. "Oh, I was going to call you tomorrow, but since you're here *now* I might as well tell you…"

Michael eyed her in anticipation.

She smiled at him. "Your offer was accepted… You have your house."

The grin on Michael's face could have lit the entire block. "That's great news." He reached his hand out. "Thank you for everything."

She placed her hand into his, giving it a light shake. "You're welcome. Congratulations."

The look in his eyes as he gazed at her was mixed with both gratitude and adoration.

Patience tried to avoid his intense stare, but found herself drawn to it. Clearing her throat, she removed her hand from his, snapping them both out of their haze. "I'll get all of the information regarding inspections, closing date and anything else, and give you a call Monday."

"Sounds good." He stood still as she backed up. "You mind if I walk you to your car?"

"No, we absolutely do *not* mind," Toni loudly interjected, before Patience had a chance to answer. She gestured to a humored Michael with her hand. "Come on Mr. Protector. Love to see it."

Patience shot a narrow-eyed look her tipsy sister's way. "You're not allowed to drink around me anymore."

Toni snickered at the threat, but didn't bother responding.

It took mere moments for the trio to exit the hotel, and for Patience to hand the valet her ticket for the car retrieval. Once her keys were in hand, Michael took the liberty of opening the driver's side door for her.

She flashed him an appreciative smile as she sat inside.

Toni also grinned as he opened her door, allowing her to enter. "Protective *and* chivalrist…" She stared up at the car ceiling, confused. "No wait, that's not a word. Chival—Sis, give me another word to use."

"Please shut her door Michael," Patience pleaded, nudging the giddy Toni back in her seat.

Holding his hand on the door, Michael quickly peered inside. "Good night. Drive safely."

"Night… I will," Patience returned. Once he closed the door and stepped back on the curb, Patience put the car in gear.

Grinning, Toni lightly smacked the arm rest. "See? I *told* you you'd have a good time."

"Shut up, and it's chival*rous*," Patience spat, pulling off.

Chapter Eleven

TAKING NOELLE BY THE HAND, Patience and her daughter crossed the busy shopping district street, heading straight for the restaurant on the corner. Opening the door, Patience allowed Noelle to enter before stepping in behind her. Noelle gleefully swung her mother's hand as Patience spoke to the hostess. Within moments, the two were seated at a booth near a window and handed menus.

The little girl held her hands out and examined her nails, gleaming.

Looking up from reading the items on the menu, Patience caught the joyful look on Noelle's face. It drew a smile from her. "You really like your nails, huh?"

"Yes," Noelle beamed. She moved some of her lavender and white beaded braids over her shoulder. "The little bunnies are so cute."

Patience remembered how excited her daughter had gotten when the sweet nail tech had said that she could paint little white bunny faces for her. "They're adorable."

Noelle pointed to Patience's hand. "Why didn't *you* get bunnies on yours?"

Holding her own hand out, Patience examined her coffin sculpted, lavender tipped nails, before returning her eyes to the menu. "Because my love, bunnies are *your* thing."

With Patience taking on even more new clients, while keeping up with the final property sale processes for her current clients, she found herself with very little free time to do anything fun with Noelle over the past couple of weeks. So that Saturday afternoon, Patience had cleared her day and taken Noelle out on a mother-daughter date.

The two had gotten manicures and pedicures, gone to an art museum, and made a stop at the mall where Noelle had snagged a new toy bunny to add to her collection, along with a few new outfits and accessories. Patience had even treated *herself* to a new outfit and a few accessories. Now, tired out and hungry, they were wrapping up their outing at a restaurant.

After chatting away, the food that they'd ordered nearly twenty minutes ago had arrived at their table. Noelle dug into her breaded chicken sandwich and sour cream and onion chips, while Patience worked on her blackened fish tacos.

Hearing her phone beep, Patience removed it from her purse. She had a new email from the contractors working on Michael's house. Quickly scanning the text, she focused on four words in particular.

The house is finished.

She typed out a quick reply, before putting the phone away. She'd be sure to call Michael once she returned home to let him know, so that the inspection could be scheduled. *He's going to be so happy about this news*, she thought as she looked out the window. She quickly forgot about her tacos as she stared at the scenery outside. Within a matter of seconds, her mind had become consumed with Michael. Had it been the first time he'd infiltrated her thoughts, she would've been shocked. But it wasn't.

Michael had been popping into Patience's head ever since she'd taken him on as a client. She'd recall something he'd said while making dinner, or found herself laughing at a joke they'd shared while she commuted to work.

However, since their run-in at the mixer three weeks ago, Patience couldn't help but think of him more often, and for *longer* periods of time. Now instead of just random recollections, she was thinking of *him*; his face, his smile, his intelligence, his personality, his infectious laugh—Patience couldn't help it…she liked him.

The sound of a dish falling in the background snapped her out of her daydream. It was just as well. Once they closed on the house, that would be the end of her time with Michael Carter.

"Mommy, can I ask you a question?"

Patience turned her attention to Noelle. "Sure, what is it?"

"Have you ever been to camp?" Noelle asked.

Thinking for a moment, Patience shook her head. "I can't say that I have." She took a quick sip of her lemonade. "Why?"

"My art teacher was telling us about art camp."

Patience raised an eyebrow. "Art camp?"

Noelle nodded. "It'll be during the summer—July I think," she replied. "And…I'd like to go."

Putting a hand to her chest, Patience took a moment to compose herself. Noelle had never been away from her for more than a weekend, let alone *weeks*. And July was merely four months away. The thought unnerved her, but she didn't want to just shoot the request down. "Umm… Let me talk to your teacher and find out more information first," she said. "*Then* I'll make my decision."

Noelle's eyes lit up. "I hope you say yes."

Patience chuckled. "Yeah, I'm sure you do."

She finished a taco, while Noelle ate more of her food. Patience watched as her little girl poured over her nails once again, while dancing in her seat and simultaneously eating a chip. She made a mental note to do more self-care activities with Noelle. It was something that Patience didn't get to do much of with *her* mother.

"When I talked to Jordan this morning, she said that she was going to ask Aunt Toni to take her to look for a dress for her daddy-daughter dance," Noelle spoke.

Patience successfully concealed a laugh. She could only imagine how her sister had reacted when her niece had asked her.

She could hear the words, *'Girl! That dance isn't until September, if you don't go somewhere,'* fly out of Toni's mouth.

"Oh yeah?" Patience replied.

"Yes." Noelle brushed chip crumbs from her hands. "She asked me if I was going."

A chill ran through Patience. She knew Noelle would hear about the dance eventually. She eyed her daughter, tilting her head slightly. "And what did you say?"

"I told her no." Noelle shrugged. "Then she asked why, and I said, 'because I don't have a daddy to go with'."

A low sigh left Patience's mouth. The initial chill was quickly drowned out by a surge of guilt and sorrow. What Patience had said to Toni was true; Noelle didn't seem too saddened by the fact that her father wasn't in her life. But now that she was getting older, Patience was beginning to wonder if that was changing. The thought of her daughter's feelings being hurt, crushed her.

"Bunny…" Patience saw that Noelle's attention was on her plate. "Look at me sweetie," she urged, tone soft and caring.

Noelle looked up at her.

Patience took a breath. "How does that make you feel?" she carefully asked. "The fact that your father isn't in your life—*our* life… Do you feel sad, or angry?"

Noelle's eyes lifted to the ceiling as her mind tried to find the words. "No," she finally answered, returning her eyes to her mother. "I don't know him. So, I'm not sad, *or* mad."

"Are you sure?"

Noelle nodded. "I have *you* Mommy, so I'm happy."

A wave of emotion filled Patience, tears pricking the back of her eyes. She doubted that Noelle had any idea exactly how much those words meant to her. She quickly blinked back her tears to avoid blubbering in front of her child and the restaurant full of people.

Instead, she reached her hand out for Noelle's, who placed it into hers. "I'm happy to have you too," she said. "And I want you to know that if you *ever* get to a point when you *do* feel sad or angry, or *anything*…you can always come talk to me. Okay?"

"Okay."

Patience gently tapped Noelle's cheek with her finger. "I love you."

Noelle smiled. "I love you too." She went back to eating her food, while Patience sat back in her seat just rethinking the past few minutes. "Oh Mommy?"

"Yes?" Patience placed her glass to her lips.

"I heard Aunt Toni tell Uncle Rob that she thinks you met *your* new daddy."

Eyes wide in horror, Patience choked on her drink. "What?!" she exclaimed, between coughs.

Noelle watched with concern as her mother repeatedly patted her chest with her hand. "Are you okay?"

Patience put a hand up as her coughing subsided. "Yes, I'm fine," she managed to get out through a raspy voice.

"What does that mean?" Noelle probed. "Do I have a new granddad?"

"No, it—" Pausing, Patience pinched the bridge of her nose, letting out a deep sigh. *I'm going to kill Toni!* She snatched the phone from her purse. "It means that I'm going to have a little chat with Aunt Toni, *and* that *you* shouldn't eavesdrop on grown-ups' conversations."

Noelle shrugged as she reached for her juice. "Okay. I won't."

"I'm *so* excited for you," Jill gushed, passing Michael a basket of dinner rolls from across the dining room table.

Taking a soft, warm roll from the basket, Michael's face beamed. "Thanks Mom."

Gary took a quick sip from his frosted glass of water. "You're closing in a few days, right?"

Michael nodded. "Wednesday to be exact." He spread a bit of butter on his roll. "If it weren't for the fact that I still have a ton of stuff to pack, I'd wish for the days to move faster."

Setting his glass down, Gary chuckled. "Don't even worry. *Because* you have so much stuff to do, time will move quicker than you want it to."

"I'm sure you're right." With closing only days away, Michael was thrilled. His parents had even invited him over for dinner that Thursday evening to celebrate.

Michael grabbed the bottle of Merlot from the middle of the table, pouring himself a little. "I tell you, I appreciate the dinner invite." He set the bottle back in place. "I've been missing a home-cooked meal. My kitchen is so cluttered, I can't bring myself to cook anything in there."

"Do you need any help?" Jill asked, scooping a smothered turkey wing out of the ceramic dish. "I'll have everything organized for you in no time."

Gary tapped his wife's shoulder, prompting her to look at him. "You know how you're always telling me to chill out and relax?" he reminded. She stared, unblinking. "*You* need to do the same. That man doesn't need you shuffling around in his way."

Jill waved a flippant hand as she turned away from him. "Packing plates is *not* the same thing as pulling up weeds and pruning a damn tree, so stop it," she threw back. "And *you're* one to talk about shuffling. I move quicker than *your* sluggish behind."

Erupting with laughter, Gary gave his wife a loving pat on her arm.

Michael laughed at the banter. "Thank you for the offer Mom, but I've got it. I honestly don't have too much left. I'm just eager to get the move over with and get settled."

Jill nodded, but as she went to speak, she heard someone calling her from the living room. "Dante, Kenya that you two?"

"Yes," they returned in unison.

"We're in the dining room," Jill replied.

Michael gave his brother and sister a head nod as they entered the dining room. "Mom made her famous smothered turkey wings."

"Oh my God, *yes!*" Dante rejoiced, rubbing his hands together.

Gary pointed a warning finger as Dante pulled a chair out and plopped down. "Hey, don't you even think about taking all of our leftovers this time, you hear me?"

"Pop, don't worry, I won't." Dante grabbed a plate from the middle of the table. "Because there won't be any leftovers to *take*."

Gary narrowed his eyes. "Make me put you out before you get a taste, hear?"

Kenya laughed as she took a seat next to Michael. "Still haven't learned to tame the trash talk until *after* you get the food, huh Dante?" Turning her attention to Michael, who was concentrating on his food, Kenya gave his arm a light tap. "You're not still mad at me about leaving you hanging at that event, are you?"

Kenya hadn't seen Michael since, due to both of their hectic schedules over the past few weeks. Though she'd already apologized to him via text *and* phone call, even getting his acceptance days ago, Kenya couldn't help but wonder if he was still upset.

Michael looked up from his food, fixing Kenya with a stoned stare. He relished the worry on her face for a few seconds, before relaxing the expression. "No, we're good."

Running a hand over her bun, Kenya breathed a sigh of relief. "Okay good, because I was stressing."

"Yeah, I'm sure you were." Michael set his fork down. "But as annoyed as I was at the time, I ended up enjoying myself, so you're off the hook."

Kenya grabbed a plate. "Well… At least *one* of us enjoyed that night," she griped, piling food onto it. "If it makes you feel any better, my date turned out to be a damn dud, and I winded up leaving his sorry ass at the restaurant."

"That *does* make me feel better, actually." Michael's jest earned

113

a playful nudge from Kenya. "No, but in all seriousness, do I need to break his neck?"

"Absolutely not. I would've done it myself if needed," Kenya replied.

"Kenya don't bring any of those *duds* around us," Gary jumped in, earning a backhand from Jill. "I'd hate to *accidentally* shoot one of them with a nail gun."

Bringing a hand to her face, Kenya blew out a huff. "Dear God—Mike are you all packed up?"

Jill laughed at the sudden subject change. "Smooth baby girl, smooth."

Kenya shot her mother an amused look.

"Oh yeah, are we still on to move you next Saturday?" Dante chimed in.

Michael nodded as he sipped his wine. "Yes. I'll be picking the truck up at nine that morning."

Dante scooped food onto his fork. "Okay, I'll be ready."

"*I* won't be lifting anything, but I'll be there directing y'all with coffee and donuts," Kenya slid in. "I'll even buy lunch afterwards."

"Oh *hell* nah, you're moving *something* princess," Dante sneered. "Otherwise, why bother coming?"

Michael chuckled at the defiant look on his sister's face. He knew Dante's rants were going unfazed. "The company *and* coffee and donuts will be appreciated sis," he said. "Don't worry about lunch, it'll be on me."

"*Thank* you Mike." Kenya delivered a light pat to Michael's back. "This is why you've always been my favorite brother." She giggled when Dante rolled his eyes.

The room was silent for a bit as the family concentrated on their dinner. That is, until Dante piped up. "Aye guys, did Mike tell you that he has a crush on his realtor?"

Michael shot him a narrow-eyed look as all eyes laid on *him*. "Seriously?" he grunted at his brother.

Kenya nearly dropped her fork on her plate in shock. "Wait, *you* have a *crush?*"

"Oh, sweetie that's wonderful," Jill added, her eyes glowing with glee.

"Face be lit up like a Christmas tree when he talks to her on the phone," Dante teased, holding his glass of iced tea to his lips. Flashing a taunting grin at Michael, he took a long sip.

Jill clasped her hands together. "Have you asked her out?"

Michael put his hand over his face, shaking his head. "God—" He pointed at Dante. "I'm about to fire you."

Dante spat his drink out.

Eyeing the tea droplets on the table, agitation flashed in Gary's eyes. "Boy!"

"Sorry," Dante coughed, wiping the table with a napkin.

Ignoring the side conversation caused by Dante's silly behavior, Michael turned to Kenya. "Yes, I am intrigued by my realtor—" He looked over at his mother. "And no Mom, I haven't asked her out."

"*Will* you?" Jill pressed, eager. "I'm sure she's pretty."

Michael exhaled deeply as thoughts of Patience bombarded him. "She's *beautiful.*" His voice was almost breathless. Clearing his throat, he picked his fork back up. "Let's change the subject, okay?"

Kenya grabbed the wine, pouring herself a healthy serving. "We'll grant that wish for now. But *trust* it'll be brought up later, because *this* is monumental."

Michael made a face at her. "Funny. Real funny."

Chapter Twelve

"I BELIEVE EVERYTHING IS IN order, do you have any other questions, Michael?" Patience asked, gesturing at him.

Michael's eyes lifted from the papers in front of him. "No, I'm good."

Patience nodded. "Great, so just sign, here, here, and here." She pointed to the flagged lines on the paper.

Picking up his pen, Michael did as he was instructed. He felt like he'd signed a hundred papers already, nevertheless he was happy to sign these last few. A little over a month after finding his perfect home, Michael was at Clayborn Realty, sitting in a conference room with Patience, the sellers and attorneys to finalize the closing.

Finishing up, Michael closed the folders and set the pen down.

"Congratulations." Picking up the set of keys in front of her, Patience handed them to Michael. "You are now a homeowner."

Clutching the keys in hand, Michael beamed. "Thank you." Standing up along with the others, he exchanged handshakes and pleasantries with the gentlemen. When they exited the room, he turned his attention to Patience, who was gathering items from the table.

"I'll make copies of everything for your records," she said. She looked up to find him staring at her.

Michael stepped forward, extending his hand.

Patience placed hers into his, shaking it.

"Thank you again," he said, sincerely.

She smiled back. "You're welcome." She went to move her hand, but paused when Michael gently placed his other hand on top of hers.

He eyed her intently. "No, really."

She stared back, her hand secure in his. She didn't want to move it, but knew that she had to. "Sure." Removing it from his loose grip, she moved around the table to the door. "You can wait in my office while I make these copies."

"Okay." Taking the opportunity once Patience left the room, Michael slipped out of the building and sprinted to his car. Opening the passenger-side door, he grabbed two boxes from the seat—a small pink one and a medium-sized white one—before closing the door. He slipped back inside, placing the items in a seat next to him, before sitting down.

When the door opened, Michael stood, facing Patience as she entered the office.

Patience approached, folder in hand. "Here's everything. You're all set."

Michael took the folder. "I appreciate it."

"It's a beautiful house." She moved around him towards her desk. "I know you'll make it a great home."

Michael watched as she clicked the mouse on her laptop. *I can only hope that you'll eventually be there with me to make it even better.* The thought shocked him. He hadn't even asked the woman on a *date*, yet he was already picturing her living in his home. "Before I go, I have something for you," he said.

Patience peered up at him. "Oh yeah?"

"Yes." Michael set his folder on the desk before picking up the boxes, holding them out for her. "Just a thank you gift."

Eyes wide, Patience took them from him. "Aww, Michael you didn't have to do this." She set them on her desk.

"I wanted to." Shoving his hands into his pockets, he shifted his weight from one foot to the other.

Placing a hand atop the smaller box, she raised her brows in question. "Do you... Do you want me to open these *now*?"

He chuckled. "If you wouldn't mind."

"Okay then." Smiling, Patience started with the pink box. Opening it, she gasped. "Oooh." Sitting inside was a lemon cupcake topped with lemon icing and a candied lemon slice on top, accompanied by two deluxe-sized lemon cookies—one covered in lemon icing and the other sprinkled with sugar crystals. "These looks *amazing*. Lemon is my—"

"Favorite," he finished.

Patience shot him a look that mixed confusion and surprise. "What?"

Michael put a hand on his chest as he gathered his words. "I know you don't remember me from the bakery... But *I* remembered *you*."

Box still in hand, Patience tilted her head as he spoke.

"And I remembered our conversation about pastries." He smiled as the sweet memory flooded in. "And that you favor lemon desserts so..."

Patience was taken aback, and it showed on her face. "Wow..." she breathed, eyeing the treats again. "This is..."

"Crazy?"

"No, it's sweet." She locked eyes with him. "Really...thank you."

Michael was pretty sure he was blushing under her gaze. "You're welcome."

Closing the dessert box, she set it aside before opening the bigger box to reveal a beautiful assortment of lavender and white flowers in a crystal vase. "Michael...these are beautiful." Her eyes sparkled as she picked the vase up, examining it. "Did you somehow find out that my favorite color is lavender?"

Michael's eyes lit with surprise. "I had no idea. You never mentioned it." He'd spent nearly an hour yesterday looking for the perfect bouquet for her. He was happy that his intuition had told him to pick *that* one. "It's good information to have, though."

Patience felt the flutter of butterflies in her stomach. Clearing her throat, she carefully set the delicate vase on her desk. "So, it seems we had the same idea."

Michael's eyes creased with curiosity. "Same idea?" He followed her progress to a small closet. Watching her open it, his brows shot up when she pulled something from it.

"I got you a gift too." She held one of the items—a small houseplant—out for him to take.

Gratitude flooded Michael's face. "You didn't need to do this. You've done enough for me."

"I appreciate that, but I wanted to get you a little something to warm your house." She gestured to the potted plant. "Something to sit in one of those beautiful windows."

Michael eyed her with adoration. "Thank you, Patience." He looked back at the plant, touching a leaf. "I know exactly which window I'll put it in."

"Oh yeah?"

He nodded. "And I'll think of you whenever I look at it."

Patience's eyes drew down at her shoes, trying not to blush. "You have one other thing." She held out a white box.

Michael set the plant on the chair, then took the box. "Jessy's Gourmet Bakery and Café," he read aloud.

Patience nodded as she watched him open it.

Laying eyes on the treat inside, he smiled. "A fudge drizzled brownie," he said. "This is one of *my*—"

"Favorites," Patience finished. When he shot her the same look she'd given him not that long ago, she nervously twisted a ring around her finger. "I *do* remember you."

Standing there in stunned silence, Michael felt his heart jump.

"I recognized you when you walked in here the first time," she confessed. "And I'm sorry that I didn't confirm that for you when you asked me at that event. I think…" She took a deep breath. "I was just caught off guard when you mentioned it."

All Michael could focus on was the fact that she *did* remember him. It didn't matter to him that she didn't tell him then; she was telling him *now,* when she didn't even *have* to. "You don't have to apologize… But thank you for telling me."

She smiled warmly. "Enjoy your dessert and…everything," she responded. "It was good seeing you again."

Michael stood before her, exhaling deeply. "The pleasure was all mine."

Patience ran a hand down her arm. She was about to say goodbye to Michael for the last time. She'd miss seeing his face, hearing his voice, being in his presence. But she knew that this was business. Even though she'd been dreading this part, her job was done. "So, if there is nothing else…enjoy the rest of your day and good luck to you."

Michael's eyes lowered as she moved back behind her desk. He couldn't lie to himself; he felt a connection with Patience. And although it seemed that she did with him as well, he wasn't foolish enough to assume it. But he *also* wasn't foolish enough to walk out that door, without at least shooting his shot.

Michael set the brownie box down on the chair. "There *is* something else."

Shooting a curious glance his way, Patience tucked some of her hair behind her ear. "What's that?"

He hesitated for a moment as he collected his nerve. *Go for it.* "Will you go out with me?"

Her head jerked back, brow furrowing slightly. "I'm sorry?"

"I'd like to take you out."

Patience looked like she'd just been asked to go bungee jumping. "You—you want to go on a *date*?"

"Yes."

The confusion on her face had not waned. "Seriously?"

"Yes." Michael initially felt that her reaction to his question was because she didn't believe that he was serious. However, as she stared at him, he began to wonder if her reaction was because she didn't *want* to go out with him. "Please understand that there's no pressure here, Patience," he said, tone deep but caring. "If you don't want to—"

A hand shot up, halting his words. "No, it's— It's just that—" Patience let out a short breath. "Michael, you remember that I'm divorced right?"

Michael gave a nod. "Yes, I remember."

"And you remember that I have a child, right?"

"Yes, Patience, I remember." Confusion appeared on his face. "I'm sorry but... I'm not sure I understand why you're asking."

Patience's eyes drifted to the desk, yet she didn't respond.

A thought forming, Michael's brow gathered. "Wait... Do you think that your situation is somehow a *deterrent* for me?"

"It is for most men," she threw out, meeting his eye. "And me being a single mother means that I won't have as much time for you as you'd want or *need*. I have a schedule and homework to help with and—" Pausing, she rubbed her forehead. Since meeting Michael, Patience had internally toyed with the idea of dating again, yet she was still apprehensive. What she had told her sister a while back was still true; Patience did not want to waste her time going through a talking or dating phase that would lead to nowhere. She didn't have it in her.

Patience let out a sigh. "Look, I'm flattered. But I just don't think you understand what it'll take to really date me."

Michael stood there, his caring eyes fixated on her. "First... Even though you didn't say it, I'm assuming that you've had to deal with a few—immature *boys* in the past," he began. "And for that, I'm sorry."

Patience admired him as she listened.

"*I'm* a grown man and I understand that this is your life, and it doesn't scare me," he continued. "It doesn't make me view you as anything other than the amazing, beautiful woman you are. Someone who I have the upmost respect for." He took a step forward. "And regarding time...I'm on *yours*. So, whenever you're available, I'll make *myself* available."

Patience's face flushed at his words—the way he spoke of her had the ability to make her melt, but she quickly gathered herself. "I wasn't exaggerating before; it's been a while since I've dated."

Michael's shoulders rose and fell subtly. "Likewise." His lips curled into a grin. "So how about we get back on the bike together?" The smile left his face after a moment, seriousness replacing it. "I like you, Patience. Seriously, and I know I can *say* it all day, but I'd rather prove it to you... If you let me, of course."

Patience stared at Michael, pondering whether to try and drudge up some other excuse as to why she couldn't go out with him. But she didn't have one. So far, Michael seemed well worth dipping her toe back into the dating pool for. *So...you're really about to do this again?* Running a hand over her hair, she glanced away, trying to ignore the nervous flutters in her stomach.

Michael stood watching her, unwavering. "Do you have any more questions or concerns for me, Ms. Harvey?"

"Uh, no. No I think I'm good on those for now."

"Good." He rested a hand on her desk. "So, what do you say?"

Patience faced him, and after a moment let a smile come through. "I say yes... You may take me out."

Feeling his heart race, Michael released a subtle exhale. A glowing smile followed. "Perfect." He scratched his head. "This would probably be a good time for me to get your personal number."

"Yeah, you're probably right," she chortled back, grabbing a pen from a cup on her desk. She jotted down her personal cell number on the back of a business card and handed it to Michael, who didn't hesitate to secure it in his wallet. "So, if there is nothing else—"

Michael let out a laugh. "No, we're definitely all set now."

She giggled in return. "I guess I'll talk to you later."

"Most definitely." He picked up his folder and gifts, then backed towards the door. "See you soon Patience."

A coy smirk crossed her face. "I guess you will." She waved to him. "Bye Michael."

"Bye."

Patience watched him walk out the door. It wasn't until it closed that she felt her legs get weak. Sinking down in her seat, she rested one hand on top of her head, and the other on her chest. "Why the hell is my heart beating out of my damn chest?"

Leaning back, she recalled the day's events. She'd closed on a house and opened herself up for a date. Both drew a smile across her face.

"Oh my God, are you serious?!" Toni squealed.

Embarrassed by her sister's outburst, Patience's eyes darted around the restaurant, taking notice of the staring patrons.

"About *time*. When did he ask you? When are you going? *Where* are you going?" Toni fired off.

Patience scratched her head. If she'd known that Toni was going to make such a fuss *plus* ask twenty questions about her date with Michael, she would've waited until they were somewhere more private. Not the crowded outdoor restaurant they had met for lunch that Monday afternoon.

Patience grabbed her glass of iced lemon water. Taking a sip, she set it back down. "He asked me last week, we're going out this Friday and…I don't know. He hasn't shared that bit of information yet."

Toni grinned. "Ooh, a 'just be ready at this time' date." She smacked the table with her hand in delight. "I love those."

"Pretty much," Patience uttered, poking at the lemon slice in her glass with her straw.

Toni took a long sip of her drink, then having a thought, she arched her brow. "Wait…" She put a hand up. "If he asked you out last week, why are you two just going out *this* Friday? And *why* the hell am *I just* hearing about it?"

"Because he and I *discussed* it, and that's the day that works for me. And I didn't tell *you* right away because I needed to wrap my head around all of this first, *and* I knew you'd do what you *normally* do and that is be *extra*," Patience threw back. Toni's mouth fell open. "You just startled half the damn restaurant."

"My loudness shouldn't stop people from minding their own goddamn business." Eager to get back to the subject at hand, Toni flagged her hand, curbing any further flippant response about onlookers. "Anyway, are you excited?"

Patience rolled her eyes. "Come on Toni."

"*What*? It's a legitimate question." Toni reached for her fork. "I'd think *so* since you accepted the invitation."

Patience sat back in her seat, folding her arms as her eyes lowered to the fresh spring rolls on the plate in front of her. "I am excited."

Toni eyed her, picking up on her low tone. "Then why don't you *sound* like it?"

Patience looked up at her. "I *am*." Her lackluster tone had not changed. It was the truth; she *was* excited. But that excitement was overshadowed by other feelings that she had. Ones that were driving her a bit crazy. "I... I like him, Toni... I mean, I know that so far it's been surface level but..." She let out a sigh. "I *like* him, and that scares the *shit* out of me."

Toni's eyes held a look of concern. "*Why* sweetie?"

Patience let out a light huff as she tried to pull her thoughts together. "Because he's the first man since my divorce that I can actually picture myself with—"

"And what's *wrong* with that?"

Patience put her hand up. "I'm not finished."

Toni gestured for her to continue, taking a bite of her food.

"Which *means* that after all this time of closing myself off, I have to open myself *up* again to let this man *in*, so that we *could* be together, and…" Patience clasped her hands together, resting them on the table. She looked at her sister, question in her eyes. "What if it doesn't work out?"

Tilting her head slightly, Toni eyed Patience with sympathy.

"What if under the surface it's not what I thought? What if *he's* not what I thought?" Patience questioned. "Or for him, *I'm* not what *he* thought… What if he's not *ready* for everything that comes…with me?"

Taking in everything her sister had said, Toni searched for the right words to say. She rested her fork on her plate, eyeing Patience intently. "Sis listen to me, I understand why you feel the way that you do—"

"T, I know you *want* to, but I don't think you really *do* understand."

Toni went to speak, then paused for a moment. "Well…I'll let you think that right now." She moved some breeze blown hair away from her eyes. "Listen, you have every right to feel how you feel. This is something new for you, and as scary as that can seem at first, it's also exciting."

Patience stared, a glint of hope lighting her eyes. "Yeah?"

"*Absolutely.*" Toni rested her hand on the table. "And from what I can tell, there's already a connection there between you two, and you haven't even gone on a date yet, so in my book, that's a great sign."

Glancing back down at her hands, Patience let out a deep sigh. "Yeah."

"That being *said* Pace, just relax and go with the flow." Closing her hand into a fist, Toni squeezed her eyes shut. "*Please* just go with the flow."

Eyes widening with both shock and amusement, Patience folded her arms once more. "Why did you have to repeat it?"

Toni put a hand up. "Because, you *know* you'll over analyze every little thing, and before you know it, you'll be digging for red flags in a yard that has none."

125

"Well, excuse *me* for learning from my past mistakes."

"Go…with…the…flow, I *said*," Toni maintained. "That fine ass man you got pining over you is nothing like your *mistake*. You know you can see that shit already."

"Yeah, yeah." Patience waved a hand in Toni's direction. "You may or may not have a point."

"Oh I *have* the *point*." Toni reached back for her glass. "You better not run off a potential brother-in-law that I actually *like*."

Patience rolled her eyes. "Girl, we haven't even had *dinner* yet, and you're already talking about *marriage?*" she sneered. "Who says I'd even *want* to get married again?"

"We'll revisit the marriage topic in a year. Don't you worry." Toni punctuated her prediction by sipping her beverage.

Shaking her head, Patience picked up her spring roll. "Oh, and thank you for agreeing to watch Noelle Friday, even though you didn't initially know the reason why I needed a sitter."

"Girl, I already told you I don't need a reason to watch my niecey pooh."

Patience smiled. "You irritate my spirit, but I do appreciate you."

Toni threw a taunting wink her way. "I know." She speared a piece of orange chicken. "By the way, I know that I'm just supposed to watch her for a few hours, but she can always spend the night…" A sly smile formed. "You know, just in case you need the privacy."

Patience caught the look on Toni's face and knew *exactly* what she was implying. "That will *not* be necessary, nasty," she scoffed. "I have absolutely *no* plans on sleeping with Michael on the first date."

Bursting with laughter, Toni put her hands up in surrender. "I was just putting it out there."

Chapter Thirteen

STANDING BEFORE HIS BEDROOM MIRROR, Michael cradled his phone to his ear with his shoulder as he fiddled with the tie. "I promise I'll let you know when the curtains get here Mom." Making a face, he tossed the printed accessory to his bed. *Nah, no tie.* "My windows are oversized, so I had to have them custom made."

"You just *better*, because I'm still coming to hang them. So have my little step stool ready," Jill instructed. Her son had been a homeowner for a little over a week, and she was eager to see the space.

"Mom, you don't have to *do* anything in order to come over." He retrieved a watch from his dresser. "I know my schedule was hectic this past week, but I'll have some time tomorrow." Placing the watch on his wrist, he fastened it. "So, you and Pop please come visit, I'd love to have you. I'll make us lunch."

"Oh, we'd love that." Her enthusiasm was hard to miss, even over the phone. "We'll be there with a congratulatory Devil's food cake."

"No, Mom—" Michael paused, shaking his head in amusement. "As much as I love your baking, just bring yourself. Don't go through any trouble." He glanced around his room, eyeing the filled bins. Making a mental note to do a bit more unpacking before his parents' arrival tomorrow.

A soft giggle came from Jill. "Okay, okay… Anyway, I won't keep you any longer darling, I know you're getting ready for your date tonight."

Michael put the phone on speaker, setting it on the dresser. "I'm ready actually." He grabbed a bottle of designer cologne, giving himself a few sprays. "I'll be heading out in a few."

"Are you excited?"

Michael couldn't help but chuckle; his mother was practically beaming through the line. She'd lit up the same way when he'd revealed that he'd asked Patience out. "I am."

"Nervous?"

"I am…probably more than I *expected* to be." The butterflies in Michael's stomach had been rampant ever since he'd awoken that morning. Though he'd interacted with her on a business level, and since last week had spoken every day on the *personal* level, Michael couldn't shake the nervousness.

"I completely understand," Jill prattled on. "But you have *nothing* to be nervous about. You're a *wonderful* man and I'm sure she'll see that."

Michael smiled. "Thanks Mom."

"Of course, baby," she replied. "Well, you have a wonderful evening with this lovely woman, who I hope to meet one day soon."

I cherish the thought. "I will. I'll talk to you tomorrow. Love you."

"Love you more."

Hanging up, Michael pocketed his phone, then his wallet, followed by keys. Bolting over to his walk-in closet, he slipped on a pair of black dress shoes from the rack, giving himself one last look over in the mirror. He'd opted for a black button-down shirt and pants, paired with a gray sports jacket. Glancing at his watch, he hurried out of his bedroom and down the staircase.

Passing through the living room, Michael retrieved a bouquet of flowers from the coffee table on his way to the garage. Hitting the unlock button on his vehicle, he climbed into the driver's seat before carefully placing the bouquet on the passenger seat next to a small gift bag. Pressing the button on his dash, he waited for the automatic garage door to open before starting the car. As the engine ran, Michael retrieved his phone.

Dialing Patience's number, he smiled when she picked up. "Good evening... I'm just calling to let you know that I'm on my way... Is there anything you need while I'm out?... Okay then, I'll see you soon."

Hanging up, he set the phone in its mount, then keyed Patience's address into his car's navigation system. As the directions bellowed through the speaker, Michael expelled a deep breath. *Calm down, Mike.* He sat for a second, then laughed quietly to himself. "I'm only going out with the woman of my dreams. What's there to be nervous about?" he joked to himself as he pulled off.

Retrieving a pair of crystal drop earrings from her glass jewelry box, Patience hung them in her earlobes before moving to the floor-length standing mirror in her bedroom.

Noelle and Jordan laid on her bed, staring as she examined her figure from the side.

"You look so pretty Aunt Pace," Jordan gushed.

Noelle smiled adoringly at her mother. "I agree."

Patience glanced at them through the mirror, grinning. "Thank you, babies."

Resting her elbows on the bed, Jordan placed her face in her hands. "Where are you going?"

Patience opened her mouth to answer, but was drowned out by Toni, entering the room with a glass in hand. "She's going to mind her business, *that's* where she's going," Toni stepped in.

Jordan looked up at the ceiling for a moment, then at her mother, confused. "Mom, that doesn't make any sense."

Patience snickered as Toni shot an amused look her daughter's way.

"You're lucky I love your little smart butt," Toni threw back, prompting a giggle from her daughter. Shaking her head, Toni approached Patience.

"But to answer your question Jordan *and* Noelle, since I'm sure you're thinking of asking next, I'm just going out with a friend," Patience informed. She had decided not to tell her daughter that she was going on a date. She figured she'd give it some time before bringing up the subject.

Toni sucked her teeth as Patience faced her.

"What?" Patience asked, perplexed by the attitude.

"You should've stuck with the 'minding your business' answer," Toni sneered. Patience waved a dismissive hand. "We're supposed to be a unit against these kids."

Patience couldn't help but snicker. When Toni held the glass out for her, Patience peered down at it. "What's that?"

"Ginger ale, it'll settle your nerves."

Bewildered, Patience scratched her head. "What kind of nonsense—*you* drink it, it might settle your foolishness."

Toni shrugged, then sipped it. Holding the cool glass to her chest, she observed Patience placing a tennis bracelet on her wrist. "You look beautiful. Love the dress."

"Yeah?" Patience smiled when Toni gave an eager nod. "Thank you." Returning her gaze to the mirror, Patience gave a once-over of her completed look. A spaghetti strap, lavender pencil-hemmed dress that fell below her knees hugged her body. The silver stiletto open toe shoes, and shimmering jewelry, complemented her attire. Her long curly hair flowed just right, and her makeup only enhanced her beauty.

It had been nearly a half hour since Michael had called to let her know that he was on his way. As the time ticked by, Patience felt herself growing anxious. She took a deep breath. "Shit, is it hot in here?"

"No." Toni fanned her sister's face. "Relax."

"I am trying *so* hard to." Patience placed a hand on her stomach. "I'm too damn old to be this anxious."

Toni giggled. "Anxiety doesn't expire with age, kid. The *good* thing is that you're already—" She shot a quick look over at the girls, who were chatting amongst themselves. Not wanting to take any chances on them overhearing, she leaned in close to Patience, lowering her voice to a whisper. "You're already familiar with him, so the hard part is over."

Patience frowned. "I sold him a *house*, that is *not* the same thing."

Toni gave her a blank stare. "Do you want a shot of something to calm you down?"

"No," Patience ground out.

"Auntie Pace?" Jordan called.

Smoothing her hand down her dress, Patience exhaled. "Yes?"

"Do you want to try my new lip gloss?" Jordan held up the pink tube. "It's bubblegum flavored."

Patience faced Jordan as Toni turned and left the room. Seeing Jordan approach with said gloss, Patience grimaced. She could tell from the tube *alone* that the bright, glittery pink gloss would not look good with her outfit…or on her *period*. Besides, she already had her go-to deep mauve lip liner and gloss combo on. Yet she hated to turn down a face that adorable.

She leaned forward, allowing the girl access to her lips. Resisting the urge to flinch when the heavy, sticky applicator touched her mouth.

Dabbing the wand on Patience's lips, Jordan stepped back, proudly examining her contribution to her aunt's get up. She made the okay sign with her fingers. "Perfect."

Patience stood up straight just as Toni reentered the room holding a wet washcloth.

"Nice job my love, now go back over there with your cousin." Toni directed her daughter back to the queen-sized bed with Noelle. As Jordan trotted over, Toni grabbed Patience's arm, turning their backs to the girls. "Pace, wipe that shit off."

Patience broke into a fit of laughter as she took the cloth from Toni.

"You look like you've been smacked in the mouth with pink icing," Toni teased as the laughing Patience wiped the substance from her lips. "So sweet of you to entertain that, but no sis."

"I know right." Patience swiftly reapplied her original lip combo. "I could tell just by *looking* at it, that it was going to be a mess."

Folding her arms, Toni shook her head. "She only puts it on when she's playing dress up in the damn house. Her normal gloss is clear and not *nearly* as sticky."

"Yeah, I bet." Patience tossed a few items, gloss included, into her silver clutch. Hearing the doorbell ring, a chill ran through her. "Okay," she whispered to herself. Grabbing the clutch from the dresser, she went over to the bed, giving Noelle a hug followed by Jordan. "I'll see you a little later. Love you."

"Love you too," the girls spoke.

Patience tapped Toni on the arm. "Feel free to cook whatever you want—"

"Girl, we're ordering pizza, if you don't get down there," Toni chuckled, then patted Patience's arm. "Have fun."

Patience left the room. "I will."

"I *mean* it," Toni hurled at her departing back.

"I *will*." Taking a deep breath, Patience descended the staircase. Crossing the living room, she approached the door. She peered out of the peephole for good measure, a smile crossing her face when she saw *his* face on the other side.

Opening the door, her eyes roamed Michael's figure as he stood on the front step. *Damn, he looks good!* "Hi," she said instead.

Michael, bouquet of roses and small gift bag in his hand, didn't speak right away. The words had gotten caught in his throat. *You are absolutely beautiful.* Snapping out of it, he smiled back. "Hi… you look absolutely beautiful."

Patience turned away to keep him from seeing her blush, but quickly recovered. "Thank you." She held her clutch to her stomach. "You look handsome yourself."

"Thank you." He held the lush bouquet out for her. "I bought these for you."

Patience's eyes lit up at the two-dozen lavender roses. "Oh wow." She took them from his grasp. "I don't think I've ever seen a lavender rose before."

Michael nodded. "They're pretty rare, but not impossible to find."

She carefully touched one of the full blooms. "Well, thank you for finding them. They're beautiful."

"You're more than welcome." He briefly glanced down at the bag in his hand. "I bought this for you too."

Patience eyed the black bag as Michael handed it to her. "What's this?"

He expelled a quiet laugh. "You have to open it to see."

She giggled, "Good point." Cradling the flowers with her arm, she stuck her hand into the bag to find a sixteen-ounce, three-wick candle in frosted glass. "A scented candle, I love these." Removing the silver lid, she put it to her nose. Inhaling the fresh scent of lavender with hints of lemon, she closed her eyes. "Oh my God, this smells *so* amazing."

Michael stood, pleased. He'd spent a pretty penny on both the custom roses, and the luxury candle. Just seeing how much she liked them made them worth every bit. "I'm glad you like it. I remember you mentioning how you'd light a candle while reading so, I just figured…"

Patience looked at him as she put the top back on it. Her eyes crinkled with a smile. *This man really pays attention to what I say.* "Thank you…" A soft breeze swept past her, swaying her hair, which she promptly maneuvered over her shoulder. "Uh— Give me a second while I take these inside?"

"Of course, take your time."

Patience stepped back inside the house and closed the door, only to be startled by Toni standing in the living room looking at her. "What the fuck?!" Patience belted out, clutching her flowers to her chest.

Fighting not to laugh at the stunned look on her sister's face,

Toni put a hand up. "I didn't know you'd be coming back inside," she explained. "I was making popcorn for the girls, and I heard the door open."

Gathering herself, Patience waved a hand. "It's fine, can you put these in water for me?"

Toni stepped forward, taking the flowers from her grasp.

"And please put this in my room on my dresser." Patience handed Toni the precious candle.

Toni beamed at her sister's gifts. "Of course. Now *go*."

Patience waved on her way out the door. "Ready," she announced to Michael as she closed the door behind her.

"Is everything okay in there?" Michael asked.

"What do you mean?" Quickly realization hit her. "Oooh, you heard my 'what the fuck?', didn't you?"

Michael nodded. "It was pretty loud so, yes."

Covering her face with her hand, Patience shook her head. She could only imagine how the muffled outburst sounded to him. "Everything is fine." She returned her eyes to him. "My sister—*Toni* startled me by standing in my living room looking like a stalker."

Letting out a quiet laugh, Michael extended his arm for her. "Well, now that I know you're good, let's be on our way."

Patience placed her hand on his arm, and together they walked down the steps.

Michael opened the passenger side door, allowing Patience to get situated inside before closing it and moving over to the driver's side.

Patience put her seat belt on then settled back against the soft leather interior as Michael started the car.

Smoothly pulling out of the parking spot, he drove down the street. "Do you prefer the air conditioning or the window down?"

She adjusted the bracelet on her wrist. "Unless you want all this hair blowing in your face, let's stick with the air conditioning."

Adjusting the air volume, Michael smirked. "I can think of worse things than having your beautiful hair in my face."

Twisting a curl around her finger, Patience successfully concealed her own smirk. "Noted."

"Are you okay with the music? Just let me know."

"The music is perfect. I happen to love R&B." She peered over at him. "I appreciate you asking though."

He shot her a quick glance while at a stop sign. "Of course, I want you to be comfortable."

She gave him a smile. "So." She returned her eyes to the road. "You have yet to share where you're taking me. Normally, I would've required that information before agreeing to a date."

Michael chuckled a bit as he kept his eyes on the road. "So does this mean that you have a dislike of surprises?"

"No, not at all. I appreciate a good one," Patience amended. "Though I've had very few of them in my life."

"Well, here's hoping I can change that."

Maybe you can. Folding her arms to her chest, she shot him an inquisitive look. "So, are you going to tell me or what?"

Amusement spanned his face. "You don't trust me?"

Raising an eyebrow, her head lingered to the side. "*Should* I?"

"Oh, you definitely should." Stopping at a red light, he gazed at her. "I'm taking you on a dinner cruise."

Patience didn't reply right away, yet her face showed that she was impressed. "Huh," she drew out, returning her focus out the front window.

"It's a two-hour cruise. Fine dining, live music…" He put his foot to the gas as the light changed. "I just figured that since we *technically* shared dinner together already, I wanted to do something a bit fancier than a normal restaurant for our date."

"Impressive." Though her tone was unflappable, she was beaming with excitement on the inside.

Michael found her ability to be coy *and* nonchalant, humorous. "You think so, huh?"

She reached over and put a hand on his leg. "I do."

Michael felt a tingle surge through him. With his free hand, he put it over hers, his eyes sparkling. "Good to hear."

"This way," the smiling suit-clad man spoke, gesturing to the two-level cruise ship in front of them.

Michael took Patience's hand, holding her secure as the pair navigated the lit ramp up to the door.

"Walking up that ramp in these heels wasn't as bad as I thought it would be," Patience quipped. Her stylish heels—though beautiful—weren't exactly the best for walking on a slant.

Michael smoothed his free hand down the front of his shirt as they moved through the short ballroom to a set of winding stairs. "I'm not going to lie, I felt bad when I saw the ramp." He shot her a sideways glance. "I was prepared to carry you if need be."

Eyes crinkling with amusement, she shrugged slightly. "Oh don't worry, you still might *have* to," she said, earning a chuckle from Michael. "Going up is one thing, coming *down* is another."

"Just say the word, and I got you."

The trip up the steps was far better for Patience. But even if it *weren't*, once they'd entered the massive glass enclosed dining deck, all she could focus on was the stunning space.

Floor to ceiling crystal-clear windows surrounded them, allowing a bird's eye view of the Virginia harbor and the landscape of the city. The night sky provided the perfect backdrop for the beautiful skyline. The live band played their instruments to perfection, engulfing the room with smooth jazz, while fellow diners conversed at their designated tables.

Eyes brightening with awe as they were escorted to their table, Patience drank everything in. "It's beautiful in here."

"It is," Michael agreed. "The website photos certainly didn't do this place justice." Reaching a premium spot—an intimate table for two right by the window—Michael promptly pulled Patience's chair out, allowing her to sit before moving to his own.

"The ship will set sail in a matter of moments. Once we're away from the dock, the server will come around and take your dinner orders," the host informed. "We have an amazing surf and turf selection this evening, however there are plenty of other food options for you to choose from." He flashed an enthused grin. "May I ask if you are celebrating anything special this evening?"

Michael and Patience glanced at one another. "First date," they spoke in unison.

"A wonderful choice of venue for the occasion," the host nodded. "I hope you have a pleasant evening."

"Thank you." Michael let out a relaxed sigh once the host walked away. "This would be a good time to ask if you have any issues with being out on the water."

A soft laugh left Patience's throat. "Lucky for *you*, even though this is my first time on a ship, I have no fear of the water. I would've said something when you mentioned a cruise if I wasn't comfortable with it." The glimmer of the crystal napkin ring caught her eye; she lightly touched it. "Can you imagine if I *had* though?"

"I would've promptly turned around and found somewhere else to take you," Michael stated. "Then would've silently berated myself for not asking you that in the *first* place."

"Don't worry about it. I'm happy you choose it."

Michael smiled at her, preparing to offer up a witty comment. But watching her brown eyes flicker in the candlelight had him at a loss for words. So much so that he felt the earth move. Then it hit him, it was the *ship* moving.

"Ooh, that was…that was weird." Patience brought a hand to her chest, feeling her heart race. "I wasn't ready for that."

Michael held his hand out for hers, and she promptly took hold of it. "Are you all right?" He covered her hand with his free one when she nodded. "I'm sorry, I should've warned you. The initial movement is a bit of a shock if you're not used to it."

"Are *you* used to it?"

"Nope," he threw back, voice laced with laughter. "I've only been on two cruises in my life, so no, not at all… The feeling will pass though as we keep moving."

She gave his hand a gentle squeeze. "Okay, I'll trust you on that."

An hour into dinner, any nervousness that Michael or Patience had felt at the start of their evening had long since faded away as they enjoyed each other's company, conversation, and the exquisite meal.

Michael speared the last piece of his Wagyu filet mignon. "This place has exceeded my expectations." He took his time with his meal, savoring the rich flavors.

Swallowing the last bite of her own filet, Patience nodded in agreement. Picking up her wine glass, she took a quick sip of the Chardonnay to wash it down. "It definitely has." She peered over at the view outside. "And you were right, the motion of the boat moving *does* fade over time."

"Yeah, I've always associated the feeling with being on a plane." He took a quick sip from his wine glass. Returning the glass to the table, he fixed Patience with a gaze. "I'm enjoying myself with you."

Eyeing him back, a sensual smile graced her lips. "Likewise." Her eyes lowered to the empty plate in front of her after a passing moment, her expression turning sober. Patience *was* having a good time, but knowing that their evening was nearing its end, the apprehensions that she'd tried to suppress were starting to creep in. "Michael, may I ask you something?"

Michael wiped his mouth with a napkin, then set it down on the table. "Of course you can." He leaned back in his seat, providing his undivided attention. "Anything."

"What are your intentions…" She looked back up, meeting his attentive eye, "with me?"

Michael tilted his head slightly. Though the question had caught him off guard, it was one that he had no issue answering.

"Honestly," Patience softly prompted.

"You don't think I'd be honest?"

"I'd hope that you *would* be," she threw back.

"Patience, I meant what I said when I asked you to go out with me." His tone was sincere. "I like you; I'm *intrigued* by you and I only hope to get to know you better."

"Okay…" She twirled the napkin ring around on the table. "I can say that the feeling is mutual."

Michael's heart fluttered. "Really?"

She nodded. "Yes." Leaving the napkin ring alone, she clasped her hands on the table as she prepared to ask her next question. "So, the follow up to that question is…" She fixed him with a stern stare. "What are your expectations for *tonight?*"

"Meaning?"

"Are you expecting me to sleep with you?"

"No," Michael answered without hesitation. He was taken aback when she arched an eyebrow in disbelief. "Is that what you think I want from you? Is that why you think I *really* asked you out?"

"I *don't* Michael, but I needed to ask." Patience's tone was firm. "I've had to end a few past *dates* because of what those men thought they were going to get from me, in exchange for a dinner."

"I can assure you, you won't need to worry about that with me," Michael said. "I don't expect anything from you, and I would never *pressure* you for anything, let alone sex. You might not believe me, but at this age and where I am in my life, I'm not looking for a casual fling."

"Neither am I," Patience declared. "However… I'm not looking to *rush* into a relationship either."

Michael listened intently.

"I just want you to understand that if dating me is what you really want—"

"It *is*." His voice radiated genuineness.

Her words became trapped; the intensity in his gaze, and the deepness of his voice confirming everything she wanted, made the butterflies stir up in her again. But knowing that she needed to make her point, she refocused. "I want to take my time," she continued. "...I *need* to take my time."

"I hear you Patience, and I understand." Michael leaned forward. "I want you to feel comfortable not only with me, but with the idea of *being* with me, if that's what you want. And I know it's something that'll take time." He smiled warmly. "Time is what I have, and I'm on yours."

Like his voice, his smile delayed her reply. Michael had a way of not only making her feel secure, but she felt heard; like what she thought and felt mattered to him. And to top it off, none of it seemed forced. This man was genuine, and that alone broke through her defenses. "I appreciate that."

"Of course." Michael reached back for his glass, taking a sip. "Is there anything else you want to ask me? Like I said before, I'm an open book."

Smirking, Patience folded her arms. "Really? You'll answer *any* question?"

He set the glass down. "Anything." He gestured to her with his hand. "Come on with it."

Moving her head, sending her hair behind her shoulder, she pondered the challenge. "Hmm."

He chuckled when she stalled. "Are you about to ask me how many women I've slept with?"

Patience quickly put a hand up, shaking her head. "God no. I believe *that's* an answer nobody really wants to know."

"This is true," Michael agreed, voice laced with humor.

"But I *will* ask… In your past relationships…have you ever cheated?"

Michael shook his head with certainty. "No. I'm a firm believer that if a relationship has reached the point of no return, you just part ways." His eyes lowered for a moment. "No need to hurt them further by cheating."

Patience twirled a ring around her finger, nodding slowly. "I agree."

Lifting his eyes, Michael met her intent stare. "Have *you?*"

"No." Rolling her eyes slightly as memories of her failed marriage seeped in, she recrossed her arms to her chest. "I just… left." Peering out the window, her shoulders rose and fell stiffly. "I was married for five years, and…" Patience didn't want to go into details, but she knew that she needed to give Michael something. After all, he had no issue with being open to her line of questioning. "Eventually I realized that I deserved better than what I was getting, so I left."

Michael held steady, comforting eyes on her. "That's commendable. Not many people can do that." He pondered for a moment on whether to probe further. "This may be a stupid question but…did it at least end amicably?"

She turned her head, facing him again. "No."

The coldness in Patience's eyes, and disdain in her voice when she answered, sent a chill through Michael. It *also* sent him into a protective mode. *What did he do to you?* He opened his mouth to ask, but quickly decided against it. He didn't want a repeat of what had happened back at the house showing, when he'd asked about her marriage.

"Did *your* past relationship end amicably?"

Expelling a weighted breath, Michael paused as he thought back. "I won't say that there weren't hurt feelings involved," he admitted. "Let's face it, there's nothing nice about a relationship ending. However, I can say that overall, the endings have been fair."

Patience raised an eyebrow in curiosity. "Fair?"

Michael gave a nod. "Yes." He was unsure if he should go into

141

detail. He didn't want to bring the date down, but he needed to be truthful. "I'm sure in the dating rule book, this is frowned upon, but I want to be honest with you about why things ended in the past for me."

A slight frown forming, Patience's body stiffened. *Oh shit, what did this man do? Please don't tell me I got my hopes up for nothing. Go with the flow, my ass!* Yet, she *needed* to know. "Go ahead."

Patience's stoney expression, and rigid posture, weren't lost on Michael. Sensing her concern, he put a hand up. "Please don't worry. I didn't harm anyone, or anything of that nature."

The prelude relaxed Patience just a bit. *Must've read my mind.* "So, what *was* it then?"

Michael took a deep breath. "To be honest…the reason why my past relationship—*ships* ended, was because I wasn't a good partner."

Head leaning to one side, she fixed him with an unblinking gaze. "Meaning?"

"Meaning that I neglected the women in my life for my own interests," he confessed. "I was hyper-focused on making sure that I achieved my goals—from finishing college to grad school, then on to my career." He ran a hand over his head. "I wasn't attentive. I didn't make time for them, I wasn't a good communicator, I just—I wasn't a good boyfriend. Wasn't a good companion." A heavy sigh escaped him. "So, understandably, the relationships ended."

Feeling water creep up her eyes as a result of not blinking, Patience finally did. Blinking several times to clear the subtle tears, she was silent as she mulled over Michael's confession.

Her silence drew another deep sigh from Michael, and regret began to slip in. He wondered if he'd shared too much too soon. *Damn, I hope I didn't blow this by opening my big ass mouth.*

"If you don't mind me asking," she spoke finally, drawing Michael's attention. "What was it that made you entertain a new relationship after the last one ended? …If admittedly, you weren't mentally or emotionally ready to handle what it takes to be in one?"

Michael stalled for a moment. "That's a good question… One

that three years ago, I wouldn't have an answer for. But now that I've had time to reflect, I believe that even though I wasn't ready for one…I still longed for it." He paused. "Longed for a relationship like the ones I grew up around with my parents, my grandparents… healthy, happy, long-lasting relationships."

"I can understand that." Patience thought back to her own past, and how she'd longed for a healthy relationship. But unlike Michael, she'd never had a good example of one. "And I'm not just saying that." She fiddled with the bracelet on her wrist. "Besides, it seems like you've learned from your past mistakes. Some people never do."

He breathed a sigh of relief, thankful that she hadn't gotten the urge to get up and flee. "I can assure you I have." Eyes locking with hers, Michael took a moment to take her all in. "Now…I'm in a place where I'm *ready* for the relationship that I've always wanted."

Her posture relaxing, Patience offered a small smile. "That's nice to know… I appreciate the honesty."

He smiled back. "I'll always be honest with you Patience. I appreciate *your* understanding."

Patience nodded. "Of course." It wasn't a lie; she *did* appreciate his honesty and the fact that he'd owned up to his past mistakes. In fact, she respected him for it. She grabbed her nearly empty glass of wine, lifting it. "Here's to overcoming past mistakes."

Michael raised his glass. "And to not letting them affect the future." He touched his glass to hers.

"Amen."

Michael took a long sip of his drink, as Patience sipped hers. Setting his glass back down, he gazed out the window. Exhaling, he felt like a weight had been lifted. Turning back to Patience, who was admiring the view herself, he rested a hand on the table. "Do you want to step out onto the deck with me?"

Facing him, she mulled the proposal over. "I don't know." A twinge of humor crossed her face. "Will I start to feel the ship moving if I get up?"

He chuckled. "I doubt it. But if you do, you can always hold on to me."

Patience peered behind her at the glass doors, before looking back at him. "Okay. Let's go."

Michael stood and rounded to her side. Extending his hand for hers, he helped her from the seat. Hand in hand, they approached the door, which was opened for them by a smiling crew member.

Stepping outside onto the lit deck, Michael and Patience walked a few steps away from the other passengers, standing a safe distance from the edge of the boat. Her hand secure in Michael's, Patience took in the city lights and the moonlight dancing on the calm waters. The view paired with the steady spring breeze provided a serene, romantic atmosphere.

As the peaceful minutes passed, Michael found himself captivated not by the scenery, but by Patience. Focusing on how her eyes gleamed and her skin glowed under the moonlight, he inhaled the captivating scent of her fragrance. Standing beside her, he replayed how they'd met, and every conversation and interaction leading up to this moment. He looked down to their hands, where their fingers were twined together. Returning his view to her face, he had no choice but to be honest with himself. This woman had already captured his heart.

Noticing her shiver, Michael snapped out of his blissful haze. "Are you chilly?"

"Just a little." Patience crossed her free arm over her chest, kicking herself for electing not to bring another layer. "I was fine earlier, but I didn't take into account how different the air is this close to the water."

Michael promptly removed his jacket, wrapping it around Patience's shoulders. "That better?"

Bringing her hands up to her shoulder, she touched the soft fabric and glanced back at him. "Yes." Her tone had dropped an octave. "Thank you."

His eyes smoldered as they locked with hers. "You're welcome."

The voices and music around them were all but muffled as the two stood, lost in each other's eyes. Seizing the moment, Michael leaned in. Patience closed her eyes, tilting her head up to allow him access to her lips. There he planted a soft, sensual, lingering kiss.

Michael had fantasized about this ever since meeting her; feeling her lips on his felt at long last like a dream. But as much as he wanted to deepen it, to taste them even more, he refrained. *She wants to take things slow*, he reminded himself. Pulling his lips from hers, he opened his eyes, then touched her face.

Patience stared at him as he lingered in front of her; a burning sexual tension building, she expelled a shaky breath. That kiss, though simple, sent a surge of heat and a long-forgotten desire through her body. His hand caressing her face, *his* inches from hers—she almost regretted her decision to move slow. *Turn away Patience, turn away.* Listening to her inner voice, she broke eye contact, returning her focus to the water.

Michael put his arm around her shoulder, securing the jacket to her and guiding her closer to him. Patience reached up and took his hand in hers. As the sound of the waves echoed through the air, she rested her head on his shoulder.

Pulling up in front of Patience's home, Michael put the car in park before turning off the engine. The clock read one-thirty a.m. on the dash. Though he hadn't intended on keeping Patience out that late, he had to admit that the past few hours had gone by much too fast.

After sharing their intimate moment on the ship's deck, Patience and Michael had returned to their table, sharing conversation and laughs over decadent desserts, before partaking in a few dances as the boat docked. They'd capped the beautiful evening off by taking a leisurely walk along the waterfront. They'd gotten so lost in each other's company that before both knew it, it was after midnight.

Gathering her clutch from her lap, Patience turned to Michael, locking eyes with him. Her mouth curved into an alluring smile. He threw one right back.

The shimmering moonlight beaming through the car windows illuminated her face, etching it and everything about her into Michael's memory. "Thank you for spending time with me tonight," he crooned. "I'd love to do it again soon."

"Me too." Patience touched his hand, which was resting on the arm rest between them. "Thank you for asking me."

His heart pounded and his eyes gleamed with adoration. "You're welcome." He undid his seat belt. "Let's get you inside." He exited the car, then quickly approached her door, opening it and escorting her to the top of the front steps.

Facing Michael, Patience removed the jacket from her shoulders. "I should probably give this back." She handed it to him.

"Oh, right." His eyes crinkled with humor. "Completely forgot that you had it." He slung the article over his arm. "I'll call you in the morning?" *I have no doubt that you'll be the first thing on my mind when I wake up.*

Leaning her head to the side, a sultry grin brushed Patience's lips. "You *better.*"

Her reply extracted a soft laugh from Michael. "Yes, Ma'am."

Opening her purse, Patience removed her keys. "Get home safe."

Michael nodded. "I will." Gently taking her free hand, he raised it to his lips, kissing it. Initially planning on releasing her hand right away, he found himself holding it secure in his.

Patience seemed to feel the same, because she didn't pull her hand free. Instead, her fingers tightened over his.

Erasing the small bit of distance between them, Michael's fingers brushed over her face as he leaned in, planting another soft kiss on her lips, then kissing her one last time on the cheek.

Patience opened her eyes just as Michael stepped back, releasing her hand in the process. "Good night, Patience."

"Night Michael." Turning away from him, she unlocked her door, then threw a glance over her shoulder. "Text me when you get in okay? So I know you made it home."

"I will." He stood in place, watching as she entered the house and shut the door behind her. Hearing the lock turn, he ambled down the pathway.

As Michael walked to his car, the evening replayed in his head. It couldn't have been more perfect, and neither could the woman he shared it with. The visions of Patience drew a smile from him—a smile that seemed to come straight from his heart. *I've never felt this way before...about anyone. Didn't even think it was possible.* Opening his car door, he gave one last glance to her house, expelling a satisfied sigh, before getting in.

Patience stood at the door, eye on the peephole, watching Michael leave. She lingered there until he pulled away from the curb, saying a silent prayer for his safe journey home.

Leaning her back against the door, she stared out into the space in front of her, reflecting on the past few hours: the date, the conversations, the laughs, the revelations...*Michael.*

Bringing a hand to her stomach, Patience felt the familiar flutters. The smile that radiated from her as Michael consumed her thoughts, came deep from within. *Yeah, this is different... He's different.*

Chapter Fourteen

PATIENCE WAS PERUSING OVER THE fruit selection at the grocery store, but her mind was on anything but produce.

Toni, having just placed a small bag of grapes into her basket, noticed the intensity on her sister's face. "Why are you staring at the fruit like it stole something from you?"

Patience chuckled a bit. "I'm trying to decide if I want to buy anything while I'm here, or wait until I go grocery shopping tomorrow." She gave the watch on her wrist a quick glance.

Toni flicked a hand. "If you're contemplating it, then that means you already want to." She selected a bag of pistachios, placing them in her cart. "Plus, this store has a much better selection."

Shrugging, Patience pulled a few clear plastic bags from the roll.

Patience and Toni had ventured to the nearby whole foods store that Tuesday afternoon to grab lunch and a few other items.

After collecting a small horde of fruit—pomegranates, apples, oranges and mangos—Patience twisted the bags closed. Secured in her hand basket, she ambled over to Toni in the prepared food section.

"Ooh, they have sushi!" Toni practically sprinted over to the station, hunger in her eyes. "You want to try some?" She leaned in to get a better look at the selection.

Folding her arms, Patience shook her head. "No, I think I'm just going to get a sandwich." She turned away from the display.

"Besides, I went to a sushi restaurant a few days ago, and I doubt *this* stuff tastes as good."

Toni giggled. "It probably doesn't." She chose a spicy crab roll, adding it to her basket. "But I'm still going to eat it."

Patience shook her head in amusement.

"*Speaking* of you frequenting fancy restaurants with that handsome man of yours—you need to make a list of the places you've been," Toni brought up. "Rob and I need new places to try."

A smile brightened Patience's face as pleasant thoughts of Michael swarmed in.

They'd been dating for a little over two months, and Patience was enjoying every bit of it. From the date nights, to the meetups for an outing between work, to the phone calls—quick "check-in" calls during the day, and late-night conversations that could go on for hours. Each interaction revealed more, drawing them closer. It was a welcome change in Patience's life. "I will," Patience promised.

Toni tucked some of her hair behind her ear as they navigated the store. "I don't even have to ask you how's it been going with Michael, because I can *tell* that it's been great." She gave Patience a soft nudge. "The smile that always shows up when he's mentioned, and the fresh flowers I see in your office every five minutes are a dead giveaway."

"Yeah well, it *has* been going well so far. I've been enjoying his company." Stopping at a station, Patience briefly scanned the prepared sandwiches. Quickly choosing a roasted turkey and cheese on ciabatta bread, she placed it in the basket. "As a matter of fact, I'm meeting him after I get off work this afternoon." She took a bottle of water from the refrigerator, adding it to the cart. "Noelle has art club today. I don't have to pick her up until five, so Michael and I are meeting up for a little bookstore date."

Toni smirked. "Yeah, you're *definitely* the bookstore date type." She giggled when Patience cut her eye at her. She put a teasing finger to Patience's cheek. "Aww, that's adorable though."

Patience casually moved Toni's hand away. "*Anyway*. I forgot how nice it was to date…someone *worth* dating that is."

"Oh, I know." Toni loaded a few snack items into her basket. "There's nothing like being with someone who treats you like you deserve to be treated."

"Yeah…and I don't feel any pressure, you know? I mean, yes we're seeing each other, but he understands that I want to take things slowly."

Moseying towards the checkout, Toni shot her a side-glance. "Soooo," she scratched her head. "In a nutshell he's not your *boyfriend* yet?"

"No, not yet." Patience raised a hand when Toni opened her mouth. "And before you start, it's not like I don't *want* him to be, or that I'm not leaning towards it, but…"

"What's stopping you from moving forward?"

Patience looked at the ceiling for a moment, as if her answer was there. "Well…" Her eyes met Toni's. "For one, I haven't introduced Noelle to him yet."

"What's stopping you from *doing* so?" Having a thought, Toni halted her steps, placing a hand to her hip. "Patience—you're not still looking for *red flags*, are you?"

Facing Toni, Patience rolled her eyes. "*No* girl, I'm not looking for red flags…" She pushed her hair over her shoulder. "I just… I want to be sure this thing between us is going in the direction I *hope* it is, before I bring him into Noelle's life." Her head leaned faintly. "All of this is new to me, and I just want to be sure, you know."

Toni's eyes softened. "I understand that." Her tone was sincere. "I know I joke a lot, but I want you to be sure too."

Patience delayed her reply as she watched Toni's facial expression morph from compassionate to mischievous.

"So… I guess that means you two haven't had sex yet—"

"Yeah, see, I knew that was coming," Patience broke in. She shook her head when Toni snickered. "No, we haven't." It was true, she and Michael had not yet taken that step in their relationship. Though it wasn't from lack of want on *either* part. "Which is *so* hard by the way, 'cause that man is a *hell* of a kisser."

Toni erupted with laughter.

"It's unbelievable." Patience fanned herself with her hand. Just *thinking* about it was a turn on. "I have to stop myself from dragging him up to my bedroom when he kisses me good night."

Toni pointed at her. "Uh huh, see? And you *swore* up and down you were cool with your little vibrator." Her voice was elevated loud enough to catch the attention of a nearby shopper.

Seeing the elderly woman shoot them a judgment-riddled look, Patience's face flushed with embarrassment. "Toni—just say the shit *louder* why don't you," she spat, sarcastic.

Fixing the woman with a warning look that dared her to say anything, Toni flagged her off. "Please. *She* uses one too, I'm sure."

The comment, paired with the horrified look on the woman's face as she shuffled her cart down the aisle, would have caused Patience to break into laughter had she not been annoyed. Instead she shot Toni a rigid look. "Shut *up*."

Throwing a hand up in surrender, Toni exhaled loudly. "Okay, okay." She tapped Patience's arm. "Look, if it means anything, *I* for one believe that this relationship is *it* for you… I can feel it."

"Uh hmm," Patience muttered, bracing herself for another teasing moment from her sister.

"I'm *serious*." Toni lightly rubbed Patience's arm. "The signs aren't hard to miss…from either *one* of you."

Patience scratched her head. "Yeah, whatever the fuck that means. Come on," she bit out, walking off.

Humored by her reaction, Toni just shook her head as she followed Patience to the cashier.

After paying for and bagging their items, Toni reached for her bag. Hearing her phone beep in her purse, she stopped short, retrieving it. Eyeing the text message, she let out a groan. "God, this girl is so *anal*," she hissed through clenched jaws.

Picking up both bags, Patience handed Toni hers as they passed through the exit. "What's wrong?"

"Angie changed that damn color scheme for her dinner party *once again*." Toni's fingers moved at a quick pace across her phone screen. "I *told* her, once Rob and I get our outfits we're not changing them. So, she better make a damn decision."

Patience adjusted the bag in her hand as they navigated the sidewalk. "*What* dinner party?"

"You know, the one she's doing next Saturday," Toni replied, sending another text. "The one she's throwing as a celebration of her raggedy husband's promotion."

Patience's brow knitted in confusion. "I had no idea about that."

Toni snapped her head in Patience's direction, bewildered *herself.* "What do you *mean* you had no idea?" The feeling only intensified when Patience simply stared at her. "Pace, she sent out invitations two weeks ago."

"I never got an invitation Toni," Patience said, tone even. "Clearly, I'm not invited."

Toni stalled for a moment, disbelief on her face. "Nah." She grabbed Patience's arm, pulling her off to the side. "I'm calling her."

Patience put a hand up. "No, don't worry about it."

"Oh, I *will.*" Toni promptly video-called Angela. "I'm getting to the bottom of this shit."

Patience just sighed as the line rang. She wasn't in the mood to have this interaction with Angela, but she knew that Toni wasn't about to let up on it. Toni had always been protective of her.

Angela's face popped up on the screen. "Hey T," she beamed. "Are you calling to tell me that you're rethinking your outfit?"

"Hey Ang, and fuck no," Toni quickly hurled. "I have Patience here with me." She moved the phone, allowing Angela to see Patience.

The smile faded from Angela's face. "Oh." The easy tone was now gone. "Hey Patience."

"Hey." Patience matched Angela's unenthused voice with one of her own.

"Listen, we were talking, and the topic of your dinner party came up and it came out that Patience doesn't know about it," Toni charged. "So, tell me sweetheart, did you not invite her?"

Angela stared at the screen, displeasure clear in her eyes. "Seriously Toni?"

"*Seriously*," Toni countered.

Patience put a hand on Toni's shoulder. "Toni, this really isn't necessary."

"No it *is*, did you not *invite* her Angie?" Toni pressed.

"No, no I did *not* Toni. And thanks for bringing this shit up while I'm in the middle of planning, as if I'm not stressed enough," Angela bit back.

Toni's eyes flashed with anger. "Why *not*?"

Rubbing her forehead, Angela let out a huff. "Look, for one, this is an adult-only party and I figured you'd need Patience to watch Jordan—"

"Jordan has grandparents and aunts and uncles on her father's side, so that could've been arranged—"

"Well, *Patience* doesn't have anyone to watch Noelle, being a *chosen* single mom and all, so she wouldn't have been able to come anyway," Angela spat, cutting Toni's argument short. "And the *last* time I invited her over for dinner, she complained. Or do you not remember?"

Patience scowled. "What the fuck do you mean by *chosen*?"

"And you know *damn* well, that invite slash blind date, was some bull—"

"Nah." Patience put a hand close to Toni's mouth to silence her. "Angela, *what* do you mean?"

"Patience, I'm not trying to argue with you about your life choices, okay. I just want to have my dinner party for *my husband*,"

Angela brushed off. "And aside from the 'no kids' issue, there is the issue that this is a *couples* dinner, and you're not part of a couple so..." A hint of a smirk appeared on her face. "Another thing you *chose*."

The look that Patience was shooting Angela through the phone could have eviscerated her.

"Hold up," Toni jumped back in. "Everything you just said was complete and utter *bullshit*. Noelle could've been watched by whoever we had watching Jordan and *second*, how do *you* know that Patience is still single? As a matter of fact she—"

Patience subtly nudged Toni, stopping her. Toni glanced at her, and Patience gave a quick shake of her head. The way Angela was behaving towards her, Patience felt it best to keep the woman as far out of her business as possible.

Clearing her throat, Toni pushed hair away from her face. "You need to stop, Angie."

"Toni— Look, are you still coming after this little revelation or not? Because I have shit to do," Angela sneered.

Toni was well prepared to give her big sister a piece of her mind, but Patience immediately cut her off. "Yes, she's going," Patience said.

Toni frowned at Patience. "What—"

"You're going. Bye Angela." Patience pushed the button on Toni's phone, ending the call before Angela could say another word. "It's fine," she insisted as a wide-eyed Toni opened her mouth. "Just go support her or—whatever." She was not about to let her eldest sister ruin her entire day.

"She doesn't *deserve* my precious support," Toni scoffed, putting a hand to her chest. "Old, bitter bitch."

The offhand insult earned a snicker from Patience.

"Don't laugh Pace, I'm not trying to be funny." Though Toni would've normally laughed *herself*, this was not the time. She was upset, and it resonated clearly on her face. "I don't like how she treats you. It's weird, and uncalled for." She stuffed the phone back into her purse. "Other than borrowing a damn shirt from her without asking when you were like *thirteen*, you haven't *done* anything to her."

Toni was right; Patience hadn't done anything that she knew of to warrant such treatment from Angela. However, as much as she wanted an answer to that question, Patience didn't have the mental energy to deal with it.

Patience touched Toni's shoulder, trying to calm her. "I appreciate it, but it's okay," she said. "I'm sure the reason for her animosity will surface one of these days, or maybe it won't. But I can't and won't worry about that right now." She glanced at her watch. "I have to get back to the office."

"Okay." Toni pouted as Patience walked off. "You sure you're okay?"

"Yes," Patience threw over her shoulder. "I'll call you later."

Chapter Fifteen

MICHAEL PICKED UP A BOOK, skimming the back before bobbing his head in approval. "This seems like it's going to be good."

Patience peered over from the titles she was checking out on a shelf. "Really?"

"Yeah." Michael handed the hardcover title to her.

Reading the back, Patience nodded in agreement. "Oh yeah, this definitely sounds good." She examined the front cover. "I'm normally not a mystery reader, but this seems like something I can get into."

They'd discussed their love of reading on more than one occasion. And though their favorite genres differed, it didn't stop them from sharing their go-to books with one another.

As Michael retrieved the book from Patience, his eyes lit up. "We should both get a copy and read it together."

Putting a finger to her chin, Patience's brow raised. "That…is a great idea Mr. Carter. I've never had a reading partner before, but it sounds like it could be fun." A dazzling smile on her face, Patience lightly tapped his chest. "Good job."

Grinning, Michael grabbed an extra copy, placing both in his basket.

"I haven't bought any new books in so long," Patience said, browsing another fiction aisle. "I feel like a kid in a candy store."

"Yeah, I've read and reread the books on my shelf more times than I can remember." He scanned the shelf. "So, this trip here was definitely overdue."

Patience picked up a book, showing it to him. "Here, try this one. It's one of my favorites: A contemporary romance novel."

Michael turned the book over, reading the back. "Hmm…"

"I know romance isn't really your go-to genre, but I think you'll enjoy it." She pointed to it. "It has a few twists in it."

He looked at her. "If I can get you to read a mystery book, I can certainly try this one." He placed the book into his basket atop the others.

A smile of satisfaction crossed Patience's face. "Good."

The pair browsed the store a bit longer, choosing a few more titles each.

Patience gestured to a cluster of colorful bookshelves off in a corner. "I'm almost finished. I just want to check out the children's section for a moment."

"Sure, take your time."

Entering the area with Michael at her side, Patience browsed with care before choosing a few hardcover titles.

"Noelle likes to read too?" he asked.

"Loves it." Patience adjusted the basket in her hand. "Especially anything that has to do with bunnies." She shook her head. "That girl and rabbits."

"I take it you're not a rabbit person," he chortled, picking up on her lackluster tone.

"They're cute and all, but that's *her* thing." Lifting her hand, she brought the silver double wrap butterfly ring on her finger to his view. "I'm more into butterflies."

Resting his arm atop a shelf, Michael eyed her with intrigue. "Oh yeah?"

"I mean I don't *collect* them or anything, I just always found them beautiful, and I love what they represent." Tucking some of her hair behind her ear, Patience's eyes gleamed. "The whole transformation aspect is fascinating. To go from being stagnant and wrapped in a cocoon, to emerging as this beautiful creature that can fly, you know—" Patience grimaced, rubbing her forehead in the process. "Yeah, I just went off on a tangent about bugs, let's change the subject."

Michael shrugged. "If you wish, but I was pretty captivated." What she didn't know was that he could listen to her talk about her interests all day.

"That's cute of you to say," Patience joked, then lightly flicked her wrist. "Anyway, my child has *so* many stuffed toy bunnies. Yet every time she gets a new one, she's just as excited and grateful, as if it were her first one."

"That's adorable," Michael mused.

Patience couldn't help but smile. "Yeah, it is…Which is why I keep buying the damn things."

"Do you think she'll eventually ask you for a *real* one?"

Patience shot him a forbidding look. "Carter—please don't speak that shit into existence."

Erupting in a throaty laugh, Michael threw his hand up in surrender.

"*Toys* I can deal with, a live one, not so much."

"Understandable." Michael's laughter dwindled. "Pets are definitely work."

"Yeah, the last thing I need is another mouth to feed," Patience jeered as they made their way to the checkout line.

"Do you still have a bit more time before you have to pick Noelle up?" Michael asked as they inched their way forward.

Patience gave her watch a quick look. "Yes."

"I was thinking that once we get out of here, we can go to the coffee shop next door. Maybe grab a latte or something and sit for a bit?"

"Sure, we can do that." Patience fancied the idea of spending a little more time with him.

Gazing at her, he smiled. "Good."

Michael's dreamy stare lingered on her as he recalled the past two months—two months and two weeks to be exact. Talking to Patience every day, spending time with her, getting to know her more with each conversation, connecting with her more with each outing...he was unashamedly enamored with her. She was the first thing on his mind when he woke up, and the last thing before he drifted off to sleep.

Finally being called up in line, Michael approached with Patience beside him, placing his books on the counter. As the cashier began ringing the selection up, he held his hand out for Patience's basket. "I'll take those," he said to her.

Patience glanced at him, confused. "What?" She touched the basket with her hand. "Oh, I can hold them, it's not heavy."

Michael shot her an amused look. "I know. But I need them so I can pay for them."

Putting a hand up, Patience shook her head. "Oh—no you don't have to, I've got it."

"Patience, it's okay," he insisted. "I want to pay for them. I asked *you* here remember?"

"Umm..." Clutching her basket of books in a firm grip, Patience shifted her weight on her feet. Her tongue stalled and her face took on a pained expression as a flood of memories, ones she'd hoped to keep contained, resurfaced.

Michael's brows furrowed in concern. "Are you okay? Is something wrong?"

"I—" Seeing the patrons assembling in line behind her, Patience suppressed her mounting anxiety. "No, nothing is wrong." She reluctantly handed Michael the basket.

Studying her face and hearing the subdued tone in her voice, Michael couldn't help but feel that Patience's words weren't exactly true. But instead of pressing the issue, he just quietly removed the books from the basket, setting them on the counter.

Patience stared at the counter as the cashier began ringing

everything up. Eyeing the few hardcover books she'd picked out for Noelle, she quickly put a hand over the stack before the woman had a chance to ring it. "Wait a second. Don't ring those for him, I'll be paying for them."

Michael threw a perplexed look Patience's way. "Why?"

"Because that's way too much," she curtly threw back. "And you're already paying for mine, which again, you don't *have* to do—"

Michael put a gentle hand on hers, calming her rambles. "Patience, if I cared about the cost, I wouldn't have said anything," he soothed. "It's *okay* sweetheart."

"I *said* I got it," Patience snapped, glaring at him. "Back off."

Eyes broadening, Michael moved his hand from hers, letting it drop at his side. "Okay, I'm sorry." His face fell. "Whatever you want."

Not saying another word, Patience moved Noelle's books aside as Michael handed his card to the cashier.

Mugs of hot caramel lattes in hand, Michael and Patience carefully made their way to a cozy corner table with their bookstore bags. Patience took a seat in the cushioned chair, with Michael sitting across from her.

Michael blew on his latte, then took a careful sip, savoring the rich, sweet taste. "This is good."

Patience stared at the contents of her mug, focusing on the caramel swirl atop the milky froth. It looked delectable and she wanted to taste it, but her mind was too preoccupied.

Setting his cup down, Michael focused his attention on Patience. Her change in mood at the bookstore had gone to a glum quiet. Clearly something was bothering her, and Michael just couldn't sit and continue to sip his latte without finding out what. "Patience," he softly called.

Her eyes rose, fixing him with an emotionless stare.

"What's wrong?"

Patience shook her head. "Nothing's wrong."

"I'd like to take that as your word, but I can't," he replied. "You seem upset…upset with me—"

"Michael, can—" She paused in an attempt to check her attitude. Patience *was* upset, but not necessarily at him. She needed to calm herself, before she made an unnecessary mess of things. "Can we drop it?"

Michael gazed at her with questioning eyes. "I'm sorry, but I can't… If I upset you in any way, I need you to tell me."

The sullen look on his face made Patience feel terrible. Softening her stern expression, she released a sigh. "You didn't do anything wrong." Gaze veering off to the side, she shook her head. "I shouldn't have snapped at you like that. I just…had something on my mind, but that's no excuse."

Michael tilted his head. "Okay… So, what was on your mind? Or should I say, what *still is* on your mind?" When she didn't reply, he reached over, putting a hand on hers. "Come on Patience, talk to me…please."

Patience sighed once again, this time heavily. It was clear that Michael wasn't going to let up, so she figured she might as well talk. "Okay…" Moving her hand from under Michael's, she met his eye. She pushed the warm mug to the side, folding her arms on the table. "Look…"

Michael sat still, bracing himself for what she was about to say.

"I appreciate you paying for my items at the store. But I want you to know that I don't need you to do that."

Taken aback, Michael's eyes constricted. "I'm sorry?"

"I don't *need* you to do things for me, to buy stuff for me or my child." Her brow pleated with seriousness. "I'm perfectly capable of doing that on my own. I've *been* doing that on my own."

"Patience, I never said that you needed me to do that," Michael replied. "I never *thought* that. I did that because I *wanted* to. Everything I *do* is because I want to."

Running her hands over her hair, Patience fought to contain the anxiety reforming within her. "I understand that I just..." Breaking eye contact from Michael, she focused her attention on the commotion going on out the window. "To be honest, I have a hard time not equating acts of financial service to some sort of debt or control."

"Why is that?" Michael's unwavering gaze fixated on her. "What made—"

"Because my ex-husband was financially abusive and controlling, among *other* things," she blurted out, snapping her head back to face him.

Michael's eyes widened. *What the fuck?* Anger brewing inside of him, his jaw tightened. Yet he refrained from interrupting her.

Patience regretted her outburst, but now that she'd made it, she had no choice but to elaborate. "Before he and I got married, I had a job—it wasn't anything spectacular, but I *had* one... I had my own place; I was independent," she said. "Not long after we married, he begged me to quit and be a stay-at-home wife. Giving this whole speech about how he just wanted to take care of me and—whatever. So, I did." She rolled her eyes at the bitter memory. "That quickly turned into him controlling every single move I made. I couldn't buy anything or go anywhere that would require money, without him guilt tripping me or micromanaging me."

Michael sat there, seething in silence as he listened.

"He made sure I had no access to anything so that I couldn't *do* anything *without* him...and that was just the *tip* of what he was capable of." She glanced out of the window. "When I decided to leave, I made a promise to myself that I would never..." *I can't talk about this shit anymore.* Sighing, she turned back to Michael. "I know that my reaction had nothing to do with you. You've never made me feel anything less than respected... That was me having...PTSD. So, I'm sorry."

Michael took a deep breath. If he could punch Patience's vile ex in the face, he would do it in a heartbeat. But despite how angry he felt about the man who had hurt the woman he cared for, he knew that Patience didn't need anger—apparently, she'd dealt with enough of it.

Frown easing from his face, he once again placed a gentle hand on her wrist. "I appreciate the apology, but I don't need it," he said. "I understand now why you reacted the way you did, and I just want you to know that you don't have to worry about that with me." The sincerity in his voice was evident. "You don't owe me anything, and I would never even *try* to control you." He put a hand to his chest. "You have my word on that."

Patience nodded. "I know." Though Michael seemed okay with the situation, *she* still wasn't. *You did what you said you wouldn't do. You let your past bullshit affect you.* Disappointed in her behavior, she lost the urge to enjoy her drink…or sit in the café any longer.

"Um…" Patience glanced at her watch. "I have to go."

Michael watched as she gathered her belongings.

"It's time for me to pick Noelle up." That was the half-truth. She also needed to get out of there, before she said something else to dampen the mood—or worse, bust out crying.

Michael stood up as she rose from her seat. "I'll walk you to your car."

"No—um." She put a hand up. "Please…stay. Enjoy your drink." She slung her purse strap over her shoulder, then adjusted her bags of books in her hand. "Thank you for the outing." *It was nice, even though I ruined it.*

Michael stood before her. He could tell that she was still bothered and that bothered *him*. But he didn't want to press her to talk further. She'd revealed enough. "You're welcome." He watched as she rounded the table, making her way past him. "I'll call you later?"

Stopping, she turned to him, giving a nod before walking out of the café.

Michael followed her progress through the window until she

disappeared out of his sight. Letting out a deep sigh, he ran his hand over the top of his head as he sat back in his seat. Reflecting on the conversation and staring at both unfinished lattes, he sighed once again.

Patience unlocked her front door, moving aside to let Noelle in before following behind her. "Go start your homework while I get dinner ready," she somberly ordered, securing every lock behind her.

Taking off her sneakers, Noelle adjusted her bookbag on her shoulder. "Is my desk coming today?"

Setting her purse along with the bookstore bags on the couch, Patience shot her child a puzzled look. Then the realization set in. "Damn it." Her thoughts had been cloudy since she'd left Michael at the coffee shop earlier. So much so, that she'd forgotten that the new desk she'd ordered for Noelle was supposed to be delivered today.

Pulling her phone from her purse, she checked the tracking information. "It's on its way—" Pinching the bridge of her nose, she exhaled heavily. "Oh yeah." She realized that she had *also* forgot to remove the old desk from Noelle's room. "I'll start dinner in a few, I need to move your old desk so the delivery people can set it up."

Scratching her head, Noelle followed her mother's progress to the staircase. "Can I help?"

"You can start your *homework*, baby," Patience calmly threw back. "Do it down here for now."

Removing a book from her bookbag, Noelle set it by the couch, then peered over at the bookstore bags. "Mommy?"

Pausing midway up the staircase, Patience closed her eyes. *You're frustrated, but not with her. Breathe.* Heading her own advice, she breathed deeply. "Yes?"

"Can I move these bags so I can set my books down?"

Patience rubbed her face. The bags—the bags from the bookstore—the same store where she had embarrassed herself and snapped at the man who has shown her nothing but kindness. Who only wanted to pay for some books. A man she was sure after two and a half months of problem free dating, was now probably having second thoughts.

The cell phone ringing from her purse snapped Patience out of her mental spiral. She spun around on the staircase. *Please don't be Michael.* She was not in the head space to talk just yet. As far as she was concerned, she'd run her mouth enough.

Heading back down the stairs, Patience grabbed her purse and one of the bags from the couch. "Those three books in that other bag are for you."

Eyes widening with anticipation, Noelle dug her hand into the bag as Patience headed back for the steps. "Ooh! Thank you."

"You're welcome, you can read one to me later." Patience retrieved the blaring phone from her bag as she walked up the stairs. Eyeing the ID, she breathed a sigh of relief as she clicked the answer button. "Hey."

"Hey yourself," Toni replied. "Just being nosy—I mean checking in to see how your cutesy day-date was."

As much as Patience wanted to at least giggle at Toni's confession, she didn't have it in her. "It was fine," she muttered, stepping into Noelle's room and closing the door behind her.

"*Just* fine?" When Patience didn't respond, Toni sighed. "What happened?"

Flopping down on Noelle's twin bed, Patience set her bag and purse on it before running a hand over her hair, moving some to one side. "I'm a goddamn idiot, is what *happened.*"

"You're far from an idiot," Toni placated. "Now come on, help me kill time while I wait for these baked potatoes to finish, and tell me what happened."

Patience only needed a few minutes to give her sister the rundown of what had taken place. She'd mistakenly thought that talking with her sister about the situation would help put her at ease. It didn't. Reliving it just frustrated her further.

"You know what's even *more* foolish?" Patience ranted. "I had absolutely *no* issues with him paying for *dates*, buying me *flowers* or *anything* like that—" She fired off, counting on her fingers. "But God forbid the man wants to pay for some fuckin' hardcovers with *rabbits* and fuckin' *ponies* on them for my child, and suddenly it triggers some weird *Post Greg Stress Disorder* shit. Then I'm all 'I don't need you for shit', like—" She huffed loudly. "What the fuck is my *problem*?" She paused, glaring when she heard a familiar sound. "Shut the hell *up* Antoinette."

"I wasn't laughing!"

"There's laughter *all* in your damn voice," Patience seethed.

"No I—okay, look that whole 'hardcovers with rabbits and ponies' sentence *did* tickle me. But I'm not laughing *at* you, I promise."

Patience rolled her eyes to the ceiling as she shook her head.

"But in all seriousness," Toni continued, humor wiped from her voice. "You're not an idiot for setting a boundary—"

Frustrated, Patience pounded her fist on the mattress. "It wasn't a damn *boundary* Toni, it was *bullshit.*"

"Okay, okay," Toni soothed. "So, you had a moment. It happens to the best of us… It's not something to beat yourself up over, and it's *not* something that'll chase a good man like Michael away."

Leaning forward, Patience put her face in her hand as her sister tried to console her.

"You're not crazy and you're not an idiot… Now you said that Michael understood where you were coming from, right?"

"Yeah," Patience sulked.

"Then let it *go* babes. He gave you some grace, so give *yourself* some…and give *him* some." Toni chuckled, "After all, you practically embarrassed the man over some books, it's the *least* you can do."

Sucking her teeth, Patience stood from the bed. "You're not funny and I'm done talking to you."

Toni cackled. "I'm just saying."

"Whatever. I'll talk to you later; I need to move a desk."

There was a pause on the line. "Wait, *what?*"

"You heard me. Goodbye." Not allowing Toni to get another word in, Patience ended the call, tossing the phone on the bed.

Standing in front of Noelle's desk, Patience began clearing the items from it. With the desk now bare, she took hold of the sides, preparing to pull it away from the wall. But halted when she heard her phone beep, sending her darting for it. Eyeing the delivery message from the furniture store, she scowled. "The damn desk isn't delivered," she complained aloud.

Phone in hand, she bolted out the room and down the stairs, to find Noelle sitting on the couch doing her homework. "Bunny, did you hear anyone knock on the door?"

Eyes not leaving her book, Noelle shook her head. "No."

Scratching her head, Patience read the email again as she went to the door. As soon as she opened it, she spotted a large box perched up on the step. "What the hell?"

Noelle glanced over. "Is that my desk?"

"Yes, but it's supposed to be *assembled*, not in…" Closing her eyes, Patience clenched her jaw as a thought popped into her head. Taking her phone, she pulled up the original order; just as she suspected, she failed to select the 'assemble' option. *What a perfect freakin' end to my day.* Shoving the phone into her trouser pocket, she eyed the box that she now had to drag into the house. "Great… just great."

Chapter Sixteen

MICHAEL PULLED HIS FRONT DOOR open and greeted his guests with a half-smile. "Hey." He stepped aside for his father and brother to enter, closing the door behind them.

Gary enveloped his son in a loving hug. "Good to see you."

Letting out a quiet laugh, Michael gave his father a pat on the back before letting him go. "You sound as if you haven't seen me in months."

"Dramatic, huh?" Gary joked, earning an amused nod from Michael and Dante. "Yeah, your mother tells me that all the time."

"No, I'm joking. It's good to see you too." Michael gestured to the kitchen. "I just finished making dinner, come join me."

Waving a hand, Gary stuffed his other into his trouser pocket. "Nah, I didn't come to eat—"

"Say less. Thanks bro," Dante cut in, practically sprinting for the kitchen.

Rubbing his face with his hand, Gary shook his head. "That boy always acts like he's starving," he complained to Michael. "He just ate at *my* damn house."

"Well, this isn't new. He's always been greedy." Michael gave his father a light pat on his back, earning a quick laugh from the man.

Gary and Michael found Dante with his plate in hand, eagerly opening pot lids.

"Can you at least wait until the man fixes *his* plate first?" Gary barked at Dante.

"Pop, Mom told you about running your pressure up on frivolous things." Dante's teasing earned an angry grunt from his father. A sound that Dante found amusing.

Michael directed his father to an empty seat at the counter island. "Hey this is a *calm* space. If you're going to argue, take it to the patio."

Michael had worked to transform his house from an empty shell into a comfortable home. From picking the right furniture pieces, to the appliances, to the décor. It was the place where he was able to unwind after a hectic day—a day like today—and the last thing he needed was a silly argument between his father and brother disturbing his much-needed peace.

Grabbing another plate from the cabinet, Michael served his home cooked meal—roasted rosemary and garlic chicken, wild rice, and sautéed brussels sprouts—atop it. "So, what brings you gentlemen by this evening?" he asked, setting the plate along with silverware in front of his father, who eyed it with delight. "You want anything to drink Pop?"

"Water is just fine, thank you." Gary dug right in with his fork. "And to answer your question, Dante paid your mother and I a visit, and while he was there that gardener you hired came over and—"

"And Pop started hounding the man," Dante told, piling his plate high with food. "Standing all over his shoulder, pressing him about what pruning tools he was using—you should've seen him."

Handing his father a cold bottle of spring water, Michael shot him a firm look. "Seriously Pop?"

Gary shrugged. "I just wanted to make sure the man knew what he was doing."

"He *does*, that's why I *hired* him for you," Michael countered.

Shoving a forkful of food into his mouth, Gary mumbled something incoherently as he chewed.

Shaking his head, Michael proceeded to fix himself a plate. "You may not be dramatic Pop, but you sure *do* have control issues."

"That's exactly what *Mom* said." Dante plopped down in an empty seat at the island. "Right before she kicked him *and* me out and told us to find something to do."

Michael stopped short of taking a bite and busted out laughing.

Dante glanced at his father, who rolled his eyes. "He tried to argue with her but—"

"It was pointless, *wasn't* it?" Michael directed at Gary.

"I'm over *here* with Dante's snitching self, aren't I?" Gary jeered. He couldn't help but laugh along with his sons. "Couldn't get a *word* in."

"Yeah well, it was either take him to my place for a bit, or come here." Dante cut a piece of chicken with his fork. "Needless to say, he chose the latter."

"There was *no* way I was going to your place to listen to Lori scream at you about your inability to pick up after yourself." Gary pointed his fork in Dante's direction. "But for the record, she has a point Dante. You've gotten too comfortable."

Dante made a face in retaliation. "Yeah, yeah."

"Well, no matter the reason I'm glad you both stopped by," Michael slid in. "It's been a minute since the three of us hung out."

"Hell, I was surprised when you texted back and said you were home," Dante said. "I thought you'd be out with Patience."

Tensing, Michael rubbed the back of his neck. "Not today."

It had been three days since their books-and-latte date. Though Michael had since spoken to Patience, he could sense by her melancholy tone and the way she continued to cut their conversations short, that she was still upset. While he understood the cause, he couldn't help but wonder if she was still holding a grudge against *him* for setting it off.

"Ah yes, how *are* things going with your girlfriend?" Gary probed, snapping Michael out of his thoughts.

"We—"

Dante gestured to his brother. "They're not official yet." He flashed a simpering grin Michael's way. "They're still in the *talking* phase."

Michael scowled at Dante's mocking tone. "Is that supposed to be an insult?"

"Not at all. I was just clarifying since Pop called her your girlfriend." Dante raised his hand up. "But if you want my opinion—"

"Trust me when I say that your opinion on anything relationship wise is the *last* thing I want or *need*," Michael sneered, eyes burrowing through Dante.

Smugness on his face, Dante reclined in his seat. "That's fine. But for the record Lori and *I* were official after *one* date. *Just* saying."

Michael's lips curled into an angry smirk. "Yeah, quick to bed her, yet slow to *marry* her isn't something you should boast about."

Gary erupted in loud, boisterous laughter. "Perfect Mike, *perfect!*" He slapped the counter with glee. "I bet you won't try to tease him again, *huh* Dante?"

Dante's mouth dropped open. "Oh wow." Scoffing, he rose from his seat, snatching up his plate. "I will *not* be laughed at to my face. I'll take my food to the patio."

Ignoring Dante's figure stalking towards the back door, Michael directed his attention to his father. The man was wiping a tear from his eye as his laughter subsided. "Anyway Pop, Dante wasn't wrong. Patience isn't *technically* my girlfriend just yet," he confessed. "However, to answer your question, things are going well." *At least I hope it still is.*

Gary nodded in approval, unaware of the doubts swirling in his son's head. "Good to hear." He twisted the cap off his water bottle. "I assume that an official relationship is in the *plans?*"

"Oh absolutely. At least it's what I *hope* for." Michael glanced off to the side, focusing on the vase centerpiece sitting atop the counter island. "I care for her Pop...deeply."

Gary produced a sincere smile. "Mike, you have no idea how

happy your mother and I are that you have someone special in your life. A relationship—with the *right* person—is a beautiful thing."

Michael released a sigh, his mind still heavy. "Yeah."

Leaning forward, Gary placed his hand on the table. "I'm assuming you haven't met her little angel yet?"

Michael looked at him, smiling gently at the term of endearment. "Not yet." He'd made it no secret to his family that Patience had a daughter, revealing it to his parents just days after their first date. The news drew a warm reaction from the elder Carters.

"Does it bother you that you haven't yet?"

Shaking his head, Michael folded his arms on the countertop. "Not at all. I'm sure when Patience feels the time is right, she'll introduce me."

"I have no doubt that she will." Gary's eyes lit with elation. "Sounds like things are headed in the right direction."

Though Michael's thoughts were still bombarded with "what if's" when it came to his current standing with Patience, he feigned a smile to keep his father from probing further. "Yeah…they are."

Pinching the bridge of her nose, Patience held the office phone to her ear. "Karrin, you know we're five days away from closing on this house, right? No, let me correct myself, we *were* five days away from closing on the house…" She rolled her eyes at the question coming through the line. "Because, as I previously informed you and your husband, the lender will run your credit report again before closing, and if they spot any big purchases, it could be a problem. And now that you went and purchased a *car*, that impacts your financials. So *now* we have to go *back* to underwriting. Which I can't guarantee will come out in your favor this time…" Balling her fist, she lightly pounded it against her forehead, as the distraught woman on the other end of the phone ranted into her ear.

As much as Patience liked her job, there were times when it

frustrated her. No matter how many times she stressed the processes and procedures of home buying for her clients, for some, her words went in one ear and out the other.

"I understand that you hired movers and ordered furniture, which I *also* advised you not to do until after you closed… There is nothing I can do. We have to start the process again and if I'm being completely honest, there's a possibility that the mortgage won't be finalized…" She sighed as the wails blared through the phone. "Karrin—crying won't help, I'm sorry… I'll let you know when I hear back."

Slamming the receiver into the cradle, Patience groaned aloud, rubbing her face with her hands. "I swear to *God*, I'm not in the mood for this shit today."

The clock on her laptop screen read three o'clock—she'd been on that dreaded call for over an hour. She then eyed the unopened container of turkey taco bowl and pita slices on her desk…the one she ordered for lunch…at twelve. The one she'd ordered despite not having an appetite.

Ignoring the now ice-cold meal, she grabbed her cell phone. Scrolling through, she read the text message from Michael that he'd sent three hours ago.

I hope you're having a good day.

Leaning back in her seat, she stared at the words. She *wasn't* having a good day, and what was worse, she'd never replied to him.

For the past week, Patience was finding herself taking longer to reply to texts from Michael, even cutting their conversations short when they *did* talk. On top of that, when he'd tried to schedule a date over the past weekend, she'd made an excuse so that she wouldn't have to face him. Not because of him, but because of *herself.* She couldn't shake her sour disposition, no matter how much she wanted to.

Opening her text box, she began to type out a reply, but halted when her phone vibrated in her hand. The name flashing on the screen baffled her. So much so, that it drew a frown from her. Hesitantly, she put it to her ear. "Hello?"

"Hey Patience, it's Angela."

Patience shook her head not only at Angela's reply, but at the flat tone. She could only imagine what the woman was calling her about. Especially since her name hadn't graced Patience's phone screen in what seemed like forever. "Yes, I know. I *do* have you saved in my phone."

"The sarcasm isn't necessary," Angela hissed.

Rolling her eyes, Patience exhaled loudly. *God, help me.* "What can I do for you sis?"

"Listen, about my dinner party taking place on Saturday…"

You mean the one I wasn't invited to? "Uh huh," she muttered.

"Well, one of my invited guests can't make it. So…" Angela let out a quick breath, "if *you* wanted to come…there's a space for you."

Patience sat still, eyes constricted, mouth slacked. Not only had Angela left her off the guest list in the *first* place, *now* she was calling just *days* before the event, with this half-hearted place-filler invitation. "Angela…as sweet and thoughtful as that invitation was, I'll be declining," Patience bristled. "I have to go."

Angela's astonished gasp sounded through the line. "Now wait just a minute, you're really not going to *come*?"

"Would *you*?" Patience's eyes blazed as she tightened her grip over the cell. "No wait, I'll answer for you, you *wouldn't*. So stick with your original plan and leave me out."

Angela sucked her teeth. "Oh grow up, Patience. I gave you my reasons for leaving you off the list. I changed my mind, so get over it," she snarled. "Stop being a damn brat and come on. Toni can get her in-laws to watch the girls."

"The girls and I will be just fine at *my* house on Saturday."

"You know what, *fine*. Be that way," Angela huffed. "I don't even know why I bothered calling you."

"That's a question you and I both have in common. Have a good day, Angela." Patience ended the call before Angela could get another word in, flicking the phone on her desk. "Bitch."

Rubbing her hands over her face once again, she leaned back in her seat. Patience didn't think it was possible, but the phone call from Angela had made her day even worse. So much so, that her eyes began to tear up. "Shit," she sniffled as a few spilled down her cheeks.

Snatching a tissue from a box in her drawer, Patience dabbed her cheeks and eyes dry before tossing it in the trash. Picking up her phone, she scrolled to Michael's number, hitting call.

"Hey," she said when he picked up.

Michael immediately picked up on her somber tone. "Hey yourself... Is everything okay?"

"Umm..." Fresh tears stung Patience's eyes; she reached for another tissue. "Not really."

The sound of loud banging hindered Michael's response. "Hold on just a sec." Signaling to a member of his team, he stepped out of the house he was working on. Moving out onto the lawn, he adjusted his earpiece. "I'm sorry for the noise, I'm on site today."

Her eyes widened. She'd completely forgotten that Michael had mentioned he'd be working on a site all week. "Oh, I—"

"No, no don't worry, what's the matter?" He made no attempt to mask the concern in his voice.

I feel like I'm losing my mind, is what's wrong. "I'm just having a bad day." Patience desperately tried to keep the shakiness of her voice at bay. She wiped her eyes, sighing in the process. "It's actually been a bad *week* if I'm being honest."

"I'm sorry to hear that." Hearing the sadness in her voice and not being there to comfort her was torture for him. "Do you want to tell me about it? I have time."

"I *want* to, but... I can't really talk at length right now." Her eyes lowered to the damp tissue in her hand, closing her fist around it. "I just wanted to hear your voice for a minute."

Michael closed his eyes, releasing a heavy sigh. If he wasn't tempted to abandon his work and go to her before, he surely was *now.* However, he knew that he couldn't. "I wanted to hear yours too, sweetheart. More than you know."

Shutting her eyes, Patience covered her face with her hand. Remorse consumed her. Michael's heartfelt response made the reality of how Patience had been treating him lately even more vivid. *He doesn't deserve this. You need to be honest with him.*

"Michael, I—" The flash from her in office phone caught her attention. "Damn it," she muttered. "I'm sorry, I have to go—I'm getting a work call. Can I call you back later?"

"Of course, you can. At any time."

"Thank you…Bye." Hanging up, Patience set the cell down and took a quick second to center herself, before grabbing the phone from its cradle.

Chapter Seventeen

"TONI, YOU KNOW IT'S A school night," Patience fussed at the cell phone lying on the kitchen counter.

"It's *not*," Toni shot back. "Their last day of school was *yesterday*. They're out for summer break."

Dumbfounded, Patience stared blankly at the wall in front of her. "Not going to lie, that *completely* slipped my mind." She'd been in such a daze, that school was far in the back of her mind. "Noelle would've been *hot* with me if I would've tried to get her up for class tomorrow."

"Hell, rightfully *so*—oh side bar. You know that Rob works from home most days, so Noelle can hang out here with Jordan while you're at work."

Patience rubbed her forehead, sighing. "Thank you. I'll take you up on that, but it won't be often; I can arrange my schedule to work at home for a few days during the week." Closing her eyes, she lowered her head. "Damn it, that means that art camp will be here before you know it."

Toni giggled at her sister's whine. "Aww, I know you're going to miss her, but it's good you're letting her go. It'll be a good experience for her."

"I know, I know." Patience tapped her nails on the countertop. "I checked into it, it's a good camp. Her art teacher is a director there, and she's kind of amazing." She exhaled. "She'll be okay... *I'll* be okay."

"Jordan is going too."

"Oh, thank God," Patience breathed, leaning over with a hand to her chest. Toni laughed. "Don't laugh at me Toni. You don't know how much better I feel, knowing she'll have Jordan with her."

"Yeah well, mini me bugged her father and I, until we decided that letting her go would be a better alternative to drop-kicking her," Toni jeered, earning a chuckle from Patience. "No, but you're right, the program *is* great, and Jordan is excited… I told you they're inseparable."

Patience moved towards the refrigerator. "Yeah, I know."

"But back to the reason I called. The early release of the movie Jordan's been prancing around, running her mouth about is premiering now, and I figured I'd take her and Noelle to see it *tonight*, before the theater gets bombarded with everybody and their mama over the weekend."

Patience opened the refrigerator. "Yeah, Noelle's been talking my ear off about it too." She removed a pack of steak strips, onion, and green pepper.

"See? Perfect timing. They'll have a good time."

Grabbing her chopping board from a hook, Patience set it on the counter along with her ingredients. "I'm sure they will."

"*And* you won't have to worry about cooking dinner tonight. I plan on taking the girls out to dinner before the movie," Toni added. "So put the ingredients away and order yourself some takeout—I know you're about to dice something up right now."

Eyeing the items on her counter, Patience made a face. "You don't know my life."

"Oh, but I *do* kid…" Toni giggled when Patience sucked her teeth. "Come on, what do you say?"

Leaning against the table, Patience pondered. "Well…" Pushing herself from it, she picked the phone up. Taking it off speaker, she headed out of the kitchen putting it to her ear. "Let me see what she wants to do."

"Girl—you're about to waste a question. You already know what the answer will be."

"Uh huh—Bunny, can you come here for a moment please?" Patience called.

"Yes," Noelle answered back, shuffling down the hall. She trotted down a few steps, stopping in the middle of the staircase and eyeing her mother curiously. "Yes?"

"Aunt Toni would like to take you and Jordan to see that movie you've been going on about."

Noelle's eyes lit up with excitement. "It's out *today?*"

"Yes," Patience nodded. "Do you want to go?"

Tossing her arms in the air, a loud squeal erupted from Noelle. "Yes!" She bolted back up the steps at record speed. "I'm going to get ready."

Patience stared at the now empty staircase. "She doesn't even know what time the damn thing starts," she mumbled into the line.

Toni laughed. "See? I *told* you," she boasted. "It starts at seven-thirty by the way."

"Very well." Patience went back into the kitchen. "Thank you, you're saving me the torture of taking them my*self* Saturday." She returned the ingredients to the refrigerator. Now that Noelle was going out to eat, Patience no longer had the desire to prepare her pepper steak stir fry.

"Anytime—oh and *speaking* of Saturday." The humor left Toni's voice. "I know you told me not to curse her out, but I *did* tell Angie that she was full of shit and a ragged heffa for that nonsense she tried to pull on you earlier."

Patience's eyebrow lifted. "That was you *not* cursing her out?"

"Sure was, because I had plenty *more* to say." Toni was *still* livid about Angela's sorry invitation. "I'm about ready to not go *myself.*"

"I appreciate it, but that won't change anything." Patience sighed. "Just go and make sure you and Rob drink up all her wine."

"Oh don't you worry. We're drinking the wine *and* that top-shelf liquor," Toni promised. "*And* I'm leaving out of there with a bottle or two. She got me fucked up." The sound of Patience's soft laughter made Toni laugh a bit herself. "Anyway, I'll be there shortly."

"Okay, see you in a bit."

Stepping foot outside his home, Michael paid for and retrieved his take-out order from the delivery driver. Door closed and steamy bag in hand, Michael passed through the house into his kitchen. After a strenuous workday, Michael didn't hesitate to refresh himself with a shower and a change of clothes. He was now looking forward to enjoying his meal in peace.

Grabbing a knife and fork from a drawer, followed by a bottle of apple juice from the refrigerator, he sat down at his counter island in front of his platter. Opening the container, the savory aromas of oxtail, rice and plantains filled the kitchen.

As he began to scarf down the tasty food, Michael read the six-fifteen p.m. time on his phone screen. It had been hours since he'd spoken to Patience. Though she'd replied to the text he'd sent once he was able to leave the site, the, *I'm okay for now, heading home,* reply didn't satisfy him.

With only worry for Patience on his mind, Michael set his fork down and dialed her number, putting it on speaker.

Patience picked up. "Hey you. Funny, I was getting ready to call you."

"Perfect timing." Moving his platter aside, Michael crossed his arms on the countertop. "I was calling to check up on you... to see if your day had gotten any better." Though judging by the dejected tone still in her voice, he was almost certain that it had not.

"It's..." Sighing, Patience adjusted her position on her couch, the muted TV show playing on the screen in front of her. "The *work* part is better because I'm not there right now. Thank you for asking."

"You don't need to thank me for that," Michael's smooth voice brimmed with compassion. "Your well-being is important to me."

Patience brought a hand to her heart. "You're so sweet... Likewise." *Even if I haven't been acting like it.* "I had planned on calling you back earlier, but figured I'd give you some time to unwind from work first. Which was just as well because I ended up having to get Noelle together at the last minute."

Twisting the cap off his juice, Michael eyed the phone in curiosity. "Is everything okay?"

"Yeah, it was nothing serious. Toni came by to pick her up." Patience grabbed a few strands of her hair, twirling them around her finger. "She took her and my niece out to dinner and a movie so..."

"That's nice of her." Michael took a quick sip of his juice, setting the bottle back down. "You have a few hours to yourself."

"Yeah." She sighed once again. "Normally that would be a *good* thing, but..."

"What's different this time?" Michael probed when she trailed off.

"Let's just say that being alone with your own thoughts isn't a good thing all the time."

Michael's eyes lowered to the marble counter. *If I had the ability to take all your worries and troubles away, I swear I would.* "I hate that you're feeling down Patience... I wish that I could—" He halted briefly as an idea jumped into his head. "Hey, how much alone time do you have left?"

Confused by the unexpected question, Patience peered at her watch. "They're at dinner now and the movie doesn't start until seven-thirty. So, three hours maybe...Why?"

"Would you be opposed to hanging out with me for a little while?"

Patience sat up in her seat; the idea of seeing his face made her heart skip a beat. She'd missed him. "No, not at all."

Michael stared at the phone in disbelief. Given the past week, he'd expected her to decline. "Really?"

She nodded, forgetting for a moment that he could not see her. "Yes."

His face brightened. "Good, I'll be there shortly." Rising from his seat, he quickly put his leftovers away. "Did you eat dinner yet? I can pick something up on the way."

"No need sweetie, I ate already." Patience had wound up making her planned stir fry anyway, enjoying it over rice. After a long, awful day, it was a comfort to cook herself something nice.

"Okay, I'll see you soon." Michael moved swiftly through the house, darting upstairs in search of his wallet.

"Are you going to give me a hint as to where we're going?"

Michael chuckled. "Someplace I think will cheer you up."

"Sounds perfect." Standing from the couch, she stretched. "I'll be ready."

Patience rushed to the door as soon as she heard the bell. There was only a quick peek through the peephole before opening it. A smile flickered in her eyes. "Hi."

"Hi," Michael smiled back. He enveloped her in a hug, planting a tender kiss to her cheek.

Patience held on longer than either one had anticipated. She hadn't realized how much she'd needed a hug…or *him*.

He relished the feeling of having her in his arms, wishing that it could last. Finally parting, he held a small box out for her. "I know you said you ate dinner, but figured you could use something sweet for later." He gestured to it. "It's just a slice of lemon meringue pie."

Patience retrieved the pastry box with an appreciative grin. "Thank you. I certainly can and *will* eat this later." Moving aside, she signaled for him. "Come in for a second."

Michael stepped in, closing the door behind him.

She moved towards the kitchen. "I'm just going to put this in the fridge."

"Take your time." Shoving his hands into his pockets, Michael waited by an accent chair. Eyes roaming over the living area, Michael remembered when he'd first made it past the corridor after their third date. Patience had invited him to wait inside because she'd run a little behind schedule to get ready. While sitting on the plush light gray couch, amongst the lavender and yellow throw pillows, he took in how warm and inviting the space was. She was not only great at selling homes, but she was also great at decorating them.

Noticing a large flat box propped up against a wall, Michael moved closer to get a better look at the picture on the front. "Nice desk."

"What did you say?" Patience asked, emerging from the kitchen.

He pointed to the box. "The desk. It's nice."

Patience rubbed her forehead. "Oh, thanks." She approached a small nearby closet. "To be honest, I forgot that thing was there. It was delivered last week, and I'm *dreading* putting it together."

Michael looked at her. "Oh yeah?"

"Yeah." Recounting her blunder, she shook her head. "I forgot to choose the 'assembled' option when I ordered it." Waving a hand, she dismissed the thought. "Anyway, I'm ready." She grabbed a pair of shoes from the closet. "You still haven't told me where you're taking me. Should I wear sneakers or heels?"

"You can wear whatever you're comfortable with… You're just going to have to take them off to put skates on anyway."

Sneakers in hand, Patience spun around to face him, eyes wide. "*Skates?* You said skates, right?"

Michael chuckled. "I did."

"As in those things with four wheels that you have to balance on?"

"That would be correct." Folding his arms, Michael's lips formed a playful smirk. "Sounds like a good time, doesn't it?"

Placing a hand on her hip, she shook her head at him, a twinge of humor on her face. "Yeah, you're crazy."

Michael let out a laugh. "Oh come on, it won't be that bad."

"Look, I haven't been in skates since I was *fourteen*—"

Gathering her nerve, she put a hand up. "*However*, I'm no punk, so I'll get in that rink." She pointed a warning finger at him. "But just know, if I fall…I might yell at you."

Cocking his head to the side, he fixed her with a cool stare. "I won't let you fall."

Bending, Patience stepped into a sneaker. "I admire your confidence Carter, but I wouldn't make that promise if I were you." She peered up at him. "Just so you know, I take people down with me."

Michael shook his head in amusement, happy that her playfulness seemed to have returned. "Duly noted Ms. Harvey."

Chapter Eighteen

"I CAN'T BELIEVE YOU GOT me doing this." Patience pulled the skate onto her foot. "Do you know how many times Toni has tried to get me to go skating again?"

Tying his size fourteen skate, Michael laughed a bit. "I should feel special then, huh?"

Crinkling her nose, she playfully nudged him. "Yeah, you *should.*"

Twenty minutes from the time that Patience had left her house with Michael, they'd arrived at the skating rink in the next town over for adult-only skating hour. The DJ was playing popular tunes; paired with the light food and drinks being served, it had drawn a nice-sized crowd that Wednesday evening.

As Patience finished putting on her other skate, Michael appeared before her, crouching. "I'll take that as a win," he mused, lacing up her skates.

The sweet gesture drew a smile from Patience as she leered at him. *He's so adorable.*

Tying the second pair of laces, Michael rested his hands on Patience's ankles, glancing up at her. "You ready to get back out there?"

Clearing her throat as she snapped out of her starry gaze, she tucked her hair behind her ears, "Yep, let's go."

Standing from the floor, Michael extended his hand for her and gently pulled her to her feet. When she stumbled a bit, he secured her by putting an arm around her waist. "You okay?"

"Yup, I'm fine." She clutched his arm in a firm grip. "Just have to get used to being on wheels again."

At a snail's pace, Michael guided Patience to the rink. He stepped onto the smooth surface, while she carefully followed suit. The pair stood as Patience tried to get acclimated to balancing herself, watching fellow skaters glide around. Most skated with ease, others…not so much.

Patience hated to admit it, but witnessing some of the adults wavering across the floor eased her self-consciousness. Taking a deep breath, she gave Michael's hand a light pat with her free one. "Okay, I'm ready."

With her go-ahead, Michael began to carefully glide with her at his side. Glancing over, he saw her inching alongside him, muttering an arsenal of profane words. He couldn't help but be a bit humored. "You want to stop?"

She quickly shook her head, a determined look on her face. "No, I'm going to get the hang of this." She tried to glide. "You go ahead."

"You sure?" he asked, feeling her pull her hand from his.

"Yeah, I'll catch up to you."

Reluctant, Michael began to skate off.

Wobbling, Patience let out a squeal. "Wait!"

Arms crossed at his chest, Michael watched Patience with satisfaction as she skated a circle around him. "Looks like you've gotten the hang of it."

"I know right, and it didn't even take a whole hour." Spinning around to face him, Patience grinned. "I'd forgotten how fun this used to be."

He threw a proud smile right back. "I'm happy that I was able to remind you."

In no time at all, Michael had witnessed Patience go from cautious and frustrated as she shuffled along, bumping into the padded wall on occasion, to cruising at a safe speed as she made her way around the rink, to gliding with ease. On occasion, she was even surpassing him.

Her determination impressed him. The times when she'd let him comfort her after she'd hit those walls moved him, and her laughter when he'd make one of his tired jokes to ease her mind was like music to his ears. Michael was having fun with her, and as much as he knew that Patience had needed it after the week she'd had, he quickly realized that *he* had needed it too.

"You up for one more go round?" Michael asked, gliding.

Nodding, she moved next to him. "I think I can go a bit faster this time."

Michael's brow shot up. "Uh…" He scratched his head. "I admire your confidence."

She shot him a challenging look. "What, you think I *can't*?"

"I didn't say that." His tone displayed a hint of laughter.

"That elevated eyebrow on your face said it *for* you."

Michael snickered. *Read me like a book.* "It's not that I don't believe you, I just don't want you to hurt yourself."

Patience rolled her eyes. "Yeah, yeah, you're just digging yourself into a bigger hole Carter. I got this." She delivered a tap to his hand. "Tag, you're it." She punctuated her words by skating off at a hurried pace.

"Oh, so you want to play?" Amused, Michael took off after her.

They both soared through the rink, successfully maneuvering around the other skaters. Patience wasn't bluffing, she *could* skate faster, and *was*. Michael went from trying to catch up to her to tag her back, to forgetting about the task all together, just focusing on the way she moved. The sway of her hips, the strength in her legs, the way her hair blew as she floated across the floor. In his mind, everyone else on the floor had vanished; she was the only one who had his undivided attention.

"Watch out bro!"

Michael snapped out of his daze just in time to see a man stumbling and flailing straight towards him. His eyes enlarged in panic. "Shit!" As he tried to pivot, he lost balance. Sending his body colliding with the hard floor, a loud groan sounded from him.

Hearing the commotion, and Michael's elevated voice, Patience spun around. Her eyes widened at the sight of him sprawled out on the floor. "Oh my God!" She dashed over. Crouching down beside him, she put a caring hand on his arm. "Are you okay?"

Michael sat up and looked at her. "Yeah, I'm good." He rubbed his hands together, getting the dirt particles off. "Am I embarrassed like shit? *Also* yes."

Patience covered her face, trying to hide her building amusement. She touched his arm again, giving it a rub. "Aww, I'm sorry." She might have been humored, but she felt bad. After all, his embarrassment had been caused by her challenging him.

"No need to be. It serves my overconfident ass right."

Giggling, Patience stood upright as Michael picked himself up. "I say our skating session is now over."

Michael brushed his shirt clean with his hand. "Yeah, you may be right."

It took less than ten minutes for the pair to leave the floor, return their skates, and retrieve their belongings. Outside of the rink, they walked to Michael's car.

Patience moved her hair away from her face as she ambled alongside Michael. Lifting her wrist, she read the eight o'clock time on her watch.

"Are we on schedule?" Michael wondered, cutting through the silence.

She put her arms behind her back, clasping her hands. "Perfectly. With about an hour and a half to spare."

Michael gave a quick nod. "Good."

Feeling the warm summer evening breeze caress her face, Patience let out a relaxed sigh. "It's such a beautiful night."

"Yeah, it is," Michael agreed. As they approached his car, a thought entered his mind. He gazed at her. "Do you want me to take you home now, or would you mind going to one more place with me for a bit?"

"This other place isn't an ice-skating rink by any chance, is it?" she joked, earning a chuckle from him.

"No, nothing like that."

She met his hopeful eyes with a dazzling smile. "In that case, I'd love to."

After pulling off from the rink, Michael had driven them another twenty minutes to the local park. Walking across the illuminated pathway hand in hand, the pair located a vacant bench with a full view of the tree-filled manicured grounds. The peaceful night had brought out evening joggers, dog walkers, and other couples moseying along.

Patience lifted her eyes towards the sky, taking in the clear view of the twinkling stars and the half-moon. Closing her eyes, she inhaled deeply, allowing the fresh air to fill her as Michael sat quietly beside her, people watching.

"How often do you come here?" she asked him.

"Not too often. Mostly when I just need to take a few minutes to clear my head." He shrugged. "I prefer the evening. Less people, less chaos."

"Makes sense." Patience stared out at the trees in front of her, rethinking the past hour and a half. "Thank you for tonight... I needed it."

"You're welcome." Michael glanced up at the sky for a moment. "I used to go skating often as a kid."

She looked at him. "Really?"

Facing her, he nodded. "Whenever my siblings and I would get into arguments—which was *often* at that age. My father would say, 'aye, shut up, put whatever you took back, let Dante out of the damn pantry and get y'all asses in the car now'."

Patience busted out laughing. Not only at Michael reliving his father's demand, but at the exaggerated deep voice he'd used to imitate the man.

Michael laughed with her. "He and my mother would take us to our neighborhood skating rink, and turn us loose," he remembered. "By the time we were finished skating, falling, playing and laughing...we'd forgotten what we were arguing about." He peered down at the grass under his sneakers. "It was just something that always made us—*me* feel better." He gazed at her. "And I wanted to share that with you."

All traces of amusement gone from her face, Patience just stared at him, listening.

"I know you've been having a rough time, and while I knew that putting on a pair of skates wouldn't completely eliminate whatever's been troubling you, I just wanted to take your mind off it for a bit." He put a hand on her wrist. "To be honest, I've been worried about you."

Patience took a deep breath as she looked out in front of her. This man, after having a long, strenuous day himself, had put his own need for rest aside to cheer her up. The *least* she could do was be honest about what had put her in a funk in the first place. "I know you have," she softly spoke. "And I know that I haven't exactly been that receptive to you lately. I'm fully aware that I've been standoffish, and I know I made it *seem* like it was due to work stress, but... that's not entirely true." She moved hair away from her face. "Truth is, I've been *frustrated*, and it stemmed from the situation at the bookstore...how I reacted to you."

Michael was afraid to ask his next question. But it had been on his mind, and he needed to know. "Patience, I know you've said that this wasn't the case, but I have to know... Are you still upset with me?"

Expelling a heavy breath, Patience turned to Michael. Seeing the question, the *worry* in his eyes, was eating at her. "Michael, I was never upset with *you*," she confessed. "I was—no I *am* pissed at my*self*."

Brow furrowed, Michael asked with all honesty, "Why?"

Patience slowly shook her head. "I've worked *so* hard in the years since my divorce to rebuild not only my life, but *me*... To heal, to regain the ability to trust, to open myself up again. I was happy—I *am* happy, and for some *stupid* ass reason I got triggered and it *sickens* me." She clenched one of her fists in frustration. "And I feel like after all the work I put in on myself, that I took a step backwards and it's embarrassing..."

She paused for a moment, trying to keep herself composed. "I know you said that you didn't take it personally. You've been *so* great, and *patient*, I just—" Feeling herself get flustered, she took a deep breath. "I'm disappointed in myself... For not only what happened, but for not being honest with you before now." Her eyes trailed down to her hands. "I made you feel that it was your fault and for that I'm deeply sorry."

Though Patience had just unleashed what had been burdening her, she still felt a bit heavy. Michael's silence was unnerving to her. She couldn't help but wonder if she'd just cost herself this new relationship.

Michael sat hanging on to every word that Patience had said. He could tell from her body language and the tone of her voice that her confession had not come easy, but he knew it was necessary for her to share. And he felt the need to do the same. "Patience...I'm about to tell you something that I haven't told anyone."

Eyes still fixed on her hands, she twisted a ring around her finger. "What's that?"

"Remember when I told you that my past relationships ended because I wasn't a good companion?"

"Yes, I remember."

Michael let out a sigh, "Well, while that was true, what I *didn't* tell you was that my first relationship—my first *serious* relationship, ended because my girlfriend at the time had gotten pregnant by someone else."

Patience's head snapped up at Michael, both shock and sympathy resonating on her face. "Are you serious?"

He nodded. "Very." He rubbed his arm. "I mean, I knew that the relationship wasn't perfect—that *I* wasn't perfect..." He shook his head, "but I never thought it was bad enough for her to not only cheat, but create a life with someone who wasn't me... What made it worse was that at that *time*, I'd planned to ask her to marry me."

Putting a consoling hand on his arm, Patience gave Michael her undivided attention as he spoke.

"I mean, at twenty-one years old, I didn't know anything about marriage," he continued. "I met her in college and I *thought* I was in love. So needless to say, what she did hurt...and it messed me up for a long time." He shrugged. "I was by myself for a while, before I started dating again and well... You already know how those ended." He took a deep breath. "It wasn't until I swore off dating for those few years that I had time to really sit and reflect... And I realized that the reason why my relationships after her suffered, was because I was still holding on to that hurt, anger, and mistrust."

"I'm sorry you had to go through that," Patience finally spoke, voice caring and soft.

Michael offered a small, soothing smile. "I appreciate it, but I *have* healed from it. So, my past sabotaging of relationships is not a factor with you... You have my word." He gently took her hand, holding it. "Patience, the reason why I shared that with you is to let you know that I've been there. So, I don't judge you." He gazed into her eyes as she stared back at him. Bringing her hand to his lips, he gave it a sweet kiss before holding it to his chest. "I *understand* you."

With Michael's comforting words, his reassurance, Patience finally felt the weight of burdening thoughts over her actions lift.

She hadn't ruined anything; in fact, it seemed to bring them closer. Squeezing his hand, her expressive eyes fixed on his. "Thank you," she murmured. "Not just for trusting me with your story, but for being understanding."

"Of course." Reaching his free hand out, he lightly brushed her cheek. "And I want you to know that you can talk to me about anything, at any time. I mean that Patience... I care for you."

She covered his hand with hers. "I care for you too."

Michael felt his pulse race. Her confession and the yearning way she was looking at him... If he'd been standing, he was sure his knees would have buckled out from under him. His words were true...he cared for Patience. However, he knew that his feelings for her ran deeper than that. Yet as much as he wanted to confess to her just *how* deeply, he was apprehensive. *We've only been dating a short time; she might think it's too much too fast.*

Her hand still secure in his, he kissed it once more, before resting it on her thigh. "Do you feel better?"

Patience gave a nod. "I do." Exhaling deeply, she prepared to say her next words. "I meant it, I do care for you Michael, and I trust you. You've been nothing short of amazing to me...and that's why...I want to introduce you to my daughter."

Michael's eyes widened. "You're serious?"

Patience nodded. "I am. I feel like it's time." She tilted her head. "Are you okay with that?"

"Oh, yes—of *course*." Though his face displayed pure elation, on the inside lay a mix of both excitement *and* a bit of nervousness. He knew that this was a huge step for her, and he prayed that it would go over well. "Just let me know when."

Patience's smile was bright. "Okay. I'll talk to her first, and then we can set up something."

"Sounds good." He noticed her look at her watch. "Time to go?"

"They're not back yet, but I should get back and get settled before they do."

"Well, let's get you home." Michael rose from the bench, with her following suit.

Michael was silent as he turned the car off in front of Patience's. Patience on the other hand, was on a phone call.

"Wait, they want to do *what* now?" Pinching the bridge of her nose, Patience shook her head as Toni spoke. "Lord," she sighed. "Well…at least I won't be the only one with a cranky child tomorrow…" She giggled at Toni's reply. "Yeah, it's fine. Let them have fun… Okay, I'll see you in a bit… Bye."

Hanging up, Patience placed the phone into her purse. "Well, it looks like I could've stayed out longer *after* all."

Michael looked over at her. "Oh yeah?"

"Yeah." She ran a hand over her hair. "Apparently one of the pony characters from that movie is there at the theater due to it being the premier, and of *course* the girls just *have* to make my poor sister stand in line with a bunch of other kids to take pictures."

Michael laughed. "Oh, I'm sure Toni is enjoying that."

Patience joined in with her own laughter. "I can picture the frown on her face now." She stretched her neck from side to side, then met Michael's eye. He looked like he was thinking of something. "You okay?"

"Sure. I was just wondering how much time you have before they get back?"

"Probably about another hour. Toni said the line was pretty long and it takes about twenty-five minutes to get back here from the theater…" Patience's head drifted lazily to the side. "Why? Do you want to take a ride somewhere else?"

"Trust me, I'd love to." He ran his hand over his chin. "But for now, why don't you let me put that desk together for you?"

Her eyebrow arched. "After the day you've had? You really want to end it by putting together a kid's desk?"

"*Because* it's a kid's desk, it won't take me long." He shrugged. "I'll have it set up and be out of your hair before they get back." When she opened her mouth, he pointed a playful finger at her. "And before you say it, I promise you, it's no trouble."

Squinting at him, Patience pursed her lips. "Just read me why don't you." When he chuckled, she let her own inward laugh fly. "I mean if you *insist*... I *am* tired of looking at that box."

"Well then, I'll get right to it."

Michael followed Patience to her door, then inside the house once she opened it. He eyed the box. "Two questions," he said, folding his arms. "Where do you want the desk, and where are your tools?"

Patience moved to the coat closet. Opening it, she pulled a toolbox from atop a shelf. "Tools are here, and the desk will be going in Noelle's room."

Lifting the box, Michael carried it up the staircase behind Patience.

Standing in the hallway, Patience watched him effortlessly carry the heavy box. She focused on how defined his biceps looked as they flexed under the weight. It only took but a moment for Patience's mind to go from the desk, to imagining what it would be like for him to lift *her*. Lift her high enough for her to wrap her legs around his waist...or around his *shoulders*.

She was so lost in her fantasy that Michael calling her name startled her. A hand to her chest, she fixed him with a wide-eyed look. "Huh?"

"Which room is Noelle's?"

Clearing her throat, she pointed to a door on the left. "That one right there." As Michael entered the room, Patience trailed behind, silently berating herself for zoning out. *Pull your shit together.*

Michael laid the box on the floor, then retrieved the tools from Patience's grasp.

Stepping back to allow him space, Patience folded her arms. "Do you need any help?"

Slicing the box open with a box cutter, Michael let out a quiet laugh. "No thank you, I got it."

Covering her face with a hand, she shook her head. "Silly question huh? You can probably do this in your sleep."

"Nah, nothing you ask is silly." He flashed her a smile. "I *do* need your company though."

Patience sat on the edge of Noelle's bed. "You've got it."

Michael hadn't exaggerated; he put that desk together in record speed. Patience didn't know exactly, for she wasn't watching the clock, but she was sure it took him only a half hour. Or maybe the time just flew by due to the conversation they were having while he worked.

Michael positioned the newly assembled furniture piece where Patience wanted it, then retrieved the toolbox from the floor, handing it to her.

She clutched it with both hands. "I really appreciate you doing this."

Michael touched her arm. "No problem." Feeling her bare skin under his hand, Michael lost his train of thought for a moment. "Umm—" he removed his hand. "The old desk, is it still around? Do you want me to throw that out with the trash?"

Waving a dismissive hand, she shook her head. "I already moved it to the spare room. I'm waiting for my brother-in-law to pick it up for my niece, but thanks."

"Sure." He gathered the empty box, placing all the discarded packing material inside. "*This*, I *will* take out to the trash though."

"Before you do that, let me get you something to drink," Patience offered.

"Okay." Michael *had* worked up a bit of a sweat. He followed her downstairs, placing the box by the door, while Patience returned her tools to the closet.

She gestured to the couch. "Have a seat."

"Thanks," he replied, doing as she commanded.

Pausing on her way to the kitchen, Patience faced him. "Do you want water, lemonade or iced tea?"

"Water is just fine, thank you."

"Okay." Patience disappeared into the kitchen. In less than five minutes, she reappeared with a tall glass of ice water in one hand, and a small plate of dessert in the other.

Sitting down next to him, Patience handed him the water, which he immediately began to guzzle down. "So, as a small token of my appreciation for tonight, I'd like to share my dessert with you."

"Sharing, huh?" Setting his empty glass on the coffee table, Michael eyed the plate of lemon meringue pie in Patience's hand. "I know how you are about your desserts, so this is *definitely* an honor."

"It *should* be," she threw back, humor lacing her voice. "I know you're a chocolate guy, but I don't have any so..." She handed him one of the two spoons she'd brought out, before cutting a piece of the pie and putting it into her mouth.

Michael, spoon in hand, watched her close her eyes as she slowly chewed, savoring every morsel. "You make that pie look *damn* good."

Snapping her eyes open, she covered her mouth to hold the chewed piece in as she giggled. "Stop it," she got out upon swallowing.

"Hell, it's true." He cut a sliver of the pie, then held it at eye level, examining it. "You know, I've never had lemon meringue pie before."

Setting the plate down, Patience shot him a stunned look. "You're kidding."

Michael shook his head. "Fruit desserts were never my thing, but I'm open to try it." Placing the pie into his mouth, he chewed, allowing his pallet to adjust to the sweet, yet tangy flavors.

His head leaned to the side, concentration on his face as Patience eyed him. "Well? What do you think?" she asked.

Smiling, he gave a slow nod. "That's pretty damn good." He took another bite. "Yeah, you're on to something here."

Tossing her arms in the air, Patience let out a squeal of delight. "I've converted you to the lemon side."

Michael let out a deep laugh. "Now, I wouldn't go *that* far." He rested the spoon on the plate. "I won't be giving up my chocolate desserts any time soon, but I *am* interested in trying more lemon ones now."

Shrugging, Patience offered a smug look. "Well, I at *least* got you to try it, so I must be special."

Eyeing her, Michael shook his head in amusement. But it soon left his face as the intensity in his eyes grew. "You *are*." His voice was low, deep.

The smile left Patience's face as she looked into his eyes. The way Michael was looking at her matched her own longing. It nearly took her breath away. "So are you."

Michael gently took hold of her hand. Feeling her fingers squeeze his, he leaned in close, his lips just barely grazing her own. The tension built higher and higher before he gave in, pressing his lips to hers. Closing his eyes, he deepened the kiss. Patience caressed his face as she eagerly returned it.

She allowed Michael to guide her back until her head rested against the cushioned arm. Michael's kiss was passionate, hungry and fully welcomed. Patience felt her body heating; she let out a soft gasp as he moved his lips to her scented neck.

Letting her eyes shut, she relished the feeling of his lips on her skin. If his *kisses* felt this good, she could only imagine how good he was at everything *else*. Her hands reached around Michael's back as his body pressed against hers.

As Michael worked his kisses down to the collar bone, Patience took hold of his hand, directing it beneath her shirt. Her breath became ragged as his hand slowly inched over her torso. When she felt his bulge press against her thigh, it only sent her desire into overdrive.

Michael's fingertips caressed Patience's bare stomach as he

reclaimed her lips with his. Guiding the fabric of her shirt up further, his hand moved from her waist to her chest. Pulling his head back, he laid eyes on the satin lavender bra that concealed her breasts. An insatiable spark in his eyes, he ran his finger along the top of the bra before slowly pulling it down, exposing an erect nipple.

A low whimper left Patience's lips as Michael's tongue brushed against it. Wetness formed between her legs as Michael's tongue began to flick. When he gently bit down, she allowed a moan to escape. Clutching the fabric of Michael's shirt with one hand, and moving the other up his bare back, she concentrated on the pleasure building inside of her as he moved his mouth to her other breast.

Kissing her, tasting her skin—Michael wanted more. Lifting his head, he returned his craving lips to hers, cupping her face with his hands. "I want to taste you so bad," he breathed against her mouth.

"Please do it," she panted.

Patience grasped the back of the armrest as Michael kissed his way down her body, stopping at her jeans. Unbuttoning them, he hooked the fabric with his fingers, pulling it down just enough to allow a peek of her underwear. Michael licked his lips before running his tongue just above the satin fabric.

The breath got caught in Patience's throat and her mind began to cloud over as she felt Michael gripping the sides of her jeans, pulling them down to her knees. She anticipated the feeling of his tongue on the most precious part of her body. She wanted it, she longed for it, she *ached* for it. So much so that when her phone rang, she tried to ignore it. Tried to block the annoying sound out as Michael guided her underwear down, revealing her delicate flesh while planting tender kisses to it.

Hearing the ring again, Patience finally snapped out of her lustful haze as realization set it. Her eyes jolted open. *Shit! It's probably Toni.*

Thrashing her hand on the coffee table, she grabbed the phone. "Shit. Michael wait," she gasped.

Lifting his head, Michael peered at her. "What's wrong?" She showed him the name on her screen. Giving a nod, he sat up as she answered the phone.

"Hello?" Patience barely had any breath in her. Grabbing a belt loop of her jeans, Patience tried to wrestle them up as Toni spoke.

Michael aided her by taking hold of her arm and guiding her upright. Adjusting his position next to her, he sat in silence.

"Fifteen minutes? ...Okay." Patience readjusted her bra then fanned herself with her hand. "What? ...Yes, I'm fine why? ...My breathing? Nothing, I was doing umm—jumping jacks."

A loud snicker erupted from Michael, earning him a stiff backhand to his arm in retaliation.

"I'll see you then...bye." Hanging up, Patience released a deep sigh as she sat the phone back on the table. Running a hand over her hair, she turned to Michael, the disappointment clear on her face. "Perfect timing huh?"

He offered a shrug in return. "Nah, it's fine." A smoldering look in his eyes, he fixed her with an intent stare. "I'm sure we'll get another opportunity."

She returned his lustful gaze with one of her own. "Yeah... we will."

Michael hoped that was true. That he'd get another opportunity to show Patience exactly how he felt about her, by showing her body all the attention that it deserved. "I'll see you later then."

"Later." She closed her eyes as he placed another kiss to her lips, which instantly heated her up all over again. If he didn't leave now, she'd make him stay. Touching his face, she pulled away. "Good night."

"Night." Rising from the couch, Michael headed for the door, grabbing the box of trash.

"Let me know when you get home," Patience said.

Looking back at her one last time, Michael winked. "I will."

Patience watched him leave, giving a wave as he closed the door.

Alone again, she buttoned her jeans and pulled her shirt back in place, resting against the sofa cushions. Staring up at the ceiling, she hoped that her body would cool off before Toni arrived.

When the memory of what nearly took place on that couch flashed in her mind, that familiar ache pulsed between her legs. Patience jumped up. "Nope, I need a cold shower like *right* now."

Chapter Nineteen

"THIS PLACE IS BEAUTIFUL," JILL gushed, observing the lush flowers and plants lining the restaurant balcony. With the sun beginning to set, the vibrant sky added to the tranquil vibe. "I'm glad we decided to sit outside."

Michael picked up his menu. "Yeah, I figured you'd like it better than inside." Wanting some quality one-on-one time with his mother, Michael had picked her up that Saturday evening for an Italian dinner.

Perusing over her menu, Jill let out a light, relaxed sigh. "This is nice. Thank you for bringing me."

"Of course," Michael replied warmly. "With Pop out playing poker with his buddies, I figured you could use some company, and of course, I missed you."

She pointed at him. "See? *This* is why you're my favorite," she said, earning a laugh from Michael.

"I believe you." Michael set his menu down as the waiter came over and filled their empty glasses with ice water. He gestured to his mother. "Are you ready to order Mom?"

Jill peered up from her menu. "Oh certainly."

After placing their orders, the waiter left the duo to their conversation.

"So…how have things been?" Jill asked.

Michael smiled, thinking back over the past few days. Specifically, the evening he'd shared with Patience three days ago.

He hadn't been able to get it off his mind. Or *her* for that matter. "Things have been great."

Studying her son's face, a grin appeared on Jill's. "You're not talking about *work*, are you?"

He smirked. "No," he leaned back in his seat, "You called it. I'm referring to Patience."

Jill clasped her hands together. "I just love how your eyes sparkle every time you mention her."

Squinting, he gestured to his eyes, a jovial look on his face. "They sparkle, really?" He laughed when she pursed her lips at his teasing. "No, I know what you mean, and I agree… I can honestly say that I haven't felt this way in a long time…*ever* really."

"I can see *that* too." Jill folded her arms on the table. "I can't even remember you being *this* smitten with that *first* girlfriend of yours— which I'm glad didn't work out by the way—I wasn't a fan of hers."

Michael winced as he sipped his water. He knew then that his mother—his *family,* wasn't a huge fan of the woman who had ultimately shattered his young heart all those years ago. "Yeah, this is something *completely* different."

"I can't wait to meet her."

"Yes, I know. Soon enough." Michael knew how eager his family was to meet Patience. He wanted them to meet her as well, but he knew he needed to have his *own* meeting first. "But in the *meantime,* Patience told me that she's ready to introduce me to her daughter."

Releasing a gasp, Jill clapped her hands.

"She's going to have a conversation with her, and depending on how it goes, we'll be planning a meet up soon."

"That is just *wonderful,*" she squealed. "It's a *huge* step. Are you nervous?"

Michael nodded, chuckling a bit. "It sounds silly, but yes."

Jill waved a hand his way. "Son, I'm sure you'll have nothing to worry about. Children are amazing little judges of character, and *your* character is perfect, so I'm sure you'll have no issues winning her over."

Though his stomach was still in knots, Michael just smiled. "I'm sure you're right."

Reaching across the table, Jill patted Michael's hand. "I *know* I am." She followed up her optimistic reply with a wink.

A plastic bin in hand, Patience hauled it into her living room. "Do you want to paint, draw, or color?"

Sitting on the loveseat, Noelle examined the purple plastic bracelets on her wrist. "Color, please."

"Okay."

It was Monday evening after eating dinner, and Patience and Noelle were settling in for one of their art sessions.

Setting the bin on the floor, Patience took out coloring books, boxes of crayons, and coloring pencils. She then placed the items on the coffee table, before sitting on the floor in front of it. Noelle followed suit.

"You can choose which book we'll work on," Patience said.

Sifting through the pile of coloring books, Noelle settled on a butterfly species one. "Since we did the animal book before, we can do the butterfly one this time." Opening the book, Noelle gestured to the images. "I'll color this side and you can color that one."

Giving a nod of approval, Patience opened the color pencils and crayons. Placing them in the middle of the table, both chose their preferred instrument and got to work.

As Patience began shading part of the butterfly image on the page, she peered over at Noelle, who was coloring the image on her side. Pausing, she stared at her daughter, trying to figure out how to start the conversation she knew she needed to have. A conversation she'd tried playing out in her head on several occasions, though she knew it was in vain; she had no idea how it would turn out in reality.

Noticing that her mother's hand had stopped moving, Noelle pointed to the page. "Mommy, you're not coloring."

"Sorry." Patience resumed, though after a long moment, she exhaled deeply. "Noelle, I'd like to talk to you about something."

"Talk to me about what?"

"Well..." Patience collected her words. "You know how over the past few months, Aunt Toni watched you some evenings while I went out?"

Eyes not leaving the paper, Noelle nodded. "Yes."

"Well...I've been going out with a friend."

"Is it that same friend you went out with when you had that pretty lavender dress on?" Noelle recalled.

Patience raised an eyebrow. *Memory like a damn elephant.* "Yes, exactly. The same friend." She chose another color pencil, then continued her shading. "Well, those outings have actually been *dates,* and that friend...is a man—his name is Michael."

Pausing her coloring, Noelle studied the progress she'd made. "Oh."

Stalling her hand, Patience fixed Noelle with a stare. "How do you feel about that? ...About me dating."

Noelle's shoulders rose and fell. "I think it's nice," she answered. "My friend from school said that her dad has a girlfriend, and that she's nice. They go out for ice cream."

Patience smiled. "Oh yeah?"

Noelle nodded once more, then rested her arm on the table. "Is Mr. Michael your boyfriend?"

"Umm, not *officially*...not *yet* anyway." Patience tucked some of her hair behind her ear. "If I'm being honest, I'd *like* him to be, but there's something that needs to happen first. Which is the *other* thing that I want to talk to you about."

Eyes meeting her mother's, Noelle brought her coloring to a halt. "*What* other thing?"

"Well..." Feeling her stomach flip, Patience set her pencil down. *Just spit it out.* "I'd like for you to meet him."

Head leaning to the side, Noelle blinked several times, yet didn't speak.

The silence would've worried Patience. However, there was no anger, sadness, or confusion resonating on Noelle's face. It was more curiosity than anything. "It's just…" Patience placed a hand over Noelle's. "Noelle, you are the most important person in my life, and I'd never want to move forward in a relationship with someone, without you getting to know them."

Noelle pondered her mother's words for a moment. "Do you like him?"

The smile that appeared on Patience's face was radiant. Liking him was an understatement. "*Very* much."

"Is he nice?" Noelle followed up.

"Of *course*. I'd never introduce to you someone who *wasn't*."

Returning her eyes to the image on the paper, Noelle's head bobbed in a slow nod. "Then I'd like to meet him."

A light gasp unexpectedly slipped out of Patience as her eyes widened. Though she'd hoped, she couldn't predict Noelle's reaction to her request. She gave Noelle's hand a gentle squeeze. "Are you sure? Because I don't want you to feel that you *have* to. There's no pressure on you at all."

"I don't feel pressure Mommy." She looked up at her mother. "You said you like him and he's nice."

"Yes, I did."

"So, if *you* like him then I know *I* will. And because I'm an awesome kid, he'll like me too." Noelle followed up her prediction with a bright smile.

"You are the *best* kid any parent could ask for." Patience held her arms out. "Come here, Bunny."

Not hesitating for a second, Noelle moved into her mother's embrace.

"Thank you." Patience kissed the girl's forehead, smoothing curly tendrils from her face. "I love you."

"You're welcome. I love you too." Resting her head on her mother's chest, Noelle played with the fabric of Patience's shirt. "Do you think we can go for ice cream when I meet Mr. Michael?"

Patience giggled. "I think we can arrange that."

Chapter Twenty

MICHAEL RETRIEVED SEVERAL PLASTIC CONTAINERS from his countertop, placing them into a large, insulated wicker basket. This was followed by a few bottles of water, and an assortment of juices. After surveying every item in the packed basket, he closed it and took it in hand.

Passing through the living room, he snagged his phone from the coffee table. Dialing Patience's number, he waited as the line rang. "Hey sweetheart...I'm heading out the door now. I'll be there soon..." He smiled at her reply. "Don't worry, I'm not. See you in a bit."

Hanging up, he picked up a cloth bag from the couch before exiting the house.

Opening the car door, Michael carefully placed the basket and the bag in the backseat. Settling behind the wheel, he adjusted the gift bag and flowers on the seat beside him before pulling off.

His favorite song blaring through the car failed to tame Michael's jitters. He'd taken the drive to Patience's home many times already, yet this time he wasn't just picking Patience up to whisk her away. He was driving to her home to be introduced to her daughter.

Turning a corner, a soft laugh overcame him. "Never imagined that a child would have me shook."

Finally, he put the car in park in front of the familiar residence. Taking the items from the passenger seat, he made his way to the door. Expelling a deep breath, he rang the doorbell.

A moment later, the door opened and Michael was greeted by Patience's beautiful smile. "Hi," he spoke.

"Hey." She motioned to him with her hand. "Come in."

Closing the door behind him, Patience turned around to be met by a bouquet of a dozen roses. Taking them, she offered a soft, albeit quick kiss to his lips. "Thank you."

"You're welcome." Michael clutched the gift bag in his hand as he scanned the living room with his eyes.

Sensing what he was looking for, or *who* for that matter, Patience tilted her head. "She's upstairs." She laughed. "She suddenly realized that she can't leave the house without her sunglasses…and not just *any* sunglasses, her purple and white ones."

Setting the gift bag on the accent chair, Michael chuckled a bit to himself. He was shifting his weight from one foot to the other, running a hand over his head.

Patience touched his arm. "I thought you said you weren't nervous," she said, softness in her voice.

He winced. "It's obvious, huh?"

Placing a hand under his chin, she caressed his beard. "A little."

A little over a week ago, Patience had informed Michael that she was ready to make the introduction. Though she'd expected to be a bit nervous *herself*, she was overcome by a sense of calm. "Children smell fear, so you should probably get it together."

Michael shot a humored look her way. "I know you're joking, but I can't help but believe that's true."

"I promise you'll be fine." Giving his arm a reassuring rub, Patience faced the stairs. "Noelle," she called.

"Yes?" Noelle answered back.

Michael couldn't help but smile at the sound of her innocent voice.

"Come on down, sweetie." Patience put her flowers on the coffee table. "Our company is here."

"Okay." The sound of footsteps hurrying down the hallway commenced.

Patience approached the steps as Noelle descended. When she reached the last one, Patience held her hand out, which Noelle promptly took.

Michael watched as Patience smiled down at her daughter, who smiled back at her. It was one of the most endearing things he'd ever seen.

Taking a few steps forward, Patience glanced at Noelle. "Noelle, this is my friend Michael…"

Noelle's eyes traveled up his frame, landing on his face. *Oh wow, he's really tall.*

Patience's attention veered to Michael. "Michael, this is my daughter, Noelle."

Taking a cautious step towards them, Michael's face displayed a genuine smile. "Hi Noelle." He extended his hand. "It's so nice to meet you."

Putting a finger to her chin, Noelle studied this man. This man her mother liked. The man who'd been taking her on all these dates, bringing her flowers. *He looks nice enough.* She peered at her mother, almost as if she was asking permission to respond.

"It's okay, baby," Patience soothed, prompting Noelle to return her sight to him.

Before Noelle could speak, Michael had a thought. "Yeah, I *am* kind of huge compared to you, so…" He crouched down to her level, extending his hand once again. "Is this better?"

A giggle escaped Noelle. "Hi." She placed her hand in his. "I wasn't scared of you, by the way."

"Well, *that's* a relief to hear." Michael gave her hand a quick, gentle shake before releasing it. "So, Noelle—that's a pretty name by the way."

"Thank you." Noelle toyed with her bracelet. "Mommy named me that because Christmas is her favorite holiday."

Baffled, Patience's eyes drew to Noelle. "That's not exactly—" Putting a hand over her face, she shook her head, then looked at Michael. "Christmas *is* my favorite holiday, but me naming her Noelle had nothing to do with it... I'm starting to think she just likes telling that story."

Noelle's head bobbled in a dramatic nod, her ponytails bouncing. "I do. It's my favorite one to tell."

"Yeah, I bet," Patience muttered in return.

Michael couldn't help but laugh at the exchange. "Is Christmas *your* favorite holiday as well Noelle?"

Releasing her mother's hand, Noelle nodded. "Yes. Every year, we get matching pajamas and bake Christmas cookies. Then we have hot chocolate with marshmallows in it." She gestured to her mother. "Mommy doesn't like marshmallows, but she lets me put them in her cup anyway."

Humor resonated on Patience's face. Noelle was as chatty as ever.

"That sounds like a great time. I haven't done the 'matching pajama' thing, but I *do* like baking cookies, *and* I like hot chocolate." Michael eyed Patience, making a face. "We have the marshmallow thing in common, Patience."

Giggling, Patience winked at him. From what she could tell, Michael's nerves seemed to have dissipated. *This is going so well.*

Finally rising to his feet, Michael smoothed his hand down his shirt. "Your mom tells me that you two have been on a few picnics before, so we thought that the three of us could go on one *today*."

"We figured instead of staying in the house and talking, we can take advantage of this nice weather and picnic in the park," Patience followed up. "Are you okay with that, Bunny?"

Noelle grinned. "Yes."

Michael reached for the gift bag he'd brought in. "Before we head out, I have something for you Noelle."

Clasping her hands together, Noelle's eyes widened with anticipation. "Really?"

"Absolutely," Michael affirmed.

Patience leaned her head to the side, staring in wonder. She'd seen the bag when he'd brought it inside, but had no idea what was in it.

"I heard how fond you are about a certain animal." He reached inside the bag. "So, I figured…"

Noelle's mouth dropped open when she saw what Michael had pulled from the purple bag. "Ooooh, it's a rainbow sparkle bunny!" She reached for it as Michael handed it to her. "Thank you, thank you!"

"You're very welcome." The pure joy on the little girl's face warmed Michael's heart.

Patience was just as surprised as *Noelle* by the gift. Bringing a hand to her chest, she looked at Michael. "Michael, that's so sweet of you."

Blushing under Patience's adoring gaze, he placed his hand on his own chest. "It's not a problem."

Noelle was so occupied with smushing her face into the colorful, oversized, plush toy rabbit, that she completely missed the adults making googly eyes at one another. "It's so prettyyyy." Her voice was muffled by the fabric.

Shaking her head at the display, Patience touched Noelle's shoulder, bringing the cuddle fest to a halt. "Okay child, go put your new friend upstairs with the others, so we can get going."

"Can I bring her with me?" Noelle pleaded, brushing her hand over the ears.

Patience shot her a firm look. "No ma'am. You don't want it to get dirty. You just got it."

Pondering the explanation, Noelle's lips pursed. "Good point." She took off running for the stairs. "I'll be right back."

With Noelle out of sight, Patience closed the distance between herself and Michael, wrapping her arms around him. A silent gesture of gratitude, one that Michael practically melted under as he squeezed her back.

"Can I pick the spot in the park where we sit?"

Breaking the embrace, both Patience and Michael turned around to the sound of Noelle's voice echoing down the stairs. "Sure," Patience replied at the same time Michael said, "That's fine with me."

"Yay." Noelle skipped to the door, with an amused Patience and Michael close behind.

The breeze was light, the weather was warm, and the sun was brilliant—a perfect Saturday for a picnic in the park. Under a tree, Michael, Patience, and Noelle sat atop a checkered blanket. They had dined on homemade breaded chicken sandwiches with lettuce, tomatoes, and pickles on fresh brioche buns, potato chips, fruit salad, an assortment of cookies, and small bottles of water and juices as they sat, enjoying the pleasant atmosphere and each other's company.

Patience beamed, while Noelle sat back in her arms, gobbling down chips. The past hour and a half had made her heart swell. Michael had remained engaged, answering every question that Noelle threw at him with kindness and enthusiasm. Her daughter was being her normal bubbly self and seemed to take a liking to Michael. Their meeting had been everything Patience had hoped for.

Noelle fixed her inquisitive gaze upon Michael, who was drinking the last of his juice. "Mr. Michael, Mommy said that you build houses?"

Swallowing the last sip, Michael nodded. "Your mom is right; I do build houses for a living. I split time between running the construction company and doing the actual building," he replied. "I knew when I helped my father build a tree house at thirteen years old, that it was what I wanted to do when I grew up."

"That's so cool. Did you build *our* house?"

Patience let out a chuckle. "No, baby, he didn't build our

house," she stepped in. "If he *had*, I'm pretty sure we'd have a bigger kitchen."

Michael shot a breezy look at Patience. "I'm still waiting on you to allow me to remedy that for you, by the way."

A cheeky smirk forming, Patience simply shook her head at him. The silent gesture prompted a tickled Michael to put his hands up in surrender.

"But yeah Noelle, it's a pretty cool job. I still enjoy doing it after all these years," Michael directed back at the little girl.

Noelle patted her mother's hand, which was resting on her waist. A grin was forming. "Do you enjoy it as much as you enjoy hanging out with my *mom*?"

Putting a hand over her face, Patience shook her head. "Good Lord—" She lightly poked Noelle's arm, who in turn giggled. "Bunny, don't put him on the spot like that." She shot an apologetic look Michael's way. "You don't have to answer that, Michael."

"I have absolutely *no* problem answering it." Michael raised his knee, folding his hands over it. "There's no comparison between the joy I get from hanging out with your mom and work." He smiled. "Simply put, I enjoy being with her more."

Patience didn't speak, but the adoring stare she gave Michael said everything.

"Yeah, *I* like hanging with her too." Noelle took the last chip from the bowl. "She's pretty amazing."

Michael met Patience's eye. "Yes, she is."

Blushing under Michael's impassioned gaze, Patience brushed some of her hair away from her face as she broke eye contact. "You both do wonders for a girl's ego, I tell you," she coolly threw out. "And I'm lucky for it."

Michael winked at her. *I'm the lucky one.* "Okay so now that Noelle and I have embarrassed you with your well-deserved adoration, I think it's a good time to bring out the activity that I brought for us to do."

As Michael began to gather the empty containers from the blanket, Patience made a move to assist, but Michael placed a hand over hers, stopping her. "Sit back sweetheart, I've got it," he said.

Conceding, Patience relaxed while Michael gathered the mess, placing it back inside the picnic basket. Moving it aside, Michael seized the bag from where it sat, bringing it to the middle of the blanket under the curious gazes of his company.

"Are those more toys?" Noelle craned her neck, trying to get a peek inside the bag. "Or games?"

"Neither, but I think you'll enjoy it anyway." Reaching inside, Michael grimaced through a silent laugh. "I *hope* you will anyway."

Patience squinted. "What do you have up your sleeve, Carter?"

"Well..." Beaming, Michael pulled out three small canvases, followed by three easels. "Since you both love to draw, I figured we could have a little art session."

"Ooh yay!" Clapping her hands, Noelle surveyed the objects. "Mommy told you that I like art?"

"She did," Michael nodded. "In fact, she showed me one of your drawings. You're talented, Noelle."

Noelle smiled. "Thank you. Do *you* know how to draw?"

Michael shook his head with vigor. "Umm, no. But I'll happily embarrass myself today."

From the bag, he laid out paintbrushes, small bottles of paint in a variety of colors, brush cups, and miniature paint palettes.

When he looked up, Patience was leering at him. "Too much?" he whispered at her. He didn't want Patience to feel that he was trying too hard. He hoped that she knew he was being genuine.

Eyes locked with his, Patience shook her head no with a smile.

Michael's face flushed under her penetrating gaze. His heart was hammering in his chest.

"Do you have regular paint or watercolor?" Noelle asked, cutting the stare session between them short.

Michael picked up the small bottles, checking them for good

measure. "Umm, looks like I picked up acrylic paint." He looked up from the paint, question in his eyes. "Is that okay?"

"Oh, that's perfect." Patience reached for a brush. "Our favorite kind."

"I can't wait to put my new painting on my wall," Noelle sang, entering the house. She swiftly removed her shoes as Patience stepped in behind her, with Michael following. She turned to Patience, who'd just set her purse on the love seat. "Can you hang it for me?"

"Yes. Put it on your desk and I'll do it later," Patience promised. "Go get ready for your bath."

"Okay." Before retreating for the stairs, Noelle gave Michael a quick hug, one that he returned. "It was nice meeting you Mr. Michael."

"You too, Noelle." He waved as she darted up the staircase. When she was out of sight, he covered his mouth to stifle a yawn.

Patience smirked. "Tired you out, huh?" It had been a long day. Between the initial meeting, the three-hour picnic and painting session in the park, followed by a trip to the ice cream parlor, she didn't blame him.

Michael stretched. "Not at all, I'm good." He let his hands drop to his side. "I enjoyed myself today."

Patience's eyes sparkled as she stared at him. "Likewise." She folded her arms. "Are you going to hang *your* picture?"

Michael let out a laugh. "Nah, I think my sad attempt at a picnic basket will be better suited for the recycling." He shook his head. "I can paint the hell out of some walls, but I completely underestimated drawing objects freehand."

Patience tried to fight the building laughter, because Michael *did* give painting his best shot. But remembering the distorted, blotchy images, she folded. "I'm sorry." She put a hand to his chest as her laughter subsided. "Poor thing, it was a good effort."

"You don't have to lie just because you think I'm cute."

She gave his chest a playful poke. "Stop it."

Humor subsiding, Michael lightly touched Patience's hair, before moving in for an embrace. Holding her close, he leaned into her neck, inhaling her lavender noted fragrance. Patience held on tight, reluctant to let go.

Pulling back from their embrace, Patience's hands rested on his arms. "Thank you again for today."

"My pleasure." Michael gave her lips a kiss. "I'll see you later."

"Later. Be safe." Patience held her hand on the door as Michael left. Standing with the door cracked, she watched until he pulled off. Once he was out of sight, she locked up and leaned her forehead against it.

"Is Mr. Michael your boyfriend now?"

"Shit!" Patience spun around, finding Noelle sitting on the steps. Patience's eyes went wide. "How long were you there?" Had her little girl happened to see her and Michael kiss?

"I just came down when I heard the door open. I'm sorry for scaring you."

Hand to her heart, Patience gathered herself. "It's okay." She approached. "I thought I told you to get yourself ready for your bath."

Noelle pointed to the bathrobe in her hands. "I turned the bath water on, but the shower came on," she replied. "That's why I came down to get you."

Patience ran a hand over her face. She'd forgotten to turn the shower back to tub mode after getting out that morning. "Oh yeah," she rubbed the back of her neck. "I'll come up and fix it."

Noelle swung the belt of the robe back and forth. "So…is he your boyfriend now?"

Patience looked at her. That was a question that had been on her mind too. One she knew she needed to answer. "Well…" She rounded the staircase, taking a seat on the step next to her daughter. "It's something that he and I will talk about. But I feel that's where we're headed… How do you feel about that?"

"About you having Mr. Michael as your boyfriend?"

Patience nodded. "Yeah."

"I think it's cool." Noelle smiled. "You were right, he's nice… I like him."

Patience smiled back. "He liked you too. But I knew he would, because you're all sorts of amazing." She adjusted a bow around Noelle's ponytail. "It's always been just the two of us, you know."

Noelle fiddled with her robe. "I know."

"And now, it'll be this other person in our lives, and I just want to make sure you fully understand what that means," Patience tried to explain. "Especially if things *keep* progressing between he and I."

"You mean like if you get married?"

Patience rapidly blinked several times. "Umm…"

Noelle's head leaned slightly when her mother trailed off. "*Do* you think you'll get married?"

"Let's—let's just focus on one thing at a time, okay kid?" She patted Noelle's hand. "No, but seriously Bunny. He'll be around more, and it's important to me that you're okay with that."

Noelle nodded. "I'm okay with that Mommy, I promise." She touched Patience's arm, giving it a light squeeze. "Are *you* okay with that?"

Patience jerked her head back. Her daughter had caught her off guard, but Noelle made her ponder. She'd spent the last nine years of her life without a relationship. No man had even made her think *twice* about being in one—until Michael.

Though she'd been cautious in the beginning, Patience had reached a point where the feelings that she had for him were unlike anything she'd ever felt before.

A smile coming through, Patience let out a relaxed sigh. "Yes, I can honestly say that I am."

Chapter Twenty-One

"GIRL, I WISH YOU WOULD'VE been at that dinner party," Toni prattled between chews of her steak quesadilla. She sipped her iced tea to wash it down.

Patience picked up her slice of Mediterranean pizza. "Was it that bad?"

"*First* off, the company was horrible. Angela and Trevor have some of the *dullest* friends." Toni set her bottle back in place. "Not one damn laugh exchanged the entire freakin' night."

Though the dinner party had been over two weeks behind them, Toni had put off talking to Patience about it. She knew that her sister had other, more important things to deal with. Like introducing Michael and Noelle. Now that she knew it had gone smoothly, Toni felt it was a good time to spill details over lunch in her office.

Covering her mouth, Patience tried to force her laugh back down while chewing her food. "You're so damn rude," she said upon swallowing.

"They were *corny*. Rob and I were talking shit about them in code all night." Leaning back in her seat, Toni crossed her legs. "But I can't lie, the catering was good, the décor was immaculate, and Angie looked beautiful of course…ol' stank heffa."

Patience motioned her hand at Toni. "See? I knew you could pull something positive out of your ass." She smirked. "It's nice that you went. Good girl."

"Yeah, yeah." Toni flicked a sliver of pepper across her tray. "Still wished *you* would've been there though."

"Why? So I could've been bored to death *with* you? I appreciate the sentiment, but I was perfectly fine at home." Hearing a notification, Patience grabbed her phone from the desk.

Holding the last piece of quesadilla to her mouth, Toni observed the radiant smile forming on her sister's face as her fingers moved across the phone screen. "That's Michael, isn't it?" she assumed. "You don't even have to answer, I *know* it is. He's the only one who can get you to cheese that hard."

"Yes nosy, it's him." Patience set her phone down. "He's just confirming plans for our date Friday."

Toni quickly finished up the last of her lunch before wiping her hands with a napkin; she tossed it and the empty food container in the trash. "Where are you two going this time?"

"Well…I'm going to his house."

Toni's brows shot up. "Oh *really*?"

"Yeah. He wants to cook dinner for me."

"O-kay, a man who can *cook*." Toni snapped her fingers. "I love that. It's why I married Rob."

Patience stifled a chuckle. "Please, you married Rob because he's the only one who's willing to put up with your bullshit."

Toni made a face in retaliation. "That's just *one* of the reasons… bitch." She shook her head when Patience snickered. "Anyway, that's sweet. Cooking can be romantic, you know?"

Patience tilted her head. "*Can* it?"

"Oh absolutely." Toni leaned forward, eyes gleaming. "*And erotic. Especially* if he eats the food *off* you."

Patience stared blankly at Toni for several silent seconds. "I can think of *nothing* erotic about a piece of meat being eaten off of me."

A cackle erupted from Toni.

"Seriously, can you imagine someone trying to eat a rib and some macaroni and cheese off your damn back?" Seeing Toni doubled over, Patience couldn't help but laugh. "You *know* it sounds foolish and unnecessary."

"I was talking about *dessert*, Pace." Toni cleared her throat as her laughter dwindled. "And you *knew* that. You were just being a smart ass."

Crossing her arms, Patience just shrugged.

"So…" Toni folded her arms on the desk. "The big question… will you be spending the *night* after this home-cooked dinner?"

Patience stalled for a moment. "Maybe."

Toni's eyes blinked in rapid motion; she'd been expecting a hard no. "*Maybe?*"

"Maybe." Staying the night with Michael had been on Patience's mind since their date night in had been planned. Though Michael hadn't brought it up yet, she knew that should *she* bring it up, he wouldn't be opposed. "We'll cross that bridge when we get there."

"Well, since Rob and I are taking the girls to our beach house this weekend, you might as well spend the *weekend*." Toni grinned. "We'll be back Monday."

"Yeah, I'll keep that in mind," Patience replied. As Toni checked something on her laptop, Patience sat in silence. Her *thoughts* however, were far from quiet. She had something on her mind, something she was uncertain of, and it wasn't sex. "Sis, can I ask you something?"

"Sure." Toni turned away from the screen, giving Patience her attention. "What's up?"

Moving her hair behind her shoulder, Patience exhaled quickly. "How soon is too soon to…" Though the look on Toni's face showed that she was ready and willing to answer whatever the question was, Patience had second thoughts about asking it. "Umm…"

"How soon is too soon to what? Have *sex*?"

Eyes narrowed, Patience shook her hand in Toni's direction. "No, that's not what—"

"Or were you going to ask how soon was too soon to tell me you've already *had* it?" Toni cut in, eyes fixed in a stern stare.

221

The confusion was clear on Patience's face. "What the hell are you talking about?"

"Was it the night I took the girls to that movie?" Toni pointed a finger at her. "You told me that Michael put that desk together for you. Did he put something somewhere *else* afterwards?"

Patience's eyes expanded in amusement. "What?!"

"Yeah, you're not slick. I *knew* you weren't doing no fuckin' jumping jacks when I called."

Unable to hold it any longer, Patience busted out laughing.

Toni playfully tossed a balled-up napkin at her. "Come up with something *better* next time."

Knocking the tissue away from her, Patience rose from her seat, slinging her purse over her shoulder. "I don't have time for your foolishness. I have to get back to work."

Toni followed her progress to the door. "I *will* be calling you later to finish this conversation."

Patience yanked the door open. "And I'll be sure not to answer," she threw over her shoulder as she sauntered out.

Pulling the oven open, the delectable aromas hit Michael's face. Carefully, he removed the roasting pan from the rack, before closing the oven. Then he checked the contents simmering in the pots on the stovetop. Satisfied they were finished, he turned the burners off.

After racking his brain for days over what dish to prepare for Patience, Michael had settled on roasted duck breast over a creamy polenta, paired with roasted season vegetables as the entrée. It was the first time he'd attempted the dish, and he was pleased with the outcome.

He'd been on pins and needles for hours as he'd prepped and prepared the meal. Since his house was already spotless, he'd used the time while his entrée was in the oven to set the dinner table and get himself ready.

Giving the watch on his wrist a quick look, Michael rubbed

his chin. "Twenty minutes," he uttered aloud. The anticipation of knowing that Patience would soon be in his presence once again sent waves through his stomach. Putting a hand over it, he released a deep breath. *Focus Mike.*

Michael tossed the arugula starter salad in a homemade vinaigrette dressing, then covered it. Grabbing a torch lighter from a drawer, he headed to his glass enclosed deck and flicked a switch. The soft lighting from the string lights illuminated the room. Moving to the round dinner table set in the middle, he lit the two pilar candles and smaller tealight candles he'd previously arranged. Rotating the fresh floral arrangement in the middle one last time, he then adjusted the charger plates, cloth napkins, silverware, wine glasses and water glasses—and the flat square box that he'd set on the table earlier—ensuring that they were perfect. Stepping back, he assessed the space.

The open windows gave a full view of the manicured lawn of Michael's fenced in backyard, and the evening sky. The hanging potted plants added a nice feel to the already romantic area.

Checking his watch once more, he left the deck. Giving the entire downstairs a walkthrough, he ensured that everything was in place.

Patience had not seen the inside of Michael's house since he'd moved in; he had always gone to her house to pick her up for their outings. Though he had a bit more to do décor wise, he'd done plenty already and was excited for her to see it.

Sprinting up the steps, Michael entered his bedroom. Retrieving his pressed burgundy button-down shirt from a hanger, he slipped it on. After buttoning it, he gave himself several sprays of his favorite cologne. On his way out the room, he checked his appearance in the mirror, approving of the final look.

Once downstairs, he turned the stereo on with the remote, then adjusted the volume to a comfortable level. Old school R&B music filled the first floor. Humming along, Michael returned to the kitchen to begin carving the duck. Before he knew it, the doorbell rang.

Practically sprinting for it, Michael peered through the peephole. Smiling from ear to ear, he opened it. "Good evening," he crooned, stepping aside to let Patience enter. "You look beautiful as always."

Patience flashed him a seductive smile. "Thank you." The fabric of the spaghetti strap, pencil cut dress fell just above her knee, clinging to her body. The sunny yellow color complemented her shimmering skin. Running a hand over her flowing hair, she eyed his attire as he locked the door. "You don't look so bad yourself."

Spinning around to face her, his face flushed. "Thank you." Closing the distance between them, Michael opened his arms to embrace her. Instead, she held a bag up for him. "What's this?" he asked.

"Dessert."

Shaking his head, Michael let out a slight laugh. "I thought I said to just bring your*self*."

"I *heard* you say that, and I countered your request with a homemade chocolate cake." Patience removed the cake tray from the bag. Watching Michael's eyes light with hunger as he leered at the decadent chocolate drizzled bunt cake through the clear plastic top, her mouth curled into a smirk. "I take it you're glad I didn't listen, huh?"

"Oh, I sure am." He took the cake from her hands, then leaned in, placing a kiss on her glossed lips. "Stubborn ass."

His response drew a giggle from Patience, before her attention was captured by the living room's décor. "Oh wow, I love what you've done in here."

"Thank you. Would you like a tour of the rest of the house?"

"Absolutely I would." She flung her hair over her shoulders. "I never get to see the finished look after selling a house, so this is pretty exciting for me."

Setting the cake on the coffee table, Michael took her by the hand. "Then let's go."

Michael escorted Patience through the entirety of the living area, den, basement, and the upstairs. He showed her the remodeling he'd done—from the new paint choices, to the updated lighting fixtures and cabinet refacing he'd done in the master bath, to the shelving units he'd added.

"I'm impressed at how much you've made a move-in ready home look ten times better," Patience complimented, descending the stairs. "Your property value has already increased."

Trailing behind her, Michael smiled at her words. "I appreciate that. That means a lot coming from you." He made a beeline for the coffee table to retrieve the cake. "There's a few pieces that I still want to get for the den, and I'm also trying to decide what to do with the other guest room, but overall, I'm happy with how everything is coming together."

"You *should* be." Patience folded her arms. "Not only can you decorate, but you're also the most organized man I've ever met."

"Thank you. I'm sure my mother would be pleased to hear that at least *one* of her children picked up that trait."

Patience giggled. "Coming from someone who also has that trait and has passed it to my *own* child, I have no doubt she would be." As she followed Michael into the kitchen, the delicious aromas billowed towards her. "Whatever you've prepared smells amazing."

"Thank you." Putting a hand to the small of her back, Michael gestured his head towards the back door. "Come on, I'll show you to the table."

Noticing the direction of his motion, Patience pointed to the dining room on the opposite side. "We're not eating in here?"

A smile building, Michael shook his head. "You look nervous," he observed when she shot him a puzzled look.

Her eyebrow arched. "*Should* I be?"

"Not at all."

Yielding, Patience walked alongside Michael as he directed her to their eating area. Any question she may have had immediately flew out of the window once Patience set foot on the deck. Zoning in on the beautifully set table, she let out a soft exhale. The gleam in her eyes, the smile that lit her face, and the way she touched Michael's arm as he led her to the table spoke volumes.

Patience faced him. "You…have been *busy*," she said, earning a small laugh from Michael. "This is beautiful." It was clear to her just how much effort Michael had put into the evening.

"I'm happy you like it." Michael retrieved the box from the table. "Before I get the food, I have something that I want to give you."

Fixing her eyes on him, Patience tilted her head. *Yeah, I want you to give me something too.* "Do you?"

Peering at the box in his hand, Michael gestured to it with the other. "When I saw it, I thought of you… It reminded me of something you told me."

Patience didn't have a chance to ask, because Michael had opened it. Inside was an amethyst and diamond butterfly pendant, attached to a dainty white gold chain. "Oh my God," she gasped. Her eyes shot up, locking with *his*. "You remembered I like butterflies." Her voice was almost breathless.

"Yes," he murmured. "The way your face lit up when you told me about them is something I could never forget."

Patience found herself at a loss for words. For the life of her, she couldn't find the right ones to express just how much the gift meant to her. How much *he* meant to her.

As Michael removed the necklace from the box, Patience turned her back to him and lifted her hair, allowing him to secure the delicate chain around her neck.

Michael lightly brushed his hand across the fastened clasp, his fingers grazing her supple skin. He immediately imagined himself putting his lips to it. As she let her hair tumble down her back, he pictured himself running his hands through it. Eyes trailing down her back, the curves of her hips, her behind—all he could think about was stripping the dress from her body and finishing what they'd started in her living room.

Facing Michael, Patience brought her hand to her neck, touching her gift. Adoration filled her eyes as she finally formed something to say. "I love it, thank you."

"You're welcome." He'd barely gotten the words out before Patience pressed her lips to his, kissing him tenderly and sending a rush of heat through his body. Michael was so caught up in the moment—he nearly forgot about the food.

Snapping his eyes open, he pulled back, taking a breath. "I should probably fix the plates, huh?"

Patience grimaced. "Probably so."

Michael pulled her chair out, allowing her to sit before backing towards the entrance. "I'll get on that. Hang tight."

Patience followed his progress through the door, before turning her attention to the view outside. As she focused on the tree leaves swaying in the breeze, she couldn't help but be grateful that Michael had remembered the food, because *she'd* nearly lost all train of thought when her lips touched his again.

Before long, Michael reappeared with two plates in hand, a bottle of red wine tucked under his arm. "Here's your starter salad," he said, setting a plate in front of her. He set his own down, then held the bottle of cabernet sauvignon out for her to see. "Wine?"

"Please." Once the bottle was uncorked, Patience held her glass out for him.

He doled out a healthy measure to each of them. Sitting down across from her, Michael raised his glass. "To a beautiful date, and what I *pray* is a good meal."

A soft laugh escaped Patience as she raised her glass. "I devoured the sandwich you made for our picnic like it was my last meal. Trust me, you have nothing to worry about."

Michael let out a laugh before taking a sip of wine.

Michael's prayers were answered. Patience thoroughly enjoyed her dinner, and didn't hesitate to tell him how much as they settled into their normal date night routine. Through the starter salads and entrée, the pair talked, laughed, and flirted as they usually did.

At long last, Michael briefly retreated to the kitchen to retrieve dessert. As he prepared their final meal portion of the evening, he couldn't help but feel a twinge of nervousness seep in. Michael had something on his mind, in his *heart*. For a while now, he'd wanted to have a specific conversation with Patience, but knew it wasn't the right time before. However, from the moment this date had been planned, he knew this was it.

I'm really about to do this. Those words hammered in his head as he released a deep breath. Grabbing the bowls from the counter, he headed back to the deck.

Patience took another sip of wine as Michael entered the room with dessert: her homemade cake paired with a scoop of vanilla ice cream.

He set a bowl in front of Patience. "I warmed the cake up a bit."

"Perfect," she replied, eyeing the bowl's contents.

Michael took his seat, picking up his spoon. Patience watched in anticipation as he scooped a healthy serving. His eyes were practically rolling in the back of his head as the rich, decadent cake melted into his mouth, Michael leaned back in his seat. "This cake is *so* good."

Patience did a happy dance in her chair. "Success," she sang.

"Seriously, it's amazing." He ate another scoop.

"Thank you, thank you." She playfully bowed her head forward. "Not going to lie, making that had my pressure up."

He shot an amused look her way. "Why?"

"As *much* as you love chocolate? Yeah, I was determined to make this thing perfect."

He chuckled. "I promise I would've liked it either way."

Patience scooped a piece of cake, followed by a bit of ice cream. "Smart answer."

Letting out a subtle laugh, Michael ate another piece.

As they polished off the dessert in comfortable silence, Michael felt flutters in his stomach. The feeling only intensified when he looked up at Patience, whose attention was on the scenery just beyond the glass. *I need to bring this up before I lose my nerve.* Setting his spoon in the empty bowl, he rested his hands on the table. "Patience," he called, voice low, deep.

Patience's eyes shifted to him. "Yes?"

"I think it's time we talk."

Her body stiffened. *Oh shit. What's wrong?* Luckily the calmness on her face didn't allude to her inner panic. "Talk about what?"

Michael stalled, trying to keep his nerves at bay. "About... where this thing between us is going."

Ooooh. Pushing her empty bowl aside, Patience inhaled deeply before expelling the breath. "Okay."

"We've been seeing each other exclusively for three months, and things have been going great—" Michael put a hand to his chest. "*I* believe they have, anyway."

"They have," Patience agreed.

"And given that...while I've been happy dating you, I no longer want to *just* date you."

Patience just sat there, eyeing Michael attentively as he spoke.

"I'm ready to be in a relationship Patience...with you."

Feeling her heart begin to nervously race, Patience tried to keep herself contained. "Are you sure?" As soon as the words left her mouth, Patience felt like smacking herself. *Yeah, like he hasn't been showing you that's what he wants all this time.*

Michael, however, was unfazed by the question. "I'm sure. I don't need to test any waters. I don't need to see what else is out there—I know what I want Patience, and it's you." He gazed into her eyes, the light of the candles reflecting between them. "I have deep feelings for you, and I want to *be* with you."

Patience didn't speak, instead she glanced off to the side,

replaying Michael's words in her head. For little did Michael know, she felt the exact same way. The idea of solidifying their relationship had been heavy on her mind, and if he hadn't brought it up, *she* would have. *This is really happening.* Both excitement and anxiety consumed her at the reality of entering another romance, after all this time. Nevertheless, there was no doubt in her mind that she was ready to take this next step with him. Patience faced him. "Okay… you have me."

Michael stared at her in disbelief. "You're serious?"

"I'm serious." Bringing her hand to her neck, she fondled her necklace. "I have feelings for you too Michael. And while you were… *unexpected.* You've become someone I can't see myself without."

Michael's smile could have lit the entire neighborhood. He couldn't have asked for a better end to this date, or a better woman than the one who was sitting across from him. "I feel the exact same way."

Chapter Twenty-Two

LOADING THE DISHWASHER, MICHAEL PEERED over at Patience as she rinsed a plate in the sink. "Sweetheart, you don't need to help me clean up. Go ahead and relax."

"I know I don't need to. I *want* to." She handed the plate to him, then lightly nudged him with her shoulder. "So just hush and let me."

Michael dipped his head at her in acceptance, humor on his face. "Whatever you say." Closing the dishwasher, he grinned at her. "I *do* appreciate the help though…*and you.*"

Turning the water off, she smirked. "I know." Not more than twenty minutes after their dessert and their heartfelt conversation, the couple were in the kitchen tidying up.

As Patience wiped down the countertops and Michael put the leftover food in containers, the R&B music continued to play in the background. Hearing a familiar song, Patience paused her task. "Can you turn that up a bit?"

Michael glanced at her. "What, the song?"

"Yes."

Placing the lid on a container, Michael grabbed the speaker remote from the counter, increasing the volume.

"Oh my God, I haven't heard this in years," Patience mused of the smooth tune. She rinsed the dishrag out, then hung it on the faucet. "This is still one of my all-time favorites. I used to play this all day, every day in high school."

"Yeah, I remember blasting this while driving to school in my raggedy car." The memory drew an inward laugh from Michael as he placed the last of the food containers in the refrigerator. "The radio was the best thing *in* that piece of shit."

Patience's soft laughter filled the room. "Well, you've certainly upgraded since then."

"Indeed." Michael watched her sway to the music. Approaching her, he held his hand out. "Dance with me."

She smiled at him. "Love to." Placing her hand in his, she allowed him to pull her close. She put her arms around his neck as he wrapped his around her waist. Slowly, they danced.

Patience rested her head on Michael's shoulder as he buried his face in her neck. She closed her eyes, only to snap them back open when she heard Michael's baritone voice softly singing along. Her eyes broadened; he sounded *good.*

"Wait—wait just one damn minute." She pulled her head back, prompting him to do the same.

He stared at her, eyes crinkling in amusement. "What?"

"I didn't know you could sing!"

Michael shrugged. "I call it carrying a slight tune."

She playfully tapped his chest. "Well, you sound good. Like you could've been on this *record* good."

"I'll surely take that. Thank you."

"You *better* because it's the truth." Returning her head to his shoulder, Patience chuckled when he resumed his singing. "Careful now, I just might make you sing me to sleep."

Michael's hand caressed her back as they rocked. "If it'll make you happy, I'll do it."

"You say that *now*, but when I call you every night to actually *do* it, you'll change your tune."

Michael pulled his head back once more, looking into her eyes. "If it'll make you happy...I'll *do* it." His tone was low, soothing.

Succumbing to Patience's tender stare, Michael emitted a light, shaky breath. "I love you."

Eyes wide, Patience's breath became trapped in her chest. *Wait what? He said what?!* "What did you say?" she breathed out finally.

Michael stood unwavering, arms still secure around her waist. He'd spoken the words; the words he'd been holding in for weeks. The ones he had tried to talk himself out of admitting, for fear of scaring her off. He'd questioned them the moment those feelings had arrived. Wondering if he was falling too fast, wondering if she was even close to feeling the same. But as he stood there in his home with her in his arms, looking into her beautiful eyes, all his questions flew out the window. There was no doubt. He knew. "I said that I love you... I'm in love with you."

Patience stood still, eyes shifting as she processed what she'd just heard. The music that had filled her ears moments ago was replaced with the sound of her own breathing. *I wasn't hearing things. He said it. He said that he loves me—Michael loves me.*

"Patience," Michael softly called, prompting her to look him in the eye. "Does that scare you?"

Eyes transfixed on him for a moment, Patience lightly shook her head. "No, it doesn't scare me." Her voice was almost at a whisper. "Because...I love you too."

Michael blinked several times. "You do?"

"Yes." Patience knew that her feelings had been growing deeper for Michael over the past weeks. She knew that what she was feeling wasn't just infatuation. Yet she still questioned it.

It had taken her over a year to feel like she'd loved her ex, and yet with Michael it had only been a few months. But him professing *his* love, knowing that he felt the same...she'd found her answer. This man had unexpectedly seized her heart and finally she could allow herself to accept it.

Michael stared at her with longing. He couldn't believe it; this was real. It was like he was in a dream, one that he didn't want to wake up from.

Patience brought her hand to his face and Michael covered it with his. When he leaned in, she lifted her chin, meeting his lips with hers. The sensual kiss swiftly deepened as Michael held her. Enveloping her arms around his neck, she returned it with equal passion.

Unlike the last time they'd shared a kiss this intense, there were no chance of interruptions.

Michael moved his lips to her neck and Patience closed her eyes, tilting her head back to allow him more access. Her body temperature elevated, and her breath became shallow as his kisses moved to her collarbone.

Michael felt himself rise against Patience as his hands roamed over her, aching to touch beneath her dress. Slowly, he backed her against the counter island. Before Patience could react, he lifted her up onto the countertop, bringing her at eye level. He kissed her lips again, before moving back to her neck.

Bracing herself on the counter with one hand, Patience grabbed hold of Michael's shirt with the other as his lips traveled to the swell of her breasts, just under the neckline of her dress. She felt his tongue brush across the top, then he stopped. She opened her eyes just as he brought his lips back to hers.

He kissed her softly, then cupped her face in his hands. "Do you want me to keep going?" he breathed against her lips.

Patience grabbed his hands. Closing her eyes, she nodded.

"Tell me." A hand traveled down the front of her dress. "Tell me to keep going."

She felt his fingers brush against her thigh, sending tingles racing through her body. "Keep going."

With her permission secured, Michael kissed her neck, trailing down to her chest. Patience grabbed at the buttons of his shirt, which he aided in unfastening. Eyeing his broad bare chest, Patience reached out, caressing it with her soft fingers.

Michael lowered the straps of her dress, letting them fall at her arms, revealing her flesh-toned lace strapless bra. He lustfully eyed her hardened nipples through the fabric, before brushing one with his tongue, making Patience gasp.

Michael unhooked the bra with one hand, pulling it down and away from her body with the other. He kissed her skin, taking her breast into his mouth.

As his mouth worked over her, Patience's breath quickened, until she finally let a moan escape her lips. She ran her hand over his head. "Keep going," she begged.

Michael's lips journeyed down the dress fabric until he reached the bottom hem. As he kissed her thigh, Patience stretched her legs for him. Michael gripped her, pulling her closer to the edge.

Shutting her eyes, Patience held her breath in anticipation, until she felt Michael's lips brush against her inner thighs. Softly, he kissed her skin through the dainty fabric of her lace panties, before his fingers slipped under the band. When he moved them to the side, she felt his tongue touch her heated flesh and drew in a sharp breath. Clutching the edge of the counter, she panted softly as his tongue flicked against her.

Michael took his time getting her acclimated to his tongue. The sounds of pleasure that were coming from the woman who'd consumed his thoughts and his heart, was exhilarating. He could stay in this moment forever.

The fantasies Patience had about Michael pleasing her, failed in comparison to the real thing. He went from flicking against her to pressing his tongue closer, giving her deliberate, intense, steady licks. Feeling a climax steadily building, Patience clutched the back of Michael's head with her hand. "Keep go—God," she moaned out as her body was overcome with an intense orgasm that left her legs shaking, and her body wanting to go limp.

Michael kissed her inner thighs before standing up. He wrapped his arms around Patience's waist, pulling her to him to steady her. He gently caressed her face as she finally opened her eyes, meeting his gaze. The look on her face was almost as if she was in shock as she tried to catch her breath.

Oh my God, what the fuck? Patience thought as she stared at him. Though she'd experienced oral on several occasions—having it done to her on a *countertop* was a first. And so was an orgasm *that* intense.

Michael stroked her hair. "Are you okay?"

Still trying to regulate her breathing, Patience nodded.

Michael stared into her eyes. He'd finally tasted her, and now he wanted *all* of her. "Stay with me tonight." It was more of a question than a command.

Patience felt her body heat up all over again. She eagerly nodded. "Yes."

Michael kissed her cheek, before lifting her from the counter with one swift motion. Patience wrapped her arms and legs around him as Michael carefully, and effortlessly, carried her through the living room and upstairs.

Entering his bedroom illuminated only by the moonlight, Michael pulled back the covers and laid Patience down on the king-sized bed. He removed her clothes, and she helped him out of his. Tossing the articles aside, Michael loomed over her. Taking his time, he attentively explored her entire body, kissing her, caressing every inch of her. He familiarized himself with every curve, taking note of the spots that made her gasp and moan.

Patience ran her hands down Michael's back, soft moans escaping her lips as his tongue and mouth worked over each nipple. She couldn't remember the last time she'd experienced this much pleasure, and he hadn't even entered her yet.

Michael trailed down her body, his head reclaiming its position back between her legs. He secured her hips with his arms as he pleased her with his attentive tongue for the second time.

Patience held the sheet beneath her in a vice grip. Her moans growing louder, her back arching and hips raising, she pressed Michael's face closer. Patience felt like the soul was leaving her body as he brought her to yet another explosive climax.

As Patience caught her breath, Michael kissed up her body. Reaching into the drawer of his nightstand, he pulled out a foil packet.

Opening her eyes, she watched him roll the barrier over his erection. Her breath stalled as her eyes fixed on him, mesmerized. Feeling him through the fabric of their clothing was one thing, *seeing* him—*all* of him was another. It had been years since she'd had sex, and as much as she wanted him, she was starting to wonder if she'd be able to *take* him without being uncomfortable. She threw her reservations out of the window when he pressed his body down on her.

He kissed her lips as he positioned himself, then gently pushed inside. Hearing the gasp that left her mouth, and feeling her body tense, Michael paused. Eyeing her with concern, he asked, "You okay baby?"

"Yes...don't stop."

Michael held her hips as he carefully guided himself inside of her, filling her to the brim. He closed his eyes and held still for a moment, allowing her to adjust to him, and allowing *him* to focus. To focus on the wetness bathing him, the tightness around him. Then gently, he began moving his hips.

Patience squeezed her eyes tight, holding onto Michael as he moved inside of her. The feeling was so intense, yet felt so good, that she was holding her breath.

Feeling her body tense once again, Michael opened his eyes, focusing. Noticing both the look of pleasure and pain on her glistening face, Michael halted his movement, holding steady.

When Michael touched her face, Patience's eyes fluttered open.

"Breathe," he crooned against her lips, causing her to immediately release her breath. He moved his hips, plunging a long stroke deep into her body, causing her to suck in another breath. He softly kissed her parted lips. "Breathe baby."

Opening fully to him, Patience let out whimpers of pleasure as Michael laid claim to her body. She took everything that he gave, and her body was responding with all-consuming pleasure. She didn't know how much longer she'd be able to hold on without succumbing to another release.

The sounds of ecstasy from both filled the room as their relationship moved to a new level.

Taking hold of one of Patience's hands, Michael's fingers linked with hers as he quickened his thrusts. Being with her was everything that he'd imagined and more. He groaned against her neck as he clung to the sheets, the two of them moving in sync.

Tightening her free arm around Michael's back, Patience's back arched as she came for a third time that night, releasing her cries into the air.

Hearing her voice against his ear and feeling her constrict around him, Michael found it impossible to hold on. Succumbing, he erupted inside of her before collapsing onto her body.

Fingers twined, they lay together as they caught their breath.

Finally lifting his head, Michael moved the tousled hair from Patience's face. Staring into her half-lidded eyes, her flushed face, full lips—she was breathtaking. And when she smiled at him, his heart melted. *There's no doubt in my mind how much I love her.*

Rolling off her onto his back, Michael pulled Patience to him. As she lay on his chest, Michael covered them with the blanket and kissed her forehead.

In each other's arms, they drifted off into a satisfied slumber.

Chapter Twenty-Three

THE SUN PEEKING THROUGH THE sheer curtain woke Patience from her restful sleep. She blinked several times to adjust her eyes before stretching. Glancing over, she found the spot where Michael had slept the night before to be empty. However, the subtle movement she heard from downstairs through the cracked door alluded to where he was.

Rolling over on her back, Patience held the covers close to her naked body. Staring at the ceiling, she replayed every single moment from the previous evening. From the romantic dinner to solidifying their relationship, to the confessions of love, to the night of long-awaited passion, to falling asleep secure in Michael's arms.

Recalling every explicit detail of their sexual encounter sent a pleasure-filled ache surging through her. Then when she shifted her position, Patience felt *another* ache which was yet *another* reminder of their tryst. *Yeeaaahhh, that's not shocking.* Patience had no doubts that her body would soon become accustomed to the well-endowed Michael.

Sitting up, she surveyed the room, lingering on their discarded clothing scattered along the floor. Patience was grateful that her intuition had told her to pack a "just in case" overnight bag, which was still in the trunk of the car.

Pushing the comforter back, she gingerly got out of bed.

Michael, clad in a pair of lounge shorts, was preparing breakfast.

He'd awaken nearly an hour ago, feeling like he was still in a fantasy. Seeing Patience sleeping soundly beside him, he was reminded once again that his dream had become his reality. If it weren't for his full bladder forcing him out of bed, he would've stayed.

As he mixed the blueberry pancake batter, the sound of light footsteps above him drew a smile. *She's awake.*

Patience moved down the hallway, last night's dress held to her body by her hand. Nearing the staircase, she stood just out of the line of sight. "Michael?"

Pausing his task, Michael swiftly moved to the living room. He stood at the bottom of the staircase, peering up in hopes of getting a look at her; yet he didn't. "Yes?"

"Can you do me a favor, please?"

Michael folded his arms over his bare chest. "Anything."

"I have an overnight bag in the trunk of my car—" She cleared the hoarseness from her throat. "Can you get it for me please?"

"Of course I can—" When she cleared her throat again, Michael's forehead creased with concern. "Are you okay?"

Face flushing, Patience scratched her head. "Yeah, my throat is just a little scratchy. It isn't used to being so loud— Umm, yeah, my keys are in my purse on the couch."

A flush of warmth shot through Michael. The reminder of the gratifying sounds that Patience had made in the height of pleasure threatened to stir him right then and there if he didn't move. "You got it. I'll be right back with your things."

Retrieving the lavender bag from the car, Michael brought it inside and carried it upstairs. He knocked on the closed door. "I have your bag."

The door cracked open, and Patience's arm shot out. "Thank you."

Michael placed the bag in her open hand. "You're welcome." Rubbing his chin, he smirked at the blatant display of "morning after" shyness. "Patience, you *do* remember that I've already seen you naked, right?"

"Trust me, I remember that and everything *else*. Go busy yourself please."

Her lighthearted command tickled Michael. "Yes ma'am," He adjusted the string of his shorts. "I'm preparing breakfast, so come down whenever you're ready, okay?"

"I will."

Michael trotted back downstairs to resume the task of cooking.

Patience took her time getting herself together: taking a soothing bath, doing her skincare routine, brushing her teeth, and moisturizing her body. Throwing on her cotton shorts and matching short-sleeved top, she fluffed her hair then left the bedroom.

Descending the staircase, she was greeted by smooth jazz music and the sweet smell of food. Standing at the kitchen entrance, she watched as Michael carefully plated their breakfast. Although she was famished and couldn't wait to eat, her stomach rumbles failed in comparison to the beating in her chest as she held her adoring eyes on him.

Snapping out of her trance, Patience entered the kitchen. "Morning," she said, voice soft.

Michael looked over at her, a loving smile crossed his face. She was even more radiant than usual, almost as if she had a glow. "Good morning." Setting the prepared plates on the counter, he closed the distance between them, enveloping her in an embrace.

Patience clung to him, inhaling his fresh scent. Pulling back, she allowed the tender, intimate kiss that he bestowed upon her.

"How did you sleep?" he asked.

"Well, thank you." She ran her fingertips across his chest. "You?"

"Same. Best sleep of my life." Michael placed a kiss on Patience's cheek as she blushed under his yearning gaze. *If I don't go get these plates now, I'm going to make her my breakfast.* "I made blueberry pancakes, eggs and beef bacon. Coffee just finished brewing."

"Sounds great. Can we eat out on the patio again?"

"Of course we can. The table is still out there." Grabbing their plates from the counter, Michael took them to the table as Patience promptly prepared cups of coffee for them both.

As the summer sun shined through the windows, Patience and Michael ate their breakfast in calming silence in between sips of coffee.

Tapping her fork on the empty plate, Patience stared down at the streaks of leftover syrup as her mind raced. "So, we're really doing this, huh?" she said.

"What do you mean?"

"This relationship—you being my boyfriend, me your girlfriend." Her eyes rose, locking with Michael's. "We're doing this right?"

Michael gave a nod. "We are. I meant everything I said to you last night, Patience. I love you and I want this." His head leaned to the side as a thought infiltrated his mind. "That is… unless you've changed your mind."

Reaching out, Patience touched his hand on the table. "No, no I haven't. I love you too, that's not why I brought it up." Her shoulders lifted then fell in a subtle shrug. "I guess me saying it out loud just makes it a bigger reality for me you know? Not that last night *didn't*—"

"I understand what you mean. I woke up in a dreamlike state *myself*, so I get it. We took a couple huge steps last night. Which I have zero regrets about."

Trust me, neither do I. "Yeah, we did." She gestured her head to the kitchen. "Including one that happened on that counter in there."

A smirk forming, Michael rubbed his chin. "Trust me, I can take *that* step and the other, all *over* this house and anywhere *else* you want it."

Face flushing, Patience squeezed her thighs together to put an ease to the throb. She cleared her throat. "Yeah, I'll umm…take you up on that."

Placing his hand over hers with a warm squeeze, a seriousness came over Michael. While he had every intention of making good on that promise, he had an idea what Patience in this moment needed even more. "Listen baby, I know that neither of us expected this to happen—if my normal routine had gone as planned that day months ago, I wouldn't have had the pleasure of meeting you. But I'm happy I did… I'm *grateful* that it happened and that we've gotten to this point. I'm in it for the long haul with you."

Patience released a relaxed breath. Michael's confession was hugging her like a warm, secure blanket, reassuring her feelings were mutual. "Me too, Michael."

Placing a kiss to her hand before releasing it, Michael retrieved his half-empty coffee mug. He raised it to her with a grin on his face and a gleam in his eye. "To riding the bike."

Patience giggled. Raising her own mug, she tapped it to his. "To riding the bike."

Chapter Twenty-Four

PATIENCE MANEUVERED HER CAR DOWN the street en route to Noelle's school. "Do you know what you want to do for your upcoming art project?"

Zipping her bookbag, Noelle peered at her mother from the backseat. "No, not yet."

"That's fine. Just let me know when you do, so I can get the supplies."

"I will." Noelle watched the passing snow-dusted scenery out the window, as her mother drove her to school that Friday morning. "Ms. Janet said that the top graded projects will be entered into this year's art fair."

Patience's eyes brightened as she glanced at Noelle through the rearview mirror. "Really?" She smiled when Noelle nodded. "That's exciting. Though I'll be proud of you no matter what, I have no doubt yours will be included, and I'll be there, right in front."

Flashing a wide grin back, Noelle twirled a braid around her finger. "If I get to go, do you think Mr. Michael will come too?"

"Of *course* he will." Patience's voice radiated with confidence. "He'd love it."

It had been eight months since Patience and Michael's relationship had become official, and it had been everything Patience had hoped it would be. Not *only* was Michael the ideal partner for *her*, he'd become a wonderful father figure to Noelle as well. One that Noelle seemed genuinely happy to have.

Pulling up to the building, Patience parked, turning around in her seat to face Noelle. "You got everything?"

"Yes." Undoing her seat belt, Noelle grabbed her bookbag. "Oh, I almost forgot to ask you if I can start taking the bus to school?"

Bewildered by the question, Patience leaned her head to the side. "Why? You don't like riding with me anymore?"

"I do, but now that I'm nine, I think it's time I ride to school with my friends."

Patience's eyes became slits. "You *just* turned nine *three weeks* ago." She shook her head when Noelle's giggle was followed by a shrug. "I'll think about it. Now get inside."

Adjusting the knit hat on her head, Noelle leaned forward, giving her mother a peck on her cheek. "See you later."

"See you. Have a good day at school. Love you."

Noelle waved. "Love you too. Have a nice day off."

"I will." Patience watched Noelle disappear through the school's doors before pulling off.

The central heat hit Patience as she entered her home, thawing her out. In the short walk from her car to her front door, the frigid February weather had chilled her to the bone.

Removing her coat and boots, she put both in the closet and headed straight for the couch, plopping down on the cushions. Grabbing the remote, she flipped the television on as she rested her head against the decorative throw pillows. She planned to take full advantage of the free morning by lounging and watching her favorite morning shows.

She was twenty minutes into the game show before her cell rang. Scooping it up from the coffee table, she answered. "Hey T."

"Hey sis, I'm sure you're back in bed—"

"No, I'm just chillin' on the couch, watching TV," Patience cut in, twisting strands of hair around her finger. "What's up?"

"Oh. Well, I'm just calling to see if we're still on for tomorrow."

Patience rolled her eyes. "You mean taking the three-hour drive back to Mom's house in the middle of winter, because big sis decided after all these years that she wants to sell it and needs us there to take inventory of what needs to be removed?" She pulled her feet up on the couch. "Yes, we're still on."

"Her petty ass won't so much as let us step *foot* in there without her, now she's just willing to hand it over to some *stranger*?" A sigh emitted from Toni. "I'm not going to lie, I at *least* hoped she'd pass it down to the girls, or her *own* child should she ever decide to have one. I mean, times may not have always been good there, but it was still part of our lives, and I'd hate to see it go."

"Yeah, well Mom left the house solely to Angie when she died, so neither you *nor* I have any say so in what she does with it." Patience examined her manicured nails. "Though for the record, I don't want her to sell it either."

"Hmm, maybe *she* could move back there, should she ever get sick of Trevor's ass and leave him," Toni sneered.

Rubbing between her eyes with two fingers, Patience shook her head. "Toni—"

"I know, I know you don't have to say it. I took it too far."

"Well, at least you admitted it this time." Patience stretched her free arm. "Anyway, I'll meet you at your house tomorrow by ten."

"Sounds like a long ass day, but a plan." Shuffling of papers resonated through the phone. "Enjoy your day off and yes, I'm jealous. It's tax season, so my ass is being taken through the ringer. Damn near every client has been stressing me out...except your man, of course. He has his shit together."

Patience chuckled a bit. "He'd be happy to hear that."

"When is he getting back in town?"

Releasing a sigh, Patience eyed the framed photo of him

and her on the end table. "Late tonight. His flight is supposed to get in around ten-thirty or so." Michael had been out of town on business for the past week, and to say that she missed him was an understatement. Shifting her gaze to the roses blooming in a vase next to the photo, Patience's lips formed a pout. "He's so sweet. Even though he's been gone, he still had flowers sent to me."

Toni scoffed. "Yeah, rub in the fact that you still get flowers every week."

"Don't do that, Rob still does sweet things for you even after all these years," Patience reminded, humored.

"I know, I'm just mad I'm at work and needed something to bitch about. Anyway, I'll talk to you later."

"Bye." Ending the call, Patience tossed the phone down on the couch, before returning her attention to the show.

Stepping off the plane, Michael walked down the corridor. Slinging his carry-on bag over his shoulder, he stretched his neck from side to side as he passed through the terminal, en route to baggage claim.

Checking his watch, he took note of the eleven thirty-five a.m. time. The flight from Chicago had been quick, and though he'd had a productive time during the weeklong business conference, Michael was elated when the plane's wheels touched down in Virginia.

Grabbing his suitcase from the turnstile, Michael made a hasty retreat out the glass doors to the parking garage. Once he'd loaded his bags into his car, he slipped inside and pressed start. He adjusted the heat before making a call.

"Hey you," Patience answered.

Her sultry voice drew a smile from Michael. It was one he never got tired of hearing. "Hey baby."

"I wasn't expecting to hear from you again until later," she said. "The session ended early today?" During the past week, Patience had gotten accustomed to talking to Michael during certain times of the day, due to his hectic conference schedule.

"Yeah, since it's Friday they cut the morning session short." Activating the blue tooth in his car, Michael put the phone in the holder, before pulling out of the parking spot. "We'll pick up later for the afternoon session as normal."

"Oh okay…I miss you."

His heart jumped. "I miss you too. More than you know." Stopping at the parking booth, Michael quickly paid the fee. "Are you enjoying your day off? Are you out, or did you decide to stay in?"

"Yeah, it's fine so far, I'm home. Came right back after I dropped Noelle off at school. It's too damn cold to do anything outside."

Michael chuckled as he pulled out of the garage. "Yeah, I don't blame you. It's freezing here too." *I'll be there to warm you up soon enough.* "Yesterday it was so cold here—what the fuck?" Michael slammed his hand on the horn at a reckless driver who was trying to squeeze into his lane, nearly sideswiping him. Glaring at the car, it swerved away from him.

"What's wrong?" Patience charged. "Was that a car horn?"

He grimaced. *Shit.* "Nothing, everything's fine, and no— Listen honey, someone is trying to get my attention," he stammered. "I'll call you back as soon as I can, okay? I love you."

"Okay. I love you too."

Michael released a deep breath as the call dropped. Maneuvering his vehicle into the next lane over, he prayed for traveling mercy while on his way to his destination.

Putting the finishing touches on her sandwich, Patience took her plate and glass of lemonade to the living room. Having had enough of the TV, she'd decided to read a few chapters from her current book selection, until hunger pangs sent her into the kitchen for a midday meal.

Visit the Cafe!

Now through 5/31/2024

Buy 1
Fresh Baked Cookie
Get 50% OFF a
2nd Cookie

Mix or Match any flavor!!!

See Cafe for details.

Reclaiming her position on the couch, she set her frosted glass on the end table and the plate on her lap. Retrieving the book from the couch, she held it to her face with one hand, while her other reached for the sandwich.

Her escape into the pages of a mystery novel was brought to an abrupt halt when her doorbell rang. Setting both plate and book aside, Patience gave the door a curious side-eye. Her daughter was in school, her boyfriend was still out of town, and her sister—the one she got along with—was at work. She had *no* idea who the unexpected visitor could be.

Rising from the couch, Patience smoothed her hand down her sweater as she advanced to the door. Peering out of the peephole, she let out a gasp of delight. Snatching open the door, she came face-to-face with a welcomed surprise. "Hi you."

Grinning from ear to ear, Michael entered the house. "Hi baby." Shrouding Patience in his arms, he lifted her in a hug, simultaneously shutting the door with his foot.

Patience tightened her grip around him. "What are you doing here? I wasn't expecting you back until later tonight."

"The conference wrapped last night." Michael set her down, but he still hadn't let go. "They wanted to use these last few hours to go bar hopping or do *whatever* it is they planned on doing, and I was like hell no I need to get home."

Patience giggled.

"I booked the first flight out for this morning as soon as I got back to the room." He softly brushed her jawline with the back of his hand. "Left the airport and came straight here…I wanted to surprise you."

Patience flashed a dazzling smile at him. Running her hands up his chest, she brought them to his shoulders. "You've succeeded. I'm happy to see you."

Michael grinned, his hungry eyes leering at her. "Yeah?"

"Umm hmm." Eyes drawing to his full lips, Patience pressed

her lips to them, igniting a searing, passionate kiss that sent tingles through her body. To avoid stripping him right there at the door, she placed a hand on his chest, pulling her head back. "You hungry?" she panted.

Still holding her close, Michael drew his bottom lip between his teeth. "You have *no* idea."

Recognizing the ravenous look on his face, Patience's mouth dropped open. "That's *not* what I *meant*." She playfully slapped his chest when he busted out laughing. "Nasty."

"You love it though."

Her eyes trailed down his jeans, lingering on the imprint she'd become all too familiar with. "Umm hmm." Snapping out of her own erotic thoughts, she broke from him. "You said you came straight from the airport. Did you eat anything? Do you want me to make you something?"

Michael removed his coat, hanging it in the closet. "Now that you mention it, all I had was a bagel before getting on the plane." He rubbed the back of his head. "*Speaking* of the plane, I need to wash it *off* of me."

Patience emitted an inaudible laugh. "Yeah, I don't blame you." She crossed the living room heading for the kitchen. "Go get in the shower and I'll make you something to eat."

Shooting a look of gratitude her way, Michael backed towards the stairs. "I appreciate you."

"I know you do," she threw over her shoulder.

Fresh from his invigorating shower, with a towel secured around his waist, Michael entered Patience's bedroom. Pulling open a dresser drawer, he retrieved a few clothing items which Patience kept at her house for him—a pair of boxers, sweatpants, and t-shirt. A knock sounded on the door just as he set the items on the bed. "Yes?"

"Are you dressed?" Patience asked.

Michael eyed the door, a hint of amusement on his face. "No, but don't let that stop you from coming in. There's nothing in here you haven't seen."

Opening the door, Patience made a face at him as she walked in. "Very funny."

Letting out a subtle laugh, Michael placed a hand to his chest. "Don't mind me, I'm just teasing."

"Yeah, yeah." Closing the door, Patience rested her back against it. "I didn't come up to rush you. I wanted to tell you that your lunch is ready—it's a turkey and cheese panini with some leftover tomato soup that I made last night."

"That's sounds great." Though Michael's lips were moving, his eyes were steady on Patience, taking in everything about her. As if he was reminding himself that the woman before him was real, that she was his, that these past months with her weren't a dream.

"I can bring your food up here if you want," Patience said. When he didn't answer her, she leaned her head to the side, arching an eyebrow. "Michael."

His movement shifted slightly, eyes gradually traveling up and down her body. "Yes?"

"Are you okay?"

Michael approached her. "Umm hmm." As the distance between them became shorter, food became a non-factor. There was something else *far* more satisfying that he wanted.

Standing before her, Michael cupped her face with his hands and sensually worshipped her lips with his.

Patience's hands ran up Michael's bare chest as the kiss intensified. His body grinded against hers as his hands brushed over her breast, traveling to her waist. When he tugged on the fabric of her shirt, she pulled back to aid him in pulling the shirt over her head. Taking it from him, she tossed it aside as Michael unhooked her bra, pulling it off with one smooth motion.

As Patience untied the string of her sweatpants, Michael's

tongue trailed down her body. Crouching before her, he took the pants down and off, followed by her underwear, leaving both at her feet. Michael was practically salivating as his eyes lingered on the most intimate part of her body. Licking his lips, he rose, standing before her.

Patience took hold of the towel that secured Michael's manhood from her. Untucking the fabric, she let it cascade to the floor. Seeing him standing at full attention, a quaking breath escaped her. The anticipation of everything she knew he was going to make her feel was almost unbearable.

Before Patience could make her move, Michael hooked his arms under her thighs, lifting her to his waist. When she went to wrap her legs around him, he lifted her higher, igniting a shriek. Grasping at the door frame with one hand and the back of his head with another, her eyes bulged. Being *that* high was new. "Shit! Wait—Michael *please* don't drop me."

"I got you, baby," Michael crooned, resting her back against the door. He secured her hips with his arms as her legs dangled over his shoulders.

The initial shock of her elevated position quickly dissipated once she felt Michael's tongue touch her. Holding the back of Michael's head in her grasp, Patience closed her eyes as she focused on the pleasure that this man was bringing her.

Michael pleased Patience as if he was a starving man—he missed her; he *craved* her and made it his mission to make sure she knew just how much. The deepness and loudness of her desire-filled moans, and the trembling of her body as he brought her to her peak, let him know that he was accomplishing this task.

As her body relaxed, Michael ran his tongue over her, tasting the juices that flowed before lowering her to his waist. Holding her, he walked her over to her bed, laying her down. Grabbing her hips, he pulled her to him, entering her with one swift, deep stroke.

Patience clenched his arms as Michael moved in and out of her. And when he took her legs, resting them on his shoulders, she tightened her grip as he drilled deeper. Her sensual cries and his groans of pleasure consumed the room. It didn't take long for Patience's body to surrender to another orgasm.

Pulling out, Michael guided Patience to her stomach. Bringing her to her knees, he penetrated her once more from behind. Patience's nails dug into the covers as she took every powerful thrust that Michael was giving her, and was giving it right back to him.

Michael moved faster, stronger—his body surged with pure passion. He couldn't get enough of her. Yet as much as he wanted to continue, he could go no longer. Throwing his head back, his body tensed, and he groaned as he released.

Heavy breaths of satisfaction replaced the carnal sounds as the two came down from the intense session.

Opening his eyes, still holding his position behind Patience, Michael observed her as she tossed hair back from her face. Leaning forward, he wrapped his arm around her waist. Pulling her back to him, he put his other hand across her chest.

Covering his hand with hers, Patience turned her head to look at him just as he leaned in. She closed her eyes as he kissed her lips.

"I missed you," he breathed.

She brushed her fingertips against his face. "I missed you too."

Chapter Twenty-Five

TONI ADJUSTED THE CASHMERE SCARF around her neck. "It's too freakin' cold to be in this house with no damn heat," she complained, shooting Angela a side-glance. "You couldn't wait until the *spring* to do this?"

"Toni, save the whining okay, I have a headache." Angela turned her displeased attention to her youngest sister, who was staring off into the dining room. "Patience."

Patience faced her, fighting the urge to not react to Angela's harsh tone. "Yes."

Folding her arms across her designer trench coat, Angela fixed her with a glare. "Make yourself useful and go check to see if the heater is working, since you're closest to it."

Moving her hair over her shoulder with a glove-covered hand, Patience's eyes flared. "Is there a reason why you're barking orders at me like I'm some subordinate of yours?"

Angela sucked her teeth. "Just see if the thing works please. You act like Toni and I are the only ones cold."

Covering her face with her hand, Toni shook her head. *God, we haven't been in here fifteen minutes and Angie is already starting with Patience.*

"It *doesn't* work because nobody *lives* here. Therefore, the electricity, water, and *heat* are *off*. You own the place, you should probably be aware of that," Patience flashed back.

Angela made a face at the reply, but elected not to respond further.

That frosty Saturday, as discussed, the sisters had driven the three hours to Chestnut Hill, Maryland to visit their childhood home. Though the overall shell of the house was in good condition, the inside was *clearly* in need of some TLC. Ever since Angela had gained control of the property, she couldn't be bothered to do anything with it.

"Look Angie, since it's clear *you* don't want to fix this place up, at least let Patience and I do it," Toni stepped in. "I may not have any desire to ever live here again, but I don't want to see it rot or *sold* either."

Taking a deep breath, Patience did her best to let the previous encounter with Angela go. "This actually would make a great rental property." She scanned the space with her eyes. "It's in a prime neighborhood, the school district is good—it could generate some extra income without you having to get rid of it completely."

Angela pursed her lips. "And what makes *you* so sure about that Patience?"

Patience stared at Angela, her expression blank. "You know I do real estate for a *living*, right?"

"I'm aware—"

"Then there's your answer," Patience cut in.

Amused both by Patience's comeback and by the salty look on Angela's face, Toni snapped her fingers. "You better let her know Pace." She snapped them again, this time right in Angela's face. "She shut your ass *right* on up."

"Toni—" Taking a breath, Angela checked her rising temper. "Okay look, I apologize for the attitude. As I previously mentioned—" She pointed to her head, "Headache."

It was clear by the phony tone of Angela's voice that the apology was far from genuine. Nevertheless, Patience just waved a hand. "It's whatever Angie."

Leaving Angela standing in place, Toni and Patience roamed about the living room. While the family had gone through and cleared out some of the clutter right after their mother had passed, there was still quite a bit left. Old furniture pieces and even some photos still remained, all under a layer of dust.

Angela had yet to utter a word while her sisters chatted with one another. She could make out bits and pieces of the casual conversation, yet she had no desire to be part of it. However, she couldn't bring herself to turn her attention away from them. When they dissolved into laughter at what she could only assume to be some joke or witty comment, Angela's eyes tightened with disdain. "Just you two off in your own little world as always," she blurted out. "Forget I'm even here."

Toni shot an amused look Angela's way. "You've been snapping since we got here big sis, we just figured you needed a minute to yourself."

Angela's lips twisted. "Yeah, cute excuse. I'm sure *Patience* was waiting for the opportunity to take your attention."

Patience opened her mouth to reply, but all that came out was a sigh as she raised her arms and dropped them to her side. *Why even fuckin' bother?*

Sensing Patience's breaking point, Toni put a hand on her little sister's shoulder. "Angie, stop it. *I'm* the one who dragged her away, and it's not like you would've wanted to be part of this particular conversation anyway."

Angela's brows shot up. "And what brought you to *that* asinine conclusion?"

A smirk curled Toni's mouth. "Because we were talking about how Patience was getting folded like a lawn chair by her man who got back in town yesterday."

Patience snickered as Toni busted out laughing.

Angela, however, did not find it so amusing. "Seriously Toni?" Angela grunted. "You could think of nothing else to converse about other than Patience's sex life?"

"We weren't talking about that Angela, she's lying," Patience admitted.

Toni pointed to Patience. "But am I lying about the *folding*, though?"

Hilarity on her face, Patience shook her head with vigor. "No."

Scoffing, Angela fixed her judgmental sights on Patience. "How nice. So what? Do you send my poor niece over to Toni's every time you decide you want some?"

Patience's head jerked. "Excuse me?"

"Or do you actually have sex with Noelle *there*?"

"Yeah, right on the floor in the living room, while she sits on the couch eating fruit snacks." Folding her arms, Patience's eyes blazed with anger. "What the fuck kind of question is that?"

Toni was completely baffled, and it showed on her face. "What the hell Angie?"

"Oh relax. It was just a question," Angela dismissed, waving a flippant hand.

"It was a stupid, *disrespectful* ass question," Patience fumed. "What the hell are you trying to insinuate? That I would expose my daughter to what Michael and I do in private?"

Toni raised her hand, waving it. "*Hello*, you don't think Rob and I have sex in the house because we have Jordan?" She fixed Angela with a stern look. "Oh my mistake, you've never questioned *me*. It's *Patience* you question."

"You know what, the last thing I need is you two jumping down my damn throat like I'm some goddamn villain." Angela stalked towards the stairs. "I'm going to see my old room."

Toni faced Patience, who was shooting a searing glare at Angela's departing back. "Pace—hey, hey." She grabbed Patience's arm, stopping her from following Angela up the steps. "Try to calm down."

Patience's fingernails dug into her palms, her breath constricting in her chest. "I'm sick and tired of her fucking with me T."

"I know. But you're turning red, so I need you to breathe it out." Toni put her hands on her sister's shoulders as the air released from her. "If you want to leave now, I'll understand. I'll ride back with her."

"I'm not going to leave you; I just need a minute."

"Okay, I'll give you that. I'll go talk to her." Sighing, Toni left Patience alone to go upstairs. Ambling down the hallway, Toni peered into Angela's old room, finding her in there staring out of a window. "Angie, I suggest you figure out whatever your issue is with our sister and fix it," she said, entering.

Turning around, Angela rolled her eyes. "And where would I find this nonexistent issue?"

Toni's eyes narrowed. "In therapy."

"I've told you *and* her time and time again, that there is no issue between us. I asked a simple question—"

"Cut the shit before you piss *me* off," Toni bit out.

Angela folded her arms, letting out a rigid breath. "Do you know her—*boyfriend?*"

"Michael? His name is *Michael*, and yes, I do." The frustration in Toni's voice was noticeable. "He's a great man, and he's amazing to Patience *and* Noelle."

"See, I don't *know* that because I don't know *him*. I met the man *once*, and that was only because I happened to stop past your house when you and Rob had them over for a game night... One that you didn't invite *me* to by the way—"

Toni's hand shot up. "Back it up now, I *did* invite you. You turned down the invitation because Trevor was home from his 'business trip', and you made this elaborate dinner for him."

Glancing down at her shoes, Angela drug a foot across the weathered wood floor.

"Which he *didn't eat*, then ended up *leaving* you there alone to go 'shoot pool' with his friends, and it was *then* that you decided to show up at my house," Toni finished.

"What's with the damn air quotes when it comes to where Trevor has been, Toni?" Angela's nostrils flared. "You think I don't notice when you do that? What are you trying to imply?"

Toni stared for a long moment, before shaking her head.

"Nothing." *If you're going to play stupid, who am I to stop you.* "But now that we're on the topic of Trevor, let me ask you. Is *he* making you sell this house?"

Angela's head jerked back, her eyes bulging in shock. "*Excuse* me?"

"Unlike *your* question, *mine* is legitimate." Toni stepped forward. "You've held onto this house with a vice grip. Not so much as letting us step *foot* in here without you, and now suddenly you want to *sell* it?"

Angela shrugged. "It's time to let it go."

"Yeah, I think that's bullshit," Toni threw back. "Did your husband fumble a business deal, and now you need the money to bail him out? Because that would *surely* be something that you'd do."

"Screw you, Antoinette. My husband did not squander anything. His business is good, our finances are great, and my marriage—as much as you don't like it, is *perfect*," Angela hissed.

Toni gave a shrug as she shot a smug look her sister's way. "Good to hear, because the clause in Mom's will said that even though she left the house to you, you can't sell it without my nor Patience's approval."

Eyes wide, Angela pointed at her. "You're lying."

"Well, *my* husband passed the bar as an estate attorney, and I had him go over the documents last night so…it's true." Toni shrugged once more. "And umm, I think I can speak for Patience as well when I say that I don't want to sell it. So rental property it is."

Angela tapped her foot on the floor in rapid motion for several seething seconds, before letting out a loud breath. "Okay."

Toni blinked. She'd expected Angela to scream, or even throw something in anger, yet she just…relented. "That's it?"

"For now." Angela took a lingering look around the room. "Since there's nothing else to discuss or do, let's just go."

Toni stood by bewildered, as Angela brushed past her on the way out. She'd discuss this weird turn of events with Patience later.

Angela sauntered down the stairs. "Pace, I apologize—"

"Save it," Patience grunted. Leaning against a wall, she didn't even bother to look Angela's way. "You never mean it and I don't want to hear it."

Angela stood in front of Patience, forcing the woman's eyes to lay on her. "I do… I was wrong to come at you like I did. I guess I'm just in my feelings because I feel left out."

Patience's face scrunched, perplexed. "Left out of *what?*"

"Toni knows Michael. Rob knows him—I'm sure you've met and hung out with *his* family—" Angela tried to explain. "And I guess I'm just wondering why *I* haven't been given the opportunity to do the same… Hell I didn't even know you were *in* a *relationship* until you were what? Four months in? Do you really think that's right?"

Hearing Toni descend the stairs as Angela spoke, Patience shot her a glance; Toni in return just shrugged. Refocusing on Angela, Patience drew in a breath, then released it. "Angie…we don't *talk*," she reminded. "And on the rare times we *do*, what transpired *earlier*, happens. So why would I subject him to that, or myself for that matter?"

Angela successfully concealed the eyeroll she so desperately wanted to display. "Okay now look, I know the relationship between you and I has its flaws. But at the end of the day, I'm your sister, and I want what's best for you. I *just* want to be included." Her head veered to the side. "I just want to get to know the man who is obviously making you *so* happy."

Registering the tone, Patience frowned. "You think I can't pick up on sarcasm?"

"I *know* you can, because you're the queen of it, but I wasn't *being* sarcastic." Shaking her head, Angela looked away. "I'm being sincere Patience, and you're not even trying to be receptive."

Patience stared at Angela, with no idea how to read her. Angela had never cared about who or what made Patience happy. Yet she was standing before her, saying otherwise. "Angela…I really don't know what you want me to say right now."

Toni approached her sisters. "May I make a suggestion?"

"Please don't," Patience grumbled at the same time that Angela said, "*Please* do."

Toni tucked some of her hair behind her ears. "Okay...why don't we go on a triple date?" She put her hand up in caution when Patience shot her a look that in no words asked her if she was out of her mind. "Hear me out, Pace."

Rolling her eyes, Patience crossed her arms, but didn't protest further.

"Rob and I, you and Michael, and Angie and Trevor—we all go to a nice restaurant," Toni proposed. "We'll have some good food, a few drinks, we can all talk, and Angela can get to know a little about Michael."

Angela's eyes brightened up. "I actually think that's a great idea, T."

"*I don't.*" Patience could've strangled Toni for suggesting this. Angela was already tap-dancing on her last nerve. The last thing she wanted to do was sit at a dinner table with her.

"I don't understand *why* though, Patience," Angela said, while Toni tried not to shrink under her baby sister's piercing gaze.

Patience snapped her head towards Angela. "Did you *not* hear what I just said before *your* sister walked her ass down here with that dumb idea?"

"You can't disown me, you love me." Toni followed up her taunting remark by putting a hand on Patience's shoulder.

Patience immediately brushed it away. "Shut up and get off me."

Angela snapped her fingers, bringing Patience's focus back to her. "Still waiting on that reason."

"My reason is that I'm not *ready* for this. I don't trust you not to embarrass me by saying something inappropriate to me, or to Michael."

Eyes flashing, Angela's jaw clenched in anger. "I'm sorry you feel that way Patience, but you painting me out to be this malicious person who uses every opportunity to hurt you, is ridiculous."

"You see how you just came up with that all on your own?" Patience shot back.

"Okay stop it," Toni snapped, cutting the argument short. "Patience, I'm not negating how you feel or your reservations, because Angie, you *are* an asshole to her—"

Tossing her hands up, Angela puffed out a loud breath. "Yeah, take her side as always."

Toni ignored the comment. "But Pace, her feelings matter too, and she *does* feel left out. This would be a good way to include her... Who knows, it might even be a start to you two building a positive relationship with one another." She sighed when neither woman replied. "Can you just try it...for me? I hate that we can't all be in a room together without an argument. It's only us three, and the fact that we're not *all* close is disheartening."

Face relaxing, Angela gave Toni's arm a pat. "You're right T. We need this."

Both women looked at Patience, whose eyes ping-ponged from Angela's hopeful face, to Toni's pleading one. Toni was not only her sister, but her best friend. And though her reservations had not waned, the fact that Toni was affected by the turbulent relationship between herself and Angela, didn't sit well with her.

Letting out a sigh, Patience lifted her eyes to the ceiling, as if she was pulling her nerve from it. "Okay." She looked at Toni, her shoulders rising and dropping. "I'll talk to Michael to see what he thinks... If he's fine with coming, then I'll be there."

The fact that both the look on Patience's face and her tone lacked enthusiasm didn't deter the smile from appearing on Toni's face. "Thank you." She put an arm around each of her sisters' shoulders, stifling her building snickers. "Should we dress in matching colors for the occasion?"

"Toni, please don't make me leave you stranded out here," Patience sniped.

Toni laughed. "I'll take that as a hard no."

Chapter Twenty-Six

ENTERING THE DOUBLE DOORS OF her home, Angela dropped her keys and pocketbook on an end table, before crossing the hardwood floor through the living room. "Trevor?" She walked further through the room. "Honey?"

Met with silence, her face fell. "Alone yet again…cozy." Having just gotten back from Maryland, Angela had hoped to come home to her husband, but instead found only an empty house.

Stiletto heels clacking along the marble floors of her kitchen, she ran a hand along the back of her neck as she approached the sink. Giving her hands a quick wash, she went to the refrigerator, pulling open the double doors to assess the abundance of food. "What the hell am I going to make for dinner?" While trying to figure out what to prepare, her smart watch beeped, alerting to an incoming call. She promptly tapped the small screen, answering. "Hello?"

"Hey, I just got in, wanted to make sure you got home too," Toni said.

Grabbing a T-bone steak, a few potatoes and a bundle of asparagus from the shelves, Angela closed the refrigerator with her arm. "Yeah, just got in actually." She rested the items on the counter island. "I'm about to make dinner."

"Okay…" Toni stalled for a moment. "Listen, not only did I call to check on you, I wanted to also say, please don't make me regret this triple date idea."

Sucking her teeth, Angela stomped her foot on the floor. "Toni—God, give me some fuckin' credit."

"I'll give you some when I have reason to," Toni threw back. "Now I'm serious. Patience agreed to this on the strength of me, so like I said, don't make me regret it."

Angela rolled her eyes. "Don't worry Toni. I'll be on my best behavior."

"Umm hmm, that means nothing, you ain't shit."

Unwrapping the steak, Angela couldn't keep the amusement from showing on her face. "You know what, I'm still shocked that your mouth hasn't landed you in trouble over these years."

"Hell, me too," Toni chuckled. "No but, you know I love you. I just want us all to get along."

"Well T, you know who you need to talk to about that."

"Yes, I do and I *am*." Toni let out a subtle laugh when Angela sucked her teeth yet again. "Anyway, I have to go. I was out with you heffas all day, so now it's family time with my loves. Talk to you later."

The sigh that left Angela was solemn. What she wouldn't give for some quality time with *her* love. "Talk later." Clearing the call from her screen, she commenced her meal prep.

Sitting in the living room and staring at the clock on the wall in front of her, Angela held a half-empty glass of merlot. As the hands struck eleven-thirty, she gritted her teeth.

She'd cooked dinner four hours ago, and held off eating her portion for an hour after in hopes of her husband returning, so they could dine together. But when he didn't show she was forced to eat alone, like she had countless times before.

She downed the rest of the wine in two gulps, setting the glass on the coffee table. Finally hearing the front door open, Angela shifted her bitter gaze to her husband as he entered.

Shutting the door, Trevor Bishop looked up from his phone,

catching his wife's stare. Swiftly, he stuffed the device into his pants pocket as he hung his coat on the rack. "I didn't think you'd still be up."

"Don't know *why*, it's not like I don't *always* wait up for you." Her voice was menacingly low. "Where were you?"

Raising an eyebrow, Trevor loosened his tie. "I was out with work colleagues."

"On a *Saturday…all* damn *day?*" Angela hurled, her voice rising.

The brows on Trevor's sable face wrinkled. "Check the tone, Angela. These are business heavy hitters, you know they don't stick to a nine to five schedule, and neither do *I*. This house, that car you drive, and all that designer shit you have in your closet, should remind you of that."

Angela's eyes lowered to her lap as Trevor ranted.

"I bust my ass all day long, and I don't need you stressing me out every time I walk in the damn house."

Turning around in her seat, Angela watched as Trevor stalked for the winding staircase. "Trevor wait." Her soft plea halted his progress. "I don't want to fight, I just…I wanted to spend some time with you today. You're always busy… You're always—"

"What's the progress on your mom's house? When are you putting it on the market?" Trevor shrewdly cut in.

Angela went rigid. That wasn't the first time he'd interrupted her while she'd vented about his absence. "There's no progress because I can't sell it."

"What do you *mean* you can't sell it? It's yours, you can do whatever the hell you want with it."

"Well, turns out I *can't*." Angela gave a hard shrug. "Which frankly is fine with me because I never wanted to sell it."

"I've already explained to you that the money from the house can turn over millions of dollars from investments."

"Screw the damn investments, we don't need more money, Trevor. We have plenty already," she countered.

"*We?*" Trevor let out a mocking chuckle. "Last time I checked, *I* was the only one bringing money into this house."

Offended, Angela bolted from the couch. "Yeah well from what I remember, you said you wanted to be the bread winner. That you wanted to take care of me." She stormed towards the stairs. "Or is that yet another promise you forgot about in our marriage?"

Seeing that she was about to pass him, Trevor put a hand on her shoulder, stopping her. His hardened expression let up. "Okay, okay, you're right, I'm sorry." Taking hold of her hand, he gave it a stiff peck. "What can I do to make up for being an asshole?"

"Eat the dinner I spent an hour and a half cooking for you," she replied sharply.

Running a hand along the back of his neck, Trevor cleared his throat. "I would Ang, but I ate out already."

Angela tossed her arms in the air. It also wasn't the first time he'd completely disregarded a meal she took her time in preparing for him. "Fine Trevor... What you can do is agree to a dinner out with my sisters and their significant others."

He flagged the request off. "Ang—I can't make that promise. You know I'm tied up at work a lot."

"You just asked me what you can do to make your behavior up to me, and this is it, so can you *please* show up for me?"

Pinching the bridge of his nose, Trevor groaned. "Fine."

"Thank you." Despite being perturbed, Angela still hugged him. Though the embrace was brief, it was more than enough time for the fragrance from his shirt to waft into Angela's nose. A fragrance that *she* didn't wear.

"You happy now? Good night." Trevor walked away, leaving Angela frozen in place.

"Nice perfume Trevor."

Trevor stopped, peering back at her.

Angela glowered at him. When he didn't speak, instead

shooting her a stoned expression, she shook her head. "Yeah," she muttered as she stomped up the stairs.

"Good job with those swirls Noelle," Michael praised, peering over at the pan of brownies that Noelle was standing over. He leaned in, getting a closer look. "Is that a flower?"

Guiding the cheesecake swirls through the red velvet brownie batter with her plastic knife, Noelle beamed proudly. "Thank you, and yes, I drew a flower with the cheesecake stuff."

Patience looked up from her task of chopping spinach, red bell peppers, and garlic. "Look at my little artist, making our dessert all pretty."

Playfully rolling her eyes to the ceiling, Noelle smacked her forehead with her free hand. "Mommy."

The reaction made Patience giggle. "Too much?"

"Just a teeny bit."

Standing at the stove, Michael flipped salmon filets in a skillet. "Aww, you know how much your mother adores everything you do." He peered over at them. "You're her little talented genius."

"I know, I know," Noelle drawled.

Patience gestured Michael's way. "*Thank* you, baby."

Michael winked at her. "I got your back, my love."

Finishing with her swirling, Noelle set the knife aside and admired her work. "All done."

Preparing dinner together a few nights a week had become a routine for the three of them, rotating between both houses to do so. Michael's home was the meal spot that Sunday evening.

Michael checked the pasta boiling on the stove, before taking the pan of brownie batter and placing it into the oven. "Would you like to do the honor of keeping track of the time on these, Noelle?"

"Ooh, yes." Noelle looked at her watch. "How many minutes?"

Michael closed the oven. "Thirty tops."

Pushing a few buttons on her watch, she nodded. "Timer set." She gave him the thumbs up. "I got your back."

Patience smiled at the sweet exchange. Every day Michael proved more and more how wonderful of a stepfather he'd be to her daughter.

Standing from her seat, Patience walked the cutting board of chopped veggies to the stove alongside Michael. Placing the aromatics inside a second heated pan, she stirred them while Michael retrieved a carton of heavy cream and fresh parmesan cheese from the refrigerator, setting them on the counter next to her.

"Oh Mr. Michael, after we eat, can you show me how to beat Ice World on the game you bought me for my birthday?" Noelle asked, spinning around in her seat. "I got through the first two worlds, but I'm stuck on that one."

"I can certainly *try*." Michael removed the salmon from the stove. "I'll admit, I haven't played a video game in a long time."

"He'll try after you finish your homework." Patience glanced at Noelle. "As a matter of fact, while we're finishing up with dinner, go ahead and get started."

"Okay." Noelle jumped down from the stool, darting out of the kitchen. "I'll let you know when to check on the brownies."

Michael gave his boiling pasta one final check, before removing it from the burner. "Are you feeling any better from earlier?"

Still sautéing, Patience nodded. "If you mean, have I finally stopped feeling like my insides were being twisted around with a fork, yes." The last thing Patience wanted to wake up to were debilitating menstrual cramps. But alas, she had. "Day one is always a nightmare and I love you for taking care of me."

When they'd arrived at Michael's house hours ago, Patience had taken advantage of his deep bathtub with the heated whirlpool jets. While she was soaking, Michael had made her a cup of tea, heated up a heating pad, and turned down the covers on his bed for her. He'd even entertained Noelle while Patience napped. She awoke feeling ten times better.

"I love you too." Michael gave her lower back a gentle rub. "I tell you, women are so damn strong. I sprained my ankle playing basketball one time and folded like a damn child... I think I even remember crying a little."

Patience let out a snicker. "Don't make me laugh, they might start up again."

He chuckled a bit. "Sorry."

Rich aromas permeated the home as the couple spent the next fifteen minutes finishing the meal.

Setting the pan of Tuscan salmon and pasta on the dining room table, a thought popped into Michael's mind. "Oh, I meant to bring this up last night. Let me know if you need anything fixed or updated in your mother's house." He peered at Patience, who was standing across the table, plates and silverware in hand. "I know you mentioned that your sister wants to sell it. I say up the property value as much as possible first."

"I appreciate that, but at this point she won't be selling the house." She proceeded to set the dining ware atop the cloth placemats. "I still might take you up on fixing it up a bit though."

"Okay, just let me know," Michael said. "She changed her mind, huh?"

"She had no *choice* since Toni lied and said that she couldn't do it without Toni and I signing off on it." Patience recalled the look of shock and disbelief she'd bestowed upon Toni on their drive back home yesterday, when Toni had told her the story she'd fed Angela. "I can't believe Angela *bought* it though. First, Rob is a *criminal* attorney, not an estate one. And second, my mother didn't exactly have the best relationship with Toni and I after her divorce from my father."

Michael's brows elevated with curiosity. Patience had mentioned her parents briefly in past conversations, yet she'd never went into depth about them. All Michael knew was that they had divorced when she was sixteen and both parents were now deceased. Though he was curious to learn more about them, he never pressed her to go into further detail.

"Why not?" he asked.

"She didn't like the fact that we were still in communication with Dad." She shook her head as she set out the silverware. "They were…toxic as a couple. Both had their faults, but my mother seemed to always have this delusion that she was innocent. When in *reality*, she was verbally abusive, controlling, and manipulative."

Michael stood frozen, giving her his full attention.

Placing her hands on the table, she let out a quick sigh. "Anyway, long story short, when they divorced, she forbade us from talking to him… Two of the three didn't adhere to that, and as a result she pretty much disowned us…" Shrugging half-heartedly, she tapped her nails on the wood. "Toni had already left for college, so the brunt of her resentment fell onto me until I left two years later. We were still estranged up until the time she died. Never even wanted us in the hospital room with her… Anyway, she left the house and everything in it to Angela."

Not being able to hold back any longer, Michael rounded the table. Standing next to her, he put his arm around her, pulling her to him. He couldn't imagine the stress and sadness she had to endure. "Damn baby, I'm sorry you had to go through that."

She gave his abdomen a soft pat. "I appreciate it, but I'm okay about it now."

"Are you sure?"

Patience nodded. "Yeah. I don't regret my choice. My father was a good man, and I'm happy that he got to meet my daughter and be in her life for three beautiful years before he passed." Pulling the chair out, she took a seat. "And regarding the house… It's just sitting there collecting dust. I figured it could at least be turned into a rental property."

"That's smart." Michael noticed the quick subject change, but decided not to mention it. "So even though the trip up there was pretty pointless, did you at *least* have a good time with your sisters?"

When she didn't answer, instead shooting him an acerbic expression, Michael folded his arms. "I recognize that face. You *didn't*, did you?"

"Of course I enjoyed spending time with Toni, but that other one, she— She just… So look, speaking of my sisters, I wanted to run something by you."

Like the prior subject change, her avoidance of the question wasn't missed by Michael either. He knew that Patience was close with Toni; he'd witnessed their relationship firsthand. But while Patience didn't share too much about her eldest sister, she did allude on more than one occasion that they didn't share that same closeness. "What's that?"

Patience opened her mouth, then closed it. She didn't even want to say it, but knew she had to. Resolved, she clasped her hands together on the tabletop. "Yesterday, Toni suggested that we go on a triple date… You and I, she and Rob and, Angela and her husband."

Michael's head leaned sideways. "Oh yeah?"

"Yeah… Would you want to go?"

"Of course. Just let me know when."

"I will." Patience sat in silence as Michael began plating the food. While she was grateful that he was willing to go along, she almost wished he hadn't. She still had her reservations. But she had promised Toni, so she was willing to sit through it.

Looking up from his task, Michael noticed the tense look on Patience's face. "Are you okay?"

She glanced at him. *Shit, I guess my face is showing just how much I don't want to go to this damn dinner.* "Yeah, I'm good."

Noelle darted into the room, a notebook in one hand, holding the other up to display her watch. "It's time to take out the brownies."

"Damn, it's been a half hour already?" Patience said, rubbing the back of her neck with both hands. They'd been so preoccupied with the conversation that they'd forgotten about the brownies.

Heading for the kitchen, Michael gave Noelle a thumbs up. "Perfect timing."

Chapter Twenty-Seven

GRABBING HER WATER BOTTLE FROM the bench, Kenya uncapped it. "This was fun, wasn't it? I think we should do it again soon."

Sitting on the mat-covered floor, Dante rolled his eyes. "Of *course* you do. Everything is always about what you women *want*."

Sipping her water, Kenya shot Dante a look mixed with annoyance and perplexity. Michael, who was sitting on a bench, threw his *own* bothered look his brother's way.

Catching the expressions, Dante's eyes shifted. "What?"

Shaking her head, Kenya nudged Michael. "So which stage of the breakup is *this*?"

"Misguided anger I believe," Michael replied, wiping the sweat from his brow.

Kenya gave a stiff nod. "Ahh, yes, that's right."

Twisting his lip up, Dante turned away from them and grumbled incoherently.

Kenya's Thursday night self-defense class had a "friends and family" night. Seizing the opportunity to get some quality time in with her brothers, she'd invited them to attend. Though Dante wasn't as eager to show up as Michael was, both brothers partook in the hour-long advanced session, and were now lingering while trying to cool down.

Michael delivered a light kick to his brother's outstretched leg.

"Listen man, I know you're still upset about Lori, but don't take your frustrations out on all women."

"Yeah, and in her defense, all she wanted was for you to step up and propose to her," Kenya chimed in.

Snapping his head in Kenya's direction, Dante scoffed. "Oh *now* you give a shit about Lori's feelings?" He pointed at her. "Where was that consideration when we were *together huh?*"

Kenya pointed a stern finger right back. "Hey, I may not have *cared* for the woman, but that doesn't mean I didn't see her side. Nobody over the age of *thirty* wants to be in a common-law relationship."

Dante flagged her off. "Whatever, yo."

"Yeah *whatever*," she flashed back. "Breaking up with you was the consequence for dragging your damn feet and that's on *you*. Don't take your bitterness and bullshit out on *me*."

Tired of the verbal battle with his sister, Dante transferred his bitter gaze to Michael, who'd been a quiet spectator of the quarrel. "Mike, this is *your* fault, you know."

Michael jerked his head back. "*Excuse* me?"

"Yeah," Dante bit out. "You being all lovey dovey and Mr. 'she's my everything' every time you'd bring Patience around, had Lori looking at *me* talking about 'why don't you talk to *me* like that?', 'why don't you buy *me* flowers every week?', 'you see how Mike is with her daughter? *You* won't even take my little cousin'—who is bad as *shit* by the way—'to a damn park', 'I bet you he marries her before you get me a ring'. Blah, blah, blah…'"

Expression going blank, Michael took a moment to process Dante's ramblings. While he was sympathetic to Dante's heartbreak—hearing firsthand how devastated Dante was when he called Michael three months ago—Michael was now beginning to tire of the misdirected, self-pitying behavior.

"Sooo let me get this straight…" Leaning forward, Michael pressed his fingers together, "Because I treat *my* lady how she deserves in private *and* public, it's *my* fault?"

"Yep. We were *just* fine as we were until *your* romantic ass got into a relationship."

Putting a hand to his face, Michael dragged it down, deciding not to engage his brother any further on the subject.

Kenya sat on the bench beside Michael. "Anyway Mike, I'll be throwing a business brunch in the next few weeks, and I'd like to invite Patience."

Micheal glowed at the idea. "I'm sure she'd love that."

Given his sister's reputation for being hard on the women in her brothers' lives, Michael had been a bit guarded over Patience. He'd made sure to give her a heads-up too when he'd introduced her to his family at Sunday dinner, a month after they'd become a couple. He was pleasantly surprised when Kenya had taken an instant liking to Patience, and vice versa.

"*And* you're inviting *Michael's* girlfriend to events and shit," Dante bristled, hands in the air. "*Again*, where was this hospitality?"

Eyes still set on Michael, Kenya gestured to Dante. "Get him away from me before I slap him."

Letting out a chuckle, Michael pointed to the other side of the gym. "Dante, go take a walk."

Jerking to his feet, Dante stomped off without another word.

Kenya shook her head at his departing figure. "I'm telling Mom and Dad he's trippin'."

Hearing his cell phone ring from his gym bag, Michael dragged it over to retrieve it. "Hey baby... No, it's fine we've finished up. Just sitting around for a bit." As Patience spoke on the other end, Michael opened his water bottle, taking a sip. "Okay, eight o'clock you said? ...Yeah, that's no problem. Sounds good...okay, see you later. Love you."

Kenya smoothed a few damp tendrils up into her coiled pineapple. "Plans with Patience tonight?"

"Nah, not tonight." Michael returned his phone to his bag. "I mean, I'll *see* her tonight, but the conversation was about dinner reservations for next Friday. We're having dinner with her sisters and their husbands."

"Oh yeah?" Kenya folded her arms when he nodded. "A triple date...*That's* nice."

"Yeah."

Kenya stared at him. "When are *we* going to go on a *double* date?"

"When a man you're *dating* makes it pass the two-week mark."

Erupting with a deep belly laugh, Kenya playfully elbowed him. "Touché."

Patience fingered a few curls in her hair, before taking the butterfly necklace from the jewelry box on her dresser. A sigh left her as she unfastened the clasp.

Michael was adjusting the collar of his sports jacket as he entered her bedroom. He held his hand out for the necklace. She handed it over before turning her back to him, lifting her hair.

"Car is warming up," Michael said, fastening the clasp.

"Okay." Releasing her locks, Patience moved to her chair, taking her purse from it.

Michael stood watching as she opened her purse, peering at the items inside in silence. As a matter of fact, she'd barely said more than a few words all day, and Michael had a feeling he knew the reason why. "Baby," he said.

"Yes?"

Michael stepped towards her. "If you're not up for going to this dinner, you *shouldn't*."

Her gaze veering off to the side, Patience didn't reply.

"You can even blame it on *me*." He put a hand to his chest. "Tell your sisters that I ate some bad food and can't leave the bathroom for the next twenty-four hours."

Eyes returning to him, Patience gave a silent laugh. "That's *really* what you'd want me to say?"

Amusement spanned over his face as he shrugged. "Hell, it's a good excuse." He caressed her arm, seriousness coming over him. "Seriously, even though you agreed to this… I can sense you're not feeling it."

Patience breathed deeply. Michael was right, she wasn't. Though she knew it was a long shot, she had hoped that her sisters would've ditched the idea of this outing all together. But that hope had crumbled when Toni had called her to confirm the restaurant a week ago. Since then, Patience had been a bit on edge; now that the evening was upon her, she felt like she could fall off the cliff altogether.

She offered a weak smile. "While I appreciate your willingness to embarrass yourself for me, I'm okay." Cupping his chin with her hand, she stroked his beard. "We're going to have a nice evening, then we'll come back and you can tear these clothes off me."

A sly grin crossed Michael's face. "Say less," he crooned, planting a quick kiss to her lips.

"This steakhouse has some great reviews." Rob placed his arm around Toni as she leaned back in the cushioned seat against him. "The steak sandwich—heard it was supreme. I think I'm going to try it."

Toni adjusted the bracelets on her wrist. "Yeah well, for a hundred and forty bucks it just had *better* be."

Rob glanced at Toni; her sour tone wasn't missed. "You all right hon?"

"No, I'm annoyed." Toni eyed her watch. "They're forty minutes late."

Patience folded her arms. "What did she say when you called?"

"'I'm en route'." Toni's jaw clenched as she recalled the brief conversation with Angela. "That's all she said—'I'm en route'—then hung up."

She, along with her husband Rob, had arrived at the upscale steakhouse in Center City for their eight o-clock reservation. The pair were elated to see Patience and Michael already there. Yet when Angela and Trevor had *yet* to arrive, Toni had checked in with the hostess and was given the option to either be seated, or wait for the rest of her party. Thinking that they'd show up in a few minutes, Toni chose the latter. But as those few minutes turned into forty, Toni's elation had shifted into frustration.

Toni tossed an arm up, huffing in the process. "Her ass is on time for *everything else* and would pitch a fit if anyone showed up late to something she planned."

"Well…" Patience tried to find the words that would calm her sister down. "Maybe traffic was bad."

Toni shot Patience a brisk look. "Patience, I love you, but please."

Sighing, Patience gave Toni's arm a light rub. She knew how much Toni wanted the evening to go along without a hitch. She turned to Michael, who was sitting beside her. "You okay sweetie?" she asked him.

"Of course." He shot her an easy smile. "I'm sure the food will be worth the wait."

Sucking her teeth, Toni uncrossed her legs. "To hell with this waiting, my stomach is hitting my damn back. Let's go get seated." She slung her purse strap on her shoulder as she rose from her seat, along with the rest of the group.

Rob straightened his blazer as the four made their way to the hostess podium. "First round of drinks is on me."

Toni rubbed her husband's shoulder. "Your parents are keeping the girls overnight, so all of *my* drinks will be doubles."

Patience giggled. Though she didn't plan on drinking much, she was grateful that her sister's in-laws were more than happy to let Noelle stay over with Jordan, so they could enjoy their evening.

"Did the rest of your party turn up?" The hostess asked, gathering menus.

"No, but we're no longer going to sit out here waiting on them," Toni answered. "We'd like to be seated."

"Of course, right this way."

Michael and Rob gestured for their dates to go ahead of them, just as the glass doors swung open. The group turned around to find Angela and Trevor standing by the entrance. Judging by the looks on both their faces, neither was in a good mood.

Plastering a phony smile on her face, Angela sauntered up. "Looks like we're just in time to be seated."

Toni and Patience met Angela with curt glances. Angela might have felt the need to fake her mood, but her sisters had no plans on doing so. "Nice of you to finally show up," Toni grunted.

"Hello to *you too* Toni," Angela bristled. "We made it, let's just go eat, okay?"

Throwing her hands up, Toni backed up. "That's fine, you'll hear it later."

"Perfect, looking forward to it." Laying eyes on Patience, Angela folded her arms. "Hello Patience."

Moving her hair over her shoulder, Patience uttered a quick. "Hey." Glancing behind her to Michael, she gestured to Angela. "Michael, you remember Angela—" Seeing Trevor lingering by the exit, his face buried in his phone, she didn't bother making the introduction. "Angela, Michael."

A polite smile on his face, Michael exchanged handshakes with her. "Good to see you again Angela."

Angela's brows rose as she ogled the tall drink of water that was her baby sister's boyfriend. Though she'd only met Michael once, his looks had left a lasting impression. "You as well."

"Guys, the hostess is about to cuss us out. Let's get to our table," Rob cut in, signaling to the woman who couldn't help but laugh.

"Oh no, I promise that never crossed my mind. Please, follow me."

Less than ten minutes after placing their orders, the group received their top-shelf beverages, with a promise of their appetizers' arriving shortly.

Rob picked up his glass of brandy. "Michael, Toni tells me your company put a contracting bid on the old mall space over in Brandywine township." He held the glass up. "That's a huge deal, I know you'll get it."

Tipping his glass of scotch to Rob, Michael gave a nod. "Thanks man." He took a sip, then set it down. "My company is one of about twenty that bid on the space. They're looking to open a super center there, which would be a great addition to the company's resume."

Patience threw a proud look Michael's way. "I already told you you're going to get that contract. You're amazing at what you do."

Flashing a grin at Patience, he leaned in, kissing her on her cheek. "Thank you, baby."

Toni swallowed the bit of her cosmopolitan. "I know that's right, you better speak life into it. You have the experience Michael, so like Patience said, it's yours."

"Yeah…building homes is a little different than a mega store," Michael said. "But I appreciate the vote of confidence. I'm praying on it."

Rob set his glass down. "Hey, we'll be praying *with* you." Spotting their waiter approach with the appetizers, he rubbed his hands together. "Ahh, nourishment."

Toni rolled her eyes at the corny comment. "Lord."

Rob grinned. "Didn't appreciate the joke, *did* you hon?"

"It wasn't a *joke*." Toni put a finger to his temple, which he laughed at. "We've talked about this."

Though Toni and Rob's playful banter was amusing, Patience couldn't help but be distracted by Angela. Though they'd tried to engage with her ever since they'd sat down, the only time Angela had spoken was when she'd placed her order. Her focus was stuck on her husband, who was paying more attention to his phone than his wife or anyone *else* at the table. She didn't even tear her eyes away when her food was placed in front of her.

Despite her and Angela's history, Patience felt bad for her. "Angie," she said.

The aggravation on Angela's face when she was forced to tear her eyes away from the device in Trevor's hands was obvious. *"Yes Patience."*

Patience chose to overlook the snippy tone and sharp expression Angela was shooting at her. "Sis, you haven't said much. You cool?"

Angela shrugged her shoulders in dramatic fashion. "Sure, I'm *cool.* Just sitting here listening to you all talk about your careers and whatnot. Since I'm the only one who doesn't have one, I just figured it was yet *another* conversation I shouldn't be part of." She flicked her wrist at Patience. "No need to act new now."

Patience let out a drawn-out breath before responding. "We only mentioned *Michael's* career Angie. And it wasn't to exclude you."

Though Michael was quiet during the tense exchange, he studied Patience. He could tell that she was trying to remain calm. But the tightness in her jaws, and the subtle way she stiffened when Angela spoke at her, told Michael exactly how hard she was fighting. Placing a gentle hand on Patience's thigh, he hoped it offered her some unspoken comfort.

Patience glanced at him. His eyes silently asked if she was okay, and she responded by relaxing her face, and squeezing his hand.

Toni squinted at Angela. First, she was late, and now she was spewing attitude. "Angie, pick up your mojito and sip until you loosen the hell up."

Snatching up her cocktail, Angela guzzled half of it before setting the glass back down. "Happy now?"

Picking up her fork, Toni pointed it in Angela's direction. "Girl," she warned before skewering a piece of grilled shrimp.

Swallowing his bite of his wagyu beef tartar crostini, Michael cleared his throat. "So Angela, Patience tells me that you're into event planning. *My* sister is in that line of work as well."

"Um, I wouldn't exactly call throwing a dinner party here and there, event planning," Angela dully returned. "But I *am* good at it."

Michael gave a nod. "I'm sure."

Angela side-eyed Trevor, who was peering towards the exit. "Sweetie, why don't you tell Michael about *your* line of work?" she clasped her hands. "Maybe he's looking for some new investments to make."

Trevor ran a hand over the back of his neck. "The man owns a million-dollar company, I'm sure he has plenty of brokers that he already works with," he flatly dismissed.

Scowling, Toni exchanged a glance with Patience, who shook her head. It was no secret that neither woman cared for Angela's husband of sixteen years, but for the sake of Angela, they at least tried to be cordial with him. However, the blatant disinterest he was showing not only the group, but his own wife, was abysmal. Toni didn't know how long she'd be able to continue without saying something.

Angela rolled her eyes at her husband, before directing her attention to Patience who'd just adjusted the necklace around her neck. The amethyst and diamond butterfly twinkled in the warm amber overhead lighting. "That's a pretty necklace Patience."

Patience looked up from her plate. "Thank you."

"You *have* to tell me which mall kiosk you got it from." Angela picked her drink up, a smirk on her face. "I could use a few more costume pieces for when I dress down."

Patience's eyebrow arched at the snide remark. "It's not costume, and Michael gave it to me."

"How nice." Angela downed the rest of her mojito, returning the empty glass to the table. "He has good taste…in *jewelry*."

Setting her fork down, Patience fixed Angela with a glower. "You think I didn't catch that—"

"Okay—oh look, the entrées are here! Uh—nourishment,"Toni stammered. She knew how ugly this could get if Angela kept poking.

Rob looked at Toni. "You really just stole my joke?"

Toni slapped her hand on the table. "It's not a—you know what? I *did*."

Shaking his head, Rob resumed his task of devouring his appetizer.

Feeling his phone vibrate in his hand as his entrée was placed in front of him, Trevor peered at it. Typing out a message, he removed the cloth napkin from his lap. "Angela, it's time to go."

Angela shot him a wide-eyed stare. "I'm sorry?"

Pushing his seat back, Trevor removed the wallet from his pocket. "We have to go."

"Why?" Angela questioned.

"Yeah, we just got our entrées, what's up?"Toni jumped in.

Trevor shoved his phone into his back pocket. "Something came up and I have to get to the office."

Angela folded her arms. "Trevor, I don't—the office? *Really*? After nine?"

Trevor fixed her with a chilly stare. "We've been over this, and I'm not going to explain it to you again. Now I don't have time for this, let's *go*."

Angela stared him down. "*I* am not *ready* to leave."

"Well, *I* drove, so—"

"*We'll* make sure she gets home Trevor," Toni interjected, tone laced with anger. "Thanks for gracing us with your detached presence."

Rob put a hand on the small of Toni's back, giving it a rub. "Breathe hon," he whispered to her.

Trevor glared at the group, then refocused on his defiant wife. "So, you're staying?"

"Yes," she got out through her tightened jaws.

Giving a stiff nod, Trevor removed a credit card from his wallet, dropping it on the table in front of Angela. "Suit yourself."

With fury in her eyes, Angela observed her husband grab his coat and walk away from the table. He didn't get too far, before she jumped up and took off after him. "Trevor!"

Michael shook his head. The display he'd just witnessed was atrocious. He couldn't understand how a man could be that rude to his wife. "What's his deal?"

"He's a fuckin' asshole," Toni bit out. "Always *has* been."

Though Patience agreed wholeheartedly with Toni, she didn't bother cosigning. She was keeping a steady eye on Angela, who'd caught up to Trevor near the exit.

"I can't believe this shit. *First* you make us late by coming *home* late. Then you ignore me all night, and *now* you're just going to *abandon* me?" Angela fussed, poking Trevor in the chest. "We haven't been here a fuckin' hour."

Trevor brushed her hand from his shirt. "I have shit to do." He pointed in her face. "And it was *your* decision to stay, remember that."

"Where are you *really* going huh?"

Trevor ignored her, marching for the door.

Angela stomped her foot on the floor. "Trevor!"

"Don't wait up."

Angela stood fuming as he disappeared outside. Running a shaking hand over the back of her neck, she blinked back tears.

"Angie?"

Spinning around, Angela saw Patience standing there. "What do you want?"

Patience approached with caution. "Are you okay?"

"Yes, though I'm sure you'd prefer me *not* to be," Angela hissed.

"If that were true, I wouldn't be out here."

Shooting Patience a scathing look from head to toe, Angela scoffed. "Please. I'm good."

Patience frowned as Angela brushed by her, bumping her shoulder in the process. Shutting her eyes, Patience calmed her irritation. *She's hurting. You know what that feels like. Just let it go and let her be.* Breathing it out, Patience made a beeline back to the table.

Angela flopped down in her chair, snatching up her husband's credit card. "Where's the waiter? I think it's time for a shot."

Toni gave her older sister a sympathetic look. "Sweetie, you don't do shots."

Leaning back in her seat, Angela flagged her hand dismissively. "I am tonight, so get him over here."

Thirty minutes and three shots of vodka later, Angela had put the fact that Trevor left her to the back of her mind...or so she thought. The truth was, the more she sat there, the angrier she became. Picking up her empty shot glass, she closely examined it. "Anybody see our waiter? I need another one."

"No Angie you *don't*, and for the love of God, *please* eat something," Toni begged. Knowing that Angela wasn't big on hard liquor, Toni and Patience had tried to stop her, but she'd rebuffed their attempts.

"It'll be my last one."

"You've already *had* your last one, Angela," Patience calmly spoke up. When Angela glared at her, Patience slowly shook her head. "Enough."

Angela slammed the shot glass to the table, then folded her arms like a chastised child.

A hush fell over the group while most of them finished up their meal. Angela's entrée, aside from a piece of grilled asparagus she'd tried before her first shot came out, went untouched. She was too livid to eat. She'd been married the longest, and to what she thought to be the most successful man there, and yet he treated her with malice. He barely spoke to her, hadn't touched her and hardly even *looked* at her. Then he'd left to do God knows what with God knows who—it boiled her blood.

Her sisters' significant others, they'd engaged with them. They laughed, joked, and uplifted one another, displaying subtle acts of affection. She directed her piercing line of sight to Patience; the divorced single mother who had managed to land a man that Angela knew she didn't deserve. When Michael took hold of Patience's hand and gave it a kiss, Angela saw *green*. "So Michael. You've been with my sister for what? Six months?" she blurted out.

Still holding Patience's hand in his, Michael smiled. "Well, we've been in a full-on *relationship* for a little over eight months, but we dated for three months before that."

Grinning wide, Toni pointed to herself. "*I'm* the reason they met."

Patience shot an amused gaze her way. "Still determined to take credit for that aren't you?"

"Oh *absolutely*. If I hadn't gotten on your damn nerves about picking up those pastries for me, you wouldn't have met him." Tipping her empty glass, Toni winked. "You're welcome."

Michael let out a chuckle. "Thank you, Toni."

Angela resisted the urge to roll her eyes. Instead, she cleared her throat. "So, I'm guessing you've talked about marriage?"

Patience nodded. "We have."

Angela's head tilted. "Oh?"

"Yes, we have," Michael followed up. He noticed the way Angela was asking. The tone was condescending, almost as if she didn't believe them. If *he* noticed it, then Patience certainly did too.

"Well, Michael I'm sure you're aware that Patience has already been married once before, so I guess I'm curious to know how you feel about that," Angela spewed off.

Patience frowned. "How he'd feel about *what*?"

"About being cheated out of being your only husband." Angela shrugged. "I mean, the man has to compete with the fact that you had somebody *else's* last name at one point. And think about the *wedding*. Face it, there's nothing special about a *second* wedding. I mean, can you even wear a *white dress* now?"

"Oh shit," Rob mumbled in an aside to Toni, who'd hid her face behind her hands.

Balling her fist on the table, Patience's breathing intensified. Her teeth were grinding hard enough to hurt. *I'm going to hurt this bitch.*

"I don't feel *anything* about that Angela," Michael said, his voice and face stern. "Patience being divorced doesn't bother me. I'll *happily* marry her and give her everything she deserves."

Patience put a hand to Michael's arm. "You don't have to dignify her with a response Michael."

Angela snorted. "How noble of you. You'll be content with being a second husband. But what about a forever *stepfather*?"

Toni gasped out loud. "Angie, what the hell?"

"Angela…" Patience felt the blood rush through her body as her temper escalated. "I suggest you stop."

Michael shook his head. He was disgusted by Angela's behavior, her offensive questions, and her treatment of the woman he loved. As far as he was concerned, the evening was over. He touched Patience's arm, leaning in close to her. "We should leave."

Throwing her hands up, Angela lurched back into her seat. "Look, I'm just saying, Patience you tried for *years* to get pregnant while you were married to Greg, but nothing ever happened until— by some miracle—the *end* of your marriage," she spat. "Michael, I hear you're good to my niece, but I'm *sure* you'll want your *own biological* children, and I'm just letting my future—*possible*— brother-in-law know, that that might not happen. Because let's face it, lightning typically doesn't strike twice. So being a father is just something *else* you're being cheated out of—"

Pounding her fist on the table, Patience's eyes blazed with fury. "Bitch *enough!*" The eruption startled not only those at her table, but other nearby patrons.

"Oh my God," Toni choked out. Her hands were shaking, she was so furious.

"What the fuck is *wrong* with you?" Patience hurled at Angela. "You really just sat here and—what have I *ever* done to you to deserve your fuckin' hatred?"

"It's not hatred baby girl, it's the *truth*." An arrogant grin crossed Angela's face. "Not *my* fault it hurts."

In a sudden move, Patience sprung from her seat. She would have succeeded in jumping across the table, had Michael not bolted up and grabbed hold of her.

Michael pulled her back from the table. "Come on baby, let's go."

Feeling her chest tighten, and her pulse race, Patience's eyes glassed over with tears as she stared down the visibly shaken Angela. She was enraged; she was hurt. The feeling of Michael's arms around her was the only thing keeping her from blacking out.

"You guys go ahead, I've got the bill," Rob offered, putting a hand up. "Don't worry about it. Get home safe."

Michael didn't protest Rob's generous offer. He knew if he didn't get Patience out of there, she would do her sister bodily harm. Quickly gathering their coats and Patience's purse, he guided her away from the table. "Appreciate it man. Toni, see you."

Toni couldn't speak; she just gave a subtle nod. She couldn't even bear to watch Patience walk off with Michael. She felt terrible, *responsible*. Turning to Rob, who was signaling for the bill, she blinked back tears. "Babe, can you excuse us for a moment?"

Rob looked at her. "You sure babe?"

Toni nodded. As Rob pushed his seat back and walked off, her wrathful gaze veered to Angela, who was staring down at her cold plate of food. "Are you fuckin' happy with yourself?" When Angela opened her mouth to speak, Toni quickly shut her down by pointing a finger at her. "Shut up. I asked you, I *begged* you to not be a bitch, and you couldn't do it. You just can't be anything other than a spiteful, hateful—" She pushed herself back from the table. "I can't even look at you right now."

Angela watched with a pained expression as Toni stormed away. The realization that she was alone, mixed with the dizzying effects of the alcohol, finally caught up to her. She covered her face with her hands as she slumped back in her seat.

Patience squirted lotion between her palms, rubbing them together she massaged it into her skin.

They'd arrived home nearly forty-five minutes after the disastrous dinner. The car ride was silent; Patience was too upset to speak. Upon entering the house, Patience had secluded herself in the bathroom to take a bath. She had hoped that the hot water would relax her, but it hadn't. Angela had sunk to a new low tonight, and Patience knew that she couldn't overlook it as she always had.

I don't understand how my own sister can despise me so much. Closing her eyes to force the building tears back down, she stretched her neck from side to side. Hearing her phone vibrate from her nightstand, she picked it up, eyeing the text message on the screen.

Toni: I'm so sorry.

Patience sighed deeply. She felt bad for Toni, once again being in the middle of this thing between Angela and herself. She knew that the idea of this date had been made in good conscience. She also knew that Toni had probably given Angela an earful and was now hoping to talk to her. But Patience couldn't, not tonight. Moving her fingers across the screen, Patience typed out a response.

Patience: I know. Good night.

Clearing the text box, Patience tossed the phone back on her nightstand then turned the bedside lamp off. She pulled the covers back and laid down, just as Michael walked in.

He'd given her space when they'd returned, and now he was ready to get in bed alongside her. Removing all his clothing aside from his boxers, Michael crawled under the covers. She backed up against him and he wrapped his arms around her. Kissing her shoulder, Michael drew her closer.

There they laid in the dark, in silence. The evening's events were playing in both of their heads.

"Baby," Michael softly called.

"Yes?"

"I want you to know that what your sister said…" He sighed, hating that he even had to say this to Patience, all because of her sister's hatefulness. "What she was trying to imply—none of that bothers me, and none of it changes how I feel about you—how much I love you, or the future that I see with you." As much as Michael didn't want to bring it up, he couldn't go to sleep without reassuring her.

Patience released a heavy sigh. "I know…" She tightened her hands over his. "I love you too." As much as she knew it was true, that Michael loved her and her child, that he wanted to build a life with her, she couldn't help but hear a nagging voice in the back of her mind. A voice that hadn't been there until Angela had mentioned it.

When they *did* get married, this would be Michael's first. Would he feel cheated out of the experience, knowing that she'd already done it? And children, Michael made it no secret that he saw children in his future. And as great of a parental relationship he and Noelle had, she wasn't his biological daughter. And as happy as Patience would be to have another baby—to give him one should they get to that point—would she be *able* to? And if she couldn't, would he really be content with that?

The burdening thoughts were threatening to cause a headache, so Patience tried her best to suppress them, at least for the night. "I'm sorry you had to go through that," she said after a moment.

Michael brushed her cheek. "I'm sorry *you* had to."

Chapter Twenty-Eight

PICKING UP HER MUG OF hot tea, Patience blew on it for several seconds before taking a careful sip. Witnessing a certain patron step foot inside the bistro, she waved them over.

Toni approached the small round table. "Sorry I'm late."

Setting her mug back down, Patience flashed a slight smile. "It's okay. I wasn't here long."

"My damn meeting ran late." Removing her coat, Toni slung it across the back of a seat, before pulling the chair out and sitting down. "It never fails, there's always that *one* dipshit at the end of the meeting who thinks that by asking a question—a question that was already answered in the *beginning* of the meeting by the way—it'll somehow draw his lips closer to the CEO's ass."

Patience giggled at her sister's commentary. Having a bit of a stressful morning at work, Toni's silliness was welcomed during their lunch time meetup that blustery Monday afternoon. "Sounds like an eventful morning."

"*Boring* is more like it. I'd prefer doing tax prep over pointless meetings." Toni removed her gloves. "Anyway, enough about that nonsense." Reaching inside a paper bag, she pulled out a small box with a clear lid. "I picked this up for you when I stopped at Jessy's bakery for my latte this morning."

Patience's gaze zoned in on the lemon glazed donut sitting before her. Her eyes then moved up, landing on Toni's smiling face.

"How many times have I told you that you don't need to keep buying me apology pastries."

"Hey now, this is *not* an apology pastry."

"Oh?" Patience's brow raised. "Then what is it?"

"It's… Umm…" Scratching her head, Toni rummaged for a good explanation. "It's a 'your birthday is coming up, so here's a pre-celebration donut'…pastry."

Patience fixed an unblinking stare. "My birthday is in *September*."

Rolling her eyes to the ceiling, Toni shook her head. "I can never lie right—okay fine, you got me. It's an apology pastry. I can't help it; I still feel bad."

"And I already told you that you don't *need* to," Patience reminded, sincere. "I don't hold that dinner against you. I'm not *upset* with you."

Eyes lowering, Toni released a heavy sigh. "I know, and I'm sorry I keep harping on it."

It had been two weeks since the doomed triple date, and although Patience had assured her that she didn't hold the idea against her, Toni still felt an enormous amount of guilt.

Fiddling with the tea bag label on the side of her orange bistro mug, Patience studied the somber look on her sister's face. "Look T… I know how much it hurts you that Angela and I aren't close. I was never blind to it and I'm sorry—"

Toni shook her head in protest. "No, Pace, you don't have to—"

"I *am* sorry that you feel like you're caught in the middle. That you have to pick a side." Patience pushed her mug aside, folding her arms on the table. "I've always tried to ease that burden on you by trying to remain cordial with Angela…having some type of open dialogue with her, but I *can't* anymore. At least not for a while."

Toni tilted her head, sympathy written on her face as she listened.

"What she pulled…it hurt. I just can't be around her or communicate with her in any capacity right now, and to be completely honest I don't even want my daughter around her. The negativity is too much for anyone to handle, *especially* a child,"

Patience continued. "So, I'll gladly sit out of any function you have that'll include Angela, and I don't want you to feel bad about it."

Toni's reply stalled in her chest for a moment. The idea saddened her. "That's *impossible* Patience. Do you really think I'm going to host a Thanksgiving dinner, a cookout, or throw a birthday party for Jordan, and not have you there?" She crossed her arms. "Hell, even if I have to put you both on some sort of schedule, you're going to *be* there."

Patience sighed. "Toni—"

"What if I talked to her? Try to find out what her issue is?" Toni desperately cut in. "If I can get to the bottom of—"

"It doesn't *matter* at this point," Patience stressed. "Nothing you say will change her feelings towards or about me. So, to protect my peace, I'm steering clear of her, and I need you to respect that, okay?"

Toni opened her mouth with the intent of offering solace, a compromise, *something*. But she had nothing. Patience was right; nothing that Toni could or have *ever* said to Angela would help the situation. "Okay...I'll respect it."

"Thank you." Patience took another sip of her tea, while Toni dragged the menu to her. "Oh, and don't let what's going on between she and I, affect your relationship with her... She actually *loves you*."

Toni glanced off to the side. *It already has.* "I'll try not to."

Opening the bakery box, Patience took the donut from it. Breaking it, she handed half out for Toni. "Here, fix your face."

Taking the piece from her sister's hand, Toni snickered a bit. "I need to, right? I'm sure it's looking good and long right now."

Giggling, Patience bit into the gooey treat.

Sitting on Michael's bed, Patience rubbed the back of her neck, stretching it from side to side before refocusing on the laptop sitting atop the comforter. Hearing footsteps approaching from the hall, her eyes drew to the cracked bedroom door.

"Hey, you all right up here?" Michael asked, stepping inside. Offering a soft smile, she nodded.

"Dante just left. His loud mouth didn't disturb your nap, did it?"

"No, he wasn't that loud." She motioned to her laptop. "I decided to eighty-six the nap anyway and look over some work instead."

Leaving work early that day, she'd gone to Michael's house. Michael, who had taken a personal day, was more than happy for her company until it was time to pick Noelle up from school.

But when Dante had popped over for a vent session, Patience, wanting to give the brothers a chance to talk without a third party, had excused herself to Michael's bedroom. Initially she'd intended on checking a few work emails before taking a quick cat nap. But after reading an email from the company's director, Patience had decided against it.

"Is he okay?" she asked as she stretched her neck again.

Michael stepped further into the room. Placing his hands into his pockets, he lingered by the bed. "Yeah, he's fine," he answered. "He saw Lori while he was at the grocery store and got a little in his feelings. I let him talk it out, then gave him some leftovers and he went on his way."

"Poor thing…" Patience sighed. "It's good that you guys are allowing him to be vulnerable. You'd be surprised at how many families don't encourage that."

Michael nodded in agreement. "This is true." He watched as Patience went back to scanning the screen. Peeping an enlarged image, he pointed to it. "Nice house. Is that a new listing?"

"Yeah, it is." Patience glanced at him. "I checked an email from management a little while ago and learned that we acquired this seven-figure mansion not too far from the Paradise Valley area, and I've been assigned as the realtor." She rolled her shoulders back. "So, I'm just doing a bit of research on the home and the neighborhood… I'll go see it sometime next week, but I'd like to get a head start."

Michael's face lit with excitement. "That's great. That'll be a hell of a commission."

This time *Patience* nodded in agreement. "Commission from a huge sale like this is always a motivation factor. But I'm not going to lie, I'm already starting to stress a little bit."

"Why is that?"

"Well, apparently the seller is moving across the country within the next few months, and is eager to unload this property as soon as possible," she explained. "And from what I can see in these pictures, their décor is…outdated…as *fuck*."

Patience's colorful addition to the description drew a chuckle from Michael.

"So, I'll have to convince them to let me restage. I'll need to coordinate an open house—" She released a sigh, "I can handle it, but…"

"You want everything to run smoothly," Michael finished.

She gave a nod. "Yeah."

"I get that. I have no doubt it will." Sitting on the edge of the bed, Michael smiled. "If you need a buyer reference, you know you can use me."

Patience shot an amused look his way. "I appreciate the offer, but I'm not so sure a glowing review from the man I'm sleeping with would impress potential buyers."

"Well, we weren't sleeping together when you sold me this house, so…" he countered, voice filled with humor.

She lightly nudged him with her arm. "I know."

Michael opened his mouth to say something else, but was distracted by Patience putting her hand back to her neck. The tension was clear on her face. "What's wrong with your neck?"

Straightening her posture, she grimaced. "A classic case of sitting with it bent forward for too long."

Michael sat back on the bed, positioning himself against the headboard. He signaled for her to sit back. "Take a break. Let me get the knot out."

Not hesitating, Patience closed her laptop then nudged herself between Michael's legs, her back facing him.

Michael moved her hair to one side, before applying slight pressure to the nape of her neck. Closing her eyes, and letting her head hang lazily, Patience inhaled and exhaled deeply as Michael's fingers kneaded the tender spot, before massaging the area between her shoulder blades.

She relished the thirty-minute massage. The tightness now fully dissipated, Patience rested back against Michael's chest, breathing out a relaxed sigh. "Thank you. I needed that."

Running his hands across her shoulders, Michael kissed her cheek. "You're welcome."

Reaching a hand up, Patience cupped his chin as she turned her face to him, then brushed his lips with hers, her silent display of additional gratitude. When Michael's half-lidded eyes loitered on her mouth, before rising to meet her eyes, heat stirred within her. Running a finger across his bottom lip, she flaunted a sensual smirk. "You look like *you* need something."

Michael's deep searing gaze spoke volumes. "I do."

"Yeah?" She ran her hand along his thigh. "What's that?"

Not uttering a word, Michael pressed another kiss to Patience. His fingers grazed her neck before he put his lips to it.

Biting her bottom lip, Patience's hand traveled up Michael's thigh, ready to feel what was pressed against her back. But Michael took hold of her hand and gently returned it to his thigh instead.

As much as Michael wanted to satiate his own cravings, that wasn't his mission. His hands traveled down, reaching the neckline of her button-up blouse. He undid one, then another, and another until the fabric separated, falling at her sides. With one hand stroking her waist, his other slid beneath the soft fabric of her bra, fingers teasing her sensitive nipples.

Body tingling with arousal at the feeling of Michael's gentle, yet tantalizing touch, a ragged exhale left Patience. She squeezed his leg as he continued to massage down her torso, until he reached her flared skirt.

Michael gathered the fabric, pulling it up to her waist. He then guided her legs apart with his hand.

Legs thrown over Michael's, Patience shut her eyes, clasping a hand over the back of Michael's head as he rubbed her inner thighs. The touch was intensifying her want of where she knew his hands were working their way to.

Hand gliding beneath Patience's panties, Michael slipped his fingers inside of her. Holding steady, he savored the feeling.

Patience quietly panted as his fingers gingerly moved in and out of her. When he finally brought them to the part that longed to be touched, a gasp left her as her back arched.

Bringing his arm around her waist, holding her secure, Michael's fingers caressed her. Feeling her grind against his hand as his movements went from gradual and soft, to quicker and more intense, his own breathing became heavy.

Her body writhed, and her moans turned into deep groans as the impending climax gradually rose. Eyes squeezed shut, Patience's body stiffened as the orgasm took hold of her, leaving her trembling against him.

Michael secured Patience in his arms as she worked to steady her breathing. He kissed her cheek, then leaned in close to her ear. "*That's* what I wanted."

Letting out a faint, yet labored chuckle, Patience patted his face. "Good job."

Chapter Twenty-Nine

JORDAN JUMPED INTO THE BACKSEAT of her mother's car, practically headfirst. "Mom! Mom, guess what—"

Toni snapped her head around. "Girl—what's your deal jumping in the car like that?!" She squinted when Jordan busted out laughing. "It's not funny, crazy."

Leaning over, Jordan closed the door then straightened up in the seat. Though she'd stopped laughing, the amusement was still on her face. "Sorry, but I'm really happy."

Toni shook her head as she pulled away from the school pick-up line. "I'm happy that you're happy. But what *specifically* are you happy about?"

Jordan dug into her bookbag, pulling out a stapled paper. "I got an A on my science test." She held the graded paper high.

Toni's eyes, which were steady on the road ahead of her, broadened in joy. "That's wonderful my love." She recalled how stressed her daughter had been just days before it, even up to the last minute when Toni had quizzed her on the way to school the morning of. "See? I *told* you you'd do well."

Jordan did a little dance in her seat, examining the big red "A" and the words, "great job Jordan", etched on top of the page. "Thank you." She rested the paper on her lap. "Daddy said that if I do good on the test, I can pick out something fun to do this weekend."

"Oh *did* he?" Toni smirked. She was pretty sure that had

Jordan not gotten the A, that her father would've said the same. "Well, have you decided on what you want to do?"

Jordan fussed with one of her braids. "No, not yet."

"That's fine, there's no rush." Toni glanced out the side mirror. "In the meantime, how about we stop and get some hot chocolate with extra marshmallows?" She giggled when a clap sounded from the backseat, followed by an ecstatic "Yes!"

Michael was scrolling through images on his tablet. Pausing long enough to take a sip of coffee, he returned his eyes to the screen. Clicking a few buttons, he activated a security video of the outside of a home, before switching to the inside view. He intently examined the recordings, before clearing them from the screen.

Reclining back in his seat, he gazed out of the window, the images still vivid in his mind. "I need to take a trip up there," he said aloud. A thought crossing his mind, he grabbed his cell. Swiftly, he typed out a text, sending it to Patience.

> Hey baby, I hope your day is going well. Just a quick question, when are you able to get a few days off?

Hearing a tap on the closed door, he looked up from the phone. "Come in." He offered a polite smile to his receptionist when she stepped in as he set the phone down. "Hey Cassie. You on your way out to lunch?"

"I was, but someone just stopped in," Cassie replied. "Said they wanted to speak to you."

Perplexity settled on Michael's face. "Really? I don't have any more in-person meetings scheduled for the day." On his laptop, he pulled up his calendar just to double check. "Yeah, nothing here. Did they leave a name?"

"Yes. It's a woman." Cassie gave a quick glance to the sticky pad in her hand. "Her name is Angela Bishop."

Michael's bewildered frown deepened. *What the fuck?* He had no idea what Patience's troublesome sister possibly wanted to talk to him about. The most *important* question on his mind was, if Patience knew that she was there.

Realizing that Cassie was still standing there waiting for a reply, he rose from his seat. "Where is she?" Michael asked.

"The Annex conference room."

Michael rounded his desk. "Okay, thank you. I'll handle it, you take your lunch."

Giving a nod, Cassie walked out of the office with Michael following.

The questions Michael had only intensified when he peered into the conference room. Angela was in fact sitting in a seat, drumming her fingernails on the hardwood table.

Michael entered the room. "Angela?"

Head snapping in his direction, a hint of a smile appeared on Angela's face. "Hello Michael." Standing, she adjusted her coat. "How are you?"

"Well, thanks." He folded his arms, fixing her with stern eyes. "What are you doing here?"

Staring, Angela stalled her response. *Damn, Patience really gets to climb him whenever she wants.*

"Angela," Michael's voice inflected a bit of harshness.

She blinked several times, knocking the inappropriate thoughts from her mind. "Yes?"

"What are you *doing* here? Does Patience know you're here?"

Angela shrugged casually. "I was in the area and remembered that you worked down here, so I decided to pop in to say hi."

Michael's eyes flashed a hint of annoyance. "Angela…I never *told* you where I worked." *And I highly doubt that Patience did either.*

Angela rubbed her forehead. "Okay, you've caught me. I looked you up. It wasn't too hard. There aren't that many Michael Carters who own construction companies in Maple Glenn—"

"I'd appreciate the *point* of this visit." Michael had no idea what games Angela was playing, but he wanted no parts.

Angela threw up a cautious hand. "I just came here to apologize." She could sense that Michael was *one* second away from asking her to leave. "I know how awkward that dinner was a few weeks ago. I wasn't in a good headspace, and I don't want you to have the wrong impression of me."

Yeah, I think my impression is spot on. "With all due respect, *I'm* not the one who's entitled to your apology," he said. "And I'll repeat my question, does your sister know you're here?"

"No, she *doesn't*," Angela spat out. "My *sister* has not answered, nor returned *any* of my phone calls, so..."

Michael shook his head. He didn't blame Patience. If the shoe was on his foot, he wouldn't have answered either.

"So, maybe me extending it to *you* will show *her* that I'm offering an olive branch." Hope shining in Angela's eyes, she shrugged once more. "*Maybe*...you could put in a good word for me?"

Michael's brows drew closer. There was no sincerity in Angela's voice. And if she was *serious* about trying to apologize, Patience's job was just blocks from his. She could've ambushed *her* instead of *him*. "No. I can't do that."

Angela flinched her head back. "I'm sorry?"

"With all due respect Angela, I think you should leave." He gestured to the open door, "I'll see you out."

Leaning her head to one side, Angela fixed him with a frosty stare. "Okay then." She adjusted the purse on her shoulder. "Well, I appreciate your time, and wish you and my sister nothing but happiness..." She sauntered past Michael, leaving the room. "For as long as it lasts."

She hadn't said the last part low enough. Michael had heard it; it made his frown turn into a repulsed glare. Which he shot at her departing back. "The fuck?" he hissed to himself.

Returning to his office, Michael headed straight for his desk, promptly dialing Patience.

"Hey baby, I got your text earlier but was in a meeting, I'll check though," Patience cheerfully answered.

Michael rubbed his eyes with his fingertips. He almost didn't want to tell her what he was about to. She sounded like she was having a pleasant day. "Okay—umm honey, I just wanted to let you know that your sister just left here."

"Who Toni?"

He paused. "No...Angela."

"Excuse me?" Patience's sunny voice quickly morphed to one filled with infuriation. "What the hell was she there for? What did she *say*?"

Michael released a heavy sigh. "To be honest I don't really know, but she claimed to want to apologize to me about the dinner situation and..."

"And *what* Michael? What else did she say?" Patience pressed. By Michael's hesitation, she knew he was leaving something out.

Rubbing his forehead, Michael sighed yet again. He didn't want to further upset Patience by telling her the specific details. She had *enough* to be upset about when it came to the woman. "Listen, I didn't want to upset you or make it seem like I'm starting any trouble by telling you that she was here, but... Given the relationship between you two, I didn't want to keep this from you."

There was silence for a moment. "I appreciate that. Thank you for telling me." Patience's monotone voice had lowered. "I have to go. I'll call you later, okay?"

"Okay..." Michael couldn't help it, he felt bad. "Are you all right?"

"Sure. Talk to you later."

"Later." Even though the air had gone dead, he still held the phone to his ear for a few seconds before lowering it. Annoyed with the entire situation, he rubbed his face with his hand.

"*Four* polishes, Noelle? Really?" Patience observed as Noelle placed each bottle of nail polish into Patience's hand basket.

Moving curly tendrils from her face, Noelle shrugged. "It's for my design inspiration."

Patience chuckled. "Design inspiration, huh?" she shook her head when Noelle grinned. "Fine, I'll trust you."

"Why thank you." Noelle returned her focus to the nail supply wall. After a quick scan, she gasped, grabbing a small bottle of purple glitter from the shelf. "Ooh, and glitter…This is it; I promise."

Patience waved a hand. "If you say so." The beauty supply store was one of a few stops that Patience had planned on making that Friday afternoon. She looked at Noelle as the girl examined her haul in the hand basket. "After we leave here, we'll head to the grocery store to pick up the pizza ingredients, then head home to start our girls' weekend."

"Ooh, we have to get the ingredients to bake our cookies too."

"I checked before we left this morning, we already have everything we need for that." Patience gestured to the cashier line. "You ready?"

"Yep." Noelle bounced behind her mother as they headed for the line.

Patience was excited about their weekend plans. Probably more excited than her daughter was. It had been a while since they'd done one of their girls' weekends. Though Michael was a welcome addition to their lives, she still wanted to make sure she spent one-on-one time with Noelle that didn't include her normal motherly duties.

"I already figured out what our first movie of the night will be," Patience announced, paying for the items.

"It's not anything scary, is it?" Noelle asked.

Patience shot her a confused look. "When have I ever let you watch a scary movie?"

"Never, but one of my friends showed me a scary video on her phone after school, and I didn't like it, so…" Noelle shrugged. "Just wanted to make sure."

Staring for a second, Patience vigorously shook her head. "Don't watch any more of that nonsense." She retrieved the bag from the cashier, then motioned her daughter along. "Come on."

Patience pulled the pizza from the oven, resting it on the stove top. Her stomach rumbled at the site of the golden crust, bubbling cheese, and lightly charred toppings. She removed the oven mitt from her hand, resting it on the counter. "While this is cooling, let's decorate the cookies. They should be cool enough."

Pulling out a chair, Noelle plopped down at the table, then took a cookie from the cooling rack. "I remember the first time we decorated cookies together."

Sitting down, Patience placed a cookie onto a plate. "You do?"

Opening a tube of purple cookie icing, Noelle nodded. "Yeah, it was after we came from the park. You bought me a big cookie with a bunny on it, and I dropped it when I tried to get out the car."

Listening, Patience opened her own tube of icing.

"It broke and I started crying," Noelle recalled, squirting out a design. "You picked me up, told me it was okay, and that we would make a new one. Then later that night, you baked cookies and you let me help you decorate them."

Patience looked at Noelle in surprise. "You were only three years old then, you remember that?"

Smiling, Noelle nodded again. "Yes." She tilted her head. "Do *you* still remember that?"

"Of course, I do. I remember everything that happened leading up to that." Eyes lowered to the cookie she was drawing on, a melancholy sigh left Patience. "I took you to the park that day, and I let you run around in the grass while I watched. I umm… I looked away for less than a minute and you had run over to the overcrowded rubber turf where other children were playing…"

303

J.B. VAMPLE

Captivated by the retelling, Noelle placed her elbow on the table. Resting her chin on her hand, she stared at her mother with bright eyes.

"Right before I was able to get to you, you were knocked down by another kid, who was in the middle of racing." Moving her cookie aside, she folded her arms on the tabletop. An unexpected knot in her throat began to form, but she swallowed it, not wanting to become emotional over the memory. "You weren't seriously hurt thank God—just a skinned knee, but your little crying face… You were so upset, and I felt *so* bad because I shouldn't have taken my eyes off you."

"Aww, Mommy. It wasn't your fault that I was a super-fast runner."

Patience couldn't help but chuckle. "You still are." The humor dissipated from her face. "Anyway, after I took you to the doctor and they reassured my paranoid self that you were okay, I bought your cookie to cheer you up and you were so excited about it. You wanted to hold it, so I let you, and when we got home, I was taking you out of the car and you dropped it, and… Well, you remember the rest."

"Yeah… I mean, I know I fell and everything, but it's a happy memory for me, because I got to decorate cookies with you." Resuming her decorating, she flashed a sweet grin. "And look, we still do it."

Patience's soft eyes resonated with both love and gratitude as a smile filtered through. She'd replayed the day's events in her head more times than she could count. Going over what she'd done wrong, questioning her decisions, questioning her abilities as a mother. To learn that it was a happy memory for Noelle, relieved her more than she could ever imagine.

Leaning forward, Patience tapped Noelle's cheek with her finger. "You have no idea what that means to me, Bunny. Thank you for telling me."

"You're welcome Mommy." Reaching for a bottle of sugar crystals, she heard a distinct ringing from the living room. She craned her neck in that direction. "Can I answer my phone?"

"Sure, go ahead. I'll wait for you."

"Okay. Be right back." Noelle jumped down from the seat, rushing into the living room.

Patience took the brief silence to reflect on the past few moments. She was so lost in her own thoughts that Noelle running back into the kitchen startled her.

"Mommy, Mommy, Jordan invited me to go to the Candy World Show tomorrow!" Noelle squealed, holding the phone up. "Can I go? Please?"

"Huh?" Patience squinted. "*What* is Candy World?"

Noelle sidled up next to her, clutching her arm. "It's a candy museum, where we can get candy, play games—it sounds like so much fun. It's in DC. Can I go?"

Patience put a hand up. "Wait, wait—*tomorrow? DC?* — Where do you kids *find* these places?"

"Commercials."

Patience rubbed her forehead. "Noelle—*first*, your aunt hasn't mentioned this to me *at all*. Does she even *know* that you two are making plans like this?"

"Hi Aunt Pace, Mom knows."

Frowning, Patience's eyes lowered to the phone in Noelle's hand. "You have me on speaker, little girl?"

Noelle grimaced. "Sorry. Jordan wanted to be on the phone when I asked you."

Patience held her hand out for the phone. "Jordan, put your mother on the phone."

Placing the device in her mother's outstretched hand, Noelle stood close by, eyes wide with anticipation.

"If this is true Noelle, what about *our* weekend plans?" Patience asked.

Noelle shuffled her weight from one foot to the other. "Well…" She put her finger to her lips, trying to search for the right words. Words that would not hurt her mother's feelings. "You have me all the time… Candy World is only around for a while."

Staring at her daughter's eager face, Patience slowly shook her head. *Kids.*

"Patience, Jordan asked us earlier if she could go to this thing. Her dad told her she could do whatever she wanted this weekend as a reward for her good grade, and this is what Miss Thing chose," Toni spoke into the line. "We checked it out, and there's a show in DC tomorrow. We're going to drive up early in the morning, have breakfast, go to the show, then more than likely go to dinner or something afterward."

Patience took the phone off speaker, putting it to her ear. "Oh okay... And I'm sure Noelle is going to want to spend the night with you guys after all of that."

"Girl, you already know the answer," Toni replied. "Listen, I know you had plans with her, and I'm sorry they sprung this on you. If Noelle can't go, Jordan will have no choice but to understand. She'll be just fine."

Patience sighed. "No, no, far be it from me to disappoint *both* of these spoiled kids." She looked to Noelle, who had her hands clasped together, a pleading look in her eyes. "She can go."

Jumping up and down, Noelle tossed her hands in the air. "Yay!"

"What time do you want her in the morning?" Patience asked as Noelle danced around the kitchen.

"Umm, it'll be easier if she spends the night tonight."

"Of course." Patience stood from her seat. "I'll bring her over. See you in a bit." Hanging up, she held the phone out for Noelle. "Here. Go pack a bag. I'll drop you off tonight."

Noelle practically tackled Patience with a big hug. "Thank you, thank you, thank you."

Patience smoothed her hand over the top of Noelle's head. "Yeah, you're welcome." She stood there as Noelle sprinted out of the kitchen, leaving her there to tend to the food she'd now have to eat alone.

Chapter Thirty

RETURNING HOME FROM DROPPING NOELLE off at her sister's, Patience tossed her keys on the table. She headed for the kitchen and removed the pizza from the refrigerator. Cutting a slice, she reheated it then took a seat at the table, just as her phone rang. Seeing Michael's name, she promptly answered. "Hey."

The somber greeting didn't go unnoticed. "Hey. Everything okay?" Michael wondered.

"Yeah, it's fine." She sighed. "What are you up to?"

"Just about to put in a movie. I won't keep you because I know you and Noelle are probably deep into your *own* movie marathon, but I wanted to—"

"No, there's no need to rush off. I'm here alone." Patience took a bite of pizza.

Michael hit mute on his television. "Oh? What happened?"

She swallowed her bite. "My child ditched me for candy." Her glum voice was low. "She and Jordan are going to some Candy World exhibit in DC tomorrow. So, yeah…*candy*."

"Aww, I'm sorry baby." Michael knew how much these bonding moments meant to Patience.

"It's all right. I'm okay. She'll have fun, so that's all that matters."

"Yes, I suppose it does," Michael agreed. "I hate to hear you disappointed though. Is there anything I can do to make you feel better?"

Patience couldn't help but smile a bit. "You can come over and watch this sappy movie with me...or I could come over *there*."

"I'll come to you." Michael stood from the couch. As he took a step, he paused as something crossed his mind. "Hey, what time will Noelle be back tomorrow?"

"She won't be back until Sunday."

Michael rubbed his chin, pondering. "Hmmm."

Patience picked a sliver of bell pepper from the pizza slice. "Why, what's on your mind?"

"I think I have a better idea of how to cheer you up."

Her brows lifted. "And what would that be?"

A smooth smile materialized on Michael's face. "You'll find out...can you pack a bag?"

Baffled by the request, Patience flinched her head back slightly. "Say what?"

Michael chuckled at the reply. "Pack a bag." He moved towards the steps. "Just something for the weekend. I'll be there in a half."

Patience leaned forward in her seat. "Michael—what do you have up your sleeve?"

"I'm not taking you far, but I *am* taking you *somewhere*," he alluded. "Unless, that is, you *just* want me to come over and watch a movie. If you want that, I'll do that."

Patience was silent for a second. While she hadn't planned on leaving the house, she was certainly intrigued by what Michael had planned. "No, no. I'll pack."

"Perfect. I'll see you soon."

Patience stared out of the passenger window, watching the trees go by, as Michael maneuvered his car through the remote area. He had yet to tell her where he was taking her. Not so much as a hint when he'd picked her up from her house two and a half hours ago.

While she'd been initially content with letting Michael keep their destination a mystery, the farther they drove out, and the less residential area she saw, her curiosity began to pique.

"Okay Michael where are we going?" she asked, breaking through the music playing through the speaker. "Are we even still in Virginia?"

Eyes steady on the dark road ahead, Michael pushed a button on the dash. The song volume reduced significantly. "We are. Pine Hill to be exact... Well, we'll *be* in Pine Hill in about ten minutes."

"Oh." Crossing her arms over her chest, Patience peered out the passenger side window once again. "Just curious because we left the highway a while ago... This is a little bit more rural than I'm used to seeing."

He shot her a quick glance before returning his eyes to the road. "You're not nervous, are you?"

"No, no. I'm not nervous." She looked over at him. "You're not about to kill me and bury my body out here, are you?"

Mystified by the weird question, Michael squinted. "What the hell?"

"Well...*are* you?"

"Woman—" He shook his head. "*No,* I'm not going to kill you and bury your body."

Tickled by his reaction, she let out a quick laugh. "I'm joking. I know you'd never hurt me."

"No, I wouldn't," he assured, then chuckled. "You're something else, you know that?"

"Yes." She rested her head back against the headrest. "But seriously Carter, what's even out here?"

"I promise, you'll see in about five minutes." Michael pulled off onto an exit, then continued further down the road until they arrived in front of a structure.

As the car pulled onto a gravel covered driveway, Patience kept her focus on the small, two-story house in front of her. Or what she *thought* was a house; it was hard to tell what it was in the pitch darkness.

Before she was able to form her mouth to ask a question, Michael picked up his phone. In just a few taps, the lights turned on both inside and outside. They illuminated the pathway and the deck.

Patience marveled at the beautiful architecture. "Is this a house?"

"It's a cabin," he clarified, undoing his seat belt.

She unfastened her own seat belt. "Oh," was all that she could say as Michael exited out of the car.

Michael took her hand as she stepped out. "Watch your step." He pointed to the area around her feet. "The gravel is a bit uneven right here."

Holding her hair back from her face, Patience glanced down at said area, making sure to step over it. "I'm good." She stood watching as Michael grabbed both of their overnight bags, and a grocery bag from the trunk of his car. "Will it be just us here?"

"Of course." Flashing his handsome smile at her, Michael gestured his head towards the cabin, before leading the way up the path.

Patience shivered as she walked alongside Michael up the deck stairs. "It's so much colder here, than it was back home."

"I know. Hang on just a sec." Michael pushed several buttons on a keypad by the door, unlocking it. Pushing open the door, he put a hand on her arm. "Here, come inside."

Patience stepped through the entrance as Michael locked up behind them. Her eyes went wide at what she saw. When Michael said that they were at a cabin, she fully expected to walk into a dank, dull, pine-filled space full of dust, and outdated, dingy furniture. What she *didn't* expect was the bright, cozy, modern layout and décor. "It's beautiful in here," she gushed, unbuttoning her coat.

"Thank you." Michael set their bags on a chair, before swiftly moving to the wood burning fireplace. Grabbing a few pieces of wood from a mesh bin, he placed them inside then lit it. "This thing heats up fast, so the chill will be off shortly."

Patience rubbed her arms with her hands. "Surprisingly, it's not that cold in here."

"The pros of good insulation," he quipped, standing upright. "Come on, I'll show you the rest of the place."

Patience followed Michael through the rest of the two-bedroom, one-bath layout. Each room was decorated in the same modern yet rustic style as the living room. The kitchen was updated with state-of-the-art appliances, and a four-seater table. The quaint bathroom, with its polished clawfoot bathtub, screamed contemporary countryside.

Standing at the back door, Michael glanced at Patience as she stared out of the glass. She couldn't make out much aside from the silhouettes of the trees surrounding the property, but it didn't make the view any less calming.

"In the morning, you'll be able to see the full beauty of this place." Michael turned his attention to the window. "There's a firepit out there, and a lake a way down." He let out a relaxed sigh. "It's completely isolated…and peaceful."

She ran her hands up her shoulders. "That sounds…much needed."

"I was planning on bringing you up here after the weather broke, but when you told me about your derailed plans, I figured why wait?" Michael revealed. She looked at him, prompting him to return her gaze. "Figured, it might ease your disappointment…if not a little bit."

Patience crinkled her nose. "It's helping." Sure, Patience was salty, but Michael's sweet gesture made her feel ten times better. Moving her hair behind her shoulder, she leaned against the door. "How did you find this place? And on such short notice?"

Shoving his hand into his pocket, he shrugged. "I own it."

Her mouth dropped open. "Seriously?"

"Yes. I bought it a few years ago... It didn't look like *this*, but I saw potential in it," he explained. "I renovated it myself, little by little with the intention of eventually reselling it. But when I finished, I realized I just couldn't part with it."

Eyes roaming the kitchen, she nodded in agreement. "Yeah, I don't blame you."

"I used to come for a weekend every once in a while, to decompress." He rested his shoulder against the window. "And while I check the *security cameras* often, I haven't been up here in over a year."

Smiling softly, Patience took his hand. "I'm sure you need the decompression as much as I do."

Bringing her hand to his lips, Michael kissed it. She was right; he certainly could use the peace and solitude, and he was more than happy to share it with the woman he loved. "You hungry?"

Feeling the heat circulate, Patience finally removed her coat. "Yes." She'd barely eaten her pizza when Michael had called earlier; she'd gotten so preoccupied with packing and wondering where she was about to embark, that she hadn't bothered to finish the slice. "Is there somewhere nearby we can order from?"

Stepping away from the door, Michael shook his head. "Nah. But I brought some groceries. I'll whip something up for us."

"Sounds perfect." She slung the coat over her arm. "You didn't happen to bring wine, did you?"

Michael flashed her a satisfied look. "You think I didn't?" He headed back for the living room. "Both red *and* white, my love."

"*God*, yes," she rejoiced, earning a laugh from him.

Chapter Thirty-One

TONI POKED HER HEAD INTO Jordan's bedroom. "You two finish getting ready, we're about to leave," she announced to the girls, who were busy dancing around the room.

"Okay," they gleefully replied in unison.

Leaving them to do just that, Toni put the cell back to her ear as she entered her own bedroom. "Hey Angie, I'm back."

Cradling her own cell with her shoulder, Angela adjusted a picture frame on her mantle. "Where are you going?"

"Rob and I are taking the girls to a Candy World exhibit." Sitting on a chaise lounge, Toni glanced at the watch on her wrist. "We'll be leaving in a few minutes to drive to DC."

"Candy, huh? Sounds like a sugar rush waiting to happen," Angela jeered, then paused. "You said *girls*. Noelle is there too?"

"Of *course*. You know those two are inseparable."

Angela drummed her nails on the marble. *Yeah, so are you and Patience.* "Oh okay… Is Patience there with you?" The bite in her tone was obvious. "Is this another family outing I'm left out of?"

Toni rolled her eyes. *Girl please, like you give a damn about some candy.* "No, she *isn't*. She allowed Noelle to come with us, and *she* is upstate with Michael."

Angela's lips tightened with envy; she couldn't remember the last time Trevor took *her* anywhere. "Oh…well how nice."

"Yes Angela, it *is* nice." Toni knew that sarcasm well. "It's *nice* that our sister is happy. Even though *you clearly* have an issue with that."

Angela scoffed. "Where the hell did *that* come from?"

"Your tone and *behavior*."

"I'm not about to do this with you Toni. I just called to talk for a bit, not be accused of something so ridiculous." She sucked her teeth. "First Patience's damn boyfriend treats me like I'm *Satan* when I went to see him, and now you—"

"Woah, woah time out. Time *out*." Toni sat up in her seat. "You went to see Michael?"

Angela folded her lips inward. *Damn, let that slip right out.* "Yes Toni. I went to his office a few days ago to talk to him, and let's just say he wasn't particularly happy about that."

Mouth hanging open, Toni tried to come to terms with what she'd just heard, and the way Angela was being so *casual* about it. "So let me get this straight, after that whole dinner fiasco, you *ambushed* that man at his place of work?"

Angela examined her nails. "It was an unexpected visit, yes."

Toni frowned. "Does *Patience* know you did that?"

"I'm sure he told her."

Balling her fist, Toni put it to her forehead. "What the hell were you trying to achieve by *doing* that Angela? What were you *thinking*?"

"I was *thinking* that maybe he could pass on a message to Patience, since she calls herself not talking to me," Angela snapped. "She complained that I barely spoke to her, and now that I'm reaching out, she ignores me. But *I'm* the unreasonable one, right? —You know what, I refuse to talk about this anymore, goodbye."

Toni's eyes bulged when the line went dead. "You got it for now. Just wait," she bristled aloud. Tossing the phone on the chair, she rose to her feet. She'd be sure to give Angela a piece of her mind, and talk to Patience about it, once she got the girls settled later.

Walking to the adjoining bathroom door, Toni gave it a knock.

"Rob babe, you've been in there a while. We need to leave; I want to beat some of the crowd."

"I'm coming." Rob's voice was low.

Toni stepped back as the door opened. The look on Rob's face was sickly. "You all right?"

"Yeah, yeah, I'm good." He rubbed his forehead. "My stomach was acting funny, but I'm good now."

The unease on Toni's face had not waned. "Did you eat something bad?"

Rob shrugged. "I don't think so." He moved around her, heading into the room. "Like I said babe, I'm good."

"Okay then. I'll round up the little ladies."

Lounging in his patio seat, Michael stared out at the grove of trees ahead of him, fully visible in the morning daylight. Though the branches were bare, the sight was still something to behold. The chill in the late winter air was toned down by the fire, roaring in the stone pit in front of him. He'd been sitting out there on the cabin deck for nearly an hour, while Patience milled about inside.

Feeling a presence sidle up next to him, he looked up to see Patience standing there. She was holding mugs of something hot, steaming in the cold air. He smiled at her.

She smiled back, handing him the mug. "Here."

"Thank you."

Her own mug in hand, Patience took the empty seat next to him. Taking the throw blanket from the arm of the chair, she covered herself before resting her back against the cushion. "I just got off the phone with that child of mine."

"Oh yeah? Is she having fun?"

"Of *course* she is," Patience answered. "She told me to be prepared for all the candy she plans on bringing back."

"You'll both be eating it for days."

Patience cut her eye at him. "So will *you*, because she's bringing *you* some too." Michael laughed, and she joined him. "No, but I'm happy she's enjoying herself. She's a good kid, she deserves it."

Michael's gaze lit with admiration. "Absolutely. She's also a *happy* kid. Which is a direct reflection of you and your parenting."

Guiding some curls away from her face, Patience blushed. "I appreciate that." She tapped her nails against the mug. "My wish is that she stays happy, you know? As unrealistic as that may be."

"I know baby, and it's not unrealistic."

She threw him a smile, hoping that that would ring true. "Yeah, you're right."

"I tend to be most times," Michael joked, earning a giggle from her. He gave the contents in his mug a long blow before tasting it. "Mmm. This is good. What is it?"

Patience finished her own sip. "It's a hot spiced cider concoction that I came up with."

"I like it." He took another sip. "Can I get the recipe?"

"Hell, I don't even remember what it is," she confessed, prompting a chuckle from him. "I was throwing stuff in the pot while I was on the phone." Taking another sip, she stared out at the scenery. Taking it all in, she expelled a tranquil sigh. The combination of a cozy evening in, complete with one of their passionate love-making sessions, followed by a hearty well-prepared breakfast that morning, had Patience fully relaxed.

"Can we come up here again soon?" she asked, breaking through the silence.

"We can come up here anytime you want. Just say when." Michael cupped the warm mug with his hands. "I'll give you a key, in case you want to come up here by yourself from time to time."

"I appreciate the offer, but I don't see my jittery ass driving those backroads alone. So, you'll be my companion for these trips."

A quiet laugh sounded from Michael. "Whatever you want." He downed the rest of his beverage, setting the empty mug on a small table beside him. "I chopped up some firewood earlier. So, we'll have more than enough to keep us warm until we leave."

Patience eyed the pile of wood stacked near the deck. She'd watched him chop it from the window, and quickly found herself getting turned on. The way he'd utilized the strength in his arms and back while wielding that axe, the glimpse of his abs she'd gotten when he'd used his shirt to wipe the sweat from his face—had she not called her child to check in on her, Patience would've come out and interrupted his work.

"Okay, good," she softly spoke. The rugged scene still playing in her head, Patience's eyes left the pile of wood for Michael, who was staring out ahead of him.

"Do you want to take a trip to the next town over?" Michael glanced over at her. "It's about thirty minutes from here. They have some shops, a bakery, stuff like that."

Patience stared. Her gaze slowly lowered to his lap, lingering for a bit before rising back up to his face. Going anywhere was the last thing on her mind. "No...I'm good here." She scanned the property with her eyes. "We're completely isolated right?"

Michael nodded. "Yep. Not another cabin for a few miles."

Patience set her mug down, then stood. "Good." Blanket in hand, she moved over to Michael.

She straddled Michael's lap before he had a chance to form any other words. Not that he cared to in the moment. For all he could focus on was her. And when she leaned in to kiss him, he rose to life.

Patience draped her arms around Michael's neck as she deepened the kiss. Her temperature rose as his hands moved under her top, along her bare back. Moving back, she closed her eyes as his lips touched her neck. She grinded her hips against him as he covered her skin in his firm kisses.

Grabbing the zipper of her sweater jacket, Michael pulled it down, following the trail with kisses down her chest. When she reached beneath his sweatpants, taking him into her warm hand, a groan escaped him.

When Michael grabbed at her sweatpants, Patience lifted herself, making sure to hold the cover at her back. Michael tugged the rest of her clothes off at her request. She tossed them to the other chair, before returning to his lap.

Taking the cover from her, Michael held it against Patience, covering their heated bodies as she positioned herself against him. Patience lifted his shirt, pushing her hands underneath as she lowered herself down onto him, eliciting a lustful groan from Michael and a loud gasp of her own.

Michael pressed his lips to hers as her hips moved, drawing him deep inside. Sitting up, he secured his arms around her as her sensual movements consumed him. When she put her lips to his neck, it took everything in him to keep from finishing right there.

Pulling her head back, Patience gripped the back of his chair as she rode him harder and faster, hitting every spot inside of her. Pants and moans filled the air. With each stroke, Patience felt her end nearing.

Michael squeezed his eyes shut as Patience worked over him. What her body was doing to him, in the middle of nature, was indescribable. He clutched her back as the pleasure steadily built. "Fuck baby," he hissed.

Hearing Michael's words of ecstasy against her ear was Patience's undoing. Wrapping her arms around his neck, her body quivered as she came, with Michael following right after her.

Her eyes still closed, Patience rested her forehead against his. Their arms were still cradling each other as their breathing returned to normal. After several moments, Michael leaned back to touch her face. "Damn," he breathed out. "Yeah, we're definitely coming up here again."

Patience erupted with a breathy laugh. "Stop it."

Toni stood by a play area, watching her daughter and niece having fun in a bin full of candy-shaped foam pieces. They'd arrived at the Candy World exhibit nearly three hours ago. They'd taken in the displays, read facts about their favorite candy, and even got to watch a candy making session.

Now they were playing in the "candy bin", while Toni stood by, keeping a watchful eye. Rob was sitting on a nearby bench with his head leaned back against the wall. Toni eyed him sympathetically; he hadn't appeared to have gotten any better, despite what he'd been telling her.

Walking over, Toni sat down alongside him. "Hey you." Her tone was soothing. Rob opened his eyes as she ran a light hand over his head. "You okay?"

He rubbed his eyes. "Yeah, I'm fine."

She raised an eyebrow at his low voice. "You're a bad liar, you know."

Rob couldn't help but chuckle. "Good thing I don't try to do it often." Grimacing, he put a hand to his stomach.

"It was those oysters you ate last night, wasn't it?" Toni assumed, to which Rob protested with a vigorous shake of his head. "Uh huh, *yes* it was. I told you about eating that type of shit raw." Toni had tried to talk her husband out of ordering the delicacy while out at dinner last night, but her request had been rebuffed. "You *know* you have a sensitive stomach—"

Rob put his hand up. "Okay, okay." With that same hand, he caressed Toni's chin, before letting it fall limp at his side. "You might have a point. My stomach hasn't been right since."

"Do you want to get out of here? You can go lay down."

Rob stared at the children playing. "No, let them enjoy this… I'll be fine as long as I don't move too much."

"Are you *sure*, babe?"

"Yeah, I'm sure. Don't worry." He offered a faint smile. "Seriously."

"Okay but, we won't stay too much longer," Toni promised. "I'm sure the shit load of candy we'll be leaving with will make it up to them for the early departure."

Rob gave a slow nod of his head.

"They'll be occupied, and I can take proper care of you," she finished.

Smiling slyly, Rob adjusted his position to face her. "Oh yeah?... You want to tell me how you're going to do that?"

Narrowing her eyes, Toni stared at him. "By putting your ass to bed, making you tea and giving you *electrolytes.*" When Rob snickered, Toni tapped his leg. "Freak."

Though she'd told Rob that they would stay a few more hours, Toni decided to cut the trip short a half hour later. Racking up a pretty penny on souvenirs and treats, she hauled her family into the car.

As soon as they arrived home, she got Rob settled in bed, before coming back down to the living room where the girls were playing.

Jordan looked up as her mother approached. "Is Daddy okay?" she asked, concern showing on her face. She couldn't help but be worried when she'd learned during the drive back home that her father wasn't feeling well.

Toni sat on a chair. "Yeah princess, he's okay." She ran a hand through her hair. "He just ate something bad last night and it doesn't agree with his stomach."

"Oh." Jordan went back to playing with her toy, while Noelle colored in her new candy themed coloring book.

Toni leaned back against the throw pillow. "So…what do you little ladies want for dinner later?"

"Not what *Daddy* ate," Jordan quipped, earning a giggle from Noelle and an amused leer from Toni.

Toni pointed a finger at her daughter. "Very funny little girl."

A loud noise jerked Toni out of her sleep. Disoriented, she grabbed her phone, reading the time on the screen: one o'clock a.m. Setting it down, she rolled over, squinting when she didn't see Rob sleeping next to her.

Sitting up, she eyed the closed bathroom door. The light peeking underneath let her know that it was occupied. "Rob… You okay?" Not hearing anything, she pushed the covers back and got out of bed.

She approached the door, giving it a knock. "Honey?" Hearing a muffled voice, Toni twisted the knob, pushing the door open. Her eyes widened, and a gasp left her when she saw her husband, lying on the floor by the shower, holding his stomach. She bolted over, shaking him. "Robert!"

"Hmmm," he murmured as Toni turned him over.

"What happened?—" she felt his face with the back of her hand; he was burning up and his skin was clammy. "That's it, I'm taking you to the emergency room." She helped him sit up right, resting his back against the wall. "Hold on."

Toni sprinted out of the room straight for her dresser, in search of something other than the lace nightgown she had on. Her mind raced with worry for Rob, so much so that for a moment it slipped her mind that the children were there. Closing her eyes, she put her hand over her head. "Shit, shit, *shit*."

She couldn't leave them by themselves, and the person she'd normally call to come over was almost three hours away. Having a moment of clarity, Toni scooped up her phone, quickly dialing a number. "Come on, pick up," she pleaded aloud, snatching a sweatshirt from her drawer. A look of relief appeared on her face when the ringing stopped. "Angie—" The urgency in Toni's voice was heavy. "I know it's late, but I need a favor… It's an emergency."

Sighing, Jordan flopped down on the couch alongside Noelle.

Noelle brought her feet up on the chair, folding them inward. She looked over at her cousin, who was turning the TV on; the squinted stare at the screen and the puckered pout gave way to the girl's sour disposition. "Are you worried about Uncle Rob?"

Adjusting the volume of the cartoon, Jordan nodded. "A little. But Mom said they were just taking him to get checked out... I know he'll be okay though."

Noelle patted Jordan's shoulder. "Yeah, he will be." She hoped the cosign comforted her cousin. She knew that if *her* mother had to go to the hospital in the middle of the night, she would be a wreck.

From the time they'd been dropped off at Angela's house, the girls had been shuffled to one of the guest rooms, where they quickly drifted back to sleep. They'd awoken hours later to news that Jordan's parents were still in the emergency room. Now nearly three o'clock in the afternoon, both Noelle and Jordan were lounging in the family room, watching cartoons while the time ticked by.

Jordan crossed her arms, letting out a huff. "I'm ready to go *home*." While Jordan loved the elder aunt, she didn't necessarily enjoy spending nights at her house. Angela wasn't nearly as much fun as her mother, or Patience.

"Yeah," Noelle agreed. Her eyes left the colorful images bouncing across the screen, then began to slowly scan the array of photos lining the room walls, taking inventory and notes. "Jordan."

"Hmm?" Jordan mumbled, eyes still on the television.

"I don't see any pictures of my mom in Aunt Angie's house."

Jordan looked at her. "What do you mean?"

"I mean..." Noelle pointed to the photos. "I see pictures of Aunt Toni, Uncle Rob, you, me, Aunt Angie, Uncle Trevor and..." She squinted at an older woman in one of the photos. "I think that's grandmom."

Jordan peered at it. "Yeah, that's grandmom." While Jordan had never met her maternal grandmother, learning that she'd died before she was born, Toni had shown Jordan photos of her at one time or another.

"Right, well why doesn't she have any pictures of my mom in here?"

"I… I don't think Aunt Angie likes her," Jordan cautiously drew out. "I overheard my mom and Aunt Pace talk a while ago."

Noelle frowned. *How can anyone not like my mom? She's the best person ever.* "Mommy said it's not good to listen to grown people's conversation."

Jordan shrugged the comment off. Looking back at the picture display, her eyes brightened. "Ooh, I see a picture of me from my daddy-daughter dance. I want to wear my dress again."

Seeing the picture, and remembering how pretty her cousin looked that day, Noelle let a smile come through. "It was so pretty… I think I want to go this year."

Jordan brimmed with excitement. "Really?" she squealed. Noelle nodded. "You want to come with me and Daddy?"

"No… I want to go with Mr. Michael." Noelle tapped her finger to her cheek. "I'm going to ask my mom if she can ask him."

Jordan nodded in agreement. "He's so nice."

"Yeah, I know," Noelle beamed.

"He may be nice Noelle, but Michael isn't your father."

Heads jerking around, the startled girls saw their aunt standing in the family room entrance. "Aunt Angie, you scared us," Jordan charged.

Angela slowly approached the couch. She was on her way in the room to check on the girls, when she heard Noelle mention the father-daughter dance. "I apologize." She looked at Noelle, who was staring at her with wide eyes. "But I mean what I said Noelle. Michael is *not* your father. He's your mother's *boyfriend*, and a boyfriend can be temporary."

Noelle's little brows gathered. "I know he's not my dad, but… He's *like* a dad."

Angela slowly shook her head. "He's *not* sweetie. And personally, I don't feel that it would be fair to your *real* father to have your mother's boyfriend take you to a dance *he* should take you to."

Jordan knew better than to talk back to an adult, let alone her aunt. But she felt protective of her little cousin, and by the look on Noelle's face, Angela's callous words were saddening her. "But, Aunt Angie, Noelle doesn't *know* her real dad. She knows Mr. Michael, and he's nice to her."

Angela cut her eye at Jordan. "I understand that Jordan, but that doesn't change the fact." Both Angela's tone and face were unsympathetic. She returned her focus to Noelle, who was looking down at her hands. "Noelle."

Noelle slowly looked up, meeting her probing gaze.

Angela leaned over the back of the couch, placing a hand on Noelle's shoulder. "You may not know your father, but *I do*." She paused for what seemed like an eternity. "Do *you* want to know him?"

Noelle looked at Jordan, who vigorously shook her head.

"Jordan, mind your business," Angela curtly spat, before refocusing on Noelle. "*Well* little one? ...*Do* you?"

Noelle's eyes drew back down to her hands. Confusion was pounding in her head. She didn't know how to answer. On one hand, she was fine with not knowing her father. But on the other, she couldn't help but be a bit curious as to who this mystery person was, and why he'd never even bothered to call her. "Umm... I—" She let out a deep sigh. "I never even talked to him."

A measured smile spanned Angela's face. "Well... How about we change that?"

Chapter Thirty-Two

PATIENCE OPENED HER DOOR, STEPPING inside; Michael carried her overnight bag in behind her. She turned on a table lamp and set her keys and purse down, turning to face Michael as he set her bag by the couch.

"You sure you don't want me to take you to pick up Noelle?" Michael asked. "I'm already out."

Patience waved a hand his way. "No, baby, that's not necessary. *You* get to Sunday dinner at your parents', before your mother yells at you."

Michael playfully rolled his eyes. "I am not *afraid* of Jill Carter." He rubbed the back of his neck when Patience shot him a knowing look. "But yeah, I guess I should get going."

The couple had left their cozy cabin sanctuary a few hours ago. Now home, Patience and Michael were about to go their separate ways for the night.

"Uh huh, that's what I thought," Patience teased. "Besides—" She glanced at her watch. "I have about an hour before I have to get her. When I talked to Toni last night, she said I could pick her up at seven… Then she told me to stop calling."

Letting out a laugh, Michael rubbed her arm. "Aww, you didn't call her that much."

"I know that. She's rude," Patience jeered of her sister. "Anyway, be safe and thank you again for this weekend."

"You're welcome." He embraced Patience, planting a kiss on her. Although it was quick, the kiss did not lack passion. So much so that it left Michael flushed when Patience pulled away. "Keep playing, and I'll gladly be late to this dinner."

Giggling, Patience put a hand on his chest. "Please tell your mother thanks for the invite. I promise to make the next one."

Michael nodded. "I will."

"Call me later."

"You know I will." Michael headed for the door, grabbing the handle. "I love you."

"Love you too."

Patience locked the door once it closed, then retrieved her bag from the floor and headed up the steps.

Toni paced the living room floor before moving to the window. Pulling back the closed curtain, she peered outside. Not seeing a car or any lights coming down the block, she sucked her teeth. "Girl, where the hell are you?" she wondered aloud.

Grabbing her phone from the coffee table, she dialed a number. "Angie, where are you?" she snapped into the line when Angela picked up.

"I'm on my way."

Toni scowled. "You were supposed to be here by *six-thirty*."

"Well *excuse me* for making sure to feed the girls before bringing them back," Angela bit back. "Damn, a *thank you* would be nice."

Letting out a deep sigh, Toni rubbed her forehead with her hand. "I'm sorry for snapping. Thank you for feeding them."

"That's better."

"Right," Toni mumbled. "How long do you think you'll be?"

"Maybe twenty minutes T, relax. Why the sense of urgency?"

Toni shuddered. Patience was supposed to pick Noelle up at

seven—it was five minutes to. God forbid the women run into each other, let alone Patience finding out that her child was with Angela in the *first* place. Especially after she'd made it clear that she didn't want Noelle around her.

"It's nothing. Just get here soon," Toni deflected. "But drive safe of course."

"Yeah, yeah. Bye Toni."

Toni pulled the phone from her ear when it was clear that Angela had hung up. Stuffing it into her sweatshirt pocket, Toni released another heavy sigh. Slumping down on her couch, she ran her hands over her hair. It had been a long day, and she hadn't been back to sleep. After spending all morning in the emergency room with Rob, he was finally cleared to return home around four that afternoon.

A knock sent Toni to the door. Peering out the peephole, she grimaced. "Of course Miss Punctual is here right on the dot." Opening the door, Toni's deadpan expression came face to face with Patience's pleasant one. Toni put on an award-winning smile. "Hey girl! How was your trip? Don't you want to go back home and get that scarf I let you borrow?"

Patience's 'what the hell is with you?' face was doused with humor. "Umm, one, why are you so loud? I'm standing right *here*."

Toni's too-bright smile morphed to a nervous one as Patience spoke.

"Two, my trip was amazing, and three, that was *my* damn scarf that I finally got back from *you*," Patience finished.

Toni scratched her head. "Oh—yeah. Forget about it then."

Patience stood there for a moment, staring at Toni. The woman was acting weird, but she was too cold to try to figure out why. "Are you going to let me in?"

Toni peered past Patience to the street...still nothing. "Sure... sure, I'm sorry. Come in," she said as she stepped aside.

Removing her coat, Patience hung it on the rack by the door.

Rubbing her shoulders in hopes of taking the chill off, she moved further into the living room. Turning around to face Toni, her easy smile changed to concern as she took in the exhaustion in her sister's eyes. "Hey, you okay T?"

Running a hand along the back of her neck, Toni waved her free hand dismissively. "Oh yeah, I'm okay. Just tired."

Tilting her head, Patience fixed Toni with a sympathetic look. "Aww, I can imagine."

Toni's mouth opened wide with a yawn, stifling any reply she was about to give.

"Well, let me get my baby and we'll get out of your hair."

Toni nearly choked on her second yawn as Patience headed for the steps. *Shit!* In just those few wearied moments, she'd forgotten that Angela still had not yet arrived with the girls. "Umm—"

"Is she upstairs?" Patience asked, looking up the staircase.

Toni moved towards Patience, a hand out. "Wait, I—"

Putting her hand over Toni's, Patience guided it down. "No, you relax, I'll go get her."

"Patience wait," Toni got out, halting Patience's ascent up the stairs. When Patience looked at her with questioning eyes, Toni sighed; she couldn't prolong it. "Noelle isn't here."

Patience frowned as she stepped off the stairs. "What do you *mean* she isn't here?"

"I mean…" Toni fiddled with her hands. "She isn't here…at the house."

Patience's *patience* was wearing thin. "Well then where the hell *is* she?"

Defeated, Toni raised her arms, then let them drop at her sides. "She and Jordan are with Angela…I took them to her house early this morning. She's bringing them back here." When Patience's eyes widened in anger, Toni put her hands up in caution. "Just hear me out—"

"Are you out of your mind? Did you not hear a word I said to you not even a *week* ago?!" Patience erupted.

"I *did* hear you Patience, but you have to let me explain—"

Patience folded her arms. "What explanation could you *possibly* have for disregarding—"

"Patience, *please* just listen to me, I have a good reason!" Toni belted out in desperation.

Glaring, Patience's jaw tightened. "Fine, what's the damn reason?"

"I had to take Rob to the emergency room this morning."

The anger immediately left Patience's face; worry replaced it. "Oh my God, is he okay?"

"Yes, he's okay now, but…" Toni ran her hands over her face. "We went to dinner the other night and he ate something that messed with his stomach. He wasn't feeling good all day yesterday, but he powered through it so that the girls could have fun. Then I brought him home and got him into bed and I thought he could just sleep it off, but…" She took a breath, as tears glassed over her eyes. "I woke up at one this morning and he was in the bathroom damn near passed out, and I was scared. I knew I needed to get him to the hospital, but I couldn't take the girls with me, so I called Angela because she was the closest and I asked her if I could drop them off—"

Patience reached out, taking hold of her hand. "It's okay, you don't have to explain any further." Her voice was full of compassion.

Toni wiped her eyes with the sleeve of her shirt. "You know I respect your boundaries Patience; I would never break that if I didn't—"

Patience pulled her into a hug. "No no, stop. It's okay." She rubbed her back. "I'm sorry. It's okay sis."

Toni squeezed Patience, relieved for her understanding.

Pulling back, Patience smoothed Toni's hair back from her face. "He's okay though, right? What did the doctors say?"

"He's okay… They said it was a severe case of food poisoning. After running a bunch of tests, they finally gave him some fluids because he was dehydrated." Toni wiped the remaining dampness from her cheeks with her sleeve. "They monitored him for a few hours, then gave a prescription and instructions, and discharged him... We didn't get home until almost five this evening."

"Damn, I'm sorry you guys went through that." Patience rubbed Toni's arm. "Glad that he didn't have to be admitted though."

"Hell, who you tellin'?" Toni exhaled heavily. "Anyway, Angie was supposed to have them back by six-thirty, but..."

"It's okay... I'm not upset with you." Patience guided Toni over to the couch. "Here, sit."

Toni flopped down, relishing the feeling of the cushion at her back.

"Do you need me to do anything while I'm here?" Patience sat beside her. "Did you eat? Want me to cook something? I can take Jordan with me for a few days if you want. You know I'll get her to and from school."

Offering a tired smile, Toni patted Patience's hand. "I appreciate you, but I'm fine," she assured her. "Rob isn't eating anything but bland crackers and gelatin, and I made myself a sandwich not too long ago, so..." She chuckled a bit. "And Jordan wouldn't *dare* leave knowing that her knight in shining armor is sick. You know that girl had the nerve to ask *me* if I gave him the right amount of juice when I spoke to her earlier?"

Patience let out a slight laugh. "She's something else."

"A damn mess." Toni shook her head, then peered over at the door. "Angela should be here any moment though."

Patience sighed, the humor gone. "I'm thinking...maybe I overreacted," she mentioned after a bit of silence.

Toni looked at her. "Overreacted about what?"

"About not wanting Noelle around her." Patience glanced down at her hand resting in her lap. "I mean, I've said before that I know Angela loves her... Why should I cause a rift in their relationship, because she and *I* aren't in a good space?"

"Because that space is *toxic* and you have every right to not want your daughter to be subjected to that," Toni said. "You have the right to want her around people who think highly of you, Patience."

"I know, but I'm starting to wonder if I'm acting like Mom, when it came to not wanting us to spend time with Dad just because *she* hated him."

A seriousness crossed Toni's face. "You...are *not* Mom, and *this* is *not* the same thing."

Uncertainty showed in Patience's eyes. "Isn't it though?"

"No, it *isn't*." Toni adjusted her position in her seat, making sure she faced Patience. "Mom didn't want us to have a relationship with Dad because she was *bitter*. Dad loved us, he never hurt us, never even raised his *voice* at us, never bad-mouthed Mom, *none* of that."

Deep in thought, Patience's gaze veered off to the side as Toni spoke.

"Now, as much as I hate to face it, *Angela* is more like Mom than any of us, and I won't let you think otherwise." Toni stalled, wondering if she should mention what was on her mind. "Do... Do you know she went to see Michael at his job a few days ago?"

"I know." Patience met her gaze. "He told me."

Toni shook her head. "What excuse did she give you when you talked to her?"

"I *didn't* talk to her." Patience remembered the anger and confusion that had consumed her learning about the visit from Michael. She'd stewed in her office for nearly an hour after he'd hung up. "I *did* call her...and as the line rang, I planned this whole yelling, cuss out session in my head. But I realized that's exactly what she wanted."

Toni kept her attention on Patience as she spoke.

"She *wants* me to be frazzled, she *wants* me to be unhappy... That's why she pulled what she did at dinner, and *that's* why she went to Michael's office... She knew he was going to tell me what happened and that it would piss me off." Sighing, Patience shrugged.

"So…I hung up without so much as leaving a message… I can't give her the energy anymore."

Toni's head leaned to the side as she fixed Patience with an intense stare. "And you *still* think you could be wrong in protecting your daughter from that?" Her phone beeping drew Toni's attention, halting any words that Patience was about to say. Picking it up, Toni eyed the message on the screen.

Rob: Babe, can you please bring me up some more orange juice and crackers?

"Hang on, I need to take Rob some orange juice and crackers." Toni stood up. Just then, she saw the glare of car lights through the curtains; it could only be Angela's car. "Annnd, the girls are back."

Looking at the door, Patience rose from the couch. She might have considered changing her mind about Noelle being around Angela, but that didn't mean that she'd had a change of heart about her*self*. "T, I can take Rob his stuff."

"You sure?"

"Yeah." Patience headed for the kitchen. "Just let him know I'm coming up."

"Thank you, I will." Toni typed out a quick reply to Rob, before going to the door. She watched as Patience emerged a moment later with a glass of juice and a pack of crackers, waiting until she disappeared up the steps before opening the door.

"Hi Mom, where's Daddy?" Jordan charged, rushing into the house. Noelle, not saying a word, sluggishly walked in after her.

Toni glanced back at Jordan. "Hi daughter, he's upstairs—" She put a hand up as Jordan went for the stairs. "Hold on a sec." She turned back to Angela. "Thank you. I appreciate your help."

"Sure." Angela adjusted the purse on her arm. "I see Patience's car outside… Back from her little lover's getaway huh?"

Toni rolled her eyes. "Yes, she is. Don't start."

Angela smirked. "I don't start, but I *do* finish though… Tell baby sister I said hi." She patted Toni on the arm when the woman shot her a questionable look. "Good night."

Toni stared, bewildered, as Angela walked out of the house, closing the door behind her. Dismissing her own puzzlement as exhaustion, she just shook her head and ambled over to the kids. "Hey girls. Did you have fun at Aunt Angie's?"

Jordan pushed her hair over her shoulder. "Not really."

"Well excuse me," Toni replied, voice laced with humor. She focused on Noelle, who was just standing there, staring at the beaded bracelet she was fiddling with. "Hey sweetie, you tired?"

Noelle just shook her head, before the sound of her mother's voice at the top of the stairs prompted her to look up.

Patience smiled as she descended the stairs. "Hi Bunny." She enveloped her daughter in a hug. "I missed you."

Noelle was silent as she parted from the embrace.

Patience tilted her head at the lack of response. "Did you have fun?"

Noelle's eyes just lowered to the floor, her shoulders rose and fell slightly.

The look on Patience's face quickly morphed from bewildered to concerned. The lackluster hug, the silence, the melancholy look… This was not like Noelle at all. "Hey." She put a hand on Noelle's arm. "Are you okay?" When Noelle wouldn't look at her, Patience frowned. "Noelle, what happened?"

Jordan stepped forward; she had an idea what Noelle's issue was. "Umm, she—" Her words were cut short by both her mother and aunt snapping their fingers at her. She knew well enough that that meant for her to be quiet.

"*Talk* Noelle," Patience demanded.

"Yeah, sweetie," Toni softly chimed in. "What happened between the time you left and now?"

Rubbing her face with her hand, Patience crouched down to Noelle's level. She knew that getting angry wasn't going to help. She had to keep calm, even though her mind was running a million miles a minute over what had upset her child. Putting her hand under Noelle's chin, she lifted it, meeting her daughter's sullen eyes. "Baby... tell Mommy what's wrong." Her own eyes were pleading. "*Please.*"

Noelle took a deep breath as she fumbled with her bracelet. "I... I talked to my dad today."

Patience blinked several times, trying to register what she'd just heard. "I'm sorry, you said you talked to *who?*"

"My dad." Noelle's voice was low.

A sharp gasp escaped Toni; she quickly covered her mouth with her hand to prevent yelling something obscene in front of their girls.

Patience felt like air had become lodged in her chest. Noelle didn't have a number for Greg, and he *certainly* didn't have *hers.* "I don't— How did— *What?*"

Toni stepped forward, putting a hand on her sister's shoulder. She could sense by the stammers and the confusion on her face that Patience was about to lose it. "You need to breathe, sis."

Patience jerked her shoulder, knocking Toni's hand off. She had no interest in being comforted. "*How*, Noelle? How did you get a number for him?"

Noelle looked down at the floor.

Patience snapped her fingers once again. "Answer me!"

"Aunt Angie called him..." Noelle revealed. "She put him on the phone with me."

"Oh my God!" Toni blurted out. She couldn't believe her ears.

Patience was at a loss for words, but her face didn't mask the horror and anger brewing inside of her.

Toni turned to Jordan, who was looking back at her. "Jordan, you were there when this happened?" Jordan nodded. "Fill us in, *now.*"

"Me and Noelle were talking about the next father-daughter dance, and Noelle said that she wanted to go with Mr. Michael, and then Aunt Angie came in and said that *he* wasn't Noelle's dad, and that her *real* dad would be upset," Jordan filled in. "Then Noelle said that she didn't know her dad, and Aunt Angie said that *she did*, and then she called him and made Noelle talk to him."

Toni stood there, eyes practically the size of saucers, as she took in everything her child had told them. "Oh my God." She fixated on Patience, who had slowly stood upright. "Patience—"

Patience put one hand up to silence her sister, and the other on her stomach. She felt like she was going to be sick. The more she processed what she'd just heard, the more enraged she became, and the harder it got to breathe. If Angela had been standing in front of her, she was sure she'd kill her.

Taking notice of her sister's distraught state, Toni glanced at the girls. "Jordan, take Noelle upstairs to your room, right now."

Jordan grabbed Noelle's hand, doing as her mother commanded. She didn't know much about the situation, but she knew that what her aunt had done was wrong, and that both her mother and Aunt Patience were angry.

"Close the door," Toni added as they disappeared up the steps. Once she heard the door shut, she faced Patience. "Okay, sweetie, you have to calm down before you pass out."

Hands clenched into fists, Patience shot a piercing look Toni's way. "Call her back here." Her voice was low, ominous.

Toni swallowed hard. *Oh shit.* "Umm..." She put her hands up. "Okay, I know you're angry and trust me I don't blame you one bit, but—"

"There is no *but*, call her back here." Patience's voice rose steadily as she began pacing the floor.

"Patience, I really think it'll be in your best interest if—"

Fed up with Toni's placating, Patience stepped to Toni, getting in her face. "It'll be in *your* best interest for you to call her the *fuck* back here!"

Toni opened her mouth to find any excuse not to make that call. Patience was furious, and God only knew what she'd try to do to Angela once their eldest sister crossed that threshold. But she knew what Angela had done. Putting that child on the phone with a man she didn't know—a man who had mistreated her sister, a man who her sister had spent every year of her daughter's life protecting her from—had crossed a line. At this point whatever Angela got, was well deserved.

"Okay." Toni took out her phone. "Okay, I'll call her." Putting the phone to her ear, she ran a hand along the back of her neck as it rang, exhaling deeply when the line picked up. "Hey where are you? ...Yeah well, you need to get back here now, Patience is here... Yep, she knows." Toni rolled her eyes at the smug reply coming from Angela. "How could you be so—" She paused, rubbing between her eyes with her fingertips. "You know what...just get over here and *face* her." Ending the call, she tossed her phone on the couch. "She's on her way back."

Patience didn't speak. She just crossed her arms and resumed her pacing.

Toni followed her with her eyes for a long moment. "All I ask is that you not fight," she requested.

Patience snapped her head in her direction, looking at her as if she'd lost her mind. "You really just said that to me?"

"It's not going to *solve* anything, Patience."

"That bitch made my baby *talk to him*," Patience fumed, eyes glassing over with tears of fury.

Seeing her sister hurt threatened to bring tears to Toni's *own* eyes. "I know."

"Do you have *any* idea what that must've done to her? The pressure she probably *felt*?"

"I don't," Toni admitted.

"Then you can't *possibly* ask that of me."

Putting her hand atop her head, Toni searched her brain for any comforting words, but had none. There was nothing she could say that could soothe her sister. But there *was* something that might prevent this from escalating. "Patience, the children are upstairs. They don't need to hear a fight."

Jaw clenched, Patience just turned away.

Taking the lack of push back as compliance, Toni breathed a sigh of relief. "Let me know when she knocks. I'm going to check on Rob." She darted upstairs to do just that.

Patience leaned up against a wall, staring at the door. Her non-blinking eyes were laser focused.

A knock sounded before the doorknob twisted, and Angela pushed it open. "Hmm, that was a lucky guess. I didn't think the door would actually be unlocked," she said, stepping inside. "Do better Toni."

Closing the door behind her, Angela's eyes locked on Patience, who was staring at her.

Angela shook her head. "Oh, *now* you want to communicate with me, huh?"

Patience stood silent, her chest rising and falling heavily with each enraged moment.

"Okay then." Taking a few steps forward, Angela's lips formed a satisfied grin. She gestured for Patience to come at her. "Let's hear it, baby girl."

Patience pushed herself up from the wall, then bolted in Angela's direction. Before Angela had a chance to react, Patience pushed her down onto an accent chair. Clasping her hands around Angela's neck, Patience repeatedly slammed her head against the back of the chair, not even giving her the opportunity to get out an effective scream. Pressing her knee into Angela's ribs, Patience held Angela against the chair, her throat caught in a firm grip.

Feeling the air being sucked from her, Angela tried prying at her sister's hands. When they wouldn't budge, she resorted to clawing at them.

As Patience pressed against Angela's windpipe, she didn't see her sister, someone whom she still loved. Someone she had once—a long time ago—looked up to. All she saw was a woman who had hurt her, and who had hurt her daughter. All she saw was red. The pain from Angela's nails scratching the skin on her hands didn't even register.

Toni sprinted down the steps, eyes bulging at the scene. Patience was looming over Angela, choking her as Angela thrashed beneath her. "What the fuck!" she yelled out, barreling over. She grabbed hold of Patience's waist, pulling at her. "Let her go, Patience!" Seeing Angela's bloodshot eyes expand, she panicked. "Patience! You'll kill her." She grabbed her hands, prying at them. "*Please*! The kids are upstairs."

The reminder seemed to snap Patience out of her haze; her hands loosened just enough for Toni to pull her back.

Toni backed Patience against a wall, while Angela remained on the couch, coughing air back into her lungs.

"I can't believe you did that," Angela painstakingly croaked out. In all their years, she and Patience had argued until they were blue in the face. But other than a shove here and there, their physical altercations had never gotten to this.

Furious, Toni stood before Patience, pointing at her. "I *asked* you not to do this!"

"Get the fuck out my face Toni," Patience seethed.

In the middle of Toni and Patience's bickering, Angela pushed herself up from the couch. She placed a trembling hand on her neck. "I can't believe you put your hands on me!" Her hoarse voice only got but so loud. "You could've killed me. Have you lost your fuckin' mind?!"

Patience maneuvered around Toni to charge again, but was quickly caught by Toni, who held her in a vice grip. "Have I lost *my* mind?!" Patience screamed. "You made my baby talk to Greg?"

"Yeah, I did. So *what*?"

Patience tried to force Toni's hands from her waist. "Do you have any idea what you've done?!"

"What I've *done* is what *you refuse* to do." Angela hurled her finger in Patience's direction. "You don't think that she deserves to know her father?"

"You don't give a *fuck* about Noelle!" Patience hollered. "This wasn't you doing what you thought was best for *her*, you did this shit to provoke *me*. You couldn't get to me through Michael, so you went through my *daughter*."

Angela scoffed. "That's a lie and you know it. I *did* it because *you* seem to think that bringing some random man into her life will replace Greg... Michael is *not* her father, no matter how much you *want* him to be."

Patience jerked out of Toni's clutches. "Let *go* of me."

Angela began moving back, fear in her eyes.

Toni caught Patience's arm. "Patience, *no* I said!"

Snatching her arm away, Patience raised a hand at Toni. "I'm not going to fight her, get *away* from me!"

Toni backed away, throwing her arms up in frustration.

Patience pointed at Angela. "Greg doesn't *deserve* to be her father. You have *no* idea what he put me through. You have no idea the person he is."

"I know more than you *think*—" Catching herself, Angela took a breath. "Look even if he *was* how you *say* he was to you back then, people change, Patience."

"Not *that* fuckin' much." Patience's eyes radiated with fury. "This is the same man, who when he realized I wasn't going to stay with him after I found out I was pregnant, tried to make me *miscarry* her." The traumatic memory drew tears from her eyes. "He tried to *kill* her by hurting *me*."

Closing her eyes to hide her own building tears, Toni turned away. The phone call she'd received from a hysterical Patience that night was one she had tried to forget, but never could.

Angela stared at Patience, deadpan. "Well...I didn't know that." Catching the scalding gaze Toni shot at her, her eyes shifted away. "But that doesn't change my stance."

Patience's eyes widened in disbelief. "You're fuckin' serious?"

"You took vows, and yet you chose to walk away from your marriage. *Now* you think you can have some fairytale ending with someone *else*?" Angela spat. "You think your boyfriend is really going to marry you and play stepfather to another man's child? Well I'm sorry baby sister, it doesn't work like that. And if I had to call Greg to bring your head out of the fuckin' clouds and back to reality with the *rest* of us, then so be it!"

Hot tears spilled down Patience's face. "So...because you're not happy in *your* life, you think that gives you the right to ruin *mine*?"

Stunned by the harsh accusation, Angela's head jerked back. "That is *not* true!"

"It *is* Angela," Toni interjected. When Angela tried to protest, Toni shook her head at her, eyes riddled with disappointment. "Yes...it is. That's how it's *always* been... *You're* the only one who can't see it."

Angela shook her head with vigor as the truth smacked her in the face.

Toni pointed to the door. "It's time for you to go."

"Oh, so you call me over to be ambushed, and now you're kicking me out?" Angela hurled Toni's way, tears blurring her sight. "I always *knew* you loved her more than you loved me."

"That's not true." Toni's voice was low, tired. "But in this moment, I *do* care about her more." She stepped forward. "Get out of my house, or I won't intervene the next time she comes at you."

Biting her lip to keep it from quivering, Angela backed towards the door. "Fine, screw you Toni."

"Yeah, whatever. Fuck you too," Toni threw right back.

Angela stormed out, slamming the door behind her.

Toni turned to Patience who had finally succumbed to her tears. When Toni tried to approach her to hug her, Patience quickly backed up. "Pace—"

"No." Shaking her head, Patience wiped the tears from her

face with the palms of her hands. She moved towards the stairs. "Noelle, come on, we're leaving," she belted up the steps.

"Maybe you should sit down for a minute," Toni advised. "You're upset, you shouldn't be driving."

"I *said* I'm leaving," Patience hissed, voice strained.

Toni fought her own tears back. Just a few moments earlier, in that same room, Patience had comforted her when she'd needed it. Now Toni wanted to do the same, but her sister was too upset to allow it. Even though Toni knew *she needed* it. "Okay...I'll go get her for you."

The girls were not in Jordan's room, but her fathers. At Rob's suggestion once Toni alerted him to Angela's pending return, Toni had sent the girls into the room with him. Even in his fragile state, he'd been playing a game with them to keep them occupied.

When Toni reappeared with Noelle, Patience, not saying a word to Toni, took Noelle's hand and left. Toni collapsed on the couch. Covering her face with her hands, she let out the cries she'd been holding in.

Rob gingerly made his way down the steps. Seeing Toni on the couch, he slowly approached, placing a hand on her shoulder. "Babe?"

Toni looked up at him. Eyes red and face wet with tears, she just tossed her hands up in defeat. Her family was in shambles; it had reached the point where they were beyond repair. "I don't know what to do," she sniffled.

Eyeing her with sympathy, Rob sat down beside her. "I'm sorry honey." He pulled her into a hug, letting her cry on his shoulder.

Chapter Thirty-Three

OPENING THE DOOR, PATIENCE GESTURED to Noelle to go inside. Neither had spoken a word the entire somber car ride home.

Standing in the living room, Patience stared at Noelle, who was sitting on the couch. She didn't know how to start this inevitable conversation. A lot had transpired over the course of a few hours, and Patience was overwhelmed. Not only with her *own* feelings, but with those of her daughter. So much so that she'd fought back the urge to cry several times during the ride home.

"Umm..." Patience folded her arms. "I'm not going to lie, I don't really know what to say right now."

Noelle was playing with the hood string on her sweatshirt. "Me either."

Despite not knowing *what* to say, Patience agonized to find *something*. But the thoughts just wouldn't form well enough for her to draw out a sentence. Unfolding her arms, she let them rest at her sides.

Noelle went still as she noticed the red marks on her mother's hands. She leaned forward, frowning. "Are your hands bleeding?"

Eyes lowering to her hands, Patience held them up. It was only then that she noticed the bloodstained scratches. It was *also* then that the pain from her injuries finally registered. Touching them, she winced. "Yes, apparently they are," she replied, dryly. "But I'm okay."

Noelle leaned back. "Did you and Aunt Angie fight?"

Patience sat on the couch next to her. "Don't worry about that right now." Taking her shirt, she wiped some of the redness from her hands. "Noelle..." She breathed heavily as the question finally formed. "How are you feeling right now?"

Noelle shrugged. "I don't know." It was an honest answer, because Noelle really had no idea of how to feel about the day's events.

"Understandable," Patience placated. "What did he say to you?"

"He asked about you."

Patience resisted the urge to roll her eyes, or say something out of anger. *Of course the fuck he did.* "Did he?"

Noelle nodded. "Then he said that he wants to see us."

Closing her eyes, Patience pinched the bridge of her nose. This was too much for her to handle; she felt that she could break at any moment. *Why the fuck did I ever marry him? What was wrong with me?*

When her mother didn't offer a reply to her father's request, Noelle looked at her, recalling things she'd been told on more than one occasion. "Does... Does he really live out of the country?"

Patience gave her head a subtle shake. "No, he doesn't... He does live in another state though."

"Then how come you *said* he did?"

Tears stung the back of Patience's eyes. The conversation she'd always feared was now front and center, and she didn't know what to say. "Because I..." She drew in a breath. "I didn't want you to know your father."

Noelle's questioning eyes staring back at her was almost too much for Patience to bear. She knew that Noelle needed to know the truth, that her father didn't want her if he couldn't have her *mother*. But that would destroy her little girl's heart. And Patience would rather Noelle be upset with *her*, than have her heart broken.

"I'm sorry that I lied to you." Her voice quavered. "About him not being around because he was out of the country."

"Does he want to see me?"

A tear spilled out of Patience's eye, trickling down her cheek. *No, he doesn't.* "I—I don't know, baby."

Noelle's gaze lowered, a tired sigh sounded from her. "Can… Can I go to bed?"

By the tone of Noelle's voice, Patience knew that the request was done out of frustration. Rather than try to engage anymore, Patience granted her request. "Yes."

Standing from the couch, Noelle headed for the steps without so much as a hug or saying good night.

Not having the mental strength to turn around, Patience focused her cloudy gaze on the floor. "I love you Noelle," she said. "More than anything in this world…and I only ever want to do what's best for you. I hope you know that."

Noelle folded her arms to her chest as she walked up the steps. "Okay."

It was when she heard the door close that Patience dissolved into a fit of tears.

Laying on the couch, Patience let them flow in silence. Between being betrayed by her sister, regretting her life choices, and feeling helpless in trying to comfort her daughter, she didn't know if she'd ever be able to stop.

When her phone rang, she let it go to voicemail. But when it rang again, she jumped up in anger. Snatching the device from her purse, she answered, clearing the cries from her voice. *"Yes* Michael?"

Driving, Michael jerked his head back at her cold greeting. "Uh, is everything okay?"

She wiped the dampness from her swollen eyes. "No, everything is *not* okay and I can't be on this phone with you right now, so—"

"Wait, hold on a second." Michael's voice failed to hide his worry. He'd just left Patience a few hours ago. She'd been relaxed, smiling, *happy*. God only knew what had caused the change in her. "What happened? Do you want me to come over?"

"No, I *don't* want you to come over, I just want—" Patience paused when she realized her voice had elevated. She didn't want to alarm Noelle, yet she didn't want Michael bothering her either. She just wanted to be left alone. "I can't do this with you right now Michael. Just leave me alone."

"What do you mean you can't do this with me?" Michael's confusion was slowly building to frustration. "What's wrong with you?"

Patience's fist clenched. "I need a fuckin' break."

"A break from *what* Patience?"

"From *everything*, including *you*." Patience knew that the words she'd just hurled at Michael weren't true. But she was too riled up to care about anyone else's feelings, not even the man she loved. Had she not started dating him, had she just remained alone, she wouldn't be in this situation right now. Angela was only lashing out now because Patience had tried to be happy.

Michael pulled over on the side of the road. "Tell me you didn't just say what I think you said." His tone was brusque. "Patience, *tell* me I didn't just hear that."

Patience shook her head, her breathing heavy. "I have a lot on my plate and this thing between us is too intense for me right now so...you heard it. Goodbye Michael." She pressed "end" before Michael could say anything else.

Shutting her eyes, she massaged her temples. The ache of her tension headache was masked only by the pain radiating from her hands. Finally deciding to tend to her wounds, she retreated to the bathroom.

Snatching the alcohol and cotton balls from the medicine cabinet, Patience tried to comprehend what she'd just done. Those thoughts were short lived as the alcohol stung the moment it touched her wounded hands.

"Shit," she hissed, flinging the bloodstained cotton in the trash. Grabbing bandages from the cabinet, she ripped them open, covering her superficial wounds.

She headed back downstairs intending to turn out the lights, but the doorbell ringing stopped her in her tracks.

Glaring, she approached the door. After a quick glance out the peephole, she yanked the door open. "I said leave me alone. What are you *doing* here?"

Frown frozen on his face, Michael crossed his arms. "You thought you could just break up with me out of nowhere and I not come over here to find out why?" When she scowled at him, he stepped forward. "Yeah, you know me better than that."

As much as Patience wanted him to turn around and get back into his car, he had a point; she *did* know him better than that. Letting out a frustrated huff, she let him in.

Michael faced her as she closed the door. "You want to tell me what's going on with you?"

"No, I *don't*. I want you to *leave* though."

"I'm not going *anywhere* until you tell me what the hell has gotten into you." When she refused to provide a reply, Michael grew even more agitated. "Patience, you can't just say some shit to me like that over the damn *phone* and not give me a reason why." He pointed at her, "No, you need to start talking *now*."

Patience's eyes grew dark with anger. "You don't get to bring your ass to *my* house and make demands of me." Her voice elevated steadily. "Have you lost your damn mind? I don't owe you *shit*."

"You owe me *that*!" he hollered.

"And don't fuckin' yell at me. My daughter is sleeping!"

Rubbing his hands over his face, Michael took a deep breath. "I didn't mean to yell at you... I don't want to *fight* with you. But I need to understand." His eyes pleaded for an answer. "What happened? What did I *do?*" He took a step forward. "We were good, we *are* good. We—baby talk to me, *please.*"

Patience folded her arms, trying to block out the hurt and confusion on Michael's face. "I just…" She shrugged. "I thought being in a relationship was what I wanted… But I don't think I was ready for this…and I don't think *you* are either."

"You can't tell me what I'm ready for," Michael argued. "And you can't *lie* to me. You wanted this as much as I did."

"Maybe so, but not anymore."

"Are you *serious*—" Flustered, Michael put his hands over his head. "You're still avoiding telling me what the hell caused you to feel this way all of a sudden. Without it, *none* of what you're saying makes any sense Patience."

Frustrated, Patience stepped in his direction. "Goddamn it Michael, I'm giving you an out here, just fuckin' *take* it!" she erupted. "Take it and go."

His eyes widened in disbelief. "You think after all this time, that I want an *out* from you?" He put a hand to his chest. "Have I *ever* given you any reason to believe that I don't want to be here. That I don't want to be with you?"

Patience shook her head. "No."

"Then *why* are you doing this to us?"

"Because I can't give you what you want, and I don't know if I'll ever be able to," Patience fired back. "A happy marriage, children, hell even just a *relationship* without fuckin' *baggage*—I *can't*…" Her chest rose and fell with strained breaths. "I've been through too much and as a result, I'm never going to be what you deserve, so just… You need to find someone who *can*. Someone who'll make you happy."

"*You* make me happy!" Tears stinging his eyes, Michael closed the distance between them. "*You* do, and everything that comes *with* you. *Everything*, I *love* you." He tried to take hold of her hand, but she moved it out of the way. "Baby—look, I don't know what you're going through, but whatever it is, we'll handle it together."

Slowly rocking in place, Patience's eyes glassed over as Michael poured his heart out to her.

"I'm here for you. I'm here *with* you, and I'm not going anywhere—I don't *want* to go anywhere," he pleaded. "You're everything to me, just… Don't end us."

Patience wanted nothing more than to jump into his arms and tell him everything that had happened. Tell him how sorry she was for hurting his feelings, because she was having a hard time dealing with her *own*. But as she looked into his tear-filled eyes, all she could think was if she broke his heart now, she wouldn't have to do it later. "I'm sorry." Her voice was barely audible. "Can you please just go?"

Michael released a labored sigh, trying to keep himself from falling apart. He loved this woman with everything in him, and she was pushing him away for reasons that were still unbeknownst to him. "Just so I'm clear…you're telling me that once I walk out this door, that we're over?" he choked out. "Just like that?"

Stepping back, Patience looked away from his intense stare. "Yes," she answered after a long, tense moment.

Michael looked down at the floor. Without saying another word, he wiped his hand down his face, cleared the wetness from his cheeks, and walked out. The door shut quietly behind him.

Patience, who'd been fighting not to sob, released it as a loud gasp. "God, what did I just do?" She felt like she couldn't catch her breath. "What did I just do?" She repeated that phrase over and over as she wept.

Chapter Thirty-Four

"I WANT TO THANK EACH and every one of you for the impeccable work you do every day," Michael spoke to the conference room full of his loyal employees. Some sat in person, and others were attending via video conference. "From the contactors to the in-office workers—this company would not be what it is today without all of you."

"Being a stellar employee is easy when you have a stellar boss such as yourself Mike."

Michael managed to smile at the kind words, which were followed by a barrage of eager cosigns from the others.

"The best I've ever worked with *that's* for sure," Dante followed up, proudly.

Humbled, Michael glanced down at the table, before returning his focus to the group. "I appreciate that." He smoothed his hand down his jacket. "Congratulations again on the new contract. It'll be hard work, but I know it's nothing that we can't handle. Meeting adjourned and lunch is on me." His generosity was met with a round of applause. "And yes Dante, you may order from the steakhouse if you so choose."

Dante pumped his fist in the air. "All right bet."

"Go right ahead and be confined to the porta potty on site, after inhaling all that red meat," a man teased.

"You mind your business, Ryan," Dante threw back. He turned

to his brother as the crowd began to filter out. "Are you coming with us, Mike?"

"No, not today. Enjoy," Michael declined.

As the room finally cleared, Cassie gathered her notes. "Do you need me to place a lunch order for *you* while I'm at it, Michael?"

Shutting down his power point, Michael shook his head. "No, I'm okay. Thanks though."

"No problem." Cassie left the room, closing the door behind her and leaving Michael alone.

Closing his laptop, Michael sank down into his chair. Letting out a long sigh, he rubbed his face with his hands. That morning he'd gotten the good news that his company had won the bid on the commercial contract. He'd been able to put on a good show of happiness for his employees. But the moment he was alone, his real feelings rose back to the surface.

While his professional life was soaring, his personal one was crumbling. It had been a little over three weeks since Patience had ended their relationship out of the blue, and he was still reeling from it. He'd barely slept, had to force himself to eat most days, and found himself shedding tears when reminders of her seeped in. He couldn't even bear to open the dresser drawer in his room that still had some of her personal items in it.

She would've been the first person he'd called to share the news, and it pained him that he couldn't. "This shit fuckin' sucks," he grumbled aloud. Hearing a knock, he peered at the door. "Come in."

Cassie opened the door a crack, sticking her head in. "Sorry to bother you, but your father is here to see you."

Michael tilted his head. He wasn't expecting the visit, nor was he in the right frame of mind for it. Nevertheless, he didn't have the heart to turn his father away without at least seeing him. "Okay, you can send him in."

A moment later, Gary stepped inside, greeting his son with a smile. "Hey son."

"Hey Pop." Michael's tone matched the somber look in his eyes. "What brings you by?"

"Well, it's a beautiful day," Gary replied, approaching Michael. "So, I figured why not venture down here to take you to lunch."

Releasing a sigh, Michael ran a hand over his head. "I appreciate the offer, but I'm not— I'm tied up right now, so…"

The cheery smile faded from Gary's face as concern replaced it. Michael had been distant, and he understood why. But while he was okay at first with giving Michael his space, the time had come to check in on him. "Michael…let me take you to lunch please."

Seeing the seriousness on his father's face, Michael relented. "Okay." He stood from his seat. "Just give me a second to put my things in my office."

Gary gave a nod. "Take your time."

Michael stared at the half of roast beef sandwich on his plate. He wasn't sure how he'd been able to eat the first half while having next to no appetite. Yet he did, and even ate a few of his steak fries along with it.

"Is it good?" Gary asked, wiping the steak sauce from his mouth with a napkin.

Michael shrugged. "It's okay."

Gary grabbed his glass of iced tea, taking a long sip. As he returned the glass to the table, he fixed Michael with a sympathetic look. "Your mother is worried about you."

"I know. I'll call her, but it's just…" Michael sighed. "I know she's going to bring up Patience, and I can't handle that right now."

"I can understand that. But in your mother's defense, I think she's just trying to wrap her head around this."

Michael fixed Gary with a wounded stare. "So am *I*."

His mother had been upset and confused when she'd learned of Michael's split from Patience, in the first days after it had happened.

And while Michael did not go into detail about what had transpired, she knew that it was a sudden end to what she had thought to be a beautiful relationship. His father, however, *did* know a bit more, as Michael knew that he would be more level-headed.

"The thing is Pop, I *still* don't understand what happened."

Reaching over, Gary patted Michael's hand on the table. "I know, son."

"I mean, we had just spent the weekend together," Michael lamented. "We were great, she was happy—something *happened* to her, and she won't tell me what it is and it's…" He took a breath when his voice faltered, rubbing his face to keep the unshed tears at bay. "This shit hurts, man."

Gary was hurt *for* his son. He wished that there was something he could do to take away his pain, but he knew that he couldn't. All he could do was give him an outlet to vent. "If it means anything… you're handling it better than most would."

Michael shook his head. "Yeah, I doubt that." He gazed out of the window. The early spring sunlit sky failed to distract him from his depressed thoughts. "I met her one year ago today."

Eyes widened, Gary stifled a gasp. "Oh wow…damn."

"Yeah, damn." Michael returned his eyes to his father. "I used to smile every time I walked by the bakery where we met…" His shoulders rose and fell. "But now I avoid the block all together."

"Michael, I know things seem rough now, but everything has a way of working itself out," Gary placated. "Your mother and I have always taught you that. So, try not to give up hope."

"Is that what you told Dante when he broke up with Lori?"

Gary shook his head with vigor. "Oh no, that boy damn near slid down the wall when I even *mentioned* 'hope'."

Michael couldn't help but chuckle. "Not damn near, *did*," he recalled. "Knocked a plant over and everything."

"Like a damn fool," Gary ground out. "Then laid in the spilled dirt, talking about 'just bury me in it'."

Putting a hand over his face, Michael let out a laugh for the first time since his breakup. "That man…" His laughter subsided. "Thanks Pop, I needed that."

Returning a warm smile, Gary gave a nod. "Anytime."

"I'll be opening the doors in about ten minutes," Patience spoke into her cell phone. "Yeah, the changes really brought out the beauty in this place… I'm confident that we will… Okay, perfect. Talk back later."

Ending the call, Patience placed the cell into her handbag and rested her back against the counter. Closing her eyes, she took a few deep breaths to ease her nerves. In less than ten minutes, she'd open the doors to the mansion she'd spent the past few weeks working with the owners to stage perfectly, for the much-anticipated open house.

In less than ten minutes, Patience would have to force a smile and ooze enthusiasm to try to sell this property, while collapsing on the inside. Since breaking things off with Michael, she'd been in a fog. Between trying to handle her own pain, while tending to Noelle and *her* feelings about her father, Patience didn't know how she managed to get out of bed some days.

Running her hands over her hair, she pushed herself off the counter. *Okay, pull it together.* Heading outside on the front lawn, she adjusted the "Open House" sign, before scanning the manicured grounds. When her phone rang, she retrieved it, looking at the screen. Seeing Toni's name, she sent the call to voicemail. "Not now."

Patience had lost track of how many times Toni had called her since the confrontation with Angela. Yet she could count on one hand how many times she *answered*. She didn't want to talk; she just wanted to be left alone to grieve her life as it had been.

Seeing cars pull up into the driveway, Patience plastered a smile on her face.

Between chatting to potential buyers and doing walk-throughs, the next few hours had flown by. Alone in the client's property once again, she stood in the living room on the phone with the seller. "Everything went well. I've already received several offers…" She folded an arm around her waist as the person spoke. "Trust me, a bidding war is a good problem to have… Well, thank you for trusting my vision… Sure thing, I'll keep you updated… You as well. Goodbye."

Phone clutched in her hand, Patience, for a moment, felt a bit of relief. However, sorrow quickly filtered back in. This showing had been a major source of stress. Now that all of her hard work had paid off, there was one person she wished she could call to tell him about it.

Scrolling to Michael's photo, she stared at it. It had been weeks, and she still couldn't bring herself to delete it. Touching the image of his face, she could feel tears building in her eyes. Sniffling, she brought a hand up to the amethyst butterfly pendant that she refused to take off. As a tear fell on Michael's smile, Patience felt her heart break all over again. "I'm sorry," she whispered.

Hearing the doorknob turn, Patience cleared the image from the screen. Thankful that her back was to it, she wiped her eyes dry as the door creaked open. "I'm sorry, but the open house is closed for the day."

"I'd appreciate just a moment to look around."

Tucking her hair behind her ear, Patience turned to face them. "Sorry, but if you—" Her eyes widened in pure shock seeing the tall, slim suit-clad man standing in the living room. "What the fuck?" She managed to get out between labored breaths. "*Greg?*"

A slow, smug smile crept across Greg Moore's light brown face. "Hello Patience… Long time."

Patience found it hard to speak, even *move*. "What the hell are you— How did—"

Greg took a step forward.

Patience backed up, putting a hand out. *"Don't,"* she warned. "You don't want to see what I have in my purse."

"You mean that purse over there on the mantel?" he asked, pointing to the black purse atop the fireplace mantel, too far out of reach. When Patience began to back up towards it, Greg put his hands up in surrender as he stepped back to his original spot. "No need to be afraid of me. I come in peace."

"Peace is something I've *never* experienced with you."

Smirking, Greg folded his arms. "Yeah, well that couldn't have always been the case since you married me."

Eyes flashing with anger, Patience's jaw clenched. She despised this man and marrying him was something she'd regret for the rest of her life. "What are you doing here? How the hell did you find me?"

He shrugged his shoulders. "I was passing through Virginia, and I looked you up."

"Did you?" she challenged. "Or did my *sister* tell you?"

Greg chuckled. "Ah, Angela…the one sister of yours I actually *liked."* He rubbed his chin. "But no, she didn't tell me *where* you work, though she did allude to the fact that you worked in real estate. A quick internet search, and umm…there aren't many *Patience Harveys'* in Virginia, who just *happened* to be the realtor showing this house today so…" He smoothed his hand down the front of his jacket. "Not going to lie, I kinda hoped you would've kept the Moore."

Patience was frozen in seething silence. Her breathing became heavier and her eyes tightened the more Greg spoke. *I'll never forgive that bitch for calling him.*

"Though I never expected to hear from my dear ex sister-in-law, I'm glad she called," Greg continued. "It stirred up a long-forgotten urge to see your face again."

"Whatever reason you have for being here, doesn't matter,"

Patience spat. "Go the fuck back where you came from and leave me alone."

"You still got that goddamn mouth on you, I see," Greg sneered, then paused, staring. "Still got that sexy ass body too."

Having had enough of this interaction, Patience pointed to the door. "You need to leave."

"I will…if you agree to have dinner with me."

She looked at him as if he had twelve heads. "Are you freakin' crazy? Not a chance in hell."

Greg eyed her, cocking his head to the side. "Well then how *else* will I hold your attention long enough to talk about me meeting our daughter?"

Patience successfully kept the dread hidden beneath a mask of fury. Though on the inside, her stomach had dropped into her high heels. "You won't, because that is a conversation that'll never happen."

His brows shot up. "No?"

"*No…* You lost the privilege to know her when you did what you did to me."

Glancing away, Greg let out a deep breath. "That was a mistake Patience, and you know that. I was angry. I was *hurt*, and I deeply regret—"

"I don't *care* about your excuses, get *out!*" she erupted. "I don't know what in your screwed up mind thought that this was a good idea."

Enthralled, Greg's eyes trailed up and down her frame. He bit his bottom lip as his eyes crinkled. "Damn, I miss that fire."

Repulsed by the way he was practically undressing her with his eyes, Patience's face scrunched. "Fuck you."

Mouth open with a grin, Greg ran his tongue across his front teeth. *I'd love to fuck you again for old times' sake.* "That's fine. I'll leave as you wish." Grabbing the latch, he pulled the door open. "It was good seeing you again Patience," he leisurely threw out. "Enjoy the rest of your evening."

Once the door closed, Patience bolted towards it and turned the locks. Peering out of the window, she watched with a stifled breath as Greg got into his car and sped off. It was only then that she exhaled. Putting a hand to her chest, she felt her heart beating rapidly. She held up the other and found it trembling. Closing it into a fist, she silently begged with tears in her eyes for it to stop so she could get home safely.

Chapter Thirty-Five

PATIENCE PULLED UP IN FRONT of her house and turned the car off. Pinching the bridge of her nose, she sighed deeply. She'd waited nearly an hour after Greg had left the open house before she'd pulled out of the garage. She'd been on edge the entire hour ride home, constantly checking her rearview mirror to ensure that she wasn't being followed.

Now, she was too mentally drained to even get out of the car. Finally getting up the strength after sitting there in silence for fifteen minutes, she grabbed her purse and walked to the door. She reached into her purse and grabbed hold of her keys, putting a few between her fingers for good measure.

"Glad to know you're still breathing."

Alarmed, Patience spun around to find Toni walking up behind her. "Toni!" she barked. "Don't walk up on me like that, what's wrong with you?"

"I didn't mean to scare you." Toni folded her arms, sternness on her face. "But you have this habit of not answering my calls. So, I did what any sister who loves you would do, and popped up on your ass."

Putting a hand to her chest, Patience calmed herself. "Well... you accomplished your task." She yanked the keys from her purse, then turned for the door. "I'm still breathing, so you can go now."

"Patience," Toni snapped, causing Patience to face her. Toni stepped forward, adjusting the oversized purse on her shoulder. "Now listen, I understand that you've been through a lot... You're *going* through a lot, and I've respected that by giving you your space but..." Feeling herself getting choked up, Toni stalled for a moment to gather herself. "I can't do that anymore. I need you to talk to me. I miss you so... Can I *please* come in?"

Seeing the emotion in Toni softened the hardened expression on Patience's face. She missed Toni too.

Toni reached into her bag, pulling a bottle out. "I brought wine."

Patience gave only a quiet chuckle. "I can see that." She gestured to the door. "Come in."

Breathing a sigh of relief, Toni followed her sister inside.

With the door locked behind them, Toni swiftly went to the kitchen, pouring two glasses of the dry red wine she'd brought. She quickly returned to the couch, where Patience was sitting, staring at the door as if to check the locks one final time. Taking a seat beside her, Toni handed Patience the glass.

"Thanks," Patience dryly said.

"And don't worry about driving later, I can pick Noelle up from school for you," Toni offered.

Patience swirled the wine around in her glass. "She has art club today."

"Doesn't matter, I'll still do it."

Giving a grateful nod, Patience sipped, hoping that by some miracle it would calm her anxiety.

Toni took a quick sip from her own glass, before adjusting her position on the couch. She studied Patience for a long moment, wondering where to begin. "So...should I even bother to ask how you're doing?"

Patience rested her glass on the coffee table, before leaning back. "You can." Her voice was low, drained.

"How are you doing?"

Slowly shaking her head, Patience stared out in front of her. "Toni...I feel like I'm losing my mind."

Putting her hand on her sister's arm, Toni fixed a sympathetic gaze. "I'm sorry sweetie."

Running a hand over her face, Patience let out a deep sigh. She'd been holding so much in with no outlet. If she didn't let it out, she knew she really *would* lose it. "I... I ended things with Michael."

Toni's eyes fluttered several times. "I'm sorry you did *what*?"

"I broke up with Michael."

"What— Patience—"Toni put her hand on top of her head as she tried to form words. "When? *Why*? What happened?"

Patience closed her eyes as the scene replayed in her head. "When I got home from your place that night, he called me, and I was an enraged, emotional mess and I just..." She sighed. "It was too much happening at once, and my head was all over the place. I told him that I needed a break and then he came over and I just blew up at him..." She shook her head. "I told him it was over."

Confusion was imprinted on Toni's face. "Sis, I don't understand. You two were amazing together. He was good for you."

"I know that."

"Then why?—" frazzled, Toni tossed a hand up. "Did you really want to *do* that?"

"*No* Toni, I didn't want to break up with him!" Patience snapped. "I didn't want to hurt him, I love him."

Toni grabbed Patience's hand to try and soothe her. "Okay, I'm sorry—"

"I didn't want to, but I *did* and I can't take it back," Patience rambled, feeling her emotions coming to a head for what felt like the millionth time that week. "And at this point, why should I even bother *trying*? He's better off without me."

"Do you really believe that? Because *I don't*."

Patience looked at her with glassy eyes. "I have to...because that's the only way I can let him go."

Toni released a sigh. "Can I reserve the right to try to talk some sense into you about this?" she asked. "Because—I love you—but you made the wrong decision sweetie. That man loves you, and he loves Noelle."

"I know." Patience wiped her eyes with the sleeve of her blouse. "But it's done." She pushed her hair from her face. "And to top all of this bullshit off…Greg showed up at my house showing."

"Greg *who?*" When Patience shot her a knowing look, Toni scowled. "Hold up. Not *Greg Moore*, your trash ass *ex.*"

"Yeah." Patience's voice dropped with contempt. "One in the same."

The anger that consumed Toni at the mere thought of Greg encountering her sister again was indescribable. "What the fuck did he *want?* How did he even know where to find you? You haven't seen his ass since you left him back in Georgia. Haven't *heard* from him since your divorce was finalized."

"I know… He said he was just 'passing through' and looked me up, which isn't hard to do, because it's not like I was *hiding* from him. In all honesty, I just never expected to *see* him again. All these years of no contact and now…" Seething, Patience breathed out a hissing sigh through her clenched teeth. "What I *do* know is that Angela's sneaky ass call to him started this shit, and *now* he claims after *all* this time that he wants to see Noelle."

Toni's lips curled in disgust at the mention of their oldest sister. She hadn't spoken to the woman since she'd put Angela out of her house. "You're not going to *let* him, are you?"

"Fuck no," Patience assured. "I meant what I told him, he doesn't *deserve* it."

Toni held Patience's hand in a firm grip. "Sis…are you going to tell Noelle that he showed up?"

"*No,* I—" Patience rested her elbow on the back of the couch, leaning her head on it. "I don't know Toni. My baby is confused as to why he's not in her life, and I don't know how to fix it."

"Maybe you *don't* fix it. Maybe you help her understand by telling her the truth."

Shaking her head, Patience looked away from Toni's intense eyes. "She's too young."

"You'd be surprised at what information children can handle," Toni said. "What they can understand and *accept*." She lightly shook Patience's hand, causing her to look at her. "It's not fair for you to take the burden of her *sperm donor's* actions all on your own... You need to explain why things are the way they are...explain what he's *done*."

Closing her eyes, Patience rubbed them with her fingertips while pondering Toni's words.

"Will you at least think about it?"

After a moment, Patience nodded.

"Good." Toni's mind was moving a thousand miles a minute as she processed everything she'd just learned. But out of everything, one thing stuck out. "Patience, I don't like the fact that Greg is even in this *state*. I mean, do you think he'll pop his ass up anywhere *else*?"

Patience shrugged. "I don't know T... I don't know."

Worry registered on Toni's face. "*Please* be careful. I don't give a damn *what* Angela says, men like him, don't change. No matter *how* much time has passed."

"I know, and I will."

Picking up the freshly dried, folded clothing from the table in the laundry room, Patience passed through the hallway en route to her bedroom. Stopping at Noelle's open door, she peered inside where Noelle was working diligently at her desk.

Toni had remained with Patience until it was time for her to pick up Noelle from school. As promised, Toni did the pickup, dropping Noelle off before going home. Aside from the time spent at the dinner table eating, Noelle spent most of the time in her room.

Though Noelle's standoffish behavior towards Patience had waned a bit over the weeks, she knew that her daughter's mind was still heavy, and it bothered her.

"Hey Bunny."

Noelle turned around in her seat, seeing her mother standing in the doorway. "Hey Mommy."

Patience motioned inside. "You mind if I come in?"

Noelle shook her head. "No, I don't mind."

Stepping in, Patience set the clothes on her daughter's bed before sitting down next to the pile. She eyed the desk, seeing an abundance of paper cut outs, glue, tubs of glitter, and colored pencils. "What are you working on?"

"My art project," Noelle glanced at her cluttered workstation, before returning her eyes to her mother. "I'm almost finished."

Patience's eyes lit up. She was aware of the upcoming due date, but had no idea what Noelle had decided to do for it. The girl was determined to keep it a secret. "Do you plan on giving me a hint of what it is?"

Noelle displayed a winsome grin. "I'll show you if it gets picked."

That adorable smile almost made Patience forget about her problems. It was the first time she'd seen Noelle smile since that dreaded night. "I know it will, and I'm looking forward to seeing it."

As Noelle returned her eyes to her work, Patience sat, her eyes fixated on her, the look on her face reflecting the internal battle she was experiencing. *What am I going to say to this baby about her father? Should I even bother telling her that he showed up? What if she wants to see him?*

"Do you know when Mr. Michael will be back from his work trip?"

Noelle's question snapped Patience out of her thoughts. Feeling her heart jump at the mention of Michael, she folded some of her hair behind her ear. "Umm…" She had yet to break the news of their breakup to Noelle; she didn't know how her daughter would handle the fact that this person she'd gotten attached to, was no longer going to be around. Or the fact that it was Patience's fault. So, she'd resorted to telling Noelle that he was away on an extended work trip. "I don't know…" Patience fixed her with an empathetic stare. "You miss him, huh?"

Noelle nodded. "Yes."

"Me too," Patience uttered softly. *I need to leave this room before I bust out crying.* "I'll leave you to your work." Standing from the bed with the clothes in hand, she went over to Noelle and kissed the top of her head. "Let me know if you need anything."

"I will." Noelle turned around as her mother was leaving. "Mommy, can I ask you a question?"

Patience discreetly wiped the tears from her eyes before glancing back at her. "Of course you can."

"My dad…is he anything like Mr. Michael?" Noelle asked, hope in her eyes. "Is he nice? Does he like to do fun things? Is he good with kids?" Since talking to the man, she'd wondered if the man who used to be married to her mother, was as kind and fun as the one she was *hoping* one day would.

Patience stood in tormented silence. She knew the answer to that question, but didn't want to speak it to her daughter. "Noelle…Michael and your father are *nothing* alike…and that's all I can say right now."

Lowering her eyes, Noelle nodded. "Okay."

Patience could've kicked herself for snatching the joy out of her child's eyes once again. "I'm sorry that wasn't the answer you wanted, Bunny. I'm sorry about a *lot* of things."

"It's okay Mommy." Noelle turned back to her work. "Love you."

That was all it took for more tears to flood Patience's eyes. Noelle had no idea how much she needed to hear that. "I love you too." Knowing that if she tried to utter another word, she'd fall apart, she walked away and pulled the door closed.

Chapter Thirty-Six

"HERE ARE MY RECORDS FOR the first quarter of this year." Michael handed Toni a folder full of papers.

Toni flipped through the paperwork. "Perfect, as always." Setting them on her desk, she looked up at Michael, whose gaze had wandered off to the side. Given the circumstances, she wasn't exactly sure if Michael was going to honor the appointment they'd set a month ago, to go over tax preparation. She was pleasantly surprised when he showed up, prepared as usual. Though through his professionalism, Toni could sense the sadness in him. "So…"

Snapping out of his haze, Michael looked over at her. "Sorry, did I drift off?"

"Just a little." Toni smiled a bit, "It's okay though."

Giving a slow nod, Michael folded his hands. "I'm umm, just a bit tired, but that's no excuse." He gestured to the folder. "Is there anything else you need from me?"

"No, I think we're good for now." Toni patted the stack. "But of course, if that changes after I compare information, I'll let you know."

"Okay. Sounds good." Michael rose from his seat, extending his hand, which Toni shook. "Have a good day."

"You too." Toni watched him walk towards the door, knowing that *he wouldn't* have one. He probably hadn't had a good day in almost a month. She stood from her desk. "Michael."

Stopping short of opening the door, Michael spun around. "Found something already?" he attempted to joke.

Toni rounded her desk. "No…" She ran a hand down her arm as she stopped in front of him. "We're off the clock, right?"

"Yeah." Michael shot her a curious look. "Why?"

"Because what I'm about to mention isn't exactly business related."

Michael stood, bracing himself for the worst.

"Rob wanted to invite you to a poker night at his friend's house," she said. "When he found out that I was meeting with you today, he got excited and wanted to extend the invite."

Michael let a smile come through. The few times he'd hung out with Rob, Michael had enjoyed himself. The smile quickly faded as the cloud of his new reality loomed over him. "Please tell Rob that I'm flattered, but I don't think it's a good idea for me to be around now that umm…" He cleared his throat. "Please extend my apologies."

"I will." She took a deep breath. "Look… I just want to say how sorry I am about what's going on between you and my sister. She still loves you—"

Michael lifted his hand slightly. "Toni, I don't— I appreciate it, but… I don't think we should be talking about this." His eyes lowered. "I *can't* talk about this."

"You're right, I apologize. Overstepping seems to run in our family."

Michael ran a hand over the back of his head. "Your intentions have always been good, so no harm done." He offered a faint smile. "Take care."

Toni opened her mouth, as Michael once again grabbed for the door handle. She'd meant what she'd told Patience; she and Michael were great together. The smile that man brought to her sister's face was one she was dying to see again. "Michael, wait."

Pausing yet again, Michael turned around.

"Umm…" Toni clasped her hands together, seriousness on her face. "I know I just made that 'overstepping' comment, but I really need to say this to you."

He crossed his arms. "Say what?"

"Patience is…*going* through something right now, and—she needs you."

Brow furrowing, Michael let out a sigh. "Toni, she doesn't *want* me."

"She *does*," Toni maintained. "You have *no* idea how much—"

"Okay, with all due respect," Michael cut in, voice calm. "That's enough." He was having a hard enough time dealing with their split. He didn't need Toni filling his head with unrealistic hope.

Stepping back, Toni gave him a remorseful look. "You're right, I apologize." Her shoulders lifted, then fell. "I just hate that this happened, but please don't hold it against me."

"Never." He relaxed his face. "You're a good sister to her… See you."

"See you." Toni followed Michael's departing figure until he closed the door behind him. Raising her eyes to the ceiling, she sighed. "Please fix this."

"Yes Mom… I know, I—" Sitting on his bed, Michael ran a hand across his face. "I'm *okay* Mom…yes, I ate earlier. As a matter of fact, I'm about to make dinner so…" He massaged his temple as he sighed. Having arrived home over an hour ago, Michael had hoped to unwind in peace. But when his mother had called him, he decided against ignoring it this time around. Now an hour into their talk, he was regretting the decision. "Yes…I did enjoy my lunch with Pop a few days ago… I've apologized for not answering your calls before now, but I'd be happy to say I'm sorry again… Yes ma'am…okay, Mom— I have to go okay. I'll call you tomorrow…yes, I promise. Love you too."

Michael tossed the phone on the bed as he ended the call. Resting his face in his hands, he sat still for a few moments. He was exhausted, both physically and mentally. Working on-site that day had taken a toll on his body. Realizing that he needed to make his dinner while he still had the energy, Michael rose from the bed.

As he passed by his dresser on his way out the door, he stopped, eyes drawn to a box sitting atop it. Picking up the small velvet square, Michael exhaled a shuddered breath as he opened it. Inside was a four-carat marquise cut diamond ring, nestled on a platinum band with diamond accents.

Michael had been so excited when he'd ordered it custom made from the jeweler a month ago. Then his heart had shattered when he was finally able to pick it up, a week after his split from Patience. Feeling a wave of emotion threaten to overwhelm him, Michael closed the box, putting it back before leaving the bedroom.

An hour and a half later, Michael stared at the movie playing on the television screen in front of him. Yet as action-packed as the chase was, he couldn't care less about it. "*None* of this shit is realistic," Michael grunted.

Grabbing the plate of Salisbury steak and mashed potatoes from the coffee table, he cut a piece with his fork. Chewing, he picked up his glass of water, taking a sip to push the food down before settling back against the cushions.

Frustrated with the over-the-top film, Michael turned the TV off, opting instead to listen to the radio. Leaning his head back, Michael closed his eyes. The smooth jazz tunes worked perfectly to clear his mind.

His doorbell ringing snapped his eyes back open.

Heading for the door, he rolled his eyes. He wasn't in the mood for uninvited guests. Looking out the peephole, he released a sigh and reluctantly opened the door.

His stoney stare was met with the smiling faces of his siblings.

"What's good Mike?" Dante cheerfully greeted.

A low grunt sounded from Michael. "Did Mom send you?" He crossed his arms. "I talked to her earlier. She knows I'm good."

Kenya shrugged. "Nope, we're not here because of Mom." Her brow arched. "Are you going to let us in?"

Michael rolled his eyes. "Do I *have* to?"

Both Kenya and Dante nodded. "Yes," they replied in unison.

Sucking his teeth, Michael moved aside. "Fine."

Stepping through the front door, Kenya flipped on the light switch, illuminating the living room.

"What are you two doing here?" Michael grunted, lumbering to the couch.

"We've come to drag you out the house," Kenya answered. "It's too nice of a night for you to be in here wallowing."

Flopping down, Michael scoffed. "I put on for everybody all damn day. When I come home, I'm *allowed* to wallow."

"Not *tonight* you're not." Rounding the couch, Dante gave a stiff pat to his brother's shoulder. "Get your stuff, and let's hit it."

"I'm not in the damn mood."

Shrugging, Dante returned a smirk. "Don't worry, *we* are."

Kenya nudged Michael's shoulder. "Get *up* Mike, or I *will* call Mom, and you know she'll come over with an overnight bag."

Michael rolled his eyes yet again. As much as he loved his mother, he wasn't in the mood for her smothering and constant questions about his relationship. Realizing the alternative was better, Michael rose from the couch. "Whatever. I don't want to be out too late."

"You won't be," Kenya promised. She peered over at Dante, who'd become distracted by the leftover dinner on the coffee table. "Dante, drop the fork. Let's go."

"Damn it." Leaving the fork on the plate, Dante dashed for the door.

Sitting at a table, Michael removed the skates from his feet, replacing them with his sneakers.

Kenya appeared at the table, two bottled beers in hand. "Here."

Michael put his hand up. "Nah, I don't care for beer."

"Neither do I, but that's all this place had, so here." She pushed it in his direction.

Michael reluctantly took it. "Thank you." He took a quick sip, making a face at the taste, as Kenya sat down at the table with her brothers. "Seriously…thank you both."

Dante offered a warm smile, as Kenya tipped her bottle in Michael's direction. "You're welcome," he replied.

Though Michael had left his house and got into his brother's car without a fight, his attitude during the entire ride let his siblings know exactly how displeased he was. Yet when he saw the sign for the familiar skating rink, Michael couldn't help but soften.

During the hour session with his siblings, he'd laughed, reminisced, and for the first time in weeks, was able to keep his mind off his heartache.

Setting his bottle on the table, Michael looked around. "I can't believe this place is still standing."

"Shit, *barely*," Dante chortled, taking some chips from a basket in front of him. "I'm sure these skates haven't been washed since we were kids."

Kenya stood, tossing her half-empty bottle in the nearby trash. "This nasty beer is doing something ridiculous to my bladder. I'm heading to the ladies room."

"That did *not* need an announcement, Ken." Dante laughed when Kenya playfully nudged his arm in passing. Humor draining from his face, Dante stared at his brother, who had just taken another sip from his bottle. "Hey umm, I didn't want to get all sentimental in front of sis, but I want to let you know that I know how you feel."

Folding his arms on the tabletop, Michael fixed a somber expression. "I know you do."

"I mean, it's not the same *situation*, but..."

"I know man." Michael's eyes focused on the table, his mind filling with thoughts of Patience once again. "I bought a ring," he got out after a moment of silence.

Dante's eyes widened. "Seriously?"

"Yep." Michael looked at him. "Picked it out before our breakup... I was going to ask her to marry me." His shoulders fell. "Now it sits on the dresser taunting me every damn day."

Dante reached over, giving his brother's arm a pat. "Damn man...that's rough."

"I know." Michael sighed. "But the thing is, as much as it hurts to look at, I can't bear myself to get rid of it. It's almost as if on some level, I'm holding on to it because I'm still hoping that she'll change her mind." He shook his head when Dante just stared at him. "It's foolish I know."

"Nah, it's not. There's nothing foolish about hoping... and this is coming from someone who had *no* damn hope when my relationship ended."

Recognizing the subtle jest, Michael couldn't help but let a quiet laugh seep through.

"I mean, *none*." Dante laughed a bit at the memory. "But...I called Lori a few days ago."

Michael's brows shot up in surprise. "*Did* you?"

"Yep. We talked, and..." Dante smiled, "she agreed to go out with me."

Knowing how much Dante missed his ex, the potential reconciliation made Michael smile. "That's great Dante."

"Thanks man." Dante leaned back in his seat, "I mean, it's just for coffee, but..."

"Hell, it's a *start*," Michael pointed out. "And it's okay to be excited about that."

Dante nodded in agreement. "I tell you Mike, this time away from her has put things in perspective. I know where I lacked, and I'm prepared to step it up…should she give me the chance of course… I even suggested a few sessions of couple's counseling."

"I'm happy for you bro. Really."

Dante fiddled with a balled-up napkin in front of him. "Listen, I didn't tell you that to rub anything in—"

Michael put a hand up. "I know you didn't."

"I just hoped that it would give you some encouragement," Dante finished. "I mean, if *my* stupid ass can get a second chance with the love of my life, I'm positive you'll get one with yours…" His eyes filled with admiration for his big brother. "You've always been a better man than me, so… I *know* it'll happen, because it's what you deserve."

Michael smiled sincerely. "Me being better than you isn't true, but, I *do* appreciate it," he replied. "And I hope you're right."

"Me too." Rising from his seat, Dante exchanging a hug with Michael, before both men sat back down just as Kenya approached.

"That damn line was ridiculous," Kenya huffed. "It's like everyone had to use it at the same damn time." She focused on her brothers who were staring at her. "Y'all talk about anything interesting while I was gone?"

"Yes," Michael answered.

"Oh?" Kenya folded her arms. "Want to share?"

Michael and Dante exchanged humored glances, before looking back at her. "No," they answered in unison.

Chapter Thirty-Seven

PATIENCE'S FINGERS MOVED ACROSS HER keyboard with vigor. She'd been so focused on typing up paperwork for the past half hour, that the phone beeping was the only thing to stall her progress. Pausing, she eyed the message on her work cell. Eyes lighting with excitement at the message, she quickly dialed a number, putting the phone to her ear.

"Hello Whitney, it's Patience over at Clayborn Realty... I'm well thanks. I have some good news for you...." Her smile was bright. "The buyer accepted your counter, they want to close the deal... You're so welcome. I'll get started on the next process and will touch base with you soon... Of course. Congratulations, talk back soon."

Ending the call, Patience clapped her hands in delight. She'd sold her first seven-figure home. The news had come at a time when she certainly needed something positive. Grabbing her purse, she closed out the screen on her laptop. This called for a celebratory pastry.

Walking outside and down the steps of her building, the bright sun was a bit much after being in the office all morning; Patience shielded her eyes from it with her hand. As she gave herself a minute to adjust, a tap to her shoulder took her by surprise.

Turning around, her light sensitivity no longer mattered; her eyes had blown wide at the person before her. "You son of a—"

Greg cautiously put a hand up, cutting her rant short. "Come on Patience, you don't have to be so rude every time we run into each other."

"*Run into* each other?" she repeated, shooting daggers at him with her eyes. "No, what you *meant* to say was you popping up on me like some fuckin' stalker."

"I'm not stalking you."

Patience was taken aback by the blatant lie. "So what? You just happened to be in the area *again*, huh?"

"Well, I'm still in *town*, so I figured…" Greg shrugged. "Look my prior research aside, your office contact information was on the lawn sign outside that open house, so you really can't fault me."

Letting out a deep breath of frustration, Patience adjusted the purse on her shoulder. "Doesn't matter Greg, I told you before to leave me alone. Don't make me have to get a restraining order." She went to walk away, but was stopped when Greg stepped in front of her, putting a hand on her forearm. She jerked away from him. "Don't fuckin' touch me!"

"Whoa whoa." Hands up, Greg stepped back. "I'm not going to hurt you. *Damn*, you act like before that *one* indiscretion, that I was beating on you during our marriage."

Patience's mouth gaped open at the sheer audacity. "Did you seriously just try to *downplay* what— You know what, trying to get you to acknowledge your faults is, and has *always* been, pointless." Fighting to keep from exploding outside of her place of employment, she tried to walk off, but he blocked her once again. "Greg, *move*."

"Look, I *told* you, I regret my past actions." The irritation in his voice was apparent. "And a *restraining order* won't be necessary. I don't plan on continuing these unexpected visits."

"Then what do you *want*?"

"I want *you*—" Greg paused, putting his hands together. "I'd like to meet my daughter Patience… I think it's time."

"I *said* no Greg." She pointed at him. "*My valid* reasons aside, have you forgotten that this is how you wanted it?"

Sighing, Greg shuffled his weight from one foot to the other. "Now look, I know what I said, and I know what I did to you. But I'm not that person anymore Patience... I know you don't believe me, but let me prove it. I can start by reconnecting with you. *Calling* you maybe... Taking you out."

Patience glared as he flashed a vacant grin.

"Maybe start with dinner, or a movie. Or perhaps I could skip the formalities and take you on a weekend getaway..." Excited at the idea, he pulled out his phone, scrolling. "As a matter of fact, there's this bed and breakfast in Georgia I think you'd like. Let me show you—"

"You keep mentioning what you want to do with *me*, but I thought this had to do with our *daughter*," Patience zoned in.

The smile cleared from his face as Greg rubbed his forehead with his free hand. "Yeah—yeah of *course* it is. I mean, that's why I'm here. To meet our daughter—Noelle," he sputtered. "Forget I mentioned the getaway, I got ahead of myself... We can try that down the line." *Just you and me like old times.*

Patience just stared at him, taking in what he was saying, how he was *looking* at her. In both conversations, there had been zero sincerity on his face when he made any request to see Noelle. It was almost like he thought it was something he *had* to say. He never even asked how she was doing, what she liked...didn't once ask to at least see a *picture* of her. Thinking back to the conversation she'd had with Noelle about the phone call, Noelle had stressed that he kept asking about *her. This bitch isn't slick. I know what he really wants.* Leaning her head to the side, Patience cringed inside at the words she was about to say. "Let me think on it."

The contempt in her voice didn't seem to faze Greg; his toothy smile showed just how delighted he was. "Good, that's a start." He eyed her up and down. "When you decide to give me that chance, my number hasn't changed."

"Why would you *ever* think that your phone number would still be logged away in my phone *or* my memory?" Patience sneered.

He smirked. "Fair enough." Reaching into his jacket pocket, Greg pulled out his wallet, and from it, a business card. He held it up in Patience's view. "Hit my cell."

Snatching the card from him, Patience balled it up in her hand.

"You on your way to lunch?" He removed a hundred-dollar bill from his wallet, waving it at her. "Why don't you go sit your fine ass in someplace expensive… It's on me."

Patience rolled her eyes. "I don't want or need anything from you. In case you've forgotten."

Greg stood in place as Patience sauntered off without another word, watching her departing figure with lust in his eyes. Rubbing his chin, the memories of having her in his bed flooded back. "Nah…I certainly remember *everything*."

Toni paced her living room floor, mumbling to herself in the process. "You can't be serious," she bit out.

Patience was sitting in a chair, her body eerily still, following her movements with her eyes. "You're going to burn a hole in the floor," she calmly said.

"Fuck this floor!" Clasping her hands in front of her face, Toni took a deep breath and brought her pacing to an abrupt stop. She faced Patience. "Okay look, you need to tell me I didn't just hear what I think I heard you say just now."

Patience stared at her, deadpan. "You mean about the floor?"

"Patience!"

"Okay…" Patience folded her arms. "You heard correctly."

"So you're *serious*?" Toni's brow creased with a deep frown. "You're *actually* going to allow Greg to meet Noelle?" She'd been floored when Patience had revealed that Greg had showed up at her job the day before. But when Patience had told her that she was planning a meeting with Greg, she'd nearly fallen out of her chair.

"No T, I'm not."

Toni tossed her hands in the air. "Well, that's what you just *said*."

"That's not what I *meant*." Patience reached out, grabbing Toni's hand. "Sit down and *calm* down."

Toni flopped down on the couch with a loud huff.

"Look, I have a feeling about what Greg's *actual* motive is for showing up, but I need to prove it," Patience explained. "He's a textbook liar and manipulator, who seems to think I'm the same *idiot* who was blind to his bullshit all those years ago."

Shooting her a chastising look, Toni tapped her sister's hand. "Stop it, you were never an idiot."

"Yeah well, the jury is still out on that," Patience jeered. "But the only way to break that damn façade of his is to get proof."

"So, you think that meeting with him is the way to do it?" It was more of a statement than a question. When Patience nodded, Toni rubbed her face with her hands. "Pace… What if you're wrong? What if he demands to see Noelle right then and there?"

Looking off to the side, Patience pondered the question. "I honestly don't think it'll get to that point. I was married to that man for five years; I'd like to think that I came away with *some* knowledge of how he operates." She returned her gaze to her sister. "Trust me on this, okay."

Toni was apprehensive, but there was no way she wasn't going to support her favorite sister. She threw her hands up. "Okay so… Where are you going to have him meet you?" she asked. "Not *your* house, I hope. The last thing you need is his pin-headed ass knowing where you live."

"No." Patience fiddled with a curl in her hair as she thought. "I have access to plenty of empty properties. I can do it at one of them."

Toni shook her head with vigor. "No…you'll do it here."

Patience frowned at Toni, shaking her head in the process. "*Hell* no. I am *not* letting that bastard know where *you* live."

"My husband is licensed to carry and *does*." Folding her arms,

Toni smirked. "And so do *I*. We're good over here honey. So, Greg can start some shit if he *wants* to, I'd *love* to pop one in his knee cap."

Patience's eyebrow lifted. "Umm… I appreciate the fact that you're willing to commit violence for me but…*don't.*"

Toni eyed Patience with defiance. "Do *not* let my career, those designer clothes in my closet, or these expensive manicures fool you girl. I'm not *afraid* of spending a few hours in jail." She crossed her legs. "My man will have me out in less than two."

"Toni," Patience warned, fixing her with a stern look.

"Okay fine." Toni tucked her hair behind her ear. "I hate that I'm about to say this but…make the call. Block your number first."

Patience grabbed her phone from the table beside her. "Yeah, I know."

The barista at Fredrick's coffeehouse greeted Michael with a cheerful wave as his familiar face approached the counter. "Good morning sir, your usual? Large black coffee and beef bacon, egg, and cheese sandwich?"

Offering a smile back, Michael retrieved the wallet from his pocket. "Good morning. Yep, the usual, thank you."

"Perfect." She rang up the order, then took the cash from his hand. "Our new drip machine is a bit slow this morning, so the order will take a few more minutes than you're used to."

"That's not a problem, take your time." Michael retrieved his change, placing it in the tip jar along with a few extra dollars. "I'll be over here."

The barista nodded and set to work.

Stepping off to the side, Michael stared out the side window, trying to clear his mind before the workday ahead. Hearing the door open, he glanced up at the man who entered, before returning his focus to the hustle and bustle outside.

Greg strolled up to the counter.

"Good morning sir, what can I get you—"

"Large coffee, extra cream and sugar," Greg briskly answered.

His rudeness cleared the smile from the barista's face. "Sure thing." She quickly rang the order and gave the total; Greg set the exact amount on the counter in front of her before turning away. "Uh— Sir, our drip machine—"

Back still facing her, Greg waved dismissively. "Don't need a speech sweetheart, just the coffee."

Michael cut his eye at the jerk. He despised rudeness, especially when it was directed at a woman. Thankfully, Greg stepped away from the counter, allowing Michael to go back to his people watching.

Aside from the drip machine noises, it was quiet in the coffeehouse that morning. Until Greg started loudly drumming his fingers on a small table. Letting out a heavy breath, Greg jerked his watch up to eye level, giving it a look. "Are all the coffeehouses in this city, like this?" When Michael didn't respond, Greg gestured his way. "Hey."

Michael turned his head, seeing the guy staring at him. "You talking to me?" His voice lacked enthusiasm.

Greg let out an obnoxious laugh. "We *are* the only two customers in this establishment, aren't we?"

There were no traces of amusement on Michael's face. "What was your question, man?"

"Was just wondering if all the coffee places in this area were this lackluster." Greg glanced around. "I'm used to something flashier."

Then take your ignorant ass and go find a flashier one. Michael had no intentions of being polite, or engaging in a casual conversation with him. He just gave a haphazard shrug. "Don't really know what you mean."

Not taking the social cues, Greg continued on. "Well, it's a good thing I won't be in these parts long. I ran into an old flame of mine and plan on convincing her to come back home with me." He fixed Michael with an intense stare. "Yo boss, you ever see a woman so fine you would do anything to have her?"

Michael offered only an expression and a low "hm." He *had*, and *she* was on his mind even at this moment. But he wasn't about to divulge that to a stranger.

Shoving his hands in his pockets, Greg peered out the window, a dreamy look in his eyes. "Yeah man, my woman is something else… Going to meet up with her later. Plan on trying to rekindle some bedroom magic, if you know what I mean."

Shaking his head, Michael turned away from him. "Yeah, that's none of my business, man."

Shrugging, Greg looked at his watch once more, then directed his attention to the barista, who was putting lids on two coffee cups. "Aye sweetheart, what are you doing, grinding the coffee beans yourself?"

The young woman shot him a stunned look.

"How long is this going to *take*?" Greg harped.

"The drip is slow today, which is what she was *trying* to say to you before you cut her off earlier," Michael stepped in, tone sharp.

Shooting Michael a side-glance, Greg relaxed the frown on his face. "It's no issue boss, was just making an observation."

Michael folded his arms, fixing Greg with a firm stare. "Umm hmm."

"H—here's your coffee," the barista stammered, handing Greg his cup. As he practically snatched it from her without so much as a thank you, she looked at Michael. "Here's yours too. Sorry for the wait."

Michael headed over. "It's not a problem, really." He could tell by the look on her face that she was feeling a bit flustered. "Don't let that nonsense get to you. You're doing a great job."

Grateful for the encouragement, she gave Michael a nod. "Thank you."

Stopping short of the door, Greg took a wary sip, and

immediately spat it out. Spinning around, he scowled at the barista. "I asked for extra cream and sugar. *This* shit is black."

Michael turned to glare at him.

"I—I'm sorry, I did put extra cream and sugar as you asked," she sputtered.

Michael set his sandwich and coffee on the counter, then opened the cup. Seeing the tan-colored coffee, he knew what had gone wrong.

Ripping the top off the cup, Greg barreled straight for her. "You look at this shit and tell me if this has cream and sugar in it. What kind of incompetent piece of—"

Michael stepped in his face before he could reach the terrified barista. His eyes were blazing with anger. "Yo, what the hell is your problem man?"

Greg pointed his coffee cup towards the barista. "I was just telling this bitch—"

Michael slapped the coffee cup out of Greg's hand, sending the hot liquid flying away from them. "The only *bitch* in here is you," he snarled. "You're standing here calling this lady out her name over some goddamn *coffee*? It was a fuckin' *mistake*." He pointed in Greg's face. "You need to check that weak shit."

Eyes wide and mouth gaping, Greg eyed the liquid on the floor and the wall beside him. He then looked at Michael, who looked as if he wanted to break his jaw. Which was not on Greg's list of things to suffer through. Checking his attitude, Greg straightened out his shirt. "Your point has been noted. Apologies for the lost temper."

"Nah, it's too late for that shit, take your ass on out of here," Michael demanded.

Greg frowned. "I'm still owed a coffee."

"You're about to get something *else*, if you don't leave." Glare unwavering, Michael pointed to the door behind Greg. "I'm not going to say it again."

Greg threw his hands up in surrender and backed away. "You got it." He scoffed. "I'm not hurting for that little five dollars anyway."

Michael watched as Greg slithered out the door, before turning to the barista. The woman was visibly shaken. "Are you okay?" he asked her, tone caring.

With tears in her eyes, she nodded. "Thank you so much."

"No thanks needed." He took several napkins out of a holder. "Sorry about the spill, I'll clean it up."

She put a hand out. "No, no I'll get the janitor to take care of it." Her hands trembled as she hit the keys on her register. "I'll get you another black coffee right away."

Michael pulled out his wallet. Taking a twenty-dollar bill from it, he placed it in the jar for her troubles. "Take your time."

Chapter Thirty-Eight

PULLING IN FRONT OF A house, Greg checked the address written on a piece of paper, before comparing it to what the GPS read. Turning the car off, he checked his reflection in the rearview mirror, grinning to himself.

"Daddy's coming for you baby," he boasted to himself. Greg was pleasantly surprised when Patience had called him three days ago with the request to meet. His surprise turned to pure excitement when he found out that the meeting spot wasn't a restaurant or some other public place, but her home.

The coffeehouse confrontation from earlier that morning, with the man Greg had spitefully deemed the *goddamn coffee hero* in his head, was the furthest from his thoughts.

Patience had been on his mind ever since Angela had reached out to him, and had been on his radar ever since he stepped foot into her open house over a week ago. Every feeling he once had for her, had flooded back with a vengeance the moment he laid eyes on her. He wasn't going to let her get away twice.

Grabbing the bouquet of assorted wildflowers from the passenger seat, he exited the car. Smoothing his sports jacket down, he strolled up the lit walkway. The evening weather was pleasant, just like his mood.

Standing in front of the door, he gave it a stiff knock. The anticipation grew with each passing moment. Plastering a wide smile, Greg held the flowers out as the door opened.

His hand quickly recoiled, the smile fleeing once he saw who was standing on the other side of the door. "*Toni?*"

Standing in the doorway, Toni eyed Greg with hatred. "Antoinette to you."

He forced a smirk. "Always a pleasure," he jeered. "I see you're still stuck to your sister like Velcro. I was *so* happy when I moved Patience away when we got married. Got to have her all to myself."

Toni held her unfaltering gaze on the pitiful excuse of a man before her. "You must want me to react to that."

Letting out a deep breath, Greg checked himself. *Remember why you're here.* "Apologies Antoinette."

"Not accepted, Gregory."

"Look—" He clenched the flowers in his hand. Toni had always pushed his buttons. "Can you tell Patience that I'm here?"

"No, I can't do that," Toni replied, much to Greg's confusion.

"Toni, she's expecting me. So please stop being evil for one moment and go get her."

Toni shook her head. "Patience isn't here. But don't worry, she filled me in on everything. You're here to meet your daughter, right? She's a beautiful child." She motioned for him to enter. "Come in, she's expecting you."

"Wait wait, hold up." Greg put his hand up, his eyes narrowing. "What do you *mean* Patience isn't here?"

Toni folded her arms, eyeing him with defiance. "I mean she isn't *here*... But your *daughter is*." She cocked her head to the side. "*That is* who you're here for, right? Your daughter? I mean, you told Patience you wanted to meet her, so here's your chance."

Greg stepped back onto the concrete, running a hand over his head. "No, no Patience was *supposed* to be here." All attempts at charm had dissolved to frustration. "*That's* who I came here to see, not— Where *is* she?"

Toni gave a nonchalant shrug. "I'm afraid I can't divulge that information Greg. But again…your daughter is waiting to meet you. I mean, if you're nervous about coming inside or meeting her without Patience here…" She pulled her cell phone from her jeans pocket. "I can call her phone and you can at least say hello."

Greg's scowl grew deeper, his jaw stiffening. "I didn't come here for that. I *came* here to see Patience."

"So, you *don't* want to meet Noelle, is what you're saying," Toni goaded, staring him down. "Even though you told *Patience* you wanted to…that *is* what you're saying right? I just want to make sure I relay the message correctly."

Rolling his eyes, Greg threw the flowers onto the lawn as he turned around, heading back for his car. "Fuck this," he threw over his shoulder.

Toni eyed the discarded florals littering her yard. "You know, flowers aren't exactly a good gift to bring a *nine-year-old*," she hurled at him.

She watched Greg jump into his vehicle and speed off down the street. Shaking her head, she shut the door, locking it. Toni looked over to the side. "You were right."

Patience folded her arms from where she'd hidden just out of sight of the door. She let out a heavy sigh. "I know."

"I should've made him pick those flowers up with his damn teeth," Rob fussed, approaching his wife. He'd been watching from a nearby window.

Toni rubbed his shoulder. "Fuck him."

"You two good?" Rob asked.

"Oh, we're good," Toni assured. She then shot him a seductive look. "You know, you look sexy when you're being protective."

Rob let out a laugh. "Stop it." He headed for the staircase. "I'll be doing some work. Let me know if you two need anything."

"We will." Toni turned to Patience as her husband disappeared up the steps. She opened her mouth to say something, but was caught off guard by the tears in her sister's eyes. Concern registered on Toni's face as she put a hand on Patience's arm. "Hey. You okay?"

Patience just shook her head no. She couldn't bring herself to speak.

"I know seeing him again upset you, but you proved your point Pace," Toni tried to console her. "You were right."

Tears fell as Patience sniffled. "I almost wish that I *wasn't*, though." At first, Patience had been satisfied, proud of herself for knowing better. Yet as she stood there, listening as this man completely dismissed the idea of meeting Noelle, it broke Patience's heart. "She doesn't deserve that. My baby doesn't deserve that."

Toni pulled her into a loving hug. "It's okay, it's okay sweetie." She rubbed Patience's back as she cried on her shoulder.

"It's *not* okay." Patience pulled back, wiping her face with her hands. "It's not okay, and I feel like shit. I feel *guilty*."

Toni held her hands on Patience's shoulders. "Guilty for *what*?"

"For *choosing* that piece of shit to be her father."

Trying to keep her emotions at bay, Toni exhaled heavily and guided her sister to the couch. "Come sit down."

Patience sank into the cushions, wiping her eyes yet again. But she couldn't clear the tears fast enough. They kept falling, and along with them, everything that she'd been holding in. "I chose wrong and now she has to pay for it." She crossed her arms to her chest. "She's been cheated out of the family she deserves. All because I was too fuckin' stupid to see Greg for who he really was before I married him."

Toni adjusted her position on the couch to face Patience. "Now you listen to me. Noelle is *not* being cheated out of a family, and neither are you." When Patience wouldn't look at her, Toni poked her arm. "Hey."

Patience reluctantly looked at Toni, face still stained with fallen tears.

"So, you had a shitty first marriage. You think that negates any chance of you ever getting the marriage that you *deserve?*" Toni questioned. "We've *all* made horrible choices in partners at some point in our past, but what *matters* is that we've been able to move on from them." She pointed to Patience, who was just staring at her in silence. "Greg might be Noelle's father, but he does *not* need to be in her life for that little girl to thrive and be happy. You've already proven that by raising her *without* him. *Just* like you've proven that you can be loved and treated *exactly* how you're *supposed* to be. So, I'm going to need you to stop being so damn hard on yourself for shit that you can't change."

"It's easy for you to try and sell me all this happily ever after shit, when you've never had to go through this," Patience fired back. "I know you *want* to understand why I'm feeling this way, but you *can't.*"

"Patience I can, and I *do*—"

Patience made a move to get up. "I can't do this shit with you right now."

"Wait." Toni grabbed Patience's arm, stopping her. "I do understand because…Jordan isn't Rob's."

Snapping her head in Toni's direction, Patience looked more shocked than Toni had ever seen her. "What?"

Removing her hand from Patience's arm, Toni folded her hands over her knee. "Rob isn't Jordan's biological father," she confessed. It was a secret she had kept to herself until now.

"Toni…" Patience was at a loss for words. She couldn't believe what she was hearing. "Does Rob *know?*"

"Of *course* he does." Toni took a breath as she found where to begin. "You remember Rob and I used to date in high school, and you remember how I told you that we broke up after graduation because we both decided to see what was out there… You know, live our lives without being tied to each other."

Patience nodded.

"Well...I did." Toni shrugged. "I lived my life without him. I graduated college, worked, partied, dated, and had my fun...which included a one-night stand with a coworker from a job I worked at before I moved here to Virginia... Condom broke, pill failed, and a month later I missed my period."

Patience sat in stunned silence as her sister spoke.

"I *told* the guy that I was pregnant, and that I was keeping it... I mean for all of my protection tactics to fail, it was *obviously* meant to happen so... I made the decision to go through with it, and he didn't want any parts, which I respected," Toni recalled. "He joined the military, and I moved here to accept a job at the company I'm working for now... And three months into living here, I ran into Rob. He'd moved here to attend law school." Toni smiled at the memory of seeing her husband's face at a grocery store, of all places, after all those years. "It was like we'd picked up right where we'd left off as friends. But when I saw that he wanted to pick up the *relationship* part as well, I told him about the baby and I gave him an out... Told him that if he chose to walk away, that I'd understand and... He *didn't*." She fixed Patience with a look that brimmed with emotion. "From the *moment* Rob held Jordan, she became his. And after we got married, he officially adopted her... She is his daughter, in *every* way expect for blood."

Patience tried to gather her words. "Does... Does Jordan know?"

Toni nodded. "Yeah. He and I sat her down and told her when she was about six."

"How did she take it? ...I mean, did she understand fully what that meant?"

"Not then, but she does now," Toni answered. "And it doesn't bother her. That man is everything to her. He *is* her father."

Patience wiped the moisture from her face as the next question formed in her mind. "Why didn't you tell me?"

"Because like *you* feel guilty...back then, so did *I*," Toni revealed. "But as we grew as a family and I watched their relationship, I realized that everything that happened, happened as it was *supposed* to, and I came to be at peace with it. And by that time, so many years had passed, that I figured it wasn't even worth saying anything, you know."

"I can understand that..." Patience placed a hand atop Toni's. "Thanks for telling me now."

"You needed to *hear* it now." Toni offered a comforting smile, and Patience simply gave a nod of acceptance. Toni then moved in for a sisterly embrace. "Now here's what you're going to do," she began, parting. "One, you're going to calm yourself, okay? And while you're doing that, *I'm* going to get the guest room ready, because you and Noelle are spending the night. The girls will be back from my in-laws' soon, and I'm sure they'll be happy about an impromptu sleepover."

"Toni, I'm fine. I can go home," Patience protested.

"You can, but you *won't*. Not tonight anyway—I want to keep you close."

Conceding, Patience nodded again. "Okay."

Toni breathed out a sigh of relief. "Good." She fixed an intent stare. "And the *other* thing you're going to do is work up the courage to fix your relationship with Michael."

Sighing, Patience grabbed hold of her butterfly pendant. "I want to, but I don't know if I can... He probably never wants to see me again and I wouldn't blame him." Her sullen gaze lowered to her lap. "I made him jump through hoops to be with me and I just..."

"He jumped through them because he knew you were worth it, and he *still* knows." Toni wiped a lone tear from her sister's cheek. "He may be upset with you Pace, but I promise if you try to talk to him, he'll be receptive."

Patience contemplated Toni's prediction, uncertainty showing on her face. She wasn't so sure if Toni was right about that. However, she knew that her sister was right about *one* thing: Patience needed to at least *try*. "I'll do what I can."

A smile in her eyes, Toni patted Patience's arm. "Good."

Staring at her phone screen, Patience's fingers moved at a steady pace as she keyed out a lengthy text message. That was until another message box popped in, forcing her to stop.

> **Noelle:** Mommy, do we have bubble wrap? I need to put it around my art piece, so it doesn't break when we bring it to school tomorrow. Oh, and my Art teacher told the class about this art magazine for kids that comes in the mail. Can I please get it?

Patience swiftly typed back.

> I'll get some bubble wrap before I pick you up today, and I'll look into the magazine subscription. Now put your phone away, you shouldn't be on it at school unless it's an emergency.

> **Noelle:** Okay. Putting it away now.

Shaking her head, Patience typed out a heart emoji to her daughter before switching back to the other message. The one she'd been agonizing over and working on for the past half hour.

Patience had spent the past few days trying to gather the nerve to call Michael, but no matter how much she tried, she just couldn't. It wasn't because of lack of want; it was fear. Not so much of the possibility that he wouldn't answer—she already half-expected that outcome. But she was more afraid that once she heard his voice, everything she wanted and needed to say to him would become stuck.

So, while sitting at an outdoor restaurant for lunch that afternoon, she had decided to type up a text message to send to him. Finishing the message, she read it through silently. As her eyes scanned the paragraphs of explanations and professions, she grew irritated. "He's not going to want to read this bullshit," she murmured to herself. Vigorously tapping the screen, she deleted the text, letting her phone fall the short distance to the table.

Picking up her glass of lemonade, she prepared to take a sip when someone tapped her shoulder. She flinched, and sent her drink down the wrong pipe. Slamming her glass down, Patience erupted with coughs.

Kenya stood next to her, eyes wide with panic. "Oh my God!" She patted Patience's back to help ease her coughing. "I'm so sorry."

Composing herself, Patience eyeballed Kenya. Though she had a profane rant composed about announcing her presence *before* touching her, she refrained from spewing it. "Hey Kenya," she finally said, voice raspy.

"Hi…" Holding her hands to her chest, Kenya's eyes were apologetic. "I'm sorry, my shop is across the street, and I saw you over here—"

"It's fine." Patience picked up a napkin, dabbing her mouth. *I would choose a place to eat right across from where Michael's sister worked.* "Good to see you."

"You too." Kenya stood, staring at Patience. She hadn't seen her since the breakup with her brother, not that she expected to. However, now that she was in front of her, Kenya couldn't pass up the opportunity to chat. She pointed to the seat across from her. "You mind if I sit?"

Patience's eyes darted to the seat, before settling them back on Kenya. She could only think of one reason why Kenya would want to sit with her. She wanted to dig into her about the breakup. Patience wasn't in the mood for a confrontation; however, she didn't feel right turning the woman's request down, after everything she'd put her brother through. "No, I don't mind."

Pulling out the chair, Kenya took the seat, resting her purse on the table. She pointed to the half-eaten salmon on Patience's plate. "That looks good."

"It was."

Giving a nod, Kenya sat in silence for a moment, studying Patience. Taking in the stiffness of her posture, the creased brow, the seriousness in her eyes. "I could be wrong here, but you seem to be on the defensive."

Patience arched an eyebrow. "*Do* I?"

"You do, but I promise you don't need to be... I didn't come over here to start anything."

Face relaxing, Patience sighed. "I'm sorry, I just..." She toyed with the napkin ring beside her plate. "Have a lot going on."

"I can imagine," Kenya placated. She leaned forward in her seat. "Not going to lie, I missed you at my luncheon...was holding out hope that you'd still attend."

"Yeah, I know. I just didn't think, given everything, that it was appropriate for me to be there," Patience was grateful for the invite she'd received from Kenya over a month ago for her women's business luncheon. But given the breakup, there was no way that she could've shown her face. "I'm sure it was a beautiful event."

"Thank you, it was nice." Kenya folded her arms on the tabletop. "You know Patience, you weren't just missed at the event... Your presence has been missed by our entire family...yours and your little girl's."

Patience glanced away for a brief moment, trying to shield herself from the sullen look on Kenya's face. She was already feeling the heavy weight of her choices, and now she felt worse. It wasn't just her and Michael's relationship affected, but that of his family, who she genuinely cared about. "We miss you guys too."

Sensing that she might be prodding Patience too much, Kenya lightly tapped her hand on the table. "I've taken up enough of your time. It was good seeing you."

Patience watched as Kenya gathered her purse. "You too Kenya."

Kenya stood from her seat, but something was preventing her

from leaving that table. *Mike is going to kill me, but I need to say this.* She sat back down. "I just have one other thing to say if you don't mind."

Though bewildered, Patience gave her a nod. "Go ahead."

"Okay…now I don't know exactly what *happened* between you two—why the relationship ended…" Kenya let out a heavy breath. "But what I *do* know, is that Michael is still hurting."

Patience's eyes lowered to the table.

"When he was *with* you, he was happier than I'd ever seen him… He loved you—he *still* loves you," Kenya continued. "And I don't know what's in your mind or heart when it comes to him right now, but I can only hope that things between you both work themselves out." She let out a sigh. "I'd give anything to see that glow in him again."

Returning her remorseful gaze to Kenya, water began building behind Patience's eyes, and she prayed it wouldn't surface. "I…" She found it hard to form any words to say to Kenya. What *could* she say? "I appreciate you stopping to talk with me," was all she could muster.

Taking the hint, Kenya gave a nod. "Of course." She stood once again. "Enjoy the rest of your lunch."

Patience was grateful that Kenya had walked away in that moment, or she would've seen her tears fall. She didn't even have the mental energy to pick up the napkin in front of her. As she sat, reddened eyes focused on the iron table, Patience replayed every moment of her time with Michael. From the day they had met, to their first date, to the first time he'd told her he loved her, to the first time they'd *made* love, to the last time she saw him.

This past month without him had been torture. Unless she was willing to continue to go through life without him in it, she had to stop running.

She had to make things right.

Chapter Thirty-Nine

THICK BUBBLE WRAPPED STRUCTURE IN hand, Patience carefully loaded it into the backseat of her car. She set it within a crate to keep it from shifting.

"This thing is a little heavy," Patience mentioned as Noelle slid into the backseat beside it. "I'll carry it into your classroom for you."

Taking her seat belt, Noelle pulled it across her, securing it. "Thank you." She giggled, "I used a *lot* of clay."

Grabbing hold of the back door, Patience watched as Noelle adjusted the top-secret project which was due that morning. A project she'd worked diligently on for weeks, requiring multiple trips to the art supply store. The excitement on Noelle's face was enough to ease Patience's heavy mind, even if it was only for a moment.

"I won't ask to at least take a peek, even though I *really* want to," Patience shot a hopeful look Noelle's way.

Tilting her head, Noelle looked at her. "Mommy...nice try."

Patience couldn't help but chuckle. "Okay little miss, you got it." She shook her head as Noelle let out a laugh. "By the way, I'm proud of you for sticking to your word. Don't ever stop doing that."

Noelle bowed playfully as her mother shut the door. "I won't."

Sliding into the driver's seat, Patience started the car then pulled off. "Do you want to make tacos with me tonight?"

Noelle leaned back in her seat. "Yes. Can we make them with shredded chicken instead of beef?"

"Of course."

"Cool." Noelle watched the trees and houses move by. "I remember when Mr. Michael made his with the chicken and I liked it."

Patience's body shivered. Hearing Michael's name only increased the anxiety she was already battling with. "Yeah...I remember Bunny." She released a sigh. "Me too."

"Are you off work today?"

Peering through the rear-view mirror, Patience squinted. "What made you ask me that?"

"You're not wearing your normal work clothes," Noelle replied.

Patience quickly glanced down at the form-hugging jeans and long-sleeved shirt she had on. She had no idea that Noelle paid that much attention to her change in dress. "Observant," she quipped. "But yes, I'm off today."

"Oh. Are you doing anything fun?"

"Uhh..." Patience tried to choose the right words. "I just have something that I need to handle today that couldn't wait." She'd been on edge all night, barely sleeping. But Patience knew that she could no longer put off what she needed to do, so she'd decided to take a personal day.

"Well...I hope everything goes okay."

Patience sighed again. "Yeah, me too."

Flipping her hair over her shoulder, Patience entered a set of glass doors, heading straight for the receptionist desk. Standing before the woman whose back was turned, searching for something in a file cabinet, Patience lightly tapped the desk. "Good morning, Cassie."

Spinning around in her seat, Cassie's eyes lit up, a gleaming smile on her face. "Oh my God, Patience, hi!" She rose from her seat. "I haven't seen you come around in a while, how are you?"

Patience offered the chipper woman a melancholy smile. "I

know, and I'm..." *A damn wreck.* She cleared her throat. "Umm, is Michael here?"

"Ooh, no he's out at one of the sites today."

The disappointment was clear on Patience's face. "Oh okay... Well, thank you for your time."

"Do you want me to let him know you're looking for him?" Cassie picked up the office phone. "He has his work cell."

Patience put her hand out, shaking it. "No, no you don't have to do that. But again, thank you."

Cassie returned the phone to its receiver. "You're welcome." She clasped her hands together. "It was good seeing you."

"You too." Adjusting her purse, Patience turned and walked away. It had taken every mustered-up nerve for her to walk into Michael's office to face him. She'd have to try again another time, yet she wasn't so sure if she could be this brave again.

Her route to the doors was halted when someone called her name. Spinning around, she saw Dante approaching her.

"Hi Patience," he greeted, a cup of coffee in hand. "I saw you leaving the reception desk. Figured I'd come say hi."

Though his tone was polite, Patience eyed him cautiously. Like Kenya, Patience had no idea if Dante resented her. "Hi. It's good to see you."

"You too." Dante raised his cup. "You want some coffee? It's a fresh pot."

Patience shook her head. "No, thank you." She shifted her weight from one foot to the other. "I just came to see if Michael was here. But I know he's not, so I'm going to head out."

"Oh...okay." Dante stood in place as Patience turned to go. While he'd planned on letting her walk out the door, he knew that he couldn't. "Patience, wait."

She turned around, shooting him a curious look. "What's up?"

Dante stepped towards her. "I umm... I know where Mike is."

Patience leaned her head to the side. "Cassie said he's at a work site?"

"He is. I'm actually getting ready to head over there now." Dante tapped the cup in his hand. "You can follow me there... If you want."

Realizing what Dante was hinting at, Patience swallowed hard. She wanted to talk to Michael more than anything, but she doubted that a half-built structure would be the best place to do it. She fixed Dante with a questioning stare. "In all honesty Dante... Do you think I should?"

Dante contemplated his proposal, before releasing a deep breath. *Mike is probably going to kill me, but I need to do this.* "Yeah, I do."

Lifting a piece of drywall, Michael pressed it against a beam. Holding it in place with his hip, he grabbed the drill from a nearby table, checking the settings. Seeing that they were in place, Michael made sure his work goggles were secure before drilling a screw in.

Not wanting to sit around the office, Michael had elected to join some of his crew at one of the housing sites that day. The construction noise was a welcome distraction from his own thoughts.

Drywall secured, Michael returned the drill to the table, moving onto another slab. Seeing Dante hurry into the house, Michael looked over at him.

"Hey, I know I'm a little late—"

"It's fine. I need you on drywall duty on the second floor," Michael interrupted, lifting the slab. "I measured some of it already."

"Got you, but listen, you need to go outside real quick," Dante urged.

Shooting a bewildered glance Dante's way, Michael moved for the wall. "Why? Is there an unexpected inspection visit going on?"

"No, but there's something you need to see."

"Why don't you just *tell* me what it is, so I don't have to lose time?" Michael threw back. "I want to get this drywall up while we have the sunlight."

Dante took the drywall from his hands, much to Michael's annoyance.

"Dante, what the hell is your deal?"

"Just give me this." Dante leaned the piece against the beam. Grabbing a towel from a chair, he began slapping Michael's exposed arms with it, a vain attempt to tidy his brother up. "Dust yourself off real quick."

Snatching the towel from Dante's grasp, Michael scowled at him. "Look—"

Dante put his hands up. "Bro, just go outside. It'll be worth your time, I promise."

Michael stood, glaring at the man for a good moment, before tossing the towel aside. "You better not be playing any damn games." Snatching the goggles off, he tossed them to the chair and stormed out. Stepping outside on the material-littered lawn, all irritation drained from Michael's face. He froze. "Patience."

Standing a few feet back, Patience stared back at Michael, fighting the urge to run into his arms. "Hi," she spoke after a moment.

He still couldn't believe his eyes. Michael had spent the past weeks aching to see her again; now that she was standing before him, he didn't know how to handle it. "What are you doing here?"

"I came to talk to you." She fiddled nervously with her fingers. "I *need* to talk to you."

Her voice, the pleading way that she was looking at him, Michael was desperately trying to keep himself together. Clearing his throat, he folded his arms. "This is a work site Patience. It's dangerous, you shouldn't be here."

"I know." Patience crossed her arms. "I would've called, but…"

"Why *didn't* you?"

Patience glanced down at her shoes. "I honestly didn't think you'd answer. Not that I blame you." Her eyes rose, meeting his. "And...you deserve for me to say what I need to say, to your *face*."

"I would've answered for you, Patience."

She gazed longingly at him. "Do you want me to leave?"

His face veered to the side. "Yeah."

Patience studied him for a long moment. His hardened look was already faltering as he kept his eyes off her, shifting his weight from one foot to the other. "You're not a good liar."

Closing his eyes, Michael sighed deeply. "I know." Opening them, he stared at her, looking as if he was fighting an internal battle. As hurt as he was, he couldn't stand the thought of her walking away. "No, I don't want you to leave." Stepping off the grass to the curb where she stood, he gestured to her. "I know someplace we can sit."

Patience followed in silence as Michael led her to a shaded spot around the corner. Approaching a bench, Patience sat down as he took a seat beside her.

"So..." Michael stared out at the empty lot in front of him. "What do you want to talk to me about?"

Taking a deep breath, Patience ran her hands over her hair before resting them in her lap. "I first want to apologize for how I left things with you... How I treated you, what I said."

Michael's chest rose and fell with a heavy sigh as she spoke.

"You didn't deserve it...my anger—you *never* deserved that."

"Then why did you do it Patience?" His tone was curt. "I still don't understand what changed." He looked at her. "*Help* me understand."

Patience moved her hand to touch his arm, but returned it to its place, sure that he'd snatch away from her. "Michael, that night when I went to pick Noelle up from Toni's, I found out that Angela made her talk to her father."

Astonished, Michael's eyes widened. "Wait... She did *what?*"

"Angela *called* him, and put Noelle on the phone," she

explained. "Noelle was confused and upset, and I *lost* it on Angela... I put my hands on her." She breathed to try and calm herself. "By the time you called me that night, I wasn't in a right state of mind. Between fighting my sister, hurting for my child and feeling enraged at the thought of my ex, I just..." She shook her head. "Everything I thought I buried had resurfaced, and I took it out on you and I know how wrong that was."

Michael's eyes were locked on to her; everything she'd just revealed was swirling in his head. He was overwhelmed with sympathy, remorse and anger. He had questions; how was she feeling? How was *Noelle* feeling? What did her ex say? ...Her *ex*. Michael's brewing thoughts fixated on the dark cloud of Patience's past. The one who'd caused the trauma that still affected her to this day. "Patience...what did your ex-husband do to you?"

Patience looked away from his prying eyes. While she'd revealed bits and pieces of her past life with Greg, she'd never went into full detail as to why she despised the man. She wondered if she even should. But if they were going to move forward like she hoped...Michael deserved to know everything.

"When I first met Greg, I wasn't interested in dating him. I couldn't put my finger on it. I thought he seemed nice, but I just felt this...*apprehension*. But he persisted, and I agreed to go out with him.... After our first date, I talked myself into letting my guard down because he really *did* seem like a good man...so I did. And for the year we dated, things were good and I grew to love him," she said. "But I realized soon after being married to him that he was an extremely good liar, controlling *and* manipulative." She focused on the scenery in front of her as the unpleasant memories filled her. "When I'd express that I felt deceived and that I wasn't happy, he'd turn it around on me. Made it seem like I was projecting what I saw throughout my *parents'* marriage, on he and I... He'd always say that I wasn't seeing that we had a good relationship, because I grew up not knowing what a good one was."

Michael listened attentively, trying to keep the anger that was brimming inside him over that scum from showing. Patience didn't need his anger; she needed his ear.

"And I *believed* him... For five years I believed him. Blaming myself, wondering if *I* was the problem," Patience continued. "Then after a while...I realized that I wasn't. It was *him*, and I told him that I couldn't do it anymore. That I wanted a divorce... He didn't want that, and he begged me to stay with him. Saying that he'd be better, that we could go to counseling." She shook her head. "But I knew nothing would get better. He'd just lie to the counselor to make himself look good, then would come home, and do the same shit... I was done."

Michael reached over, placing a hand to her knee. Holding it in place, he stayed quiet as she continued.

"Throughout the time I was married, I'd never gotten pregnant... I'd reached a point where I figured I just couldn't *have* children." She gripped the bench with her hands. "...The day after I filed for divorce, I found out I was pregnant... It was some weird, twisted miracle because I was barely allowing him to *touch* me... But it happened, and I was *happy* about the idea of finally becoming a mother."

Feeling her stiffen under his touch, Michael fixed her with a concerned gaze. *I shouldn't have made her do this.* "Baby, maybe you should take a break."

Pushing out a deep breath, she shook her head. "I need to get this out... I hate it, but I need to."

Knowing that there was nothing else that he could say to comfort her, Michael moved his hand from her knee to her back, hoping that the silent gesture could provide relief.

Patience lowered her gaze to her lap. "When Greg came home that night, I told him that I was pregnant..." She felt her chest tighten. "And the look on his face was that of someone who'd gotten the biggest relief of his life. Which honestly surprised me, because when I thought I couldn't have children, he said that he didn't care to have any *anyway*. That he just wanted me to himself... But, he seemed genuinely happy about it. Then he smiled at me and said, 'Well that means you can't leave me now'."

Michael's brows furrowed, yet he remained quiet.

"I told him that I was still going through with the divorce, and that he was welcomed to co-parent with me... I never intended to keep him from his child, that wasn't my plan. My mother tried to do that with our father, and I didn't want to be like her. I just didn't want to be married to him anymore but..." Patience shook her head, glaring. "That look in his eyes quickly changed to—*resentment*...We argued for *hours*. He called me every name in the book. Told me that I was worthless, useless, said that no one else would ever love me, that I was ruined. Telling me if I left him that he'd leave me penniless, and he'd have *nothing* to do with the baby... That I'd be raising her alone."

Patience focused on the gravel under her shoes as she continued. "I just looked at him and said, 'So be it'... I didn't want anything from him. I just wanted my freedom and my peace back, and if that meant that I'd be a single mother, then I was willing to do that." Tears welled up in her eyes. "We were in the bedroom, and I remember leaving—walking down the hall to go into one of the other rooms. And the next thing I knew he grabbed me from behind and repeatedly slammed me against the wall. Then he picked me up and threw me down the stairs."

This time the rage that Michael felt would not be held back. "He *what?*" He adjusted his position in his seat, facing her. His fist was balled at his side. "Patience, he did *what* to you?"

Patience looked at him, eyes glassed over. "Yeah," she confirmed. "I remember lying at the bottom of the steps, crying and in *so* much pain... He just causally walked down the steps and stood over me." She wiped a tear from her eye. "Then he kneeled down and said, 'Now neither one of us gets what we want', and he left...

He tried to cause me to miscarry my baby because he hated the fact that I was leaving him."

Michael reached for her hand, taking hold of it. "I'm so sorry baby." He wanted nothing more than a face-to-face meeting with Greg to repay the man in kind. "I'm sorry you had to go through that."

"I just…" Patience sniffled. "I don't know how I got up with a broken arm, bruised ribs, and a concussion, but I eventually did and I called Toni, crying from the car and she told me to come to her … So, after I left the hospital, and they told me that I hadn't lost the baby, I drove from Georgia up here to Virginia and I never went back." She paused a second as the overwhelming emotions weighed on her. "It took a year for the divorce to be finalized, because he tried to contest it when he found out from the lawyer that I was still pregnant, but eventually it was… His name isn't even on Noelle's birth certificate."

"It doesn't *deserve* to be anyway," Michael seethed.

"I know." Patience exhaled deeply, locking her eyes with his. "When everything happened with my sister, it was like the flood gates opened and all the trauma, hurt, and guilt came flooding back and I didn't know how to handle it… Even my insecurities over being in a relationship—*all* of it came like a goddamn tidal wave and it made me question everything, including whether I could ever truly be happy. Or if I could make *you* happy."

"You never have to question that with me." Michael's voice was heavy with sincerity. "I told you that night that you *do* make me happy. I've never loved anyone the way I love you, and there is *nothing* that I wouldn't do for you or Noelle."

Patience's glistening eyes were filled with adoration. "I know that, Michael." Reaching her hand out, she gently touched his face. "I am *so* in love with you."

Hearing her impassioned words, Michael felt the familiar

heart flutter that only Patience could ever give him. He covered her hand with his as he stared into her eyes.

"And I'm so sorry for hurting you," she poured out. "Please forgive me."

"It's okay, baby," Michael's voice was low, tender as he wiped the tears from her face, while trying to keep his own from falling. "I forgive you. It's okay."

"I don't want to be without you anymore." She moved her hand down to his chest. Gathering the fabric with her fingers, she looked deep into his eyes. "Do you still want me?"

"I never stopped." His face close to hers, a tear dropped from Michael's eyes. "You're my *world* Patience."

Unable to hold back any longer, Patience pressed her lips to his. Closing her eyes as he pulled her closer to him, they ignited a fiery kiss. Holding on tight, Patience was sure this time she wouldn't let go.

Chapter Forty

BEAMING, MICHAEL RAISED HIS GLASS of iced tea. "To Noelle's art project being chosen for the fair."

Glass of juice in hand, Noelle's eyes were bright as both Michael and her mother clinked their glasses to hers. "Thank you."

"I'm so proud of you," Patience gushed, setting her lemonade on the table. She peered at Michael, who was cutting into his food. "The fair is Wednesday at two o'clock."

"I'll be there," Michael promised. Having learned of Noelle's accomplishment, Michael had taken them out for a celebratory dinner.

Digging into the macaroni and cheese on her plate, Noelle let out a content sigh. Not only was she excited about her project being chosen for presentation and display in her school's art fair, but she was also thrilled that Michael was back. "They're going to display all the pieces until we leave for summer break." Noelle held the food to her mouth. "Then I can take it home."

"Nice. That'll give me time to find the perfect display case for it." Patience's eyes crinkled. "You already know I'm going to show everybody."

Noelle smacked a hand to her face in mid-chew, shaking her head.

Leaning her head to the side, Patience shot Noelle a knowing look. "I'm embarrassing you again, aren't I?"

Giggling, Noelle rested her hand on the table. "No, it's okay."

Sitting back, Michael watched the endearing exchange with a glimmer in his eyes. Sometimes he found it hard to believe that he and Patience had been separated just over three weeks ago; they'd slipped right back into their family routine as if no time had passed.

He remembered sitting on that bench, holding Patience, kissing her until he was forced to return to work. Spending the time counting down the minutes until he got off so he could see her again. The pure joy on Noelle's face when he'd stepped through Patience's door later that evening warmed his heart. And the love he made to Patience that night quenched his desires, and displayed just how much he missed her, and how happy he was that they were back together.

"I, for one, can't wait to see your project Noelle," Michael chimed in. "Your mother told me how hard you worked on it."

Noelle broke off a piece of her fried fish. "I really did. It was my first time using real art clay, and not the colorful kid's clay."

Patience prepared to offer up a comment, but some new patrons entering the restaurant caught her attention. Squinting, she leaned forward, "Is that who I think it is?"

Peering over, Noelle craned her neck. Her eyes broadened when she noticed who it was. "Yay, Jordan!" Holding her arms out, she scooted up in her seat as her cousin darted over to her. Her mother and father followed right behind.

"The running girl, geez." Toni shook her head at her daughter, giving a stunned Patience a hug.

"What are you guys doing here?" Patience wondered as a waiter added the extra chairs to their table.

Toni sat down in the seat that her husband pulled out for her. "Well, Michael told us that he was taking you to dinner to celebrate Noelle, and he invited us to come join you." She scooted herself to the table. "Thought it would be a cute surprise."

Patience looked at Michael, glowing with appreciation. "It is." Michael winked at her in return.

Reaching over, Toni grabbed Patience's fork, hovering it over the ceramic cup of truffle macaroni and cheese. "Ooh, that looks good, let me try before I order."

Patience snatched the fork right before it had a chance to touch anything. "Girl, keep your hands off my food."

"Pace, just let me try *one* noddle." Toni's voice was brimming with laughter. "Come on, don't embarrass me in front of my kid."

Grabbing the menu from the table, Rob shot a humored look Michael's way. "Welcome back to the chaos man."

Spearing a bit of fish from his plate, Michael laughed. "It's good to be back."

"Anybody up for a quick game night?" Rob asked, rubbing his hands together. "The night is still young."

Standing next to him, Toni adjusted her purse on her shoulder. "Babe, the night is *middle-aged*, and the children have school tomorrow."

Rob threw a glance her way, then pointed. "*That*...was kind of funny."

"And it's *Friday* Mom," Jordan added, patting her mother's arm.

Mouth falling open, Toni put a hand on her head. She'd completely lost track of the day. "What the—I'm not drunk, am I?" She shook her head as snickers sounded around her.

Having just left the restaurant after spending the past two hours dining, the group was now out in the parking lot, figuring out what the next move was.

"If an impromptu game night is what you want to do, I'd have no problem with having it back at my place," Michael offered, grabbing his phone from his pocket. "I'll call up my brother and sister and we can just make it a thing." He glanced at Patience, who was leaning her head on his shoulder. "Are you up for that?"

Nodding, Patience lifted her head. "Yeah, sure." She moved her hair over her shoulder. "Should I make something in case they didn't eat?"

"*Hell* no," Michael scoffed, earning a giggle from Patience. "I'll tell them to eat before they get there. They'll only care about me having something to drink anyway."

Pleased, Rob clapped his hands as he shot a look his wife's way. "What do you say, T?"

"I say, I'm down for whatever." Toni shrugged. "Just get me a latte or something to give me my second wind, because *clearly* I'm trippin' thinking today was still Thursday."

"I'll be sure to get you the largest cup they have," Rob mused. "We need to stop anyway, so I can pick up a bottle to bring."

Hand over his phone receiver, Michael shook his head in protest. "Rob, man that's not necessary. I already have stuff there."

"I insist Mike." Rob pulled his keys from his pants pocket. "You already paid for dinner and are offering up your house. Grabbing a bottle of scotch is the *least* I can do."

Sidling up to Patience, Toni placed a hand on her shoulder. "While our men are competing in the 'I got it' games—"

Patience snickered, delivering a playful tap to Toni's hand.

"And the girls are busy jumping around in circles for some reason, come walk with me."

Patience walked alongside Toni to a spot feet away from the group. Fixing her with a curious stare as Toni faced her. "What's up?"

"Well first..." Toni's mouth curved into a smile. "I'm happy that you and Michael are back together."

Contentment glowed on Patience's face. "Me too... Thanks for talking the sense back into me."

"I don't need thanks for that. Just don't let it creep its ass back *out*."

"Trust me, I won't." Patience peered over at Michael, who was chatting away with her brother-in-law. "He's stuck with me."

"Good." A seriousness fell over Toni as she kept her gaze on Patience. "So...have you heard from..."

Looking back at her, Patience took note of the weighty look in her sister's eyes when she stalled her words. "Greg?" she finished. Toni nodded. "Since that night at your house, no I haven't."

"Really?" Toni folded her arms. "Not one weird phone call, no more visits?" Patience shook her head, to which Toni exhaled a relieved breath. "Good. That's good... Perhaps you calling him on his bullshit made him realize that he can't manipulate his way back into your life, and so he slithered his ass back across state lines."

"I'm praying that that's the case." Patience hesitated for a moment. "I haven't told Michael that he showed up."

Toni's eyes widened. "Pace—why *not*? That's not something you should be keeping from him."

"T, *you* didn't see the look in Michael's eyes when I told him about what Greg did those years ago," Patience explained. "If I would've told him that he came to see me and all the shit he *said*, I'm almost certain that Michael would track him down and kill him."

Bemusement on her face, Toni gestured with her hands. "And that's a problem *why?*"

Patience frowned. "Because he could ruin his *life* over someone who isn't worth it." She adjusted the purse on her shoulder. "No, I'm not letting him do that."

Toni put her hands up. "Okay, I get where you're coming from... I wouldn't want Michael to go to jail either." She folded her arms. "I didn't mean to bring the mood down."

"I know," Patience quickly threw back, some bite in her voice. "I just don't want to talk about it anymore. Greg has taken up *enough* of my mental energy."

"Then we don't have to." Toni sighed. "I just wanted to make sure you were okay."

"I am."

Toni nodded, giving her sister an easy smile. "Now let's get back so my man and I can whoop you and yours in spades."

Patience couldn't help but laugh. "You're about to get your feelings hurt, I promise you."

Letting out a laugh herself, Toni put her arm around Patience's shoulders as the two made their way back to their families.

Back resting against the headboard under the soft lighting of the bedside lamp, Patience's pencil moved along the sketchpad, her eyes laser-focused on the image she was creating. She didn't even look up when Michael entered the room.

After a successful game night at Michael's home, the guests had since left for the night. With Noelle sound asleep in one of the guest rooms, Patience was lounging in bed drawing.

"Noelle is knocked out," Michael said, shutting his bedroom door behind him. "When I passed by the room and saw that she was sleeping, I went in to turn the light off." He removed his watch, putting it on the dresser. "Then my big ass tripped over the damn throw rug on the way out and caught myself on the wall. She didn't stir *once*."

Shoulders shaking with laughter, Patience peered up from her paper. "Aww, poor baby. Did you hurt yourself?"

Michael tossed his shirt into a nearby hamper. "No, I was more startled than anything."

Patience shook her head, laughter ceasing. "Yeah, she sleeps like a log most times." She resumed her shading. "Tonight was fun."

"Yeah, it was. All my good scotch is gone, courtesy of Dante and Lori, but I enjoyed myself."

"I'm glad those two are back together," Patience said. "He looked so happy...*drunk*, but happy."

Michael let out a chuckle. "Me too." Unbuttoning his pants, he observed her. "Drawing I see."

"Yeah." Turning the pad around, she showed her progress. "It's going to be a half butterfly, half woman's face—*thing*." She shrugged, flipping the pad back around. "I see the vision in my head. Just trying to execute it."

"Looks like you're doing a good job of it already," Michael complimented. "I should probably be quiet, so I don't break your concentration."

Patience's eyes were locked to the page. "No, you're not breaking it. I've learned to focus even with things going on around me." Her eyes lifted, watching as he removed his pants. Staring at his hard body as he moved about the room, her chest rose and fell heavily. "But yeah, you can't distract me."

Approaching the bed, Michael caught her eye. He recognized that look. "That kind of sounds like a challenge."

Eyes smoldering, Patience's mouth formed a taunting smirk. "It's not a challenge, it's a *fact*." Offering a nonchalant shrug, she returned her attention to the paper. "But I mean, you're welcome to try."

A sly smile forming, Michael rubbed his chin with his hand. "Challenge accepted."

"Mm-kay," she coyly threw out. Eyes focused on her paper, Patience's hand moved with ease as she added more dimension. Not so much as budging when Michael pulled the covers back from her. Even when she felt the bed dip with his weight, and her legs being spread apart with his hands, she didn't break.

However, when he lowered himself between her legs and kissed her thighs, her hand stalled for a moment. She was forced to hold in a breath when his kisses traveled between her thighs. But, determined not to lose, she kept drawing.

Once she felt his tongue brush against her, she clutched the pencil in her hand, soft pants escaping her. When his tongue began to lap steadily, she no longer cared about winning.

Dropping the pencil and letting the pad slide to the floor, Patience grabbed the back of the headboard, closing her eyes as Michael's exceptional mouth pleased her. As her breathing became heavier and the sensation grew intense, Patience tried to scoot her body back, but Michael grabbed her hips, pulling her back to him. Keeping her still with his arms, his tongue worked her into a frenzy.

Panting getting heavier and quicker, Patience tried to keep quiet. But as the pleasure escalated, she had no choice but to slap a hand over her mouth to keep from belting out the moans that were in her throat. Eyes squeezed shut and clutching his hand with her free one, Patience succumbed to her release.

Before she had a moment to come down, Michael's tongue resumed. Catching her off guard, he quickly brought her to a second plateau that left her screaming in her hand, her satisfied body shaking. Hand over her heart, Patience's labored breathing continued as Michael finally moved up her body.

Hovering over her, Michael smoothed her hair from her face. Licking his lips, he kissed her before pushing himself back on his knees.

Patience aided him in pulling the night gown over her head, throwing it to the floor on top of her discarded artwork. Reaching under her, Michael clutched her hips, elevating her before pulling her to him. She barely had a moment to suck in a breath as he entered her with ease.

Her legs resting over his forearms, hands gripping her waist, Michael drove himself in and out of her. The steady movement inside her conditioned body brought him so much gratification that his chest tightened with the audible groan he so desperately wanted to let out.

The rapid breaths that left Patience became heavier as the intensity in his strokes grew faster. Had the headboard not been secured to the wall, it surely would have pounded against it. She tried to keep her sounds of sexual satisfaction low, but the more he hit her spot, the harder it became for her to keep quiet. Squeezing the sheets in her hands, she released her whimpers.

Holding still, Michael wrapped his arms around her, pulling her upright. Panting, he cradled her to him as he kissed her lips. "Am I hurting you?"

Tightening her arms around his neck, she shook her head with vigor. When he resumed his thrusts, Patience buried her face into his shoulder, muffling her cries as she moved against him. Tears squeezed through her shut eyes as her body surrendered to her lover.

Grasping Patience's hair in his hand, his other arm tightening around her, Michael's body followed suit, surrendering to his own climax within her.

Pulling her head back, Patience stared at him as her breathing slowed to its normal pace. When he grinned at her, she threw one back at him. Clearly, he'd won this round.

Chapter Forty-One

THE AUDITORIUM OF NOELLE'S SCHOOL had been transformed into the much-anticipated art fair. Tables of sculptures, easels of drawings and paintings, were stationed around the space while students and their families observed and praised the pieces.

Noelle skipped ahead as Patience and Michael walked through, eyeing the works in amazement.

"Damn, there's some *serious* talent in this room," Michael mused, eyes roaming.

"Tell me about it," Patience agreed. "I remember when I was in school, it felt like I was the only one interested in art. I'm glad to see that Noelle is in great company."

Approaching Noelle's designated table, they found Noelle's art teacher with her back turned. Patience tapped her shoulder. "Hello Janet."

Janet turned around, a dazzling smile on her face. "Patience, hi." She greeted her favorite student's mother with a friendly hug. She waved to Michael, who returned a polite wave of his own. "I know I've told you before, but Noelle is *so* talented."

Patience gleamed with pride as she placed a hand on Noelle's shoulder. "Thank you."

"Her project…" Janet's hand rose to her chest. "It's *beautiful*. Have you seen it?"

Patience chuckled a bit. "Uh no, my child has kept this a secret from me. This will be my first time seeing it."

"Well…" Janet winked at Noelle, who smiled back. "I think it's time you saw it." Moving aside, Janet allowed a full view of Noelle's art piece.

On the table before them sat a clay sculpture that was comprised of three figures, one above the other, each secured by what looked to be arms. Each figure was decorated with different hand-painted clay pieces, three-dimensional stickers, and charms.

Both Patience and Michael's eyes were transfixed in awe. "Bunny, this is *amazing*," Patience praised. She had to refrain from touching it, for fear of messing something up.

"Yeah, Noelle, this is beautiful," Michael chimed in.

Noelle clasped her hands together. "Do you want to know what it means?"

"Of *course*." Patience eyed her daughter with anticipation.

"Okay." Noelle held her hand out in front of the piece. "Ms. Janet said that I had to name it, so I named it 'my family'." She pointed to the smallest part. "This one, I decorated in bunnies, and that represents me." Pointing to the bigger part above it, she looked at her mother. "This one is decorated in butterflies, and that represents you Mommy."

Patience brought a hand to her chest, resisting the urge to interrupt her daughter's presentation by hugging her.

Noelle pointed to the last piece, the biggest one. Its arms were covering the smaller objects, almost like it was protecting them. "And *this* one…" She peered up at Michael. "Represents *you* Mr. Michael."

Michael stood, speechless. But his eyes showed the emotion that was bubbling up inside him. To know that Noelle saw him as an important piece of her life was everything he could have ever hoped for.

Patience put an adoring hand on his arm.

"I decorated yours with little hammers and nails because you build houses and stuff," Noelle finished.

"This is… It's beautiful Noelle," Michael managed to get out. "Thank you for including me. I'm honored."

"You're welcome…" Noelle leaned her head to the side. "Thank you for being a dad."

Patience couldn't take it anymore; she enveloped Noelle in a loving hug. "You are the sweetest— I love you so much."

"Love you too." Noelle giggled when her mother held on. "Mommy, I can't breathe."

"Oh, I'm sorry." Patience released her, wiping the happy tears from her own eyes.

Noelle gave Michael a hug, which Michael returned.

"I love you kid." Michael wiped his eyes dry with his fingertips. "I mean that."

Parting, Noelle smiled up at him. "Love you too." She looked back and forth between the two, noticing the glassiness in their eyes. "Are you two crying?"

"Maybe," Patience downplayed, the same time that Michael unapologetically admitted, "Yes."

"So, what do you want to do to celebrate? You want to go to that new arcade and restaurant that just opened down town?" Patience asked, holding Noelle's hand as they stood outside of the school, waiting for Michael to bring the car around.

Tapping her chin with her finger, Noelle pondered. "Can we go there tomorrow?"

"Sure, we can."

"Today, I'd like to go out for pizza and then ice cream cones from our favorite spot… Then we can go home and watch a movie."

Patience gave an approving nod. "That sounds perfect. We'll

do that." She watched as Noelle lightly swung her hand back and forth. "I'm proud of you, you know."

"I know. You always tell me."

Patience folded some of her hair behind her ear. "Do you ever get tired of hearing it?"

Noelle shook her head, her ponytails swinging. "Nope."

"Good, because I'll never stop telling you," Patience promised, tapping Noelle's cheek with her finger. "Do you ever wonder why I make it a point to always tell you that I'm proud of you, how much I love you?"

Noelle shrugged. "Sometimes."

"It's because my mother never said it to *me*," Patience revealed.

Eyes fluttering in surprise, Noelle fixed a curious stare. "She didn't?"

Patience shook her head. "Your late grandmother wasn't... *affectionate*, and I remember how hurtful it was growing up. So, when I found out I was having *you*, I made a promise that I wouldn't do that to you." She brushed some wispy hair strands away from Noelle's eye. "I promised to always show *and* tell you how much you're loved and how amazing you are."

Patience had never told her daughter the bad things about her childhood, or her grandmother. Never even *intended* to; it was yet another thing Patience had wanted to shield Noelle from. But at that moment, she felt it was a good time to share just a bit. Maybe it would help Noelle understand her a little better.

Clutching her mother's hand, Noelle's eyes glimmered with adoration and respect. "You're doing a good job, Mommy."

"Looks like I finally get a family reunion."

The smile immediately cleared from Patience's face, as a biting chill shot through her body. Head snapping in his direction, she inhaled sharply, eyes flashing with disbelief and fury. "Fuck, not again. Not now." Her shaky voice was barely audible.

Greg stood on the sidewalk, feet from his ex-wife and child. "Hello again Patience." He took a step towards them.

Patience pulled Noelle to her, holding her close as she stepped back. Her heart was racing; she couldn't believe this was happening *again*. "Why won't you just go away?"

Greg halted his steps, locking eyes with Patience. "Why *would* I?" His spiteful gaze lowered to the little girl, who was staring up at him with confusion in her eyes. "Hello little girl—"

"Do *not* talk to her," Patience hissed.

"What? You expect me not to talk to my own daughter?" Greg taunted. "That's right," he said when Noelle's brows gathered. "I'm your dad... I said I wanted to meet you remember?"

Noelle peered up at her mother, who was holding her in a tight grip. The fury in Patience's eyes when she looked at him, the harshness in her voice when she spoke... Noelle could tell that his presence wasn't welcomed.

Noelle's eyes then traveled back to this man, who had just revealed himself to be the father she'd never met. She leered, her forehead creasing... There was nothing about him that screamed "dad". His eyes were cold, the way he spoke to her mother was callous, and even the smile he gave to *her* lacked warmth.

Patience wanted to pick her daughter up and run back inside—anywhere that Greg wasn't. But she wasn't sure what he'd try to do if she did. "Greg, you need to—"

"Leave? Yeah, I thought about doing that after our failed 'meet up', but I changed my mind. I'm not going anywhere." Greg straightened his jacket. "And that was real cute what you pulled."

Before Patience could utter another word, Michael stepped up on the sidewalk. "Sorry it took so long, it was hell getting out of the parking lot," he said, oblivious. "The car is across the street."

Patience looked at him.

Seeing the distress in her eyes, Michael touched her arm, concern on his face. "What's wrong?"

Patience felt like she could suffer a panic attack at any second. "Umm…" She let out a quick, stifled breath. "Greg is over there."

Fire lit in Michael's eyes as his head jerked back slightly. "What?"

Patience subtly gestured to Greg, who was still standing in place, staring at them.

A surge of rage filled Michael as he locked eyes with him. Taking his keys out of his pocket, he handed them to Patience. "You and Noelle go get in the car."

"Michael," she grabbed his arm when he made a move. "Wait."

Michael looked at her, his eyes firm with urgency. "*Go.* I'll handle it."

She held his arm in a firm grasp, eyes pleading with him. She knew what Michael could do to Greg, what he *wanted* to do, and she didn't want him to go through with it. Not for Greg's sake, but for his. "We need you… Please don't do anything you can't take back."

Michael's jaw tightened. He wanted to break him in half. But seeing the worry on Patience's face, he forced himself to tame his temper. "I hear you," he promised. "Go."

With Noelle at her side, Patience did as Michael asked, taking off across the street.

Michael stood, watching to make sure his family made it inside the car, before turning his piercing stare on Greg.

A scowl on his face, Greg sized Michael up. *This bastard looks familiar.* Then after a moment, a vindictive scoff sounded from him. "Well, if it isn't the goddamn coffee hero."

Approaching, Michael's eyes were unblinking. "What the fuck did you just say?"

"You can save that macho shit, we're not in a coffee shop right now." Greg puffed his scrawny chest out as Michael stopped within inches of him. "Small world, *isn't* it boss?"

Staring down Greg, it took a moment for Michael to register what he was talking about. But as he studied the self-righteous look on his face, it finally clicked. The disrespectful coward from the coffeehouse was Patience's ex-husband. The revelation only infuriated him more. His scowl deepened. "So *you're* the weak ass bitch she was married to."

Greg's jaw clenched. "And just *who* the fuck are *you* to Patience?"

Michael cocked his head to the side. He wanted more than anything to crush Greg's neck with his bare hands, but remembering Patience's words to him, he elected not to do bodily harm. "I suggest you turn around, get back into whatever piece of shit you drove here in, and take your ass back to wherever you came from."

"You didn't answer my *question*," Greg snarled. "Who are you to my goddamn wife? What, are you fuckin' her or something?"

Michael stood unwavering as a frazzled Greg looked him up and down. He was not about to dignify Greg with a response, nor bother reminding him that he was no longer *married* to Patience.

The silence gave Greg the answer he sought; his face turned livid. "You—" He could barely get the words out. Greg huffed out a quick breath. "So, you think you can come over here making *demands*? Telling me to *leave*?" he barked. "Guess what, I'm not going *nowhere*. And neither is whatever relationship you *think* you have with her. Because guess what boss, she's *mine*. She was married to *me*, and that kid? *I'm* her father." He smacked his chest with his hand. "That's *my* family you're trying to—"

Michael took a step closer to Greg, sending him stepping back and bringing his temper tantrum to an abrupt halt. "Yeah, I thought so," Michael taunted. When Greg opened his mouth, Michael raised his hand, shutting him up. "I've lost my patience with you, so listen, because I'm only going to say this once." His voice was low and menacing. "If you so much as *look* at Patience or Noelle again…if you show up *anywhere* they are. If your phone number shows up on their *phone* screen, if you touch them in *any* fuckin' capacity, I *promise* you, I will kill you."

Greg's eyes shifted. "So you're threatening me huh? *Again*."

"I don't make *threats, Greg*... And by the look on your face, I think you know that." Michael pointed his finger at him. The sudden movement caused Greg to flinch. "Consider this your only warning."

Straightening out his jacket, Greg swallowed the lump in his throat. Like before, he didn't want to risk an altercation with this man. "Yeah, a'ight," he grunted, before turning and speeding down the street.

Michael watched Greg like a hawk until he jumped into a car several spots down. He didn't look away as the car made a U-turn and sped off. Only when it was out of sight did Michael make his way to his car.

Patience sat on her bed, head in her hands, while Michael stood with his arms folded by her closed bedroom door.

"That wasn't the first time he came around, *was* it?" Michael asked. While driving back to Patience's house, the full interaction with Greg at the coffee shop came back to his memory. Recalling how he was talking about seeing an old flame and was planning on meeting up with her. The flame, Michael could only assume, was Patience.

Sighing, Patience lifted her head. "No, it wasn't." She knew she could no longer keep this from Michael; Greg was becoming a bigger problem. "The first time he showed up was at my open house... The second, was outside my job."

Michael frowned as she spoke.

"Umm...I did *initiate* a meet up just once," Patience admitted. "I had this feeling that he was lying about wanting to meet Noelle, so I set up a fake meeting at Toni's house for him...Toni answered the door, told him that I wasn't there, and pretty much got him to admit that he was only interested in seeing me... I was there the whole time."

"Patience—" Michael breathed out to calm himself. "Do you *realize* how dangerous that was?"

Lowering her head, Patience didn't speak. She knew he was right.

"And you didn't think that was something you should've *told* me?"

She looked at him. "We weren't together then."

Michael fixed her with a firm look. "Patience, you *know* that doesn't matter," he fussed. "And even if you didn't want to say anything *then*, you should've told me when we were sitting outside on the bench, after you told me what he did to you."

"I—" Patience paused briefly. "Okay, I admit it, I should've told you. But I honestly thought I could handle it, Michael."

"It's not about what you can *handle*, it's about what type of nutjob this guy is," Michael argued. "The muthafucka is *clearly* out of his goddamn mind. He seems to think he has a right to you. He's *stalking* you. This isn't something that you can handle on your own, Patience."

Feeling overwhelmed, tears began to cloud Patience's eyes. "I know."

"You can't *keep* stuff like this from me."

"I *know* Michael, and I'm *sorry* okay!" she snapped. Adjusting her position on the bed, Patience faced him. "I didn't think it would go this far, I didn't…" Thinking about how her life was once again being turned upside down made her furious. "I'm fuckin' *pissed off* that this shit is even happening." Her voice faltering, she clenched her fists. "It's like *every* time I'm at a point where I'm happy, something or some*one* screws it up, and I don't get it."

Seeing Patience in distress, Michael's frustration over how she'd handled this situation vanished. All he wanted to do was offer her solace. He crossed the room as she stared up at him with a tear-streaked face.

"I'm tired of this shit, Michael."

Michael secured her in his arms. "I know baby," he murmured as she buried her face into his chest. Feeling her hands grip his shirt, he rubbed her back. "Breathe, it'll be okay." He kissed the top of her head. "I told you; I got you." When she pulled back from him, he held her hands, looking into her eyes. "I mean it... I'm here with you. Okay?"

Nodding, she closed her eyes as his fingers brushed the remaining tears from her eyes. "I know." She let out a deep, slow breath to calm herself. As much as she could anyway.

Sitting on the bed next to her, Michael ran a hand along the back of his neck. "Tomorrow, first thing, I'm taking you to file a restraining order against Greg."

"Okay." She ran a hand up her arm. "I knew it needed to be done the moment I saw him today... I'm just mad that I didn't do it sooner."

"I know. But it's getting done now and that's what matters." Michael eyed her intensely. "And until he *leaves*, I want you and Noelle to stay with me," he said. "Bring anything you want, I'll *get* you anything you want to make you as comfortable as you need to be, but I want you both with me. It's my job to protect you and I'm going to do that."

Patience stared at him for a long moment.

Taking her silence as hesitation, Michael gently took hold of her hand. "Please don't fight me on this, Pace."

"I won't," she promised. "We'll stay with you."

Breathing a sigh of relief, Michael kissed her forehead. "We'll go tonight. Okay?"

"Okay... Can you call Noelle in here please?"

"Sure." Michael headed for the door. Opening it, he called for Noelle. Within a few seconds, she came running,

Patience gestured for her daughter. "Come here sweetie." When Noelle plopped down next to her, Patience held her hand out, which Noelle promptly held. "Umm, you and I are going to move in with Michael for a little while... We have to go tonight."

Noelle scratched her head. "Oh...is something wrong with *our* house?"

Patience shook her head. "No."

"Then how come we're moving?"

"Because..." Patience searched for the right words. She didn't want to scare Noelle, but she knew that she needed to be honest. "Because it's better for us to be with Michael while your dad is around."

Noelle stared at her mom, trying to read between the lines of what she was saying. "Mommy..." She sighed. "My dad isn't a nice person, *is* he?"

Patience softly brushed some hair out of Noelle's face. "No Bunny, he's not."

Noelle nodded slowly. "I could tell... He didn't look or sound nice at all."

Michael pinched the bridge of his nose and let out a deep sigh. The fact that Greg's maliciousness was so evident that even his child, who was seeing him for the first time in her life could sense it, pissed him off all over again. *That triflin' son of a bitch.*

"I'm sorry that you had to experience that." Patience's soft voice was full of remorse. "I never *wanted* you to... I never wanted you to know that he was...mean."

It was then that Noelle understood why her mother was so upset about Angela making her talk to her father. Why she had kept her *from* him. "Was he mean to *you*?" she asked, her eyes wide with wonder.

Patience nodded. "Yeah, he was," she reluctantly admitted. "He...hurt me."

Hearing that her father had hurt her mother sank Noelle's little heart. She leaned her head on her mother's shoulder, wrapping her arms around her waist. "I hope he goes away soon, because I don't ever want to see him again."

"You won't have to," Patience swore, holding her close.

Pulling back from the embrace, Noelle looked at Michael. "Am I allowed to bring all my bunnies and my art desk to your house?"

"You can bring anything you want sweetie," Michael answered. "We'll take all your toys tonight and tomorrow; I'll come back with a truck and get your desk."

Patience peered over at him. "Or we can just get her another one for your house."

Michael gave a nod. "Whatever you want. I'm good either way."

Turning back to Noelle, Patience gave her leg a pat. "I'm sorry your day got ruined, but I'll make it up to you." She kissed her cheek. "Go pack baby. We'll be leaving soon. I'll be in there to help you in a bit."

"Okay." Noelle stood, then walked out of the room.

Standing from the bed, Patience released a tired, heavy sigh. Rubbing the back of her neck, she approached Michael. "Tell me again that it's going to be okay," she pleaded, standing before him.

He pulled her into his arms, holding her against him. "It's going to be okay. I promise you."

Chapter Forty-Two

PULLING AN IMAGE UP ON her phone screen, Kenya showed Michael, who was sitting across from her at the restaurant table. "Look at how beautiful lavender and gold pair together." Her smile beamed. "You agree, right?"

Michael eyed the collage on her screen. "Yeah, I do." He reached for his water. "But is there a reason why you're showing me pictures of decorations?"

Putting the phone back to her face, she clicked through a few more photos. "Just throwing out ideas in case you know, you want me to plan a wedding or something."

Michael smirked. "You are *not* slick," he said, earning a giggle from her.

"Hey, I just figured that you'll be popping the question to Patience soon enough." Kenya put her phone down. "And I'm just putting it out there that when that happens, if Patience doesn't want a full-on planner, I'll be available to her with my consulting expertise..."

Michael leaned back in his seat, sipping his water as Kenya babbled.

"Since her favorite color is lavender, I figured that could be the primary wedding color," Kenya finished.

Michael set his glass back down. "You're right, I *do* plan on asking Patience to marry me, and should she accept, I'll consider hiring you to plan our wedding under one condition."

Folding her arms, she shot him a challenging look. "*What* condition?"

"That you don't get on my nerves between now and then."

Kenya waved a dismissive hand. "Boy please." She shook her head when he chuckled. "So…" She fixed him with an inquisitive stare. "How has it been, having Patience and Noelle staying with you? Though I'm not sure why I'm even asking, you seemed to have settled into family life quite easily."

"I love having them with me," Michael answered. "I don't know how to really explain it, but this family dynamic—this routine… It feels natural you know?"

Kenya grinned. "I'm sure it does. It looks good on you."

Michael smiled. "Thanks." Finishing the last bite of his food, he took a moment to reflect. It had been a month since Patience and Noelle had started staying with him. While the circumstances as to why weren't to his liking—Greg was still nowhere to be found—Michael meant what he'd said; he loved having them with him. He just wished he had some idea as to where Greg was, so that both he and Patience could have peace of mind.

"I'm sure you're going to be sad when the renovations are finished on her house and they have to go back," Kenya added, fiddling with the napkin on the table. "Though I hope they stay."

Glancing off to the side, Michael let out a subtle sigh. After discussing it with Patience, they'd decided to tell his family that the reason for the move was due to her house needing renovations. They didn't want to cause questions and panic, especially with Michael's parents. "Yeah…I hope they stay too."

Before Kenya could say another word, her phone beeped. She picked it up. "God," she huffed out, staring at a message.

Michael peered at her with curiosity. "Something wrong?"

"Mom just texted me saying that Dad bought a new grill."

Kenya set her phone down on the table. "She said that the thing is massive for no reason."

"What's wrong with that?"

Shaking her head, Kenya grabbed her fork. "You know what's coming next." She speared her salad. "A text of Dad cheesin' next to the thing, followed by an announcement that he's throwing a cookout."

A look mixed with confusion and amusement settled on Michael's face. "I'm still lost on what the problem is." Before his sister could offer a rebuttal, both of their phones sounded.

Michael picked it up. It was a photo of his father, posing in front of his shiny new grill, grinning from ear to ear wearing a grilling apron and holding a pair of barbecue tongs, along with the text "you already know what time it is".

Michael dissolved into laughter while Kenya sucked her teeth.

"I *told* you," Kenya complained. "He's going to have us hostage at the house for *hours*, eating those nasty hot links he keeps buying."

Shaking his head, Michael retrieved his wallet from his pants as the waiter approached with their bill. "Stop complaining, and support Pop's weird hobby."

Kenya made a face. "Yeah, yeah. Just know he'll have *you* on that grill right along with him."

Hands in his pockets, Michael strolled down the street. Having paired off from his sister after leaving their lunch outing, he'd gone to Patience's office to drop off the lunch he'd bought for her. Michael was now on his way back to his office to finish the rest of his workday.

As the mid-May breeze blew past him, his mind kept reverting to the wedding conversation he'd had with Kenya. Soon his thoughts were consumed with every detail: décor, themes, family and friends, and most importantly, Patience. The idea of watching her walk down the aisle towards him to share vows nearly brought a tear to his eye.

Michael's wandering blissful thoughts came to a halt when he nearly passed by a familiar place. A place he hadn't been to in a while. He stared at the sign, then having a thought, he opened the door, walking in. Patiently, he waited while the cashier tended to the other patrons. When it was his turn, he approached the counter.

"Hi, welcome to Jessy's bakery and café. Can I interest you in one of our special pastries?" the kind woman offered.

"Hello and yes, you can. But not just yet," Michael replied politely. "I have a question."

The woman eyed him with anticipation. "Fire away."

"Is the owner here by any chance?"

"Actually...I'm the owner." A wide grin crossing her light-brown face, she pointed to the sign on the wall behind her. "*I'm* Jessy."

"Oh perfect. Love the establishment." He gestured to where he was standing. "As a matter of fact, I met someone important to me, right here over a year ago."

Jessy's eyes sparkled with delight. She clasped her hands together. "That's beautiful, I love that for you both."

A dreamy smile lit Michael's face. "Yeah." He rubbed his chin. "Which brings me to my next question... Do you accommodate special requests?"

Jessy tilted her head. "Absolutely, we do."

Toni rang the doorbell, then peered at her phone while she waited. When the door opened, she looked up.

"Hey Toni, come on in." Michael motioned her inside before closing the door. He made sure to check the locks twice.

"I'm not disturbing anything, am I?" Toni asked, facing Michael.

"Not at all. She's in the den."

Toni followed Michael through the living room, where Noelle was sitting on the couch, playing a game on the television. "Hey Bunny."

Noelle turned around, offering a wave. "Hi Aunt Toni. Is Jordan with you?"

"Not today sweetie, but I'll bring her back over soon, okay?"

"Okay." Noelle spun around, clicking her controllers.

Entering the den, Toni saw Patience sitting on a chaise lounge by the bay window, her face in a book. "You know that book isn't even good."

Patience glanced up with a smirk. "It *is* actually." She set it down on a nearby end table.

Michael walked in with his keys in hand. "I'm heading out to go check in on one of my sites. I'll pick up the stuff on your list while I'm out," he said.

Patience lifted her head to allow the quick kiss he placed to her lips. "Okay. Love you."

"Love you too." He checked to make sure his wallet was in his jeans pocket. "Call me if you need me."

"I will."

Toni followed Michael's progress as he headed out of the den. "You two are sickening," she teased.

"And?" Michael jokingly threw over his shoulder, earning a laugh from Toni.

Patience shook her head, amusement on her face. "What brings you by on this lovely Sunday?"

Sitting on a cushy ottoman in front of Patience, Toni crossed her legs. "Oh, just my usual 'nosy' visit," she replied. "Seeing how you are."

Patience grabbed her mug of tea from the table. "I'm good." She took a sip.

Toni nodded. She was furious when she'd found out about

Greg's visit to Noelle's school. Knowing that her ex-brother-in-law was still up to his nonsense had consumed her with fear. But she was able to breathe a bit since they'd begun staying with Michael. She knew that he'd protect them with his life. "You appear to have settled in nicely."

Patience nodded. "Yeah, we have." She set her mug back in place. "To be honest, I was upset at first because of the *why*, you know?"

"Oh, I understand that."

"I mean, who wants the reason why you move in with your boyfriend, to be because your ex-husband is pretty much stalking you," Patience vented.

Toni's eyes tightened at the mention of Greg. "Not pretty much, he *is*. Even *if* it's once every few weeks or so."

Crossing her arms, Patience sighed. "Right." She couldn't sleep well for nights after her last encounter with Greg. However, with each day that passed, having not seen or heard from him, Patience was beginning to feel a bit of relief. "But being here *has* been good, and Michael has done a lot to make us feel right at home," she continued. "He fully converted one of the rooms into Noelle's bedroom, furnished and decorated it to Miss Thing's liking."

Toni giggled. "Yeah, you know she's particular about her room, honey."

"Who you tellin'?" Patience ran her hand down the arm of the chair she was sitting in. "He turned this den into my own personal space," she smiled. "Built this bookshelf for me, and everything, so… yeah. It feels like we're right where we're supposed to be."

"Well, you know I'm happy to hear that. Because I was telling Rob that if Michael wasn't around, you would've been moving in with us." Toni leaned back. "And if you refused, me and my special metal *friend* would've been moving in with *you*… And I was bringing *his* too."

"Yeah, I'm sure." Patience glanced out the window. "I just hope Greg stays gone. So, I can fully enjoy...*this*."

"I know sweetie." Toni's eyes traveled down to the phone, still in her hand. "Umm... Pace, another reason I came over was to tell you something."

Patience tore her attention from the scenery, putting it back on her sister. "Okay."

"I had Rob pull some information on Greg."

Patience squinted. "What information?"

"Like, what he's been doing...specifically before he set foot here in VA," she answered. "First, he's *broke*. He lost the house you two used to live in. He was fired from his job, and is currently being investigated for tax fraud and embezzlement. Which serves his ass right, especially since he thought it was cute to not give you any money in the divorce—"

"Toni, I couldn't care less about how sorry his life is," Patience cut in, irritated. "I just want him to leave me alone."

"You might not care, but you need to hear this." Toni's eyes were laser focused on her sister. "Financial investigations aside, Greg has a warrant out for his arrest back in Georgia."

Patience's head jerked back. "For *what*? The only punishment he suffered for what he did to *me* those years ago, was anger management and probation."

The reminder made Toni's blood boil. "Which was a fuckin' joke. It shouldn't have mattered that you weren't there to press charges. His ass should've been thrown in jail."

"I know, same, but focus." Patience sat up in her seat. "What is the warrant for?"

Toni pulled up a text box in her phone, reading it. "Rob said that allegedly, he beat up a bartender because *she* refused to serve him more drinks after he was visibly drunk." She scrolled. "She was in the hospital for a week, and the police have been trying to find him."

Dread rushing through her, Patience rubbed her face with her hands. "God."

"And his ass is just strolling around like shit is sweet." Toni shook her head. "You haven't seen him at *all*, right?"

"No," Patience assured her. "Noelle's school has his picture and so does security at my job, and I'm always on the lookout when I'm out. Michael drives by my house to pick up my mail and he hasn't seen anything suspicious, so…"

Toni nodded. "Well…I didn't want to worry you, but I thought you should know."

"I appreciate it, thanks." Patience fiddled with her necklace as her gaze veered off. "I'll fill Michael in when he gets home."

"Good." Toni reached out, touching Patience's knee and fixing her with sympathetic eyes. "I'm sorry you have to deal with this sis."

Putting a hand over Toni's, Patience kept her focus on the window. "Me too."

"I'm here for you," Toni promised. "Always."

Patience turned to her. "I know."

Sitting on Noelle's bed, Patience adjusted the covers around Noelle as the girl snuggled beneath them. When she opened her mouth to speak, Patience pointed at her.

"You're not about to ask me for a glass of juice before I go, are you?" Patience asked, a twinge of amusement in her voice. "You know how you do."

Noelle let out a little laugh. "No, not this time. I was going to ask you if my new art magazine came in the mail yet."

"Oh." Brow creasing, Patience tried to think. "I didn't see it in the mail that Michael brought from the house the other day. I'll have him check it again in a few days."

"Okay." Noelle toyed with a piece of comforter fabric. "I hope it comes soon, because I already did all the crafts from *last* month's magazine."

Glancing back at a built-in shelf, Patience eyed the assortment of completed craft projects Noelle had neatly placed there. "Yeah, I can see that," she mused, then turned back to Noelle. "You sure are filling up this room with your artwork."

"Yeah." Noelle rubbed her tired eyes. "If we're going to be here for a long time, can we go take my drawings off my old wall so I can hang them in here?"

"Sure we can." Patience adjusted the satin scarf covering Noelle's hair, then let out a sigh. "Do you miss our house?"

Noelle shrugged slightly. "A little, but I really like it here too." She smiled. "My room here is bigger."

Patience flashed a warm smile back. "Yeah, I know."

"I *do* miss going to our favorite ice cream shop with you though," Noelle confessed. "I miss the colorful polka dot walls and stuff...and how we used to get the big waffle cones."

Leaning her head to the side, Patience fixed Noelle with an empathetic look. "I do too." She put a hand on Noelle's arm. "Bunny, I know this change happened fast and I'm sorry about that. But I promise you, things will get back to normal eventually."

"I know," Noelle said. "And I'm fine with other kinds of ice cream. As long as I get to have it with you."

Poking her lip out, Patience brought a hand to her chest. "Aww, I feel the same." She leaned in, kissing Noelle's forehead. "Love you. Good night."

"Good night, love you too."

Turning off the bedside lamp, Patience left the room, closing the door behind her. She journeyed down the steps to the living room where Michael was sitting on the couch.

"Yeah Mom... Sure, I'll check with her, and we'll get back to you..." Michael retrieved the remote from the arm of the chair, looking up at Patience as she walked in front of him. "Mom says hi, Patience."

"Hi Ms. Jill."

Michael put the phone back to his ear. "She says hi, Mom... Okay. Yep, I will... Talk to you later... Bye."

Patience flopped down on the couch next to Michael. "Did you start watching the movie yet?" she asked him.

He set the phone on the coffee table. "Nope, was waiting for you." He leaned back against the cushions. "Don't know *why*, you're just going to fall asleep on it anyway."

"Hey now, I'm not that bad." Adjusting her position, she laid back against the arm of the couch, resting her feet on Michael's lap. She put a finger up at him when he shot her a look. "Hush, I'm not going to sleep."

Michael laughed. "Uh huh." After hitting play on the TV screen, he set the remote down before taking Patience's foot in his hand, massaging it.

She released a relaxed sigh as his hands kneaded her tense arch. "Now, if I *do*, it'll be you and those magic hands' fault."

He smirked. "I know." As the film began to play, Michael looked over at Patience. "My parents are having a cookout next Saturday...would you be up for going?"

"Of course I would." She folded her arms across her chest. "I think it'll be fun and a nice change of scenery..." Catching the glum look on Michael's face, she regretted saying it. "Baby I didn't mean it like that."

"Oh no, I didn't take that personally." Michael began massaging her other foot. "I know you're tired of feeling like you're in a bubble...feeling like you can't come and go as you please without me hovering over you."

"You're not hovering Michael, you're being protective, and you're doing a hell of a job," Patience soothed. "I want—no, I *need* you to know how much I appreciate you."

"I know that baby. I just don't like that he's still out there." Facing the TV, his eyes narrowed into a glower. "I want to find him and handle him *accordingly*. *Especially* knowing he's out there with a goddamn warrant on his head."

Patience let out a heavy sigh. When Michael had returned home earlier, she didn't hesitate to fill him in on what Toni revealed to her. "I know you do," she said. "But I meant what I said to you. I don't want you going to jail over him. He's not worth ruining your life."

"Patience, I don't think you understand the extent of what I'd do for you. What I'd sacrifice for you," he replied, eerily calm. "You will *not* be looking over your shoulder the rest of your life."

Sitting up, Patience leaned forward, touching his face. "I *do* know, and I love you for it." She followed her declaration with a sweet kiss to his lips. "But, just let the police and my restraining order deal with him... I'm sure they'll track him down soon."

Michael looked at her. He wished he could share in her optimism when it came to Greg. But he couldn't. The man was deplorable and dangerous. And should he dare to pop up again, Michael would be sure to keep his promise. Still, he didn't want to further stress her out by dwelling on it. "I hear you," he said finally.

"Let's not talk about him anymore, okay?" she gently ran her finger across his bottom lip. "I just want to watch this movie with you, then go get in bed with you and do nasty things."

A wicked grin forming on his face, Michael grabbed the remote, turning the TV off. "Hell, we can skip the damn movie for all that."

Laughing, Patience delivered a playful tap to his chest. "No, turn the movie back *on* horny ass."

Chapter Forty-Three

CRADLING HER CELL PHONE TO her ear, Toni took a sip from her water bottle as Rob spoke on the other end.

"Are you feeling any less tense today?" Rob asked.

Putting the top back onto her water, Toni rolled her eyes. "What do *you* think?"

"I think I need to send you out for a spa day."

"I think I'll hold you to that." Toni leaned back in her office chair, sighing deeply. "I'm just worried about Patience you know? I mean, I know she's in good hands—*great* hands, but the fact that Greg is still on the damn street..." She clenched her fists. "It's like he has control over her life *again* and it's pissing me *off*."

"I know honey," Rob soothed. "I know, and trust me, I have my friend down at the station on it. They have feelers out. In fact, I spoke to him the other day, and they've been checking every hotel and motel in the city to see if he's staying there."

"His broke ass probably can't afford to stay in any hotels at this point." Toni lightly pounded the desk with her fist. "I'm sure he blew through whatever money he had just bringing his ass *up* here and on those cheap ass flowers he brought to our house."

"He'll be caught slipping, guys like him always are," Rob placated. "But in the meantime, like you said, your sister is in good hands with Mike. Everything is going to be okay."

Toni spun around in her seat. "Your optimism is sickening

sometimes, but I love you for it," she jeered, earning a slight laugh from him. "Anyway, I have an audit to finish up, so I'll see you later."

"Okay. I'll have dinner ready when you get home."

"You're the best. See you." Hanging up, Toni began clicking a few keys on her laptop. When a knock sounded on her door, she looked up. "Come in." She offered the admin who opened the door a quick smile. "Hey Isaiah."

"Hey, a client is here looking for tax prep information."

Toni scratched her head. "Uhhh, okay. I normally don't take walk-ins, but I can spare a few minutes to answer some questions." She moved her laptop aside, grabbing a notepad. "You can send them in."

"Sure thing."

Toni grabbed a pen from a holder as Isaiah disappeared around the corner. Jotting a few things on the notepad, she made a quick list to make this meeting more efficient. Upon hearing the door creak, she glanced up, frowning at who entered.

Angela closed the door behind her, shooting her a pleading look. "Toni—"

Tossing the pen down on the desk, Toni sucked her teeth. "Bitch, you know damn well you don't need no taxes done."

"It's true, I didn't come here for tax advice," Angela confessed. "I just didn't know another way to get your attention."

Rising from her seat, Toni pointed to the door. "Angela, go play with someone else's time."

"I'm not leaving until you talk to me." Angela stepped forward. "It's been *months* Toni."

Toni looked at Angela as if she'd lost her mind. "I don't *give* a damn. I have *nothing* to say to you."

Running a hand over her hair, Angela let out a long sigh. She'd spent the past three months since her fight with Patience feeling isolated. Not only had Patience not so much as spoken a word to her, but Toni hadn't either. The latter was crushing; Toni had always been quick to forgive and resume their normal relationship. "Look

T, I *know* you're still pissed at me for the whole calling Greg thing. I get it—"

"No, I don't think you *do* get it Angela," Toni interrupted, her eyes blazing with contempt. "Because of *you*, Greg's unstable ass has resurfaced and is *stalking* Patience."

Eyes going wide, Angela went rigid. "What?"

"Yeah, you heard what I said." Toni crossed her arms. "She and Noelle are staying with Michael while he's still out there—and yeah, as much as you *hate* it, Michael *still* loves her and they're *still* together."

Angela rolled her eyes. "I don't hate that they're together, Toni."

"Do you not remember your own words? Or are you *that* goddamn delusional?" Toni argued. "'You think your boyfriend is really going to marry you and play stepfather to another man's child?' Does that ring a fuckin' bell Angela?"

Closing her eyes, Angela lowered her head. She remembered, word for word.

"Oh and guess what? Greg doesn't care about having a relationship with Noelle at *all*. So, you can add turning your niece's world upside down and exposing her to the piece of shit our sister was trying to *protect* her from, to your rap sheet."

"Okay, okay, I know what I did was wrong." Angela put a hand to her chest. "I *do*, but I honestly didn't know that Greg would do this, I just—"

"It doesn't *matter* what you knew!" It was when Angela flinched that Toni realized she'd just yelled. She took a deep breath to bring her temper down; her office wasn't the place for a screaming match. "It doesn't matter what you knew. It matters what you *did*, and *why* you did it." Though her tone was lower, it was no less harsh. "You did it to hurt our sister for *no* reason and you should be fuckin' ashamed of yourself."

Angela opened her mouth to speak, but couldn't find the right words. Toni was right, she *did* do what she did to hurt Patience, and she didn't know how to fix it. "What... What can I do to make things right?"

"You can get out of my office."

Angela's face fell even lower. "So, you're saying that you're just never going to talk to me again? That *our* relationship is never going to go back to what it was?" Her voice quivered. "You can really live with that?"

Toni's scowl deepened. "You can save the manipulation tactics you learned from your husband and carry your miserable ass out of my face."

Adjusting the purse strap on her shoulder, Angela turned on her heel towards the door.

"Angela," Toni called.

Stopping, Angela turned around to see Toni approaching her. She had a sliver of hope that Toni finally had a change of heart, until she was met with the piercing look in her sister's eyes.

"You better pray that Greg doesn't harm one hair on my sister's head," Toni warned, standing chest to chest with Angela. "And I do mean *pray*."

Swallowing hard, Angela's eyes shifted under Toni's gaze. *I will.* Electing to keep her promise to herself, Angela dipped her head and walked out.

Toni barely let Angela get out of the door before forcing it closed. Resting her forehead on the door, she closed her eyes and released a deep breath, before going back to her desk in hopes of getting some work done.

Laying on the plush rug by the fireplace, sketch pads and pencils laid out, Patience and Noelle were drawing. After dropping Patience and Noelle off at home that Thursday afternoon, Michael had headed back to his construction site, leaving the two to settle into their afternoon routine. Now early evening and having finished dinner, Patience and Noelle were capping the day off with an art session.

Pausing her drawing, Noelle peered over at Patience's paper, scrutinizing the sketch on the page. "Is that supposed to be a rose bush?"

Shaking her head, Patience made a few marks on the paper. "To be honest, I don't know *what* this thing is turning out to be." She leaned her head to the side, examining it. "But I'm sure I'll know soon enough."

Noelle gave an approving nod. "*Abstract* art, cool."

Patience giggled as she continued to move her pencil down the paper. Her phone beeping stalled her hand. Grabbing it from nearby, she read the text.

Michael: Hey baby, I finally left work. I'm taking Dante home and will probably chill for a minute, then I'll be heading home. Do you need anything while I'm out?

Patience texted back right away.

Okay, tell Dante I said hi, and nope, we're all good here.

Michael: I won't be too long but call me if you need me. Love you.

Patience: I will. Love you too, see you soon.

Setting her phone down, Patience picked her pencil up to resume her sketch.

Aside from the sound of lead dragging across paper, it was quiet as both concentrated on their work.

Until Noelle piped up. "Mommy, now that my dinner has settled, can I have some dessert?"

"Sure." Patience didn't bother looking up from her paper. "What do you want? We have cookies, and some brownies I think."

"Umm…" Noelle tapped the pencil to her chin as she weighed the options. Neither piqued her interest. "Do we have any ice cream?"

"No sweetie, we're out."

"Okay." Noelle rested her chin on her hand. As she began shading her picture, an idea popped into her head. Her excited eyes darted to her mother. "Oh, can we go out and get ice cream at our place?" She clasped her hands together. "With the big waffle cones?"

Patience paused, eyes still on the paper. Not because she was ignoring her daughter; she was dreading looking into her hopeful eyes, knowing that she'd have to turn down her request. With Greg still at large, Patience was leery about making unnecessary trips alone.

"*Please* Mommy?" Noelle begged when her mother didn't answer.

"Noelle…" Running a hand over her hair, Patience let out a sigh. "I don't think it's a good idea to go right now sweetie. It's late."

"But it's only like seven o'clock," Noelle whined.

Patience shot her a stern look. "Not *now* Bunny. We can go another time, or we'll get some ice cream tomorrow and make cones here."

Eyes lowering to her paper, a small sigh left Noelle. "That's okay." She spun her pencil around on the paper. "I'll just take some cookies."

Patience stared at Noelle, guilt consuming her. Her daughter had been a trooper throughout this entire ordeal, handling every change thrown her way without complaint. All she wanted was to go for an ice cream cone with her mother, and Patience had to turn her down.

I can't keep doing this to her, it's not fair. Dropping the pencil in the box, Patience moved to get up. "You know what, on second thought, let's go get that ice cream."

Lifting her head, Noelle's smile was bright. "Really?" When Patience nodded, Noelle tossed her pencil in the box and jumped up from the floor. "Yay!"

"Do me a favor and put this stuff back in the case." Patience moved towards the stairs. "I'm going to get my purse, then we can go." Darting upstairs, Patience headed for the room she shared with Michael. Removing her purse from the closet, she checked inside to ensure her essentials were there: her wallet, license, keys, mace, taser, and the pocketknife that Michael had given her.

Zipping the purse shut, she closed her eyes, exhaling deeply. "We won't be out long, it'll be fine," she whispered to herself, then left the room.

Chapter Forty-Four

NOELLE WAS FULL OF GLEE as she finished up her vanilla ice cream in a chocolate dipped waffle cone, with sprinkles and chocolate syrup.

Finishing up the last of her own, Patience chuckled at the sight. "Enjoyed it, huh?"

"It was so good." Noelle tossed her napkin in the nearby parlor trash can. "The ice cream here always tastes different than the kind we buy at the store...*better* actually," she said as she sat back down at their table.

While the pair normally ate outside, Patience had opted for indoor seating for a bit of increased safety. "Yeah, I suppose it does." She'd been careful to keep her eye on the front door while they ate, but so far it had been a lovely visit to their favorite ice cream parlor. Patience folded her arms on the table. "You ready to head back?"

"Yes." Noelle stood up. "I can finish my drawing before bed."

"Sounds like a plan." Standing from her seat, she took Noelle's hand as they exited outside into the night air. Standing in place on the step, Patience scanned the entire area that her eyes could reach. There were plenty of shadows for someone to hide in, but so far all was still. Yet it didn't calm her down an inch.

This shit is driving me crazy, Patience thought as she surveyed the space another time for good measure. Not seeing the dreaded familiar figure or his vehicle, they walked to the car.

Getting situated inside, Patience started the engine, preparing to pull off.

"Oh Mommy," Noelle said, putting a finger up. "Can we do one more thing before we go?"

Patience rubbed her eyes. "What's that?"

"Since we're near our house, can we go check the mail to see if my magazine came?"

"Shit," Patience hissed, her voice low. Michael had been working later hours this week, therefore Patience had told him not to worry about grabbing the mail until the weekend. She'd completely forgotten that Noelle was waiting with bated breath for that magazine.

"What did you say Mommy, I didn't hear you?" Noelle innocently asked.

Patience hesitated to reply as she went back and forth in her mind about what to do. She wanted to get back to the safety of Michael's house, but they *were* already in the area.

Stretching her neck from side to side, Patience released a sigh. *It'll take less than five minutes, just get it over with.* "Okay, we'll stop and grab it."

Pulling up to the curb, Patience put the car in park. She eyed her front door, and found the porch light had gone out. "I need to replace that damn bulb," she muttered. Grabbing her keys and phone from her purse, she opened the car door. "Stay in here, I'll be just a second."

"I want to come with you," Noelle piped up, removing her seat belt.

Patience turned in her seat, glancing back at her. "I'm just going to the door."

Stalling, Noelle fiddled with her fingers as a worried look

appeared on her face. "I…just don't want you to walk by yourself," she finally got out.

Patience's brow knitted, confused by the change in Noelle's demeanor. Then as her words registered, Patience's eyes widened slightly. "Wait… Sweetie are you afraid that something is going to happen to me if I go alone?"

Noelle's eyes lowered to her lap. "I just need to come with you."

Closing her eyes, Patience exhaled deeply. Her gut told her that Noelle should stay in the car, but her heart wanted to ease the little girl's mind. "Okay…you can walk with me."

Satisfied, Noelle unlocked the door, and was getting ready to open it until her mother told her to wait. Which she did, watching Patience as she rounded the car to her door.

Giving a scan of her surroundings, Patience opened Noelle's door. "Stay close, okay?"

Nodding, her daughter grabbed hold of Patience's hand as they walked up the path to their door.

Standing on the dark step, Patience scrutinized the keys dangling from the ring in her hand. *Why didn't my dumb ass have the mailbox key ready before I got out the car?* She handed Noelle her phone. "Hold this for me, please."

Taking the phone from Patience's hand, Noelle clutched it to her side.

"Finally," Patience blurted out, finding the key. A subtle sound in the distance caught her attention. She paused, closing her hand around the jingling keys so she could hear better.

It took a split second for it to register that the sound was footsteps, walking across grass. A foreboding feeling seeped in. *Shit! No, no no!* Patience grabbed Noelle's hand, preparing to make a run for the car, but was stopped when Greg jumped in front of her, blocking her path.

Patience was terrified into silence; Noelle let out a little scream.

Patience swiftly moved Noelle behind her. Securing her with her arm, Patience stood face to face with Greg.

"I figured you'd show up eventually," Greg spoke, his voice unnervingly calm.

Eyes locked with his, Patience's breathing intensified. She was kicking herself for not going straight back to Michael's. "Shit."

"Yeah, *shit* is right baby." Greg moved in, leaving Patience no personal space. "Can you imagine the pain in the ass it's been, driving past here every hour hoping to see you…while avoiding your *dog* of course." When Patience opened her mouth to speak, Greg immediately cut her off. "I'd like to talk to you…inside." He gestured his head towards the door. "So why don't you open the door."

Though petrified, Patience scowled at him. "I don't think so." When Greg grabbed her arm, she tried to snatch away, but he tightened his grip. She opened her mouth to yell for help, but Greg put a finger to his lips.

"I'd advise you not to scream."

Closing her mouth in fear of what he'd do if she went against his warning, Patience could feel Noelle gripping her shirt tight. Her little girl's face was plastered to her back, her little breaths quickening. "You're scaring her, you bastard."

Unfazed, Greg yanked Patience's arm. Pulling it to his hip, he pressed her hand to it. "You feel that?"

Feeling something hard beneath her fingertips, Patience's heart dropped into her stomach. *A gun! He has a gun!* Swallowing a cry, Patience's eyes pleaded with him. "Greg—"

"You should open the door." Greg tilted his head. "I just want to talk."

Patience tightened her grip on Noelle. She didn't want her to go inside that house with Greg. "At least let her wait in the car."

Greg shook his head. "Nah, she shouldn't be left out here by herself, right?" He released her hand. "Open it, it's getting chilly."

Cursing under her breath, Patience unlocked the door, pushing it open so hard that it slammed against the wall. With Noelle still clutched to her, she walked in with Greg following.

As Greg closed the door, Patience faced him. Seeing him in the light, she took notice of his rough appearance. The clean cut, well-dressed man who had showed up at her open house months ago was gone. Before her stood a scruffy mess who clearly hadn't slept *or* showered in days. The white T-shirt and light jeans he had on were wrinkled and dingy.

Looking at the smug look on his crusty face, Patience's fear quickly turned into anger. "We're in…*now* what?" She hissed at him.

Greg folded his arms. "Why don't you send the kid upstairs so we can talk in private."

Glaring at him, Patience took Noelle's hand. As much as she didn't want to be separated from her, Patience knew that it was in Noelle's best interest not to be downstairs with them. She didn't want Noelle bearing witness to whatever he had planned.

Guiding Noelle from behind her, Patience crouched down to her daughter's level. Holding her hands, she looked into Noelle's tear-filled eyes, and tried to keep from tearing up herself. "Listen Noelle, I want you to go upstairs—"

"Mommy no." Noelle's voice broke, tears spilling.

Patience's face grew wet with her own, but she had to stay focused. "Listen, it's okay," she promised, holding her voice together. "I'm just going to talk to your father. So, I want you to go upstairs, close the door and lock it okay?"

Noelle's eyes lowered as she cried.

Patience cupped her face with her hands. "I'll be okay Bunny."

Greg let out an exasperated huff. "This is taking *way* more time than needed Patience."

Patience snapped her head in his direction, eyes blazing. "Don't *rush* me!"

Throwing a hand up, Greg let out a maniacal chuckle. "Damn, my bad *mama*. As you were."

Turning back to Noelle, Patience swaddled her in a hug. Pulling away, she lifted Noelle's chin with her finger. "Go baby. It's okay."

Sniffling, Noelle took off running up the steps.

Pushing herself to her feet, Patience watched the steps until she heard the door close, before facing Greg once again.

Noelle slammed the door shut and jumped on the bed, tears cascading down her face. She didn't know what to do. Her mother was downstairs with someone dangerous, and she wanted to help, but she didn't know how. Her bedroom was too high for her to try to sneak out the window to go to her neighbor. She felt helpless.

Hugging her knees, Noelle buried her face into them. "I'm sorry Mommy. I shouldn't have asked to go for ice cream," she sobbed.

Lifting her murky gaze briefly, something caught her eye. Her mother's phone was on the end of the bed. She'd never given it back to her, and must've dropped it when she'd landed on it.

Scrambling, Noelle scooped it up, scrolling through the contacts until she found the right one.

"It's been real watching you make cinnamon rolls for the past hour and a half, but I need to get home," Michael told Dante, who was pulling a pan from the oven as he danced to the music blasting through his speaker.

"Come on man, you haven't tasted one yet." Dante fanned the steam away with a potholder. "It's my first time making these from scratch. Of *course*, I want the cooking master to try them."

"Wrap it up for me." Michael peered at his watch. "I'll try it later and let you know."

Dante moved for a cabinet, opening it. "All right, I guess that'll do." He took a roll of foil out. "I'll send one for Patience and little mamas too. Y'all can try them at the same time."

Michael looked at him, eyebrow lifting. "Yeah, *I'll* try it first… wouldn't want you to poison all *three* of us."

Making a face, Dante playfully tossed the potholder Michael's way. "Funny, jackass."

Hearing his phone ring, Michael pulled it from his pocket. Checking the ID, his face lit up. "Speaking of Patience, this is her now." He placed the device to his ear. "Hey baby, I'm about to leave now. Dante made us—" He frowned, perplexed by the voice on the other end. "Noelle? What's wrong sweetie? Where's your mom?" His eyes widened with rage at the answer coming from the hysterical, sobbing child. *No, no no! Fuck!*

Bolting from his seat, Michael charged through the living room at top speed, the phone still to his ear. "Hang tight okay, I'm coming right now." Though his voice was composed so as not to further upset Noelle, Michael was rattling on the inside. *Patience, I'm coming baby.*

Stepping out of the kitchen, Dante looked on in concern, as his brother yanked the front door open. "Bro, what's wrong?"

Michael ran out without so much as looking back. "I have to go!"

"Whatever you're going to do, *do* it and get it over with," Patience hurled at Greg, who was slowly pacing back and forth, staring at her.

He had yet to speak or *do* anything. He was just taunting her with his deliberate silence.

"What? You want me to cry? *Beg* you? I'm not giving you the fuckin' satisfaction."

Greg finally halted. "You've always been impatient, beautiful." Taking a step forward, he lifted his shirt. "Very well, then." Slowly, he pulled the object from where it was tucked in his pants.

Patience held her breath, saying a silent prayer, dreading the fact that this could be the end. All she could think about was leaving her daughter; she hoped that Noelle would forgive her. But when she saw what Greg pulled *out*, she exhaled loudly.

In Greg's hand was a rectangle box.

Seeing the stunned look on her face, he laughed. "Come on P, you didn't really think I'd pull a gun on you, *did* you?" he tossed it aside. "I just needed you to *think* I had one. How *else* was I going to get you to let me in so we could talk?"

"I swear to God." Enraged, Patience stepped towards him, pointing, "You sick son of a bitch!"

Greg clapped his hands. "Hey! Chill with the name calling."

"*Fuck* you! Do you have *any* idea how you just traumatized my daughter?" Patience fumed. "What is *wrong* with you?"

"Last time I checked, she's *my* kid too." Greg crossed his arms, smirking. "As a matter of fact, I've been thinking that I should spend more time with her…maybe permanently."

Patience let out a vicious laugh. "Yeah, whatever shit your raggedy ass is on has *seriously* fucked you up even more than you already were," she hurled. "I'd kill you before I let that happen."

"Oh *really?*" Greg pointed at her. "Let's see how a custody judge feels about you threatening me."

"Judge?" Patience repeated, looking at him as if he had ten heads. "You're threatening *me* with a judge? With *court?*"

Greg gave a hard shrug. "Scared?"

Patience folded her arms, the look of disbelief intensifying on her face. This man was delusional. "Greg, I have a *restraining order* against you. Which you're *violating* at this very fuckin' *moment* by the way."

"Well, in my defense, I was never actually *served* with the order—no address and all, so that bullshit won't stand. Besides I didn't do *shit* to you outside of visiting you," he argued. "I didn't *touch* you and—before you bring up the past, I *told* you that was behind us. You are *still* overreacting, just like you did throughout our *entire* marriage."

Patience cocked her head to the side, staring him down. "Oh, I'm overreacting huh?"

Greg nodded emphatically, anger in his eyes. "Yeah, you are."

"Okay, well how about that warrant you got out for beating up that bartender back in Georgia? Am I overreacting about *that*?"

Greg's eyes widened. "How the hell did you find out about that?"

"The *same* way you found out where I live." Patience looked him up and down in disgust. "You never *could* fight a man, but was ready and willing to put your hands on a goddamn woman."

Greg's brow deepened into a glower as she berated him.

"Yeah, no judge in his right mind would grant you visitation, let alone give you *custody*."

Teeth clenched, Greg felt the little composure he had slip away. He jerked his hand at her, making her flinch. "So what, you're just going to let that guard dog you're *fucking* take my place? Take you away from me? *Huh*?!"

"And here goes the façade tumbling *yet* again." She shook her head. "Just like before, this is not about your child, this is about you still wanting to control *me*."

Greg made a hasty approach, sending her backing up. "I don't want to *control* you, Patience, I still love you!" He put a hand to his chest. "I never *stopped*! I never wanted a divorce. *I* didn't give up on us, *you* did."

Seething with fury, Patience felt her body shake. "Get the fuck out of my house Greg!"

"You know you still have love for me, just admit it." Greg beat his chest with his fist, crazed look in his eyes. "Admit it!"

"The *only* thing I admit to is the fact that I never should've married you in the first place!"

Greg stood, eyes digging through his ex-wife like a knife. There were no more thoughts, only rage that propelled him forward, grabbing hold of her.

Patience screamed out as Greg crashed her back into the wall. The impact knocked the hung pictures down, the glass shattering on the floor all around her. She tried to pry his hands off, but Greg was squeezing with everything he had in him, his face inches from hers. "Get off me!"

Distantly, she could hear the upstairs door open; Patience could only pray that Noelle wouldn't come down. "Mommy!" Noelle cried out in distress.

"Stay upstairs baby!" Patience pleaded, struggling to find a way out as Noelle's cries echoed through the hallway.

"You're really replacing me with *him*?!" Greg screeched against her face. He slammed her against the wall again. "You really think he can do better for you! You think he loves you more than I do? That he fucks you better? After everything I've done for you—bitch, I'll *kill* you before I let that happen!"

Patience managed to maneuver her leg just enough to knee Greg in his groin, causing him to yell in agony. When he released his grip on her arms, she headbutted him, sending him stumbling back until he collided with an end table. The wood buckled under him as he tumbled to the floor.

As Greg laid writhing in pain, Patience pushed herself up from the wall, trying not to let her dizziness paralyze her. Panting uncontrollably, she eyed Greg on the floor—one hand on his groin and the other covered his bloody nose—having the nerve to have *tears* in his eyes after he assaulted her. After he'd scared her daughter and tried to ruin her life for a *second* time. His pathetic scene, and the sound of Noelle crying for her upstairs, snatched the last bit of sanity she had left.

Grabbing a long shard of glass from the floor, Patience jumped on top of Greg.

Eyeballs bulging in terror, Greg grabbed hold of her hand before the glass could collide with his face. He screamed at the top of his lungs as Patience forced the weapon closer. "What the fuck are you doing?!"

The blade cut through her hand but it did not deter Patience, nor did the blood streaming down her arm. All she could focus on was trying to get that glass into Greg's face. She would've succeeded had Greg not moved his head, causing her hand to slip and plunge glass into his shoulder instead.

Patience relished the sound of his roaring cries of agony as she pressed the blade further into his flesh. But the more she pressed, the deeper the glass cut *her*. Unable to bear the searing pain anymore, she lifted her hand from the glass and backed off.

Grabbing her leg just as she tried to get up, Greg pulled it out from under her, sending Patience down and knocking her head against the floor. Not hesitating for a moment, she pushed herself to her feet and scrambled away, as Greg shot up from the floor.

"Now I really *am* going to kill you. You fuckin' crazy bitch." Glass still deep in his shoulder, Greg charged at Patience just as the door crashed opened.

A pair of strong arms grabbed hold of him before he could get the chance. Michael picked Greg up and slammed him to the ground. Dragging Greg's flailing body outside on the front step, Michael fulfilled the promise he'd made in the school parking lot. As his fists rained down, Michael spoke no words. The power in his punches, and the fury in his eyes as he connected blow after blow on Greg, spoke for him.

Finally succumbing to her dizziness, Patience stumbled to the floor. Looking up with half-lidded eyes, she watched Noelle dart down the steps, running right for her arms.

"Are you okay?" Noelle cried, holding tight.

Patience blinked slowly, holding onto Noelle. "I'm okay," she murmured. "I'm okay." Seeing a hint of red and blue flashing lights in her peripheral, Patience thought they might be a symptom of a concussion. Blinking would not clear them. It was only when she heard sirens that she realized what was happening. Her eyes widened with fear; Michael was out there doing exactly what he swore to. *God no.*

Forcing herself from the floor, she hurried out of the house, where three police officers were jumping out of two cars. Michael had a severely bruised and bloody, unresponsive Greg, pinned to the ground by his throat. By the wrath on his face, Michael had no intentions of letting up. As much as she wanted Greg gone from her life, she wanted Michael here more.

"Michael, let him go," Patience managed to belt out, holding on to the door frame for support.

"Go back in the house Patience," Michael ordered, eyes still fixed on Greg's swollen face.

"You'll kill him, let go!" Seeing the officers approach Michael, hands plastered to their holsters, Patience put her hands up. "No, don't hurt him, he's saving me. The man on the ground was trying to kill me and my daughter." She looked to Michael as the officers yelled for him to release Greg, desperation in her eyes. "Baby, *please!*"

It was only the fear in her voice that allowed Michael to grit his teeth and let go. Raising his hands, Michael stood up and backed away.

A car pulled up on the curb in a screeching halt. Toni jumped out of the passenger's side before it was even put in park. "Patience!" She tried to run for the house, but was stopped by an officer.

"Ma'am, you can't come through here," the officer said, holding her hands out.

"No fuck that, my sister is over there," Toni hollered, pointing at the woman.

Rob grabbed Toni, holding her. "It's okay baby."

"Let me go see if my sister is okay!" Toni tried to pry her husband's hands off her.

Rob looked at the officer. "Listen, please let my wife through. That's her sister over there," he pleaded. "I know Captain Warren. That man on the ground has been stalking my sister-in-law, and she has a restraining order against him. He's assaulted her before, and he has a warrant out for his arrest in another state."

The woman looked at Toni. Seeing the worry in her eyes, and hearing what her sister had dealt with, she felt sympathy. "Ma'am go to *her*, no one else."

Toni took off running for Patience, while Rob thanked the officer.

Patience had her hand on Michael's shoulder, while he sat on the ground, handcuffed. With her other arm, she was trying to block the door, so Noelle couldn't see. Another officer was tending to Greg on the ground, while the third called in an ambulance. Patience's eyes shot up when Toni barreled for her.

Toni grabbed Patience, moving her away from the melee. She pulled her into a hug, tears of relief spilling down her cheeks. When Noelle had called to tell her that she and her mother were trapped in the house with Greg, Toni and Rob couldn't get out of the restaurant they were dining in fast enough. On the way there, Toni had called the police.

Pulling back, Toni put her hands on Patience's face, examining her. "Are you okay? Are you hurt? Did he hurt you?"

Bursting into tears, Patience motioned to Michael. "They're arresting him."

Toni zoned in on the blood covering her sister's hand, a shuddering gasp leaving her. "Oh my God—I'm taking you to the hospital."

Patience snatched away from her. "I'm not leaving!"

"Baby, I'll be fine. Go to the hospital," Michael said. As the officer led him to the car, he glanced over at Patience, fighting his emotions. He wanted nothing more than to run over and hold her, comfort her. "I'm fine. Don't worry about me."

Rob patted Michael's shoulder as he was placed in the backseat of the cop car. "Don't worry about a thing Mike, I'm coming down to the station."

Patience nearly collapsed when she saw the car door close on Michael. "Don't let them take him, he didn't do anything wrong!"

"Hey, listen to me," Toni said, holding her. "He's going to be fine. Rob's got him, and *I* got *you*. We're going to the hospital."

Distraught, Patience just sobbed uncontrollably. She peered at the doorway, where a weeping Noelle was now standing. "My baby Toni. Get my baby."

Toni gestured for Noelle to come to her; the frightened little girl moved quicker than Toni had ever seen. "We need to go, now," Toni urged, guiding them to the car.

Chapter Forty-Five

SITTING ON A BED IN the emergency room, Patience held her head in her hand as she tried to will away her pain. She'd been in the hospital for hours and with her adrenaline now gone, she was feeling everything that she'd been through.

Hearing the door open, she slowly peered up as Toni walked in, a cup of water in hand. "Hey…you want some water? If not this, I can go get some tea or coffee?"

Patience gingerly shook her head. "Where's Noelle?" she asked, voice low.

Toni approached. "My in-laws came and got her." She set the cup aside on a table. "The doctors wouldn't allow her in here and I didn't want her just sitting in that cold waiting room… I knew you wouldn't either."

Patience took a labored breath. "I wouldn't."

"She didn't want to leave your side, though." Toni lightly touched Patience's arm.

"I know…" Patience ran a hand over the back of her neck, wincing. "Please tell her that I'm okay… I can't find my phone."

Toni sat on the bed next to Patience. "Noelle has it," she said. "That brilliant child called Michael, then me, while she was in her room."

Patience shook her head, tears filling her eyes as everything flooded back. "She was so scared."

"I know." Toni rubbed her sister's back. "But that was *Greg's* doing, and she knows that."

Wiping her eyes with her unbandaged hand, Patience sighed deeply. "I can't believe I was so *stupid*."

"Do *not* do that to yourself, Pace."

"I should've never left the house," Patience vented, voice cracking. "I gave Greg the opportunity to hurt me *again*, my baby is traumatized, Michael is in jail, and—*all* of this shit is *my* fault."

Toni held her hand on Patience's back, fixing her with an unwavering gaze. "First, *none* of this is your fault, okay? It's Greg's. Second, Noelle will be just fine, sweetie, I promise you. Because she will no longer have a reason to fear him coming after you, and third, Michael is *not* going to jail."

"And you know all of this, *how?*"

"Because Rob has been keeping me posted," Toni answered. "One of his best friends is the police captain, and he let Rob know that Greg is currently handcuffed to a hospital bed, and once they un-dent his *face* they'll be *arresting* his ass. He's going down for not only what he did to you tonight, but he's being shipped back to Georgia to face time for what he did to that bartender." She gently moved some of her sister's hair behind her shoulder. "Michael will be released from holding soon and no charges will be pressed… It's over sweetie."

Overcome with emotion, Patience put a hand over her face and buried herself in Toni's shoulder.

Wrapping her arms around her, Toni just held Patience as she cried. Feeling the sting of tears behind her own eyes, Toni squeezed them shut. Though it was over, the gravity of what *could* have happened to her sister was hitting her. Thinking of the alternative was almost too much for Toni to bear.

Hearing Toni sniffle, Patience pulled back. "Toni—"

"I'm just grateful that you're okay." She wiped her eyes with her shirt. "It just hit me that things could've ended differently so… I'm glad you're okay."

Patience didn't speak; if she did, she'd start blubbering all over again. Instead, she just leaned her head on Toni's shoulder once again.

A quick knock sounded on the door before it opened. "Hi Patience, how are you feeling?" the doctor asked, clipboard in hand.

Patience let out a deep breath. "Everything hurts."

"I can imagine. You've been through a hell of an ordeal tonight," the doctor replied, his voice filled with compassion.

Seeing that a call was coming in on her phone, Toni stood up. "Pace, it's my mother-in-law, I'm going to take this outside." She went to go for the door, but paused, looking back at her. "Unless you need me to stay in here with you."

Patience gestured for her to go ahead. "No. Go."

The doctor examined his chart as Toni left the room. "The good news is that there doesn't seem to be any permanent damage done," he said. "Your CAT scan came back clear of any swelling or internal bleeding. X-rays don't show any broken bones and the cut on your hand—while you did need stitches—no nerves or tendons were damaged."

Patience just stared at him, trying to absorb what he was saying. "Do I have to stay here overnight?" she finally asked.

"No, but we'd like to keep you another hour or two for observation. Just try to relax as much as you can, and I'll get you something to take for your pain."

Patience just gave a subtle nod as he left the room. She didn't want to stay in that hospital any longer than she already had. Inching herself back against the pillow, she winced. *Yeah, 'try to relax' my ass.*

Toni stepped back in just as Patience was trying to reposition herself, and hurried to her aid. Taking the pillow, she propped it behind Patience's back. "I spoke to the doctor; he said you can go home in a few hours."

"I want to leave *now*," Patience muttered.

"I know sweetie," she sympathized. "Umm, Mom-in-law is here in the waiting room with Noelle."

Patience's brow creased with panic. "What? Why did something happen—"

"No no, she's okay. She just refused to go to sleep without seeing you."

Breathing a sigh, Patience's face relaxed. "Can you bring her in here, please?"

"Of course." Toni made a hasty departure, returning minutes later hand in hand with Noelle.

Not uttering a word, Noelle immediately dropped Toni's hand, running straight for her mother's outstretched arms. She jumped onto her mother's bed, who pulled her close and held on tight.

Toni put a hand out. "Bunny wait, not so—"

"It's okay Toni," Patience cut in, hugging her daughter as the little girl buried her face in her shoulder. Hearing Noelle's little sniffle, Patience's eyes teared up. She looked at Toni. "Can you give us a minute?"

"Sure sweetie." Toni left, closing the door behind her.

Resting against the pillow, Patience rubbed Noelle's back as she rocked her.

"Mommy are you okay?" Noelle's voice quivered.

Patience stroked her hair. "I am now," she answered truthfully. "Are *you*?"

Noelle nodded. "I didn't want to go to sleep until I saw you."

"I know baby. I'm glad you're here." Patience guided Noelle beside her. Grimacing, she adjusted her position to face her. "Thank you for calling Michael and your aunt... You've been so brave and I'm proud of you."

"But I didn't *feel* brave." Her eyes shimmered with tears. "I was really scared."

Patience's heart sank even further. "I know Bunny and

Mommy is *so* sorry." Tears trickled down her own face. "I swear to you, you'll *never* have to go through anything like that ever again, okay? Because your—Greg won't be coming around anymore. *Ever.*"

"Really?" Noelle asked, hope lifting her voice. "You mean he's gone?"

Wiping the wetness from Noelle's cheeks, Patience nodded. "He's gone."

Noelle didn't say another word, though the look of absolute relief on her face spoke *for* her.

Pulling her daughter close, Patience kissed the top of Noelle's head. "We're going to be okay baby… I promise."

Fiddling with the string on her pajama pants, Patience sat in the living room at Michael's, staring at the door. Released from the hospital around three in the morning, Patience had Toni drop her and Noelle off at Michael's home. After getting Noelle settled in bed, Patience moved at a snail's pace to soak the day away in a bath, before changing into some comfortable pajamas.

Now two hours later and unable to sleep herself, Patience sat up, waiting for Michael to get home from the police station. *He should've been let out by now.*

Hearing the door unlock, she pushed herself up from the couch. When it opened and Michael crossed that corridor, she couldn't stop the tears from forming.

Shutting the door behind him, Michael rushed to wrap his arms around her, breathing a sigh of relief as he held her close. He'd been given updates on her condition from Rob while he was sitting down at the station. While he knew that she was going to be okay, he almost couldn't believe it until he had her in his arms.

"I'm so sorry," she sobbed into his chest.

"No, no, don't do that baby." Pulling back, he guided her to sit on the couch. "You have *nothing* to be sorry about."

Patience heard his words, but she could only focus on the black and blue markings on his knuckles. "Baby, your hands—are you okay?"

"I promise you, it's nothing, I don't even feel it," Michael soothed. When she looked down at her lap, he softly lifted her chin with his hand. "Patience, I mean it, *please* don't blame yourself for any of this."

"I'm trying *not* to Michael." She brushed wetness from under her eyes with her fingers. "I really am."

"I know you are, and if I have to reassure you every single day to ease that, I will." His own eyes clouding over, Michael smoothed her hair back from her face. "Are you in a lot of pain? I wanted to be there with you at the hospital."

"I know you did." Patience ran her hand along Michael's arm; grateful that he was sitting in front of her, and not rotting in a jail cell. "The pain was bad, but I took something, so it's manageable right now. The doctors said that no permanent damage was done, thank God… I'm okay." She touched Michael's face when he zoned in on her bandaged hand, his eyes tight with anger. "Hey, look at me." He did as she said. "I'm okay Michael… He's going away for a long time."

"I know…lucky for him." Michael released a deep breath. "Is Noelle okay? Where is she? She wasn't hurt, was she?"

"No, she wasn't. She's upstairs sleeping," Patience answered. "She wanted to wait up for you, but I told her she needed her rest."

"She *deserves* her rest…you *both* do."

Patience sighed heavily. "So do you."

Closing his eyes, Michael tried to force the evening's events from his mind, but it was proving to be a difficult task. Everything continued to vividly replay. From the sound of Noelle's distressed voice on the phone, to the helplessness, fury and dread that had consumed him as he'd sped to Patience's house, to barging through her door just as Greg was about to attack her. He could still hear the anguish in Patience's voice, when she'd thought the police were going to harm him for nearly taking Greg's life.

But when he opened his eyes, he focused on Patience's face. She and Noelle—his family—where safe and back home. And thanks to Rob, Michael could be there with them. He *could* rest. They *all* could now.

Cupping her face with his hands, Michael kissed Patience's lips, then her cheek, before securing her in another hug. "I love you baby," he breathed against her hair.

She held on and refused to let go. "I love you too."

Chapter Forty-Six

SITTING CROSS-LEGGED ON A BLANKET under a tree, Michael stared at Patience, who was sitting in front of him in the same position. The subtle curve of her lips told him that she was suppressing a laugh.

Hands resting on his folded legs, Michael successfully stifled his own. "You look like you want to laugh."

"I'm trying *not* to." Patience cleared her throat, then wiped the humor from her face. "This better?"

Michael opened his mouth to reply, but couldn't help it. He broke.

Patience put her hand on Michael's chest, as his shoulders shook with laughter. She turned her head as her own cackles seeped out.

Noelle, sitting a few feet from them, peered over her easel. Her eyes narrowed. "Mommy, you moved."

"Huh?" Eyes wide, Patience pointed to Michael. "*He* moved first."

Putting a hand up, Michael ceased his laughter, though the humor was still on his face. "We're sorry Noelle, we'll act right." He moved himself back into position. "Come on Pace, focus."

Patience adjusted herself. "She's so *bossy* when she's doing portraits."

Shaking her head, Noelle returned her eyes to her drawing. "I just need like ten more minutes."

Making the most of the mild September afternoon, Michael, Patience, and Noelle were enjoying one of their park picnics. Meal finished, they had prepared for another family art session. However, Noelle had revealed that she wanted both Patience and Michael to be her models so she could draw *them*.

Sitting before one another for the past forty-five minutes, Patience and Michael had remained cooperative and statue-like. That is until their silliness got the best of them.

"Okay, I'm finished," Noelle finally announced.

"Thank God, my legs fell asleep," Patience muttered in an aside to Michael as they relaxed their bodies.

Scooting over to them, Noelle turned the board around, displaying the completed work.

Both Michael and Patience eyed it. "Oh wow," Michael gestured to the picture. "Those are really good caricatures."

"Thank you." Noelle then cocked her head, bewildered. "Wait... These aren't supposed to be caricatures."

"Umm..." Michael stalled. Surely, he thought that the distorted images of them were Noelle's intention. "Forget I said that. Great job."

Grinning proudly, Noelle set the portrait on the blanket. She then grabbed a bright pink bottle from a bag. "Can I go over there and blow bubbles?"

Patience nodded. "Sure, just stay where I can see you."

"I will." Noelle trotted off.

Resting his back against the tree, Michael chuckled as Patience positioned her back against him. "Wasn't going to jump in to help me with the caricature faux pas, huh?"

"Oh no, you handled it on your own quite beautifully," Patience teased, earning a playful pat to her thigh. "She's still learning how to draw realistic people."

Relaxing against Michael as she watched her daughter play, feeling the autumn breeze caress her face, Patience felt a sense of peace she'd not found in a long time.

Four months had passed since the incident with Greg. While

she'd struggled in the first few weeks after to put it out of her mind, she was now at a place where she could go about her life without thinking about it.

Greg had been convicted and locked away in a jail in Georgia, and Michael had walked away with no charges. Noelle, with both Patience and Michael's attention, love, and reassurance, seemed to be putting the incident behind her.

Michael wrapped his arms around Patience's waist. "Are you looking forward to the sleepover tonight?" he asked.

Thinking of tonight's sleepover with Jodan, Patience laughed internally. "*I'll* be the only one sleeping. Those two little girls will be up until the wee hours."

"Yeah, I'm sure."

Patience ran a hand down his leg. "Did you plan anything for tonight? I know it's been a minute since you had one of your game nights."

"Nah, I'll be spending the evening with that novel you gave me." Michael shrugged. "Besides, I couldn't have a game night without you. You're my partner."

A giggle sounded from Patience. "This is true."

"Yeah." After a long moment of silence, Michael let out a heavy breath. "I miss coming home to you."

Reaching her hand up, Patience stroked his face. "I know... I miss it too."

Though there was no longer a threat, Patience, with mixed emotions, had moved back into her house a month after.

"I hope you know that my decision had *nothing* to do with not wanting to live with you," she said. "I loved being there. I miss waking up to you every day... I just hated that we got to that point under duress."

"I know, and I understand. I didn't like the idea of it being forced on you either." While Michael was supportive of her decision to return to her home, he'd gotten used to having Patience living with him. And even though they'd resumed their routine of at-home dinners and overnight stays, he missed the everyday dynamic. It made him yearn to have it permanently.

"We'll have that again," Patience promised. "The right way."

Michael smiled at the thought, then kissed the top of her head. "I know we will."

Patience maneuvered her car down the block. "We're going to drop these groceries off, then go pick up Jordan," she said.

Noelle looked up from her phone. "Okay. I can't wait to—" Pausing as the car pulled up to the house, she peered out the window. "Umm, Mommy... Someone is sitting on our step."

Turning the car off, Patience stared at the figure, her eyes glaring. "I see that." She undid her seat belt. "Come on."

Leaving the bags in the car, Patience, with Noelle at her side, approached the house. Stopping in front of the slumped over figure, Patience maintained her harsh gaze. "Angela, what are you doing here?"

Angela's red, glassy eyes slowly inched up towards Patience. Her puffy face was lined with tears. "I—I didn't know where else to go."

"I find that hard to believe," Patience sneered. When Angela lowered her gaze to the ground, Patience shook her head. *Great. Just great.* She had half the mind to throw Angela off her step with a few choice words. But the woman looked broken, and the small part of Patience that *still* loved her, would at least let her pull herself together before sending her packing.

Patience gestured to Angela to move. "Get up."

As Angela moved to do as her sister commanded, Noelle stepped forward, offering her a hand.

"Thank you, angel," Angela sniffled. She lightly patted Noelle's hand, while waiting for Patience to open the door.

Unlocking each deadbolt, Patience motioned them in. Shutting the door behind her, she pointed to the couch. "Sit down Angela."

Angela took the seat, hugging her arms to herself as her tears poured.

Grabbing a tissue box from a nearby end table, Noelle swiftly handed it to her aunt. "Are you okay Aunt Angie?" she asked, eyes wide with concern.

"Not really honey." Angela's voice was hoarse.

Patience stood, staring at her sister. Angela's tears didn't draw sympathy. Had this been months ago, before Angela had made the fateful phone call, she would've felt something. She would've even *hugged* her. But now, she just wanted to get the issue out of Angela, so the woman could leave. "You want some water or something?" Her tone was as expressionless as her face.

Angela nodded. "Yes please."

"I'll get it, Mommy." Noelle darted for the kitchen, reappearing not even a minute later. "Here," she said, handing it to her.

Offering a grateful nod, Angela accepted the glass then took a sip.

"Noelle, go to your room so your aunt and I can talk," Patience said. Noelle swiftly did as she said. Once Patience heard the upstairs door shut, she folded her arms. "This is the time to start talking, Angela."

Setting the glass on the coffee table, Angela tried to form the scattered thoughts in her head. Dabbing her eyes with a tissue, she couldn't bring herself to look at her sister. "Patience I... I'm *so* sorry about what happened to you... I *swear* I wanted to call you—"

"I'm almost certain that's not why you were crying on my doorstep," Patience curtly cut in. "And I don't want an apology from you. It's too late for that. Why are you *here*?"

"He..." Angela let out a shaky breath. "He got one of them pregnant."

Patience frowned. "He *who*?"

"Trevor." Angela looked at Patience. "He got one of the bitches he's been *sleeping* with...*pregnant*."

Patience relaxed her face, though her eyes were still stern. "I'm sorry to hear that."

Both she and Toni had an idea that Trevor had been cheating on their sister for years, and had tried to get Angela to see it... But their sister hadn't been so blind after all. "How did you find out?"

"He *told* me." Angela shook her head. "That bastard just said it like it was nothing... Like he didn't just break my fuckin' heart." Tears welled up in her eyes again. "I stood by as that man stepped out on our marriage time and time and *time* again for *years*, and now..."

Patience just stood in place, listening as her sister vented.

"He always said he didn't want children...and I *accepted* that even though I always wanted them, and *now* he's having a baby with someone else, and I don't know how to deal with that," she sucked in a breath. "I don't know what to do."

"You leave him," Patience replied.

"Patience, he's been my everything since I was twenty-two years old and now, I have to be *without* him? I—I don't know if I *can*." Angela's sorrowful gaze was locked on her sister. "I don't have the strength to leave...to start over with *nothing*."

Patience tilted her head. "If *I* could, so can you."

"I'm not *you*, Patience... I'm not strong like you." Angela lowered her eyes. "You've *always* been... Ever since you were little, no matter what was thrown at you, or how you were treated, you always handled it with *so* much grace... You were always determined to be happy, no matter what." She stared at the crumbled damp tissues in her hand. "You were never afraid to stand up for yourself, even against Mom... I guess that's why I've always resented you."

"So, you resented me all these years because I was *resilient*?" Patience questioned, bite in her voice.

"I resented you because you were everything that I *wasn't*," Angela admitted for the first time. "I hated you because I wanted to *be* you."

Letting out a heavy sigh, Patience rubbed her eyes with her fingertips. While she'd always suspected it, learning the truth at long last…cut. Patience returned her eyes to Angela. "I'm going to ask you something, and you need to be *completely* honest with me."

Angela gave a slow nod. "Okay…I owe you that much."

"When you introduced me to Greg…did you know how he was?"

A shiver ran through Angela's body. She raised her eyes, meeting Patience's stare. She didn't want to answer, but knew she had to. "Yes."

Scoffing, Patience balled her fists. "Are you fuckin' serious?"

"At the time… I had no idea that he would ever grow to be physically violent," Angela amended. "But I did know that he was a narcissist… He and Trevor were college roommates. They got along so well because they were *just* alike. I'd see how Greg mistreated the women he messed with in school—"

"Do you really think I *care* about your goddamn college backstory with him?"

"I'm sorry, I know you don't. I was just trying to explain—"

"Why did you *do* it?" Patience snapped at her. "If you *knew* he wasn't shit, *why* did you bring him into my life?"

Angela stared at her, eyes glassing over as guilt and regret consumed her. "…Because I didn't want to be miserable by myself."

Patience's eyes widened as she was stunned into silence.

"For the first two years of our marriage, Trevor was the perfect husband. Then it was like a light switched off, and he became cold. We stopped doing things together. He was staying at work late, and… One night I checked his phone and found out he was cheating." Angela wiped the tears from her eyes. "When I confronted him, he didn't deny it…but I couldn't leave. Despite what he'd done, I still *loved* him. So, I stayed even though I wasn't happy…but *you were*. You were out there working, dating, *thriving* on your own, and I just…" She sighed. "At one of Trevor's poker nights, Greg mentioned that he was looking for another—*prospect*. So… I told him about you."

Tapping her foot on the floor, Patience fought to keep herself composed. "I don't need to hear anymore." She shook her head. " You might have introduced me to him, but *I'm* the one who ignored the red flags in the beginning," she said, reflective. "*I'm* the one who didn't leave when I first realized that he wasn't who I thought he was... Those were *my* choices, so I can't hate you for that."

"I appreciate that, but I *deserve* your hate... *All* of it." Angela's voice trembled as she prepared to reveal another confession. "I umm...I lied to you that night at Toni's. I *did* know about what Greg did—about him hurting you... I found out the night you left him."

Patience felt like the breath was sucked out of her. "You—you *what?*"

"Toni told me," Angela confessed. "I know you didn't want her to, but she did...and I chose not to believe it. Told myself that you tripped and fell, and just wanted to blame him so it would make it easier for you to leave him." Unable to look her sister in the eye any longer, Angela turned away. "I chose not to believe it because if I *did*, then that would mean that what happened to you was my fault... Because of my vindictive plan to make you feel what I felt in my own marriage, I caused you to be put in a position where you and your unborn baby could've lost your lives and I didn't want to face it... I didn't want to face how horrible of a person—of a *sister* I was."

Shaking her head, Patience blinked back the angry tears threatening to fill her eyes. Of all the things she thought Angela would confess, that wasn't it. It just made her actions those months ago ten times worse. "Wow... And here, I thought you couldn't get any more *triflin'* than you already were."

Angela broke down sobbing. "I'm so sorry Patience. If I could take back everything—"

"Stop the goddamn pity party Angie, you knew what he did. You *knew* and you *still* made that phone call." Though Patience was furious, her voice remained neutral. "You brought someone *back* into my life who not only terrified my *daughter*, but he attacked me *again*.

This time with her *in the house...*" Her scowl burned through Angela. "For *no* reason other than fuckin' *jealousy*."

Rocking back and forth, Angela choked back her cries.

With a heavy breath, Patience calmed herself. "For the record, I do not feel sorry for what you're going through. Because this is your karma," she said. "But before I tell you to get the fuck out of my house, I *will* give you some advice."

Angela looked up at her, not daring to utter a word.

Patience fixed Angela with an intense gaze. "Get a good lawyer and file for divorce. It's time to let that shitshow of a marriage go. Move into Mom's house and while you're there, figure out how you're going to put that college degree that you wasted playing Trevor's doating housewife all those years, to good use," she ran down. "It'll take time, and you will cry a *lot*, but you *will* get over him and the life you *had with* him."

Eyes filled with gratitude, Angela opened her mouth to speak, but was shut down when Patience raised her hand.

"Now that I've said that...you and I are done."

A soft gasp sounded from Angela, her eyes creasing with confusion. "I—I don't... What do you mean done?"

"I don't want you in my life anymore Angela," Patience said. "I've let too much go with you over these years, but not this time. Just because you're my sister, doesn't mean that I have to love you, or forgive you for the shit you've done to me. You don't deserve that from me... *We*, are done."

Those words hit Angela like a load of bricks. And though they hurt, she knew that Patience was within her right to not only feel them, but to say them. Angela knew that she deserved it. Her marriage wasn't her karma, losing her baby sister was. "I understand."

"It wouldn't matter if you didn't." Patience motioned to the half-empty glass of water on the coffee table. "Finish your water. After that, you know where the door is." She punctuated her terse reply by heading for the stairs to check in on her daughter.

Chapter Forty-Seven

MICHAEL HANDED THE SERVER THE folder with his card inside. "Everything was great, thank you," he spoke to the woman.

"Glad to hear, I'll be right back with your receipt," she replied, before walking off.

Resting her back against the seat, Patience closed her eyes as the evening breeze kissed her skin. "It's beautiful out."

Michael gazed at her. "It sure is." Grabbing his glass of remaining wine, he raised it to Patience. "To a beautiful night, a great dinner, and the perfect woman... Happy birthday."

A glowing smile on her, Patience raised her glass. "Thank you, my love." She put the glass to her lips, finishing the last bit of wine.

Patience had awoken that morning in a sense of bliss. She was stepping into her thirty-seventh year of life happy, healthy, and in-love with the man sitting across from her. She'd been treated to a lovingly prepared breakfast in bed, and birthday gifts that morning, followed by a relaxing full afternoon at a luxury spa. Now Patience was finishing up her day with a birthday dinner at an upscale, open rooftop restaurant, overlooking the heart of downtown Maple Glenn. The mild fall weather was even cooperating perfectly.

"It's been a crazy year and a half, huh?" she mused, adjusting the diamond butterfly charms on the bracelet Michael had gifted her for their one-year anniversary.

"It has. But I can honestly say that the good certainly outweighed the bad."

Her eyes crinkled. "It has." When a breeze blew her hair in her face, Patience let out a giggle as she maneuvered it over her shoulder. "Damn, right in my mouth."

Michael's humor-filled eyes lit with adoration for the woman sitting before him. The woman he loved with every fiber of his being. When her eyes met his, butterflies flickered in his stomach.

Folding her arms on the table, Patience let out a light sigh. "I love this restaurant. We definitely need to come back here one day." Noticing that Michael seemed to be lost in thought, her brows knitted in concern. "What's the matter?"

"Nothing baby, everything is good." When the server returned with his card and receipt, Michael promptly signed the slip. "You ready to go?"

Grabbing her clutch, Patience nodded.

Under the moon, stars, and haze of city lights, Patience and Michael walked hand in hand along the sidewalk. Patience was so lost in the calming atmosphere, and the feeling of her fingers twined with Michael's, that she didn't hear him speak. Blinking, she looked over at him. "What did you say?"

"I have to stop at the bakery really quick to pick something up."

"Oh." Patience tucked some of her hair behind her ear. "Which bakery?"

Michael halted his steps, prompting her to stop as well. "This one."

Patience glanced up at Jessy's Gourmet Bakery and Café sign above them. "Oh shit. It didn't even register what block we were on."

Michael chuckled a bit. "Are you okay with that?"

"Of course."

"It'll only take a moment." With Patience's hand still secure in his, Michael approached the door. As he went to open it, Patience pulled back, prompting him to look at her. "What's the matter?"

She gestured to the window, and the lack of light coming through it. "It looks like they're closed."

"No, they're open," Michael assured.

Patience pointed to the small sign on the glass door. "Michael, you don't see the sign? They closed at seven. It's nine-thirty. I think you missed your order."

He put his hand on the door handle. "They're open, I promise." Pushing it open, he flashed a grin. "See, there's even some light in there."

Patience squinted. "You mean that weird *flickering* light?" When Michael just stared at her, unmoving, she tossed a hand up. "Okay fine. Let's walk into the dark establishment and get dragged to the back by lunatics over some pastries."

Michael shook his head, successfully hiding his amusement. "Let's not think morbid thoughts on your birthday, my love."

Rolling her eyes, Patience followed Michael inside. Upon entering, she let go of Michael's hand. Candles, both tea lights and pillars, had filled the quaint space, lining the windows, sitting on small tables in the corners, and on the ordering counter.

When Michael went for the counter, Patience backed towards the door. "Carter—they're having some kind of seance in here, let's *go.*"

Michael spun around. Seeing Patience halfway out the door, he softly laughed. "Patience, hold on."

She looked back at him, eyes wide. "Will you come on?"

"Will you *stop* it?" He gestured for her. "Now there's nothing satanic going on. The owner is probably cleaning or something and needed a bit of ambiance. Just come back inside. I'll only be a minute."

She pointed to the floor, eyes still fixed on him. "And the rose petals all over the damn floor?"

Michael scanned the floor with his eyes. She was right, the linoleum was littered with scattered rose petals. "Umm." He met her inquisitive eyes. "I don't have an answer for that. I'm just here to pick up an order."

Irritated by his lack of urgency, Patience pushed the door closed. Walking towards him, she smoothed her hand down her dark purple, long-sleeved, form-fitting mini dress. Standing before Michael, she glared when he smirked at her. "What's so funny?"

"Nothing, just try to relax. You trust me, don't you?"

Rolling her eyes, she let out a huff. "*Yes*, I trust you. You *know* I do."

Unfazed by her attitude, Michael leaned in and kissed her cheek. "Good." He peered behind the empty counter. "Excuse me. It's Michael Carter, I called in an order earlier." Within a moment, Jessy walked out of the back, a flat lavender box in hand.

"Hello Michael. Everything is ready for you." Jessy smiled warmly, handing him the box. "We appreciate the special donut order. These were fun to make."

Michael returned a smile of his own. "No problem." He gently nudged Patience, who was eyeing the candles. "Baby."

Patience looked at him but didn't answer, her eyes tight.

"Can you hold this for me, while I go get the car?" He held the box out.

Patience took it from him, stifling an eye roll. "*Sure*, Michael." This side quest was starting to annoy her.

Michael dug for his keys as he headed for the door. "Be right back."

Patience turned her back on him. "Umm hmm."

Jessy stood behind the counter, beaming at Patience. "That's a beautiful dress."

"Thank you." Seeing the warmness on the woman's face,

Patience relaxed her taut expression and checked her tone. "I apologize if I sound annoyed. I'm not…with *you* anyway."

Jessy waved a hand. "Oh, it's no problem. I know it's late." She leaned her elbows on the wood counter. "Those are some great specialty donuts that Michael ordered."

"I'm sure," Patience replied. "I can smell them through the box…smells like lemon."

"If *I* were you, I'd peek at them."

Patience raised an eyebrow, eyeing her skeptically.

"You're Patience, right?"

"I am," Patience confirmed. "And you know that how?"

Jessy offered a casual shrug. "Michael's order noted that they were specialty birthday donuts for his girlfriend Patience," she explained. "So, I just assumed that you were her."

"Well, you assumed correctly." Glancing down at the box in her hand, Patience was growing intrigued. She initially thought that Michael was picking them up for his parents or someone of the sort. However, learning that the treats were for *her*, she decided to do what Jessy suggested, and take a look.

Setting the box on the counter, Patience peeled back the tape. Opening the box, she was met with the familiar aromas of lemon and sugar. But she soon forgot about her sweet tooth, when she actually laid eyes on the donuts.

Through the dim light of the candles, Patience noted four deluxe lemon donuts within the box. Each decorated with an intricate design and piped wording. Her eyes deliberately scanned over each one, reading. Will. You. Marry. Me?

Her eyes fluttering in surprise, she felt a presence behind her. Patience spun around to find Michael standing before her, gazing at her. She brought one of her trembling hands to her chest. "Michael do you know what these *say*?"

Michael smiled at her. "Yes…I do." He'd seen the donuts

earlier when he'd met up with Jessy about his plans for tonight in her shop.

Still trying to register what was happening, Patience peered down at Michael's hand as he took hold of hers.

A small box in one hand, her hand secured in his other, and his heart pulsating in his chest, Michael took a deep breath. "I never expected a trip to a random bakery a year and a half ago to completely change my life," he began. "But it *did* the moment I laid eyes on you."

Patience stared at him, emotions bubbling inside of her as he spoke.

"I fell in love with you that day Patience, and it's only gotten stronger from there." Michael choked back tears as he stared into her shimmering eyes. "You're my entire world baby, and I want to spend the rest of my life proving it to you."

Patience sucked in a breath as Michael dropped down to one knee before her. "Oh my God."

Opening the box in his hand, Michael held it up, the engagement ring sparkling in the candlelight. "Patience Harvey, I love you with everything in me… Will you do me the honor of being my wife?"

Tears of happiness filling her eyes, Patience gently touched his face. Little did he know, she'd fallen in love with him at first sight too. "I love you too." She took a shaky breath. "Yes, I'll marry you."

Michael removed the dazzling ring, placing it on her finger, while Jessy's applause and cheers sounded in the background. Rising to his feet, he pulled Patience into a loving embrace, before tenderly kissing her lips.

"I can't *wait* to tell this beautiful story to my family when I get home," Jessy gushed, hands clasped together.

Michael looked at her as he and Patience held each other. "Thank you for doing this."

"Of course. It was my pleasure."

Patience's smile and the glimmer in her eyes could have lit the bakery brighter than any florescent lighting. She held her hand up, admiring her new ring. "This is absolutely beautiful Michael."

Michael blushed under her adoring gaze. "I'm glad you like it." Still holding her close, he removed his phone from his pocket. Making a call, he put it on speaker when the line answered. "Hi Noelle. She said yes."

Hearing a loud, familiar wail of delight resonate through the phone, Patience peered at the screen. Seeing Noelle's beaming face, Patience's own smile radiated back. "Hey Bunny."

"Congratulations Mommy and Mr. Michael!" Noelle squealed. "I'm so happy. I can't wait to pick out my dress for the wedding, and help you pick out yours."

"Thank you, baby, so am I." Realization setting in, Patience put a hand over her heart. "Wait, Noelle you knew he was going to do this?"

Grinning, Noelle nodded with vigor. "Yes."

Michael gazed at Patience. "I talked to her about asking you to marry me," he said. "Since she's the most important person in your life, it was only right that I asked for her blessing."

Looking into his eyes, Patience couldn't find the words to express just how much she loved and appreciated him. But she'd be sure to show him for the rest of her life. Wrapping her arms around his neck, she pressed her lips to his as her daughter's gleeful cheers once again rang through the speaker.

Epilogue

SOFT SNOW WAS CASCADING THROUGH the winter afternoon sky. Patience stood at her bedroom window, entranced by the view.

"Hello?!" Toni's loud voice through the speaker snapped Patience out of her trance.

She peered down at the phone in her hand. "I'm sorry T, I spaced out looking at the snow, what did you say?"

"What was the last thing you heard?" Toni asked.

"Uhh..." Drawing a blank, Patience grimaced. "Yeah, I've got nothing."

"Patience—I just ran down a whole *paragraph.*"

"I'm *sorry.*" Patience's tone dripped with laughter. "You have my full attention now."

"It doesn't even matter, it wasn't that important anyway. I was just bitching about being left alone."

Patience twisted some of her hair around her finger. "Rob and Jordan still not back yet, huh?"

"Girl, *no.* They've been sliding around that mall for three hours like Frick and damn Frack. But had the nerve to tell *me* that *I* would slow them down, because I'd be stopping at every store."

Patience successfully suppressed a laugh. "Well Toni...they weren't lying. That three-hour trip would've been *five* hours had you gone with them."

"Oh sure, take their side," Toni grunted, to which Patience snickered. "Anyway, they promised to bring me back a soft pretzel, so I guess it'll make up for it. In the meantime, I'm sitting here with my glass of wine, staring at this big ass Christmas tree."

"Ever think that their *goal* was to give you a few hours of peace and quiet?"

"Hmm…you may be right." Toni's voice rose with merriment. "See, *that's* why I keep you around. To talk my dramatic ass down."

"It's a twenty-four seven job, but I'm happy to do it," Patience jeered.

A laugh sounded from Toni. "Funny… All right, I won't keep you any longer. I know you've got your hands full over there."

Peering over at her bed, Patience's smile gleamed. "Yeah." She eyed the shimmering engagement ring and diamond wedding band on her left hand. "I love it though."

"I *know* you do." Toni's smile was clear through the line. "I can't *wait* to come over tomorrow to kiss and smoosh that cute little *face*."

Patience smirked. "I'm assuming you're not referring to *my* face."

Toni sucked her teeth. "*No*, I'm not referring to your damn face. But I *can*, if you want me to."

"No, I'm good on that."

"Yeah, I thought so," Toni threw back. "Anyway, I'll be in Maryland—well, Mom's house for a bit tomorrow, checking on a certain *someone* who still isn't used to spending the holidays alone. But we'll be there at your place by five for dinner."

"Okay." Keeping the promise she'd made when Angela had come to her house in distress three years ago, Patience had cut communications with her. She didn't mind Toni hinting that the woman was still breathing, but that was the extent of it. She was better off for not having Angela in her life. But while in the process of reflecting on her choices, and everything she'd endured and overcame, Patience knew that she was better for having someone else *in* her life. "Drive safe, I'll see you tomorrow. I love you and…thank you."

"I love you too, but why are you thanking me?"Toni wondered.

Patience shrugged her shoulders. "I'm just thinking about how my life turned out, and everything that got me to this point, and…" She searched her heart for the right words to convey everything she felt. "I don't know where I'd be if I didn't have you in my life. So… thank you for being here."

Other than the sound of a sniffle, the line went silent for a moment. "Pace, you don't have to thank me— *I* don't know where *I'd* be without *you*. You've been my best friend since you were *born* and that won't ever change."

Releasing a sigh, Patience dabbed away the water droplets that formed in her eyes. "Okay, let's get off the phone before we both start crying."

"It's too late, I already have tears in my wine."

Patience laughed quietly. "See you tomorrow silly."

"See you kid."

Ending the call, Patience set her phone on the windowsill before approaching the bed. Hovering over the mattress, her eyes lit up as a teeny pair of brown eyes stared brightly back at her.

"Hi Mamas," Patience cooed at her infant daughter. "Did Mommy wake you from your nap?"

Five-month-old Riley Carter, sprawled on a baby blanket in the middle of her parents' bed, stretched her little hands and kicked her feet, making happy gurgling noises.

The sweet sight made Patience bubble on the inside. "Come on, my love." Scooping Riley up, Patience kissed her little cheek before leaving the room.

She ambled down the steps of her home, the home she'd introduced to Michael years ago, and now shared with him as his wife.

She was greeted by the sight of the festive holiday décor in her living room, including a Christmas tree that was trimmed and illuminated to perfection, and the abundance of gifts that laid beneath it. With her daughter in her arms, Patience moseyed over to the tree, getting a full view of the ornaments, zoning in on a few *particular* ones. Hanging side-by-side, were four round glass ornaments. Each was hand-painted with the family's symbols: butterfly, house, bunny, and a lavender heart.

Turning Riley around to allow her full view of the baubles, Patience pointed to them. "Look Riley, your big sister made these," she said. Riley responded by making a noise, to which Patience giggled softly. "Yeah, they *are* pretty."

Heading for the couch, Patience sat, settling back against the cushions. Cradling Riley, Patience stared at her little dark brown face. Lightly stroking the soft black curly hair atop her head, she was mesmerized by her little miracle.

Though she'd hoped, Patience had no idea if more children were in the cards for her. When she'd found out she was pregnant a year after she and Michael had married, there were tears of joy shed from both her *and* Michael.

Hearing the doorknob turn, Patience looked over as Noelle and Michael entered. "Did you two have fun at the mall this ridiculously busy Christmas Eve?"

Michael chuckled as he removed his coat. "I didn't mind it, but Noelle almost lost her mind when she couldn't find more glass ornaments."

"What did you need more ornaments for?" Patience directed at Noelle, humor lacing her voice.

Noelle removed her coat, handing it to Michael when he gestured for it. "Since Jordan is coming over tomorrow, I wanted to make her one." Seeing her baby sister staring at her, Noelle happily trotted over. "Hi baby." When Riley cooed at her, Noelle squealed. "I'm going to wash my hands, then I'm coming to hold you." She sprinted for the half bathroom down the hall, throwing questions over her shoulder. "Mommy, has it been four hours? Did she eat yet? Do you want your pillow?"

Patience followed Noelle's progress, laughing softly. At twelve years old, Noelle was a loving and attentive big sister to Riley, paying close attention to everything regarding her care. "I just fed her not too long ago."

Michael approached Patience, kissing her lips, before kissing the top of Riley's head. "I'm about to make us some lunch. You want anything in particular?"

Cupping his chin with her hand, Patience lightly shook her head. "No, whatever you make is fine."

He smiled at her. "Okay."

Just as Michael headed for the kitchen, Noelle darted back into the living room straight for Patience, holding her hands out. "Hands are clean, gimme gimme."

Patience shook her head in amusement. "Sit down." Taking the receiving blanket from her shoulder, she placed it on Noelle once she sat down, before carefully placing Riley into her arms.

"When you get older, I'm gonna teach you how to draw." Noelle's voice was bubbly. Her grin only grew wider when Riley grabbed her finger.

"She'd love that." Watching Noelle hold Riley, Patience smiled. "I remember when *you* were that size."

Noelle looked at her. "Really?"

Patience nodded. "Yeah. You were the prettiest little baby, with the cutest cry—*loud*, but cute nonetheless." She chuckled when Noelle giggled. "But you were a good baby. You've *always* been good."

Noelle wrinkled her nose. "Now I'm almost a *teenager*."

"Oh God." Patience clutched her chest in dramatic fashion, earning a laugh from Noelle. "Yeah, you're growing up on me...but you're growing beautifully."

"Thank you."

"Of course. It's the truth." Letting out a light breath, Patience felt herself becoming emotional as she thought of Noelle. Her first born, her first miracle. The little girl who had changed her for the better, and had been the light of her life since the day she came into this world. "You're probably going to roll your eyes at what I'm about to say, but I'm going to say it anyway," Patience began. "No matter how old you get, no matter what you do, where you go...you will always be my baby."

Noelle stared at her dotingly. "Aww Mommy." She put a hand on her mother's arm. "No matter how old I get, you will always be my favorite person."

That did it; Patience's eyes glassed over with joyful tears. She fanned her face. "Aww, that makes me so happy to hear, and I'll hold you to that when you turn sixteen."

Noelle giggled. "It'll be true then too."

"I believe you." Patience leaned in, kissing Noelle's forehead. "I love you, Bunny."

"I love you too."

Patience removed a pan of freshly made cookies from the oven, while Noelle arranged cookie decorating items on the counter island. Standing across from her, Michael was holding Riley, rocking her while lowering the volume on the holiday music. All four were clad in matching black, white, and red Christmas pajamas. Afternoon had turned to nightfall and after having dinner, the Carter family were preparing to decorate cookies.

"We'll let these cool for a bit before we start decorating them," Patience said, removing the oven mitts.

Michael adjusted Riley in his arms. "Noelle has forbidden me from decorating the reindeer cookies," he chortled. "Apparently my art skills *still* aren't up to par."

Noelle laughed out loud.

"I've been tasked with the ornament cookies," Michael finished. When the baby started gurgling, Michael looked at her.

"You're laughing at Daddy too, huh Riley?" He kissed her cheek when she smiled at him.

Patience shot an amused look his way. "It's okay baby, you make the best ornaments."

"That's what *I* said," Noelle chimed in. "And I even picked out a mini cookie icing *brush*, since you're used to painting stuff with brushes."

Michael chuckled. "I appreciate the assistance."

"No problem." Noelle grinned at Michael, giving him the thumbs up. "See Dad? I got your back."

The happiness that Michael felt every time Noelle called him Dad, had yet to cease. Though he'd legally adopted Noelle as his own once he and Patience had married two and a half years ago, he didn't request or even *expect* her to do so. But when she'd referred to him as such the night he took her to her first father-daughter dance, he couldn't keep the tears at bay.

"I know you do, Bunny," he replied, sincere. "Likewise."

Noticing that Riley was beginning to squirm, Patience lightly tapped her husband's shoulder. "She's doing her hungry dance. I'm going to feed her." Michael handed Riley over to Patience. "You hungry my love?" Patience cooed at her as she passed through the kitchen.

Noelle jumped from her seat. "Oh wait, I'll go get your special pillow."

Patience didn't get a chance to reply as Noelle had already sprinted past her out of the kitchen. The scene made Patience laugh. "She's been on *go* ever since we brought Riley home from the hospital."

"Hell, *before* that. You remember she wanted to be at all your doctor appointments?" Michael recalled. "She's a great big sister."

"Yeah, she is." With her daughter in her arms, Patience entered the den, taking a seat on her favorite chaise. Noelle walked in, holding Patience's breast-feeding pillow.

"Here you go." She handed it to her mother, before holding up a small stuffed object. "I also brought one of my little toy bunnies to keep her company while she's eating."

"That's sweet of you Noelle," Patience replied, warmly.

Noelle rested the small white bunny on Riley's legs, before carefully placing a kiss to the wiggly baby's forehead. "I hope you get nice and full."

Patience smiled at the scene. "I'm sure she will," she said. "Go help your dad finish getting the stuff together, I'll be in in a few minutes."

As Noelle left, Patience placed the pillow around her waist, then positioned Riley. As she fed, Patience looked out the window, reflecting on her life. It was hard to believe that a few years ago, she didn't think that this outcome would be possible. Yet it had become her reality. Patience had the marriage and family she'd always dreamed of, and she couldn't have been more grateful, or deserving of it.

A tray with three mugs of hot chocolate and a plate of decorated cookies in hand, Michael entered the living room. Setting the tray on the coffee table in front of the couch, he took inventory of the contents. "Are we missing anything?"

Noelle, busy playing with Riley in her rocker, craned her neck to see. "Did you put marshmallows on top of the hot chocolate?"

Michael nodded. "Yes, *yours*."

With cookies decorated and piping hot chocolate, the family were retiring to the living room with their treats to watch a holiday movie. A tradition that had started with Patience and Noelle had become one that Michael was now part of, and it couldn't have made him happier.

As Michael turned on the fireplace, Patience removed Riley from her rocker, bringing her to the couch. She reclined back against the cozy cushions as Noelle snagged a cookie, then settled on the couch beside her.

Grabbing his mug, Michael took a seat next to his wife. "What movie did we decide on?"

Noelle picked the remote up from the table, turning the television on. "Umm…" She looked at her mother. "Mommy, do you want to watch the one Dad and I picked out, or that old clay animated one you like?"

Patience shot her a side-glance, her eyes narrowing. "Did you just call me old?"

Noelle giggled. "No…*but*—"

"Hey now," Patience jumped in, voice mixed with humor. She shook her head when Noelle busted out laughing. "We can watch whichever. It doesn't matter to me."

Noelle clicked the remote. "We'll watch the clay one first. *I* like that one too."

Patience made a face at the tween. "Don't try to butter me up after you just called me old."

Michael let out a snicker. "We're not old baby, we're just well-seasoned."

Laughing, Patience pointed at her husband. "I'll take that."

He winked at her before sipping a bit of his beverage. Setting the mug back down, Michael took the throw blanket from the arm of the chair then spread it over his family.

As the television screen lit with the opening credits of the selected movie, Michael's eyes slowly scanned around the living room. The amber lighting from the flickering fire, paired with Christmas lights lining the tree and mantel, gave him a clear enough view of the framed photos on the walls. Photos of his family, and his wedding photos.

Michael's memories flooded with the beautiful ceremony that his sister had planned. He'd spared no expense, and it had been a wedding both he and Patience had dreamed of. Watching Patience walk towards him in her breathtaking gown, was an image he never wanted to forget.

He looked over at his children, his heart swelling. Another moment that was etched in his memory was the day Riley was born. The tears of happiness he'd shed on his wedding day were the same tears he'd shed the moment he held his newborn baby in his arms for the first time. And Noelle, the child he didn't create, yet loved her as if he had.

Finally, he laid eyes on his wife—Patience: a woman he had met by chance, who had become the one who completed him. The one who had made him love and *feel* love unlike anything he had before.

Catching Michael's tender stare, Patience felt her heart flutter. "What?" she softly asked.

"I'm just thinking about how blessed I am to have you in my life." Leaning in, Michael softly stroked her cheek with his fingers. "I love you so much."

Her adoring eyes twinkling with the flicker of the fireplace, she smiled at him. "I love you too."

As the TV screen captured their children's attention, Michael brushed Patience's lips with his, igniting a loving kiss of all that they had gone through together, and the many years of happiness that laid ahead.

Acknowledgements

My family: I love y'all and I'm thankful for each and every one of you. I wouldn't be who I am without you.

Special shout outs to my husband, Stephen. I love and appreciate you more than you know. My sister, Jawhara. What is understood doesn't need to be said, but I'll say it anyway. Thank you for the constant encouragement, your listening ear, and always having my back. You already know.

My trusty beta readers, Jawhara, and Aja, thank you. The constant stalking for more chapters was much appreciated and frankly, hilarious. You are forever a part of my team.

Thank you to my editor, Suzanne L. It is always a joy working with you.

Last but *certainly* not least, my readers. Thank you so much for every bit of support you continue to give me. It means the world, and I appreciate each and every one of you.

About the Author

J.B. VAMPLE is an author who fell in love with the written word at a young age. While in her final year of high school, she came up with the concept of her new adult fiction series *The College Life Series*. After years of writing only for herself, J.B. published her debut novel *College Life 101: Freshman Orientation* in 2015. She has since written and published the other eight installments of *TCLS* and in 2022, she released her tenth novel *Right as Reign*. Which was her first standalone, and debut into the romance genre. Currently residing in Philadelphia, J.B. continues to write while managing her career as an indie author.

Printed in the USA
CPSIA information can be obtained
at www.ICGtesting.com
LVHW091231300424
778864LV00003B/305